Nati

NATIVE SOIL

Sarah Watkinson

1

The Man with a Mission

'Will the audience be very eminent? These days I feel so stupid and out of touch.'

'They'll be about ten thousand GCSE biology kids. I said we can always slip out.'

Twenty minutes later they stood in the hurtling Cromwell Road under the cliff-face frontage of the Natural History Museum. Olivia paid the taxi driver.

'That was a luxury,' said Pippa. 'I like it when my rich friends come to town. Thanks, Liv.'

When you've had your first expensive but easily disarranged haircut for fifteen months, and your feet, jammed into unaccustomed heels, cannot handle a brisk dodge across traffic, a cab is hardly a luxury. And anyhow, Olivia had little to spend on lately, alone in the wilds. Steadying herself on the pavement as the taxi vanished, she glanced up at what could be seen of the sky, to counter that nervy, hemmed-in feeling London gave her. She hoped she wasn't tired of life. There had been no cars in

Dr. Johnson's day, only lovely horses. Apes and serpents watched quietly from their stone niches in the museum's gothic arcading. What a comforting assertion by those old naturalists—that Nature deserved a cathedral in the Empire's capital. Arm-in-arm the friends dodged between four jockeying lanes of traffic and up the grand steps to the entrance.

Inside, the halls pullulated with school parties. Some were in uniformed crocodiles carrying notebooks, a teacher front and rear, others milled in clusters in a rainbow of anoraks and trainers. Teachers marshalled their groups to coalesce round the tapir, study dioramas or jostle into queues for the lavatories, or the gift shop's pocket money objects. They fingered science-fiction plastic dinosaurs, these little inheritors of mammalian supremacy, each child about the size of one of the Diplodocus's vertebrae.

Olivia's parents had brought her here at weekends during the divorce, a diversion for their tug-of-love daughter. She hated the mausoleum atmosphere of the cavernous atrium. She imagined all the life that had ended in these cold glass cases: the flittering and swooping, courting and nest-building, preening and grooming, barking and carolling; all the migrations and flockings and dawn choruses stilled in mothballed corpses.

'There's Andy! And Mark too,' Pippa waved both arms, regardless of a stare from a volunteer museum assistant in a uniform red sweatshirt. Andrew Bamberg and Pippa's husband Mark walked towards them from a cloistered side corridor, signed as the way to the lecture theatre. Mark waved back—a little shorter and tweedier than Andrew, the rural GP up on a day in town. Both men smiled.

Andrew Bamberg—in person—put out a hand. 'Mrs. Gabrieli? Thank you so much for coming to my lecture. I'm afraid you must have been press-ganged.'

He had a lean face, just like on TV, cleanshaven but with a shadow, mobile and humorous, deep-set dark eyes and a wiry frame, set off today by his lecturing get-up. He appeared smoother than the anoracked figure of *Invisible Wildlife*. A hand-made suit and white shirt, no tie. Ridiculous, how school-girlish one could become, faced with a celebrity. It was like the opposite of seeing a ghost; a living, breathing human version of the flickering TV presence that kept her company—kept her sane—in her dark and lonely farmhouse. Good God, she was blushing. She was out of practice, that was it. Normal, if one had been so long out of circulation.

'Olivia's going to put up a satellite dish on her farm,' said Pippa, sprightly. 'You were very blurry up there, Andy.'

Andrew smiled, looking at Olivia. 'I hear you're Isobel Burbank's daughter? Do you play too?'

People never understood how you wouldn't dream of competing with a virtuoso mother like Isobel.

'So you and Pippa were little girls together!' Andrew surveyed Olivia and Pippa, amused as though picturing them as children. He might have been making friends with a couple of badger cubs, thought Olivia. So much for the haircut and heels. What had Pippa and Mark said about her? Of course, decent clothes and clean shoes were normal for media people; Andrew Bamberg would look silly mucking out. Now he was glancing at his watch, offering her a faux-apologetic smile. 'Look, I have to go and get organised. You'll have to excuse me. Why don't we lunch afterwards?'

'See you then, Andy. Good luck,' said Mark, and patted Andrew on the shoulder.

'I may need it.' And he was off, down the gothic corridor, into the recesses of the building.

Mark escorted them in the other direction to the public entrance of the lecture theatre. He foiled Pippa's attempt to slide into the back row and steered the three of them into the front, as cheerleaders, he said. Olivia felt old as the noise of teenagers swelled behind them.

'It's summat about spaceships,' a youth behind them told his neighbour.

'No it i'n't. It's about bacteria.'

'Oh nooo! Bor-ing.'

'I know, the panda tickets were sold out,' said the young teacher appeasingly.

'Andy's got a hard row to hoe,' whispered Mark. 'None of them will be the least bit interested in microbes.'

Andrew started strongly with a rapid montage of repellent instances of disease and decay. There was good feedback, cries of 'Yuck!' 'Ugh!' 'Gross!', and vomiting noises. Two boys hit each other. A lavishly made-up girl ran out dramatically, hands over her mouth.

Without waiting for the hubbub to abate Andrew dimmed the lights and played false-colour videos of spectacular microbes: a space-age spirochaete in motion and Vorticellas extending and retracting their vaguely sexual trumpets.

'Wow! Unreal!'

Lights up. He addressed a girl directly. 'What's odd with this?'

The others watched. He showed the revolving sphere of spaceship Earth, a monochrome version of the iconic image.

'It's black!'

'Yes—before bacteria made us an atmosphere, the sea was black. Sulphides.'

'Is that true?' Olivia whispered to Mark. She imagined the horror of a black horizon, grey waves, sulphurous air, like *Paradise Lost*. Mark nodded.

Andrew glanced at them. 'Yes—the sea would have been black. And nothing could survive but bacteria. There was no oxygen.'

'Amazing,' Olivia, spoke out loud. Then caught Andrew's eyes on her and blushed.

Again.

Behind her, the audience fell silent.

'Yes, isn't it?' he was addressing her, but loud enough for the audience to hear. 'Bacteria do amazing chemistry. Bacteria got the oxygen out of rocks and into the atmosphere. And now plants keep it circulating. That's why we can breathe.' He changed to modern green-and-blue Earth and zoomed on Siberia.

'This is all forest—where's this?'

'America!' A confident boy's voice from the back.

He zoomed in further to show inset trees. 'This is the world we live in. You see the trees. But the vital part is out of sight, underground. Without soil bugs—no plants, no trees, no animals.'

'But moss grows without soil,' said Olivia, swept up in the debate. Then blushed again.

'It's Nicole Kidman,' somebody whispered loudly at the back. The dialogue at the front had become part of the show.

'That's true, Miss Kidman. But not many plants do that. You'll know that from your own country.'

Mark gave a snort. Pippa nudged him.

'She's Australian,' the audience whispered. There was shuffling as the ones at the back craned for a better view of Olivia.

There was dead silence when Andrew replied. 'Without soil microbes, dead stuff would just pile up. Microbes run all those cycles you learn about at school: carbon, nitrogen and phosphorus. They're microbial chemistry.'

Conversation about Miss Kidman broke out in the lecture theatre. 'They're going out.'

'It's a film.'

'We're in a film.'

'Like *Moulin Rouge!*'

'That's the camera.' A child pointed to the data projector.

'Like *The Hours*.'

'I thought she had red hair.'

'Ain't yer ever 'eard o' wigs?'

'Miss Kidman,' called a boy, 'Miss Kidman, tell us about microbes!'

'Gee, however do you guys find anything so teeny out there?' asked Olivia, trying for the accent. 'You can't put a darn great tree under a microscope.'

'Ah,' said Andrew. All eyes were on the exchange. 'That's what I was coming to. DNA.'

He put up slides with cartoon naturalists using nets, hides, cameras and binoculars. 'That's how the people who built this museum discovered the variety of plants and animals all over the world. And that's why they built this place, the variety of life was so stunning. But for microbes you need something different.'

A composite photo of a room-filling machine, a DNA model and a smiling white-coated girl in charge of a lab. 'We have the technology. And there are far more bugs out there than plants or animals, billions of kinds, too many to count. It's a new frontier. You just have to think small.'

At the end Andrew showed his credits—photos of his lab and researchers with their names. It was the cue for thanks from a teacher.

Mark stood. 'Cut. It's a wrap. We'd appreciate it if you could leave as quietly as possible by the door at the rear.'

Excited whispers ran through the school parties as they recognised the authority of the director. Everybody, including two teachers, filed out discreetly, stealing side-glances at Olivia.

It was wonderfully quiet in the staff dining room.

'I love that picture of the earth from space,' said Mark. 'Never thought of it all run by bugs, I must say. Always thought bugs were bad news.'

'It's quite a statement, isn't it—microbes rule the world?' Andrew admitted. 'But people are finding huge DNA diversity in the tiny stuff. It does look as though there are billions of unknown organisms, especially in soil and water. Another few years and we'll have the technology to monitor what they're actually doing in natural environments—if there's any natural environment left.'

'There will be if Olivia has anything to do with it,' Pippa said. 'Olivia has heather moors and limestone pavements, and the most heavenly wood.'

They all looked at her. She felt strangely self-conscious. 'What a lovely way to be described! As though I owned some idyllic kingdom.'

'Well, it's true,' Pippa said. 'The house needs work, but it's a gorgeous, unspoiled place. And I'm beginning to think of you as a farmer. Although you don't look the part today.'

'You should see me with my post rammer.'

Their soup arrived. Mark and Pippa set to. Olivia caught Andrew's eye as, shaking out his napkin, he surveyed her across the table. 'Where do you farm? Moors sound northerly.'

'Wharfedale, in the Yorkshire Dales. I haven't been at it long.'

'No, I didn't think you could have been.' He smiled. 'I'll be up north in a couple of weeks.'

'Won't your undergraduates be back?' said Mark. 'I thought you were tied down in term time.'

'It's a sweat but I can fit it in. I'm going to see a promising location. It's important to do this public understanding stuff. And helps attract good students. Outreach, you know. My boss's trying to stop me, though.'

'Your TV boss?' asked Olivia. 'Who's that?'

'No, she's lovely. I meant my university head of department. Not my favourite person. Excuse me, off the record, of course.'

'That man is a menace,' said Mark. 'He's trying to stop Andy doing his programme.'

Olivia was amazed. 'Aren't universities supposed to tell people about the interesting things they do? You'd think he would want to trade on your programme's success.'

'The university loves me! I get lots of kudos for public understanding of our work. But molecular biology takes more than kudos. Science needs cash—salaries, equipment, buildings. Government panels decide policy and who gets funded. Nigel's the head of our little department and hell bent on making his name in crop biotech, so he wants us all collaborating with agribusiness. Making fortunes out of pesticides for barley barons. It's a damn shame, and specially tough on the young ecology researchers—who need encouragement, not that sort of mindless contempt.' In his passion, he had become quite unlike the genial host of *Invisible Wildlife*.

Later they stood by the cloakroom as Olivia waited to retrieve her overnight bag. Taking it from the attendant, she glanced at her watch. 'I've got to get to Mama's by five.' She kissed Pippa. 'Thanks, Pip. It's been lovely.'

Mark bent to kiss her too, and Andrew shook her hand for the second time. It was a bony, masculine hand that took hers in a capable grip. Their eyes met. 'I've so much enjoyed meeting you, Miss Kidman. Maybe we'll meet again? Safe home!'

Waving over her shoulder, she hurried across the hall, through the revolving door and down the steps.

Uncharacteristically, she tripped, and had to be fielded by an elderly man coming in the opposite direction. Hanging to the smooth Melton cloth of his sleeve for balance, stammering apologies, she tugged the heel of her shoe out of a gap between the stone steps of the museum. No need, in London, to introduce herself and exchange pleasantries as you would in Skipton; once she had regained her shoe and poise and thanked the stranger, he tipped his hat with kind formality and went briskly on. Descending into the street Olivia wondered why, today, she should feel so disoriented, as though newly arrived in an unknown city. The same old London, familiar streets, looked distanced, vivid, almost cinematic. She could still feel the touch of Andrew Bamberg's hand. It was almost as if he had teleported her into his magic world behind the television screen, like *Alice Through the Looking Glass*. Her hero was a real person. And he had enjoyed meeting her, had said so in as many words. Hearing his amused baritone, she realised she was smiling.

'I've made up the divan for you in the drawing room,' said Isobel. 'I hope you don't mind, darling. I needed your room for an artist friend; he's doing a painting of Ben, from photographs. It's such a good likeness, I have to sit down and have a little cry in front of it. Do sort yourself out, darling, while I see to a bite of lunch for us.'

As Isobel disappeared into the kitchen at the back, Olivia headed upstairs to deposit her overnight case in the drawing room, but something—old habit, probably—led her up another floor to her childhood attic room. Turpentine mingled with, but could not disguise, the little room's scent of sorrow and old furnishings. Her bedroom, on exeats from boarding school after the divorce. Its noises took her back: the whistle-dribble of the cold-water header tank refilling; the drone of an aircraft descending to Heathrow. The little skylight was already almost dark. Thank God she wasn't supposed to sleep tonight in the narrow bed, now loomed over by a hideous rendition of Ben in Jack Vettriano style, wearing cricket whites and smirking. It was nothing like the Ben she liked to remember, her twin and ten-year-old accomplice. She backed out, clicking the door firmly shut. The drawing room smelt more as if living people had been there lately, a Sloane Square miasma of furniture wax, drains and recent cigarette smoke, mingled with Isobel's scent, *Amazone*. Extracting a small whole Wensleydale from her bag, Olivia returned to the kitchen, where her mother took down plates and glasses and received the cheese.

'Ooh, yum, thank you darling. Is it from your cows? You must tell me all about yourself and Yorkshire. We'll have a quick bite before I go and practise. Some nice people coming for drinks, it'll be a change for you after *Wuthering Heights*.' Isobel had never been happy in Yorkshire, so obviously Olivia couldn't be expected to be, either.

'I miss Pippa so terribly,' Isobel went on, as she rummaged in the fridge and pulled out a small piece of pâté on a saucer, a plastic pot of supermarket hummus and two strawberry yoghourts. 'Really, I live on scraps these days. There's a tin of tomato soup we can have, and crispbread, you like that I know. And Wojtek brought me a bottle of Champagne. Open it, would you, darling?'

Olivia drank a whole glass of Champagne while her mother went to and from the kitchen setting out an exquisite but meagre supper in the front room. Isobel never ate in the kitchen. Narrow but high-ceilinged, the dining room held a handsome small polished table dimly lit by a small high-up chandelier, and a tall glass-fronted cupboard filled with crested family porcelain, blue and gold on white. Dark blue velvet curtains muted the swish of traffic in rainy Elizabeth Street. What a contrast between this dark, elegant room and the little basement flat below, which Pippa had made so cheerful with the help of Ikea.

Pippa's space in the house had been like a small bubble of underground cosiness, a bright burrow of hope. After Isobel had left to play at a concert, Olivia would crutch her way down the wide carpeted stairs of Isobel's domain watched by family portraits hung at intervals down the walls, and then the narrower steeper ones to the basement where Pippa, her housekeeping jobs finished, welcomed her to sit on the little red Ikea sofa, provided hot drinks in red-spotted Ikea mugs and talked—about their little school in Ilkley, about Pippa and Mark's wedding plans. About anything but the accident; the horror; beautiful, brilliant Frederico who no longer existed. About being widowed, bereaved of the love of your life, your future wiped clean, at the age of twenty-eight. It was in this room, in a copy of *Yorkshire Life* Pippa's Mum had left when she'd stayed a weekend to see *The Lion King*, that Olivia first saw Oxhide farm advertised. In this room she knew at last what she wanted to do with Freddie's legacy of four million Euros.

Could you be homesick for a place you'd only lived in for months? Olivia thought intermittently about Oxhide throughout Isobel's drinks party later that evening, through the gallantries of her mother's côterie of elderly and not-so-elderly admirers, through the tiredness that threatened to overcome her after the long day. At last everybody drifted off with kisses for Isobel and noisy goodnights on the doorstep, and Olivia was free to go upstairs to her makeshift bed in the smoky drawing room. She remembered times here with Ben on the occasional weekends when their half term breaks coincided. If only he were here now, to laugh a little at their mother, and give his brotherly reaction to her meeting the famous TV presenter. He was always an affectionate teaser.

After the excitements of the day, sleep came slowly on the lumpy sofa. She lay mulling over Andrew Bamberg's lecture, walking her new farm boundaries in her mind's eye, imagining the land teeming with microscopic underground life. How did you do DNA analyses, she wondered? Falling asleep she half-dreamed the cart shed housing a lab, with Andrew Bamberg emerging with a triumphant wave to tell her about exciting results.

'I thought we'd go to the park. It would be a shame not to enjoy the sunshine. It could be the last warm sun we'll get this year. Make some vitamin D when you can.' Olivia's godmother Jane strode up Whitehall in the brown lace-ups that were the one departure from her elegant senior civil servant outline. She walked everywhere, fast, which Olivia found bracing. When they reached St. James's Park, Jane made a determined swoop for a bench with a view of the pond, sweeping dead leaves and bird shit off the space beside her for Olivia to sit.

She came straight to the point. 'How can I help? Your father said you wanted my advice.'

'Mama says I'm mad,' said Olivia. 'A girl on her own, taking on a job she knows nothing about, trying to push herself into a closed community of strangers.'

'Isobel's still bitter about being blackballed by the Ilkley Lawn Tennis Club,' said Jane. 'You're not her, Olivia. And you're not a girl any longer. It's very sad about your husband, I liked him very much. But you have your own life to live. What do you want to do on your farm? That's the first question. Answer the *what* first, then you can work out the *how*. That's what the Minister always says.'

'I want to run it as a model hill farm. On scientific principles. Show how you can make a living and respect historic landscapes. I want to make a place people will come to learn.' She didn't mention that the dream had been Freddie's; it might have struck

Jane as sentimental misplaced loyalty. Olivia glanced down covertly at the emerald ring. The green of a Tuscan meadow, he'd said, sliding it on her finger, not yet three years ago. Her mind turned inward, away from St. James's Park to a mountain meadow with purple anemones dotting close- cropped grass, the scent and feel of it under her back.

'Sounds reasonable.'

Olivia looked hard at Jane's face to make sure this wasn't a joke. It seemed not to be. Feet-on-the-ground Jane saw nothing obviously unrealistic about it. A silence was broken only by a succession of quacks from a string of mallards paddling by.

'I went to an interesting talk yesterday, at the Natural History Museum,' said Olivia.

'Aren't you needed on the farm?'

'I haven't taken over the management yet. I'm using this time to learn, the practical side and the economics. And the science. The talk was by Andrew Bamberg, you know—*Invisible Wildlife?*—and it was rather relevant, I thought. About soil bugs and how they affect life aboveground.'

'I suppose you do need to learn about parasites,' Jane conceded. Obviously she was not a Bamberg fan and still saw microbes as things to get rid of, like the dreadful boss who Andrew had described.

'But that was the interesting thing. They do good as well as harm. There are millions, and with most we don't know what they do. It's a new frontier, he said.'

'He's a clever boy. I know his mother, Vanessa.'

'Really? How?' Plain-speaking in her charcoal suit, Jane was far from a media person or boffin. The Civil Service was her milieu.

'She's a very distant cousin. Rather a nuisance to us at Defra, I have to say. She uses her position to encourage the green lobby, all those well-meaning NGO's with unrealistic ideas about bees and butterflies.'

A missed beat followed. Jane's words weren't what Olivia

wanted to hear from her supporter; the raw emotion in her godmother's voice made her seem less reliable.

'You mustn't let Isobel discourage you,' Jane went on, recovering her even, civil servant's tone. 'I think you're doing a sensible thing. Farmers are friendly on the whole, they'll help if they think you're serious. I know a few. Not in the hills, I admit.'

'So far, they certainly are being very friendly. So do you think it'll possible for me to make a living farming at Oxhide? Well, more than a living—really make a go of it?'

'Why ever not?'

Olivia decided to trust Jane. 'It's what Fred and I planned. To promote hill farming and hill farmers. I wish there'd been time for you to see our farm at Trebbia in the Apennines. We were sure there must be a way to go on using the old methods, conserve the cultural landscape and still be a viable business. So when he left me a lot of money I decided to come back to my own roots and carry on his dreams, our project, but in the Dales. There are so many parallels. Respecting old methods that have evolved in the place—and made the place. Viable and productive methods, even today, without selling out to commercial interests that contribute nothing to conserving the traditional culture.'

'That's asking a lot. Was he succeeding? Most people nowadays would say it's a tough business, specially in the hills, in England. This single payment business is a shambles. And God knows what'll happen in future. I can help you, Olivia. I'm glad we had this talk. Actually I'd have thought that was more important than going to hear Vanessa's pride-and-joy amusing schoolchildren in the Cromwell Road.' Jane stood. 'Well, this has been lovely my dear, but I can't spend all day in the park. The Minister needs his draft paper by this evening.' Then, surprisingly: 'You're doing very well, Olivia. Go and see your father. He agrees with me.'

She kissed Olivia, shyly as she wasn't naturally kissy, and strode in the direction of Whitehall. Olivia, heartened, walked back to Elizabeth Street to collect her case and take a taxi to King's Cross for the four-fifteen to Leeds. As dusk fell on the London suburbs, the darkened carriage window reflected Nicole Kidman, who smiled at her. There was a resemblance, actually—the set of the eyes, the intelligent look. How gratifying to be mistaken for a star. Would Andrew Bamberg seriously come to Oxhide? Freddie would be impressed—somebody in his league, supporting his widow, his vision. Olivia hardly felt up to receiving such a grand visitor—but one day, who knew? How extraordinary Jane was cousin to his mother, the shadowy Vanessa. The lights of midland towns thinned until, to the west, the moon showed the low profile of hills she recognised as the Pennines. Soon she was climbing into Giles's car at Skipton station, headed home to Oxhide.

When Pippa had asked her how she kept sane, alone on her hillside, Olivia had brushed her friend's concern aside and pretended to be self-sufficient. Inside, she was overturned. She lay awake at night and slept in the daytime. You had to have meals, not to eat was to give in to grief, to give up, be overwhelmed. The best times were when there was an obvious job. As Olivia swept dead leaves from the backyard and made an aromatic bonfire of them, her pleasure felt shared. Sometimes Freddie seemed to be around; her mind even supplied the hallucinatory sound of his cough, or the turn of his shoulder through a drift of smoke that swirled down in an autumn gust. On fine mornings she took her coffee on the front terrace, sat on the low wall alternately surveying her land, and tilting her hand in the morning light so his emerald ring sparked green. And then he felt so close that turning over her plans for the day's work—arrangements with the architect; the firm installing the Aga; with Mike Robertshaw about the sheep; getting in food and fuel; organising her college sheep course—was like two people in conversation. These autumn mornings the mist from the river often lay like a milky fluid blanketing the valley floor, and the morning the architect walked up out of it into her fields, his car parked invisibly on the road below, she saw him as Freddie for a whole minute, before taking a pull on her imagination. She would be faithful to her husband, but not to the point of madness. How would she carry out their plans then?

Sometimes grief enfeebled her and she would yield to a temptation to sprawl motionless on her new sofa like a teenager. When that happened she fought back by springing into activity. She bought trail running shoes and a track suit, and ran, at first along the road, but then, inspired by fell runners like the legendary Nicky Spinks, attempted to jog the circuit of her farm. After weeks her muscles grew able to keep the jog going even up the steep path through the in-bye pasture behind the house, rich with every sort of small plant—thyme, burnet, eyebright—surely a treat for grazing sheep. When she arrived, panting, at the massive drystone wall separating the bright limestone turf from dark heather and millstone grit above, she would stand atop the ladder stile and look down at her roofs, her farmhouse palace tucked into its niche on the hillside beside the cleft of the ghyll, guarded by tall ash trees shining gold with their remaining leaves.

By spring, the farm would be all bustle and change: clearing the old slurry pit, reroofing the outbuildings, wind turbines (a special mini-version, respecting the National Park regulations) on the moor; drystone walling including the huge project of buttressing the terraced front lawn, the holiday cottages, the track newly surfaced in limestone chippings. And then she always felt happy. Who wouldn't? How lucky she was, what a tribute to their love, this present from Freddie they now shared. She took to going for her run in the dusk of the November afternoons, lighting a fire before setting off. That way, wood smoke wreathed over the farmhouse in the temperature inversions of the first frosts; she wouldn't admit to herself she did it to conjure a manifestation of her dead lover.

She must look forward now: her thirties would be a new kind of life: independent, without hostages to fortune; with all the horror behind, a new Olivia Gabrieli.

2

Taking Possession

As the London suburbs thinned to fields, hitting the M1 had felt like a new life. Olivia daydreamed about Oxhide as the miles spun by. Parked in a layby for a sandwich, she studied the agent's brochure for the Nth time, coffee cooling on the dash. '*Property comprising a five bedroom period stone farmhouse and outbuildings in need of renovation, 56 acres accommodation land, 120 acres of moorland, 80 hefted Swaledale ewes*'. All hers, to carry on the life's work she and Freddie had embarked on together in Italy, the year before last.

If only that memory could be demoted to a mere nightmare. Traffic swishing by on the other side of a thin line of bushes restarted the old flashback: the autostrada speckled with snow; then, through fog, a loaded farm lorry crawling up out of the slip road ahead. Black out. Later, the two stretchers with their quickly sheeted burdens, tilted upwards and into the ambulance and driven away. That major-fourth hee-hawing of Italian emergency vehicles. Her wet skirt blood-soaked. Would this internal cinema never end? Olivia thrust sandwich crusts and banana skin back into their paper bag, and started her new CD, A

Shepherd's Life, to fill the remaining hundred miles to Wharfedale with more forward-looking thoughts.

After she'd turned west off the motorway to Otley she got caught in queues of homegoing Leeds commuters. She should have started earlier now the clocks had gone back. But her mother had shoved endless afterthoughts into the car at the last moment: the heraldic cushions, an opened bottle of gin. And just when Olivia had finally been ready to go, kind godmother Jane had rung from her office, promising to check up on her. They worried she must be unhinged by grief.

Once she arrived at the farm gate a chilly drizzle had set in and it felt more like early evening than late afternoon. There were no more street lights, not even a lighted window visible in the deep valley where the horizons of the moors rose like walls on each side. Olivia waded through wet grass in her London shoes and wrestled to undo a rope, swollen with damp, which fastened the sagging gate to its stone post. In the puddled farmyard behind the house she turned off the lights and ignition and sat a moment in the car's protective bubble, then opened the door and climbed out into rainy murk, clutching her car keys for security.

The back of the house, set close into the hillside, was dark, overarched by several almost-bare ash trees that had been in full leaf when she first viewed the farm. Water dripped from a broken gutter and ran down the back door, soaking its skin of flaking paint. She felt in her shoulder bag for the key with the agent's label still attached. It was an antique mortise type you had to fit exactly the right depth into the lock. But it turned smoothly, recently-oiled. She creaked the door open and a scurry of dead leaves accompanied her across the threshold into silence and a deeper dark.

With difficulty she located the mains electricity switch in a box high above a line of enormous iron coat hooks. Without much hope she flicked it up. The welcome stone-flagged passageway appeared, dimly lit by a single unshaded overhead bulb, with the kitchen doorway on the right. The kitchen smelt of damp and mice. What was the chance of making a meal in here this evening? Freddie would have done the unpacking and produced a spaghetti carbonara for them both by now, a much better cook than she'd ever been. He would have been at the cooker raising clouds of aromatic smoke, singing a Verdi aria accompanied by sizzling and scraping as he tossed onion and garlic in hot olive oil, while Olivia sipped wine from the Trebbia estate he'd have poured for them, marvelling again at how lucky she was. The ghostly scene was so vivid, with even an imagined waft of oregano, that for a moment she was tempted to collapse and howl. But there was nowhere to sit, and a good howl works best if you can rest your elbows on a table. So she made herself busy, fetching the rest of her possessions from the car in a series of trips across the puddled yard, bending to dart through the curtain of drops falling across the doorway.

Eventually her boxes of survival provisions, clothes and bedding were lined in the passage. Unpacking bread, butter, tea, coffee, eggs and tinned soup and her mother's gin on to the plastic-topped kitchen table, Olivia spotted a scrap of lined paper weighted under a jam jar of shrivelled roses, and made out its biro scrawl.

"Hi Olivia, Welcome to Oxhide! There's a pie and milk in the fridge. Call if you need anything. See you soon, Meg x."

That explained the oiled lock. She'd forgotten to let her kind new neighbours know she was coming later than expected. And when she tugged open the rust-stained fridge there was the milk, its surface draped in velvety-blue, and the pie, smelling toxic. Damn! How could it not have occurred to her that the Robertshaws, as well as selling her their mother's house and land on generous terms, and minding the Oxhide-hefted sheep, might even be thinking about her welfare? What a way to start a neighbourly relationship. No use crying. She tried the Robertshaws' number, etched in her mind by those calls from London about the farm purchase. Amazingly, the yellowed-plastic phone on the sitting room windowsill was connected, and even better, she got the Robertshaws' answering machine, avoiding any kind invitations to join their family supper. Much better to meet her neighbours refreshed in the morning, on her own ground, than to appear on this gloomy evening like a castaway washed up on their substantial doorstep.

She heaved her bedding and overnight case up the narrow curve of stairs. Four bedrooms lay along the corridor. The largest was at the far end. Its double window lay in a gable and commanded a view of the opposite fell side, foregrounded by Oxhide's hay meadows, their drystone walls running down to the lane that ran alongside the Wharfe. With a thump of her fist the casement creaked open, admitting a swirl of sheep-scented air into the stale room. The faint shush of the river came to her from the dark valley, and nearby the beck gurgled in its deep ghyll. How different from the last time she'd been here, finally about to sign the contract in early September, her fields green, the moor above purple with heather and the first heady excitement of being able to call all this hers. And now she was at home. Her sodden shoes freezing. Kicking them off, she felt infinitesimally warmer.

A defunct storage heater was the bedroom's only source of warmth and Olivia shivered as she made the bed. It was fine, old Mrs. Robertshaw had died in Skipton Infirmary. There were no ghosts. But when she put the photo of Freddie on the uncurtained windowsill, with only cold glass between the bedroom and the twilit valley, she was overwhelmed again with the thought that his familiar grin was nothing but photographic film, its reality unthinkably underground—don't go there, she told herself. She had to sit on the sagging bed and breathe deeply. Concentrate on the here and now, the therapist said, don't think about the past or future. But the here and now was this lonely gloom. She decided to phone her mother.

The ringtone from Elizabeth Street was reassuring. *See, I can call up reinforcements,* she told the house. Leaning an elbow on the sill, she peered out at the last glimmer of light in the sky. Eventually her mother's voice came through matter-of-factly from

Belgravia, like the mother ship answering from outer space, so distant from Olivia on her dark hillside. Isobel was in the middle of her usual social whirl, in swishy dress, on clean warm carpets. Olivia heard faint laughing and talking.

'Darling! You arrived? Are you all alone? Is anybody there to help you? You have the coffee, the lasagne? Your gin?' Her mother's throaty giggle. 'Luke's here... he says... (oh— what?—ah) ...Oh, the cab's here! We will have a long talk tomorrow, early? Look after yourself Olivia, won't you? Until then, love.'

'Uh—okay—speak to you then. Have a lovely evening, Mama . . .'

Unexpectedly, morale drained like the storm water flooding into the drain in the derelict yard. Her mother's voice had sapped her adult resolve, transforming her from a wealthy widow of twenty-nine into her homesick eleven-year-old self, newly deposited at boarding school. As she put the phone down she saw the sleeve of her cream pullover had picked up a smear of grimy fluff from the cobwebbed window ledge. Her town shoes felt sticky on the vinyl floor. A tear escaped. She wiped her cheek with the back of a hand. For her sanity she needed to get out, fast, and find light, warmth, food and living company.

Outside it had grown pitch dark but for a distant gleam from Skellside, and a few street lights glimmering half a mile down on the road by the Bell. For a moment she stood listening in the doorway. It wasn't raining any more but rhythmic drips made a syncopated pattering. The sky had partly cleared and the Plough shone through a gap in the clouds. Stars were always there, their familiar shining patterns infinite and predictable. They would be here for her as she brought this place to life again. The future would be good. It was reassuring to be outdoors after the musty silence of the dead house. It was as though you could somehow absorb energy from nature—the rain-filled beck's muffled roar down the ghyll beyond the end of the house, the ash trees rattling their twigs in the night wind.

She hurried across the yard, breathed in the lovely new-car smell of the little Fiat, switched on and swung out of the farmyard and down the potholed track to the lane, headlights sweeping stone walls and surprising a rabbit grazing the wet grass. *The Archers* came on. How could life in this remote valley, and theirs in the lush shires, both be called farming? The Archers were never lonely. Would she populate Oxhide, build a household busy with comings and goings in the farmyard, the voices of sheep and dogs and people, the kettle on the hob—as in childhood memories from walks in the dales with her parents and Ben, as a little girl when she had been happy? Did these places still exist, and could she make one, or might she end up a lonely old lady hermit?

A single string of coloured bulbs swung in the wind across The Bell's forecourt. On either side of the entrance, two lit windows proved, as expected, to be the lounge and public bars. She needed the warmth and company of the public side, but as a single woman and a stranger considered it polite to choose the lounge, at least to begin. The room was cold and smelt faintly of Dettol. From the other end of the bar, out of Olivia's sight from where she sat in ladylike seclusion, came the calm rumble of male voices. A log-effect electric fire did little to warm her, and small brownish framed views of rural scenes lined along the Artexed walls failed to cheer. Eventually the landlord appeared, and Olivia asked for a menu, and a half pint of Tetley's, which had been her father's favourite.

He drew the beer, carefully topping up the glass as the foam ran over the rim, and handed the menu across. He looked at her a moment, then smiled as he gave her the change. 'It's a bit parky this side. There are tables in the public if you'd prefer, maybe? There's a fire. Not many folks come by this late, back-end o' t'year, like.'

Relieved to have got the code right, and escape the lounge, she ordered ham, egg and chips, and took her glass through the two doors to the warm side where everybody was. About half a dozen people clustered at the bar. An older man sat at a table between the bar and a well banked-up coal fire, with a grey-muzzled collie under his chair, nose resting between its front paws. Olivia sat in the window bay at the opposite end from the bar and, so as not to make too much of an entrance, picked up an old copy of the *Yorkshire Post* somebody had left lying about. The drinkers at the bar discreetly ignored her, allowing hardly a break in their conversation. It was as though unaccompanied young female strangers turned up regularly at The Bell on a dark night.

She was afraid nobody would speak to her at all, but—

'Come far?' the barman asked.

'London.'

'Ah—on holiday then?'

'No. Moving in—I've come to live at Mrs. Robertshaw's old place.'

A hush fell. How could they all have been listening while carrying on their own conversations? Then murmured comments—*a brave old lady*—*time somebody took the place in hand*—*a bad state . . .*

'You'll be putting your husband to work then!' said somebody finally addressing her directly, from the far end of the bar.

'I'm a widow,' said Olivia, raising her voice slightly.

'That's a bad job. I'm sorry to hear that,' said a younger man, a farmer by his outdoor complexion and checked shirt. He had a longish narrow face, and a pleasant smile with small square front teeth and pointed canines. 'We ought to introduce ourselves then, seeing as we'll be neighbours,' he said—then, 'Dad!' to the old man with the collie, 'this young lady's bought Robertshaws' mum's place,' and to Olivia, 'I'm Giles, and this here's my Dad. We farm Skellside, next to you.'

'I'm Olivia.' She offered her hand and Giles shook it firmly, both of them smiling at the formality. 'Olivia Gabrieli.'

Remembering the plans in Oxhide's title deeds, Olivia knew Skellside was little more a smallholding, a few acres around a bungalow on the valley floor, without the moorland grazing rights she and the Robertshaws had. The collie must be a pet, not a working dog.

Giles's Dad gave her an assessing look, then put down his pint and stood. "'Ow d'ye do and welcome. Say hullo to young lady, Tess.'

Tess crept forward with a minimal wag of her tail. Her hypnotic pale blue eyes, odd for a dog, reminded Olivia of an older girl at school in Ilkley, who'd bullied her for being the only one with brown eyes. Tess smelled Olivia's offered hand attentively, but did not lick. A Yorkshire dog, thought Olivia, at home.

'Good dog, Tess,' she said, withdrawing her hand to the safety of her jeans pocket. She turned to Giles, businesslike. 'There's a lot needs doing. I guess I'll have a fair bit of fencing to do. Can we look at our joint boundary together some time?'

'Aye, Giles'll be round to ye,' interrupted old Yarker before Giles could reply. 'Ye'll contact Miss Gab . . . whatsit, won't ye lad? London hours, mind—she'll want to let sun come up—'

'Aye, no problem,' Giles cut his father short. 'There's a load of old posts and wire in yard. Pete can help, can't he Dad?'

'Aye, Pete knows boundaries.' The older Yarker cleared his throat bronchitically. 'Old boundaries some folks forgot, think on.'

'We can see what needs doing,' said Giles, rather quickly, with a small frown of annoyance at his father. 'Next weekend if you like.' Some murmured banter broke out at the far end of the bar and Giles turned to suppress it. 'Anyone else like to come up Robertshaws and give the lady a hand? A good deed on a Sunday morning?' Mutters and disclaimers were the only response.

Olivia laughed and went to put her glass on the bar, earning a thank you from the landlord. 'I've got plenty of help, thanks,' she said. 'I'm off now. See you on Sunday, Giles?'

Giles smiled. 'Good night then. Safe home. Mind the bugs don't bite.'

'Do you think there might be . . .' she faltered.

He looked at her for a moment, puzzled. Then laughed. 'Bed

bugs you mean? Naa, just an old rhyme is that. *Good night, sleep tight, mind the bugs don't bite.* Nobbut what that house is in a fair old state I heard. Poor old Mrs. Robertshaw, she wasn't herself at the end, was she?'

Olivia collected her jacket from the window bay, shrugged it on briskly and went out into the night. I'm a Yorkshire landowner, she thought, going home, here to stay. In the morning she would look out from her house over her new fields and half mile of fishing rights in the rushing Wharfe. Freddie would surely have applauded this evening's initiative, the first cordial contact with the locals, the engagement with the neighbour. This place already had a feel of the Trebbia farms; Giles reminded her a bit of Lanfranco, the Gabrielis' agent, and the hint of ancient boundary disputes was also familiar. Spirit Freddie would help her deal with it in due course, she felt sure. He appeared in her mind's eye, including her with a dark-eyed glance that lifted her heart, while he mollified one of the Trebbia tenant farmers in his beautiful Italian voice. No, she would not fail. She would be a faithful steward to Freddie's memory.

It was as wet and windy as ever when Giles arrived the next afternoon to go round the farm boundaries. She needed wellingtons and a hooded parka. Giles, long acclimatised, went bare-headed but wore a tightly-wound brown scarf under the collar of his waxed jacket to keep out the rain. They headed up the dale along the single lane road with its strip of green in the middle and high stone walls both sides, turning right through a field gate that needed rehanging. Crossing a stretch of level soggy turf they started up the steepening hillside towards the moor.

The northernmost boundary wall of Oxhide ran straight from the green valley floor to the dark horizon. In its shelter, Olivia's locks of escaped hair gave up thrashing her eyes and forehead, clinging to her cheeks in damp strands. Underfoot the soaked turf was close and even, finely textured with the shapes of tiny leaves—clover, thyme, burnet, eyebright and gold patches of moss. Sheep's feet had worn narrow purposeful paths that traversed the slope in gentle zigzags pocked with small hoof marks. Half-way up, a smaller field wall had partly collapsed into piles of stones, the gaps part mended with rusty wire that hung in sagging loops decorated with tufts of snagged wool and frayed orange baler twine.

'Mind thaself on wire.' His home turf brought out the Yorkshire in him; Giles trod down a slack strand and helped her over the loose stones. His hand was warm and firm.

'Thanks. Sure you've time for this, Giles? The days are getting so short now.'

'Nay, it's a treat for me, going out with you, Olivia.'

The top boundary wall contoured the moor's edge, dividing the green grass of the inbye fields from the dark heather moorland above, where millstone grit overlaid the limestone. They climbed out on to the moor over the ladder stile with its platform on top. Here they were level with the moor edge on the opposite side of the valley. You could see the matching geological strata, as if the glacier that was now the Wharfe had sliced through a layer cake of rock. Giles strode over, the old sheepdog slinking after him through the dog gap in the base of the wall. Olivia paused on the platform as she always did on her runs, to look down at the stone slate roofs of her farmhouse shining wet below thrashing ash tree tops, the farmyard with its spread of derelict corrugated iron roofs and leaning sheds huddled along a shelf in the hillside, with the trees along the ghyll marking its southern edge. In the distance, the South Eastern reaches of the dale diminished into grey lowlands; to the North West lay the misty North Pennine hills from where the gale poured over the moors, making their jackets flap like tethered sails.

'It's main raw for time o' year. Getting back-endish now,' said Giles. He made a fine figure in the landscape, reddish curly hair blowing back from a high brow, the well-worn jacket loose on his broad bony shoulders.

Once out on the open moor they scrunched along a gritty track through knee-high heather that scratched at her boots. As the slope plateaued you could see the next ridge of distant hills, and in the foreground a derelict hut with a tarred felt roof came into sight, standing in a grassy area among wiry nettles. Piles of sheep droppings had accumulated where the flock sheltered in the lee of the building.

'Old shooting 'ut,' said Giles, forcing open its rotting door with a shoulder. 'Came here for lunch, the shooting parties did. It's let out to syndicates now, they lunch at pub, don't use 'ut any more. I helped as beater when I were a young lad, got pound a day.'

Inside the door was a pile of fresh hay bales, and at the other end a fireplace with an iron grate, wooden table and benches. Crumpled beer cans, candle stumps, and a scatter of cigarette ends littered the plank floor.

'Lads from the village, or hikers mebbe,' said Giles. 'They better not set light to my hay, I keep some bales up here for the ewes. It's a ruin. But, by! It's yours, now, Olivia, happen you could do summat with it. Have picnics and that.' He smiled at her.

'Oh, I've got the farm to think about before I get round to partying,' said Olivia, conscious of Giles looking at her. 'Let's get back.' She moved towards the doorway. 'I'm sopping wet, and we've both got masses to do. The rain's almost stopped.'

Walking on with the hut behind them, Giles led the way to a grassy track that turned right along the heathery highland between dales. He opened a small swing gate and they were at the top of a small tree-filled valley Olivia recognized as the path down back to the farm, where there was an oozy spring that must be the source of the beck. Starting as a mere sandy pool edge with bright moss, a stream formed and then dropped into a gully, descending in a little waterfall that gushed into a peat-brown pool. Walking became awkward as the small valley deepened, contained between slabs of limestone. There were places where they had to walk in the stream and others where the only way down was to climb up the rocks to divert around a small gorge. Giles was in no hurry, making heavy weather of the obstacles as though he had a stiff leg.

As they descended, small cliffs of pale limestone walled them in close to the beck. A high waterfall plunged into a deep pool and dripping ash trees above made a green tunnel of the ghyll beside the farmyard. As they reached the house the late afternoon light faded. A tawny owl hooted from woods by Skellside, where lights had come on.

Olivia hadn't thought to leave a light on in the farmhouse. She would have liked company, to sit in the warmth and share buttered toast by the fire, and chat. But might Giles misinterpret it if she asked him in? Better not, yet. Giles and Tess gave her an imploring look. 'Thank you so much, Giles,' she said. 'It looks like the field gates, and that wall, need fixing.'

'Aye, I'll get Pete to come over next weekend and see what needs ordering if you like? And if I've time I could do that lower in-bye with RoundUp, sort out the weeds for you.'

'Uh, no, Giles, just the gates and walls, would be great. I'm not allowed to use weed killer. National Park rules, you know. They'd throw the book at me.' No point in just saying she'd prefer him not to use herbicides. He'd mark her as a sentimental southern fool if she lectured him about rare plants and bird habitats; the primulas, the curlew she'd delightedly watched, pronging the damp turf in her fields alongside the river. Better to invoke wrathful National Park wardens interfering with sensible labour-saving methods. Though, with Llanfranco, his Trebbia manager, Fred would just have said No. Everything was so much easier, if you were a man.

She waved cheerily as he set off across the fields to Skellside, then turned back to the darkening house. Inside, she turned on all the lights and both electric fan heaters, and lit a fire with logs she'd collected from around the yard. The fridge, cleaned and just about working, was full of eggs and milk and Wensleydale cheese. She had local bread, russet apples and six cans of Stella on the kitchen table. Things were still grubby but Meg Robertshaw's household help had promised to come round every day next week, to help her scrub floors, wash paintwork and polish windows.

She went out of the back door and round the side of the house to the front terrace where there would be a lawn next summer, but which now was shaggy with long grass, docks, dead thistles and trailing brambles. She stood in the gathering dark and felt joy at the house's solidity, looking out from its shelf of rock under the fell, its arcade of tall ash trees arching up behind the roof, sending out golden beams from its mullioned windows with scented wood smoke rising into the autumn air from one of its three stone chimney stacks. The beck sounded contented this evening and the Plough was faithfully in place.

All this was hers, her support, and her inspiration. No one could replace Freddie, but she would be happy here now, married to this place.

3

Friends and Neighbours

'I filled up the car. Don't forget to charge your phone, darling.' Mark Foreman stood in the doorway of the empty waiting room polishing his black shoes and watching his wife arranging a jug of bronze and white chrysanthemums. Pippa placed the flowers on a low table between the row of chairs along facing walls, and tidied the copies of *Yorkshire Life* and *Housekeeping*.

'Those are lovely. Thank you, love.' Swapping the shoe-polish brush for a duster, he rubbed the toecaps to a mirror shine. He was shaping up so well as her ideal of the rural GP, with his thoughtful care, his competent equanimity. It was part of the doctor's magic, to bring calm and reassurance to the fear and upset of the farmhouse sickroom.

'Smart young Dr. Foreman from London. Er—fingernails?'

'Oh. Yes, damn.' From the cloakroom, over scrubbing noises, he went on, 'I hope you'll find Olivia's managing all right. The surgery staff told me it was pretty grim there when poor old Mrs. Robertshaw was coming to the end. She wouldn't have any help, or modernise anything. Said she preferred an outdoor privy where she could sit and look at the view. D'you think these country people see indoors as a box, on the way to the final box? Pippa!'

'Yes love?'

Mark returned to the sitting room and took her in a tight hug, then sat her beside him on the little red Ikea sofa Pippa insisted on keeping as a souvenir of her snug basement flat in London, where they'd courted, both training at Guys. It looked sweetly absurd in the cool Georgian splendour of the old Skipton Doctor's House with its high ceilings and grand marble fireplaces. 'Don't let Olivia take you over, will you love? Remember she's better now.'

'I know she can be a bit bossy but it's only a mannerism. Wasn't it funny to see her so star-struck with Andy? Almost shy.'

'Well, no doing her housework. I'm sure she's a lovely girl, but she always struck me as inclined to give orders. Entitled.' He sat on the end of the little sofa and crooked one knee across the other to tie his laces.

Poor old Liv. That had been exactly how people saw her at school. Snobby Lolly, bullied for her bossiness, envied for her daring. The mill-owner's daughter with a pony.

'You saw her at her worst time, with her leg in bits, devastated at losing Fred—and her brother, too. Remember, I was paid to nurse her then—paid, as well as having that lovely little flat in Isobel's basement—so of course she was entitled to have me care for Olivia. And I still feel responsible for her, in a way.'

Mark raised an eyebrow. Pippa stood and went to tweak the flower arrangement, then faced him. 'Honestly, Liv's okay now. She loved Andy's lecture, didn't she? She's fun and brave and loyal. I want to see her back to being her old self, like she was before her parents' divorce. And I know I shouldn't speak ill of the dead, but I never liked her husband, Frederico. Far too old. Far too foreign. What she saw in him I'll never know.' Pippa pulled out a chrysanthemum stem and briskly stripped its lower leaves, dropping them in a waste paper bin.

'Why do you think she married him?' asked Mark.

It was amazing how little men knew about the female psyche, even doctors like Mark.

'Oh, it was so romantic. An older guy. They met at university, he was the foreign lecturer, and terribly handsome in that dark Italian way. Not tall, but incredibly charming. He loved her, and she fell for his whole family, that whole Florentine aristocrat thing with lots of cousins partying in big houses. The family she didn't have.'

'I love you, Pip. Tell Olivia I send her my best wishes. Don't be too late, will you love? I've got a brace of grouse. Grateful patient.'

Pippa hugged him goodbye and sneaked her Marigold gloves into the car behind his disappearing back. Poor old Liv, she must miss that warmth, the solid feel of a male body, the way your nose came level with a shoulder, the smell of clean shirt and how hair curled on his neck. That kind of innocence nice men had. Actually, had Frederico had that? Pippa slid a CD into the player, *What to Expect When You're Expecting*, and set off for the fifteen miles to Olivia's farm. In spite of her assurances to Mark she rather dreaded what she might find. It must have been six months since the last evening they'd spent together in Elizabeth Street. Olivia could walk again now, and had seemed fine at Andy's lecture—but was it possible she had recovered the morale and fitness necessary for this new life, so different, and so impulsively embarked on? Manoeuvring the car up the track to the farmhouse, Pippa glanced up for signs of life. Olivia was waving energetically from the overgrown terrace in front of the house and then running towards the farmyard gate, tugging it open for the car.

'Pippa!' They hugged. Olivia seemed taller somehow, and smelt of fresh air and sunshine. This was more like the old Olivia of their schooldays, the long legs and lean face, even the dark ponytail she had sported at twelve, before she had vanished to boarding school.

'Pippa, it's glorious here. Come in, come in and see the house.' Olivia was almost manic. Probably she had her downs too. But she seemed a different person today from the wreck she'd been in London those long months after the accident. A mother's care wasn't always best once you approached your thirties.

Pippa's own mother behaved like a proper mum, cooking and polishing her warm little house. She'd always been caustic about Isobel, and sympathetic when Olivia came to play with Pippa, plying her with cake and sympathising over small accidents and grazes. Thinking of this, Pippa said, in her mother's tone, 'How's the poor old leg now? A little better, is it?'

'The leg? Oh, fine. It's fine. I hardly notice it now. It's a bit shorter, but I've just walked a couple of miles over, up on the heather, so it must be cured.'

'A centimetre or two's differences is within normal variation. I've brought you a house warming, Liv. The bottles are from Mark and I made the cake, date and walnut, it's a Mary Berry recipe. I'm practising being a doctor's wife.'

'Oh, Pippa! What a beauty!' With the lid of the tin in hand, Olivia was momentarily overcome. She wiped her eyes with the back of her hand, quickly recovering. 'Aren't you working too? You should be, you're so good.'

'I've still got my agency job—since Mark and I got together I want to have that flexibility, specially now we're settling into the new house at Skipton. Anyway, what time did you arrive? Liv, you should have called us, we could have come over and given you a welcome.'

'The 31st of last month. Late. Oh, Pip, I was spooked, it was so gloomy. I nearly ran off to a B&B. But then when people were so nice at the pub, and I'd had my egg and chips, I braced up and managed to ignore the spooks.'

'You spent the night? By yourself? How did you stand it? I couldn't have stayed here alone for a minute. In the dark, on Hallowe'en! Wow, Liv. You always were so brave.'

'I suppose I feel nothing worse can happen. I've lost everything and if I'm fated to go too, so what? Bring it on.' She laughed. 'Actually a nice thing happened. The warmth of the storage heater woke up the bats. I was petrified until I realised what they were. They went round and round like a ceiling fan until I managed to shoo them out of the window. Come up and see my bedroom.'

Pippa followed up the creaky stairs and along a narrow corridor that gave on to a row of four doors. Olivia opened the end one, and stood aside smiling, ushering her in.

Even in its present state, the room was beautiful, golden November afternoon sunlight falling on the bed. Pippa went straight to the window, forced up the catch and pushed the casement wide open. Fresh air stirred cobwebs on the pelmet. The location of Oxhide was stunning, it would be like living permanently on one of those photo-opportunity parking places in the alps. 'Wow, what a view! Lucky old you! Better than London, isn't it? How is Isobel, by the way?'

'Mama's flourishing, as always. Missing you, of course, nobody to dust and run her errands. But I think she was relieved to be rid of me. A sad daughter's rather a downer to have around the house. Of course she does work hard, she has her own life. No, we don't miss each other, Isobel and me. I never want to hear another Beethoven piano sonata.'

'She's talented, your mum. I liked the sound of her practising. And she's so glamorous when she goes out. When are the rest of your things coming, furniture and so on?'

'Everything's in storage,' said Olivia. 'Masses of it, stuff my father's new wife Bridget didn't want, as well as Freddie's family furniture from Torralba. And this place is still full of Robertshaw remains. I'm going to get a skip, make a clean sweep and have just a few things I like. It's funny they didn't clear the house, it just didn't occur to anyone, I suppose. They'd got used to their Gran's place being in a time-warp.'

'Yes, I think they'd given up on it. Mark's Dad said old Mrs. Robertshaw became quite a hermit, frightened of change, just wanted to keep everything as it had been. Old people are like that. They get disoriented more easily.'

'But it meant the land was unspoilt. That's why I bought it. Dad was surprised— you're not supposed to be able to buy farmland in the Dales National Park. Mrs. R. didn't modernise anything, so the land never improved, as they say. No liming, no fertilizers, no draining, no weedkiller. The little stone buildings. It's beautiful, and Meg and Mike Robertshaw wanted somebody who'd take care of the old hay meadows, the rare plants and birds and proper limestone walls. And that's what I wanted, to maintain the traditional farmed landscape, as Fred and I planned at Trebbia, so it was perfect.'

Maybe this could work, after all. If anybody could do this, it was the Olivia she remembered from the Ilkley days. 'Are you going to show me round outside?'

Olivia grinned, her old smile with a gap between the front incisors. 'Yes, come on Pippa! Ridiculous to waste time indoors when my very best friend arrives at the start of my new life!'

Pale sun lit the shaggy grass on the terrace along the front of the house. A few yellow roses still in flower hung over the porch. Lucky old Liv! Pippa fetched Wellingtons from her car instead of the cleaning things she'd brought. They went out through the kitchen at the back, crossed the yard, and climbed crooked stone steps to where the main farm buildings stood, backed into the hill like sheltering cattle. The green corrugated walls of a new Dutch barn towered over the stone cowshed, stable and cart shed. A puff of wind like a breath of approaching winter fluttered a few last leaves down.

Olivia was taking over gradually, she explained, learning the ropes as she went, doing a part-time course at college but discovering far more from Mike Robertshaw and his kids. His family had farmed here since the middle ages. They ran a big concern these days, with land in the Vale of York too, so he wasn't hard-up like Olivia's neighbours down the dale, 'the poor old Yarkers' Olivia called them, pointing out their smallholding, Skellside.

The neglected farmyard lay under horrific tangles of brambles, thistles and nettles that half-concealed unidentifiable objects and equipment. Could Olivia really resist all weed killers? They fetched heavy garden gloves and secateurs. Stacks of rotting fence posts, rusty buckets, rolls of blue plastic sheeting sheltered slugs and earwigs, and even a small grey Fordson tractor, irretrievably rusted. How tiny it was. You couldn't hide a modern tractor in a bramble bush. Mark would love it, Pippa could picture him with Andy, trying to get it going again.

'It's the right scale for these fields.' Olivia pulled at a string of creeping grass and uncovered the small iron seat. 'There's one like it in the pub, in one of those old photos of local life, it looked to be about the fifties. I suppose old Mrs. Robertshaw might have been one of the little girls helping. Men hay-making, women bringing picnics, families together, one little tractor pulling a tedding machine. It might be this very one.'

In the end of a cart shed roofed in rusty corrugated iron, partly loose, they found more recent relics, testifying to the decline of the old Robertshaw parents: a grey metal filing cabinet, a drawer hanging open with curled mould-blackened papers spilling out; a child's swing, a broken garden bench, a pony saddle, stiff and floury with mould. Pippa backed off. It looked a health hazard.

Olivia had seemed better, with all her old spark, but now her shoulders drooped. It was four and already daylight faded and mist gathered in the shadows.

'I don't think there's much more we can do out here, Liv, anyway. Let's just have tea and a bit of that cake and then I'd better be off. We can watch Andy, it's time for *Invisible Wildlife* in a moment.'

'Really?' The name acted on Olivia like the promise of chocolate to a tired child. 'Oh, Andrew's my hero! Thank you so much for taking me to his lecture. I hope I didn't behave too stupidly—I used to watch *Invisible Wildlife* every week in London. I had to try and distract Mama from watching anything else when he was on. She never saw the point of it at all. In her family, wildlife's just for hunting, shooting or painting pictures of.'

Pippa laughed. It was true, Isobel used to send her out to the expensive shop at the end of Elizabeth Street for quails' eggs and partridges, and there were some horribly lifeless oil paintings of dead birds and fruit on the landing.

'There's an old telly in the sitting room,' Olivia said. 'You never know—let's have a look at it, see if it works.'

'We always enjoy watching Andy on TV. It feels so funny seeing someone you know getting famous. It's a pity Mark'll miss it because of surgery hours.'

'I wish I'd met him sooner. He must have visited you in Mama's house? To think I was moping about at the top of the house like Elizabeth Barrett, while you had all these exciting friends jollying down below.'

'He wasn't around last year; working abroad. He'll probably stay with us though, before long. He and Mark were friends long before I met Mark. They're almost like blood brothers.'

They kicked off their boots in the dark passageway. Pippa left Olivia to find TV reception, and went to collect the cake. Wondering where the plates were, she gazed around the big cold kitchen that was Olivia's future base, musing about life.

Love was such a strange thing, the way it struck. Look at Mark—not in any way gay, but forever linked by a first juvenile encounter to Andrew Bamberg; so that to Pippa, Andy seemed almost a brother-in-law. Or look at Olivia—bonded to that defunct exotic charmer Fred Gabrieli, strongly enough to declare this ridiculous vow of never re-marrying, burying herself up at Oxhide and spending all Fred's money on her weird green project. Of course, Liv had always been mad about nature. And these days, surely having the occasional fling wouldn't count as breaking a vow. All the same, it was strange. To quote Old Amos in *The Dalesman* –'There's nowt so queer as folk!'

Pippa carried her tea tray through to the front of the house.

The sitting room was cosy, in spite of its grime—long and low, facing out across the dale. Much cosier than the Doctors' House. Pippa turned on a lamp in the far corner, and there, connected by coils of dirty cable to a yellowing wall socket, was a small cubical television with an indoor aerial, a small loop of black plastic on top. It didn't look as though Mark would get a detailed report of this week's *Invisible Wildlife* this evening. Without hope she crouched beside the set, switched it on and waggled the aerial. When she looked up Olivia was watching in a concentrated way that made her feel like a circus ringmaster bringing on the highlight act. At first nothing appeared on the little screen. Poor Olivia sat crouched on the deep windowsill, watching Pippa's efforts and cradling her mug in both hands. But at last the set crackled and Andrew's figure emerged from a screenful of static snow. They pulled over two disgusting fireside chairs.

Olivia leaned forward to the picture like one long-starved of television. Pippa determined her friend should get a proper flat-screen, even if, tucked here on the hillside, it needed a satellite dish on a pylon to get a clear picture.

Invisible Wildlife wasn't billed as a children's programme, but that was how Pippa had always thought of it. Andy came across like an uncle, benign but authoritative. His helpers Julie and Dave, like ideal older cousins on holiday, rushed about full of enthusiasm and energy in their patterned jumpers and bright anoraks.

'It's amazing how little they know, when they're so enthusiastic,' Olivia observed, caustic as ever. 'I suppose they're actors. The producer's told them to grin at the camera and hang on Andrew's words as though they haven't the faintest idea about anything until he tells them.'

'They're enjoying themselves. I wouldn't have much idea about owl pellets. Would you?'

'No—but I would have looked things up first, if I was expecting to spend time in a place like that, with an expert like him.'

'But then the programme would just have been you showing off, Liv!'

'Uh?' Olivia stared at Pippa for a tense moment—then, thankfully, giggled. Years rolled back. It was a relief she hadn't lost her knack of making her friend laugh, gently teasing Olivia off her high horse.

'It's okay, Andy knows what he's doing. He does that jolly uncle act on purpose, he told Mark and me, he tries to draw the audience in, not put them down. It has to be fun, to make people watch, it mustn't sound like a lesson. He said it would be worth the effort if just somebody, somewhere, understood what's lost when marshes full of birds and frogs and dragonflies get drained for playing fields, or cow parsley on verges is mown flat in the name of safety.'

Remembering Andrew's words, Pippa saw again what a clever presenter he was, and how well he succeeded in foregrounding his subject. Places were the real stars of *Invisible Wildlife*, landscapes from fens to forests, manure heaps to mountain ranges—*ecosystems* was the proper term in biology, she remembered. Andy spoke little and was mainly positioned to the side of the frame in middle shot, never as a close-up talking head. You always saw the whole of him, but his expression was clear: humorous and genial. He spoke simply and enthusiastically and never assumed anybody would know anything already, or be as interested as he was himself.

Although, occasionally, he would insert a surprising capsule of science. 'I want correct scientific names, properly spelt,' he said now, speaking to camera so that, watching, Pippa felt almost admonished.

Olivia was delighted by his sternness. 'That's more like it. He let the mask slip. It was like a real scientist speaking. I'd love to talk to him again Pippa; such an interesting man.'

'I wonder if we could get him to make a programme about your project here at Oxhide? Shall we suggest it? It could follow the story of your farm right from the start.'

'I don't see why he should. I'm sure he's busy in London. He wouldn't want to come all the way up here. And what if the story went wrong? The wrong slant—reality TV, posh southern girl falls on her face among real folk?'

'Andy's all right,' said Pippa. 'He's terribly serious about what he does. But he has a sense of humour, too. You should see how he and Mark fool about, like little boys.'

'Tell me more about him.'

'He has this big idea about the soil. He says people think of it as just dirt but it's alive really, and terribly important for everything. Not just agriculture, but the world. Mark and he have silly arguments about bacteria—Andy loves them, Mark hates them.'

'Goodness. He doesn't look like an agricultural type. More of a scientist—it's easier to imagine him at a microscope than ploughing a field.'

'He is a scientist really, it's his main job. He's published loads of high-powered articles, too technical for me. The TV's a sideline he turned out to have a gift for. An old girlfriend got him on her programme. I've a lot of respect for Andrew,' said Pippa, refilling Olivia's empty cup. 'Even though he's not my type. A bit strange, if you know what I mean. But he is determined. A man with a mission. He wants to stop people spoiling things. Like the off-roaders on the moor you hate so much. He'd deal with them, all right.'

'I'd like to meet him again,' Olivia repeated. 'He said something about being up north soon?'

After Pippa left, Olivia sprawled in front of the tiny television with a gin and tonic, half watching the news. When football followed, she ran upstairs to her laptop and, without permitting time for doubt, shot off an email to Andrew Bamberg's university contact address.

'Dear Andrew Bamberg (if I may?)'—nice touch—'I was fascinated by your lecture at the Natural History Museum, to which Pippa and Mark kindly brought me along. You mentioned you might like to see my farm in Upper Wharfedale with a view to investigating soil biology in an undisturbed upland pasture, and I am writing at Pippa's suggestion'—had Pippa actually suggested that? Never mind—'to say you would be more than welcome. Do let me know if you would like *to fit in a visit to Oxhide on your next journey north. With best wishes Olivia Gabrieli'*

Pausing only to delete '*(Nicole!)*' after her signature as a step too far, Olivia downed the last of her gin and pressed send.

4

Roots

Olivia rang the front door bell at The Hollies a week later. It felt so familiar still, as she stood on the top of the three sandstone steps she'd dared herself to jump down as a child, twenty years ago. The steps still sparkled with mica, the way she'd loved. If you shut first one eye and then the other, the tiny glittering flecks seemed to flick from one spot to another. But Bridget and Anne lived here now, Joe's new family. Olivia felt like a ghost from the house's past. Things had changed. She imagined a time-warp, her eight-year-old self looking down from the nursery window at her grown-up version from the future, getting out of a red car and ringing her own front door bell.

Joe opened the door, looking less impressive than she remembered, in an open-necked shirt and a regrettable beige ribbed-knit cardigan with leather elbow patches, a complete change from the pinstripe tailored suit he'd always worn to go to the mill, or his weekend jeans and tweed jacket.

'Come in, Liv,' he invited, unintentionally demoting her to a guest as he opened the front door and stood aside. White carpets had replaced the hall parquet where the grandfather clock, now in Isobel's London flat, used to stand. Then, suddenly, 'Olivia!', and he was himself again, giving her a bear hug, holding her at arm's length, hands on her shoulders, studying her face, and then another hug. 'I've been waiting for you to turn up.' He turned to Bridget who had come down stairs and joined him in the hall, beaming at her.

'Olivia! How are you love? We've been wondering about you, haven't we Joe? Oh, I did hate leaving you after the funeral. I said we should have stayed, didn't I Joe?' Bridget wore the same royal blue. It shot Olivia back to the terrible day Freddie's body was carried down the aisle in its box, wreathed with cold lilies.

'And here's Anne,' Joe said, as his new daughter, model two, appeared from the direction of the kitchen, a blonde teenager in jeans ripped and creased in all the right places. They would have cost a ludicrous amount, judging from the shop windows she and Pippa had passed on their way to the museum in London. Anne looked her up and down shyly, then took the plunge and hugged her. Anne was nice, a grown-up teenager. She smelled agreeably of fresh air and offered to take Olivia's coat.

'Quite the Dales farmer,' Bridget said, clocking the waxed jacket.

Olivia assured her it wasn't a Barbour, just a snip from Skipton market.

'It looks very smart, anyway, quite the latest fashion,' said Bridget in excessively mollifying tones. Olivia told herself they weren't in London now and her stepmother wasn't being ironically offensive. Bridget was guileless; remarks that might have seemed two-edged in Isobel's drawing room were innocent, even well-meant, here. But she still found Bridget irritating, specially her next sally: 'Let's have drinks, shall we, Daddy?' *Daddy!*

Joe went off to the kitchen and a moment later they heard the pop of a champagne cork. He returned carrying a brass tray with four glasses, already gathering dew. He offered one first to Bridget, then to Anne and Olivia, and all three of the new Burbank family raised their glasses to her, Olivia Gabrieli. Three pairs of blue eyes, Bridget's nicely made-up, Anne's large and bright, and her father's slightly bloodshot and shadowed by eyebrows bristlier and more overgrown than she remembered.

Bridget and Anne produced a delicious beef Stroganoff for lunch, and a properly alcoholic trifle. After a glass or two more—the new Burbanks liked fizz and didn't stint on alcohol—he lost the slightly shamefaced deference he'd initially assumed towards Olivia, and became jovial and relaxed. Bridget was evidently a more comfortable wife for him than Isobel. After lunch Bridget suggested, with tact Olivia hadn't given her credit for, that she and Anne would take the dog for his walk. Joe and Olivia could stay and have their coffee in peace, she said, and pick up the threads.

His study had avoided Bridget's renovations. Olivia breathed in the old scent—wood, books, Pear's soap and tobacco. A friendly masculine smell, that can't be imitated by bottled scents with names like Old Spice, or Imperial Leather, because some essential component comes from the living man. At the big windows on to the garden, old green velvet curtains had faded from bottle to sage. Bookcases lined one wall from floor to ceiling. The latest exhibition catalogues joined the collection of art books on its deep lower shelves. There were his Latin and Greek texts from university days; some sets of classics—George Eliot, Trollope, Hardy—and various directories and reference books, *Fly Fishing*, *The Rough Guide to Finland. Eat Yourself Thin* and *She Never Forgave Him* must surely be Bridget's. In a space on one shelf stood a silver-framed photograph—a holiday snapshot of Bridget and Anne, all piano-key grins and blond windblown hair, sitting on a beach. A large round table occupied the centre of the room. She and Isobel had trespassed on it while he was out at work. Its big shiny surface was ideal for cutting out material. The polished grain reminded her of making a school nativity costume—tall, dark Olivia was a shepherd (only fair children were allowed to be angels). Now it held nothing but a thin report file, and marigolds in a pewter tankard. Old mismatched leather armchairs faced each other across the empty fireplace. Opposite the windows, small English eighteenth century landscapes covered most of the room's back wall. There was one in the centre Olivia didn't remember.

'That's a new one, isn't it, Dad? I don't remember it.'

'My latest extravagance, yes.'

Joe looked quietly delighted, the way he'd done when he'd landed a half-pound trout from the Wharfe. The picture was small, only about six inches square in its faded gold frame, and densely detailed. He stood and they went over to look closely. He unhooked it and brought it to the light. The harder you looked, the more you saw; and the more its tiny world drew you in. A gibbous moon shone in a twilit sky behind the spire of a village church, while at ground level it was almost dark. A small figure carried a sheaf of corn and another had a scythe over his shoulder.

'A pastoral vision,' said Joe. 'Calm and order in a perfect little landscape. Maybe a bit like your dream of Oxhide, Liv? I'd rather live in yours than Samuel Palmer's, I think. Plenty of hot water and a Land Rover in the yard—not pickled in peat smoke.'

A Land Rover. That was a thought.

He looked up from his study of the picture, straight into her eyes. 'How are things, really, Liv? Oxhide is a lot to take on. It can't be easy.'

'It's getting better. It's so beautiful. It was lonely at first. I couldn't have managed if it hadn't been for Pippa. D'you remember my friend Pippa, from Moorfield? She came to help Mummy in London. She sends you her love. She says she always liked you, when we played together, do you remember?'

'How nice of her. I can't say I do. I hope you'll be all right, Liv. A business is a worry, God knows. Getting shot of the firm was the best thing I ever did'

Olivia said nothing. It had seemed at the time more like the firm shedding Joe. The whole woollen industry had collapsed, leaving her father bankrupt.

'And getting together with Bridget,' he went on. 'I was no good for your mother, I'm afraid. Bridget's a comfort to me, and Anne.'

It was true that glamorous Isobel was not cut out to be a comfort to anybody. When Olivia arrived in London in need of comfort after the accident, Isobel had to hire it in.

'I'm so pleased to have met Anne,' said Olivia, choosing safer ground. 'She's great. Like you. Your sane daughter, Dad.'

They laughed. It was the kind of shared laugh they used to have. Olivia was assimilating the thought of Anne. She'd previously thought of her half-sister as the beautiful grown-up version of the little bridesmaid she'd been when Olivia had last met her. To Olivia then, Anne was like her father's proper daughter, an upgrade and rival. Today, Anne's unassuming friendliness had replaced this spectre with a real person. Anne hadn't chosen her blue eyes, blonde hair or annoyingly perfect teeth. And Joe was still her father, even with his new family.

'Oxhide is perfect. I'm so happy there, Dad. When I come down when it's getting light, and see the fields and the fell behind, and hear the sound of the beck close—well, it's just marvellous. The other day I opened the door and there was a mushroom in the intake field below the house, shining white, as though it had come specially for my breakfast.'

'Hmmm.' This was too fanciful for Joe. 'Sure it wasn't a golf ball? Bit late for mushrooms. How's the business plan coming?'

Olivia was about to show off the work she had done with Jane, give Joe a summary and projections, explain how Freddie's legacy was going into the business, but hopefully Oxhide would have an income in two years' time. But it didn't seem Joe was asking for in-depth analysis. He was watching her with an eyebrow raised, as he had when she'd been a small girl and, unlike Isobel, would listen to her accounts of her childish worries about difficult people at school and give advice on dealing with them. Ilkley Moor's horizon crossed the square of blue sky in the window behind his head. A great affection for him welled up, and, like a physical blow to the solar plexus, a huge, impossible longing for the past. To turn the calendar back before the divorce, before Freddie, long before jolly Bridget and Anne. To be ten again, in this room before supper, doing maths prep at her father's study table, her mother Isobel practising *Kinderszenen* on the baby grand in the drawing room, and her twin brother Ben not dead, but a little boy again, shouting and kicking his football around the garden. Why did everything have to let itself be spoiled? Before she knew it was coming, a terrible sob broke from her. Joe jumped and dropped the picture on the table. He pulled his chair beside her and took her in his arms.

'Ah, Olivia, love. I know, I know. I'm so sorry. I'm sorry.'

His hand was comforting, patting her shoulder gently, like a rider trying to calm a horse before it bolted with him. Olivia freed an arm from his embrace and dug for a tissue in her jeans pocket. She sucked in a deep breath and felt the shock of emotion ebb.

'Ridiculous. I'm so sorry, Daddy. I don't know where that came from. It was the moor—it reminded me . . .'

The moor, and the smell of the study. She wiped her eyes and nose and took another deep breath. Breathe right out, the therapist told her. Relax your muscles. Think of a beautiful calm scene. Damn, it was the moor again that did a fade-in on her mind's screen, that Open Sesame to memories. It had taken her to her childhood self, lying in bed in the nursery on long light June evenings, watching light fade on the moor side opposite. Its surface detail waned: all the landmarks she knew—White Wells, the paddling pool, the track to Panorama Woods, the Swastika Stone and Heber's Ghyll; the leafy suburban roads of Victorian villas curving up to the moor's edge. All changed to a purple-black cut-out, the moor's constant profile sharp against the navy blue sky. She would look for the first star before sleep; you could only see them from the corner of your eye, never looking straight. The moor was eternal, she thought; it would always be there, not like mutable, mortal people. She was about to share this with her father—he would have understood—but wheels on the gravel, followed by car door noises and Bridget's holloa from the hall, changed the atmosphere.

A Cairn terrier ran in shaking and spraying a muddy shower at Bridget's cream-fronted kitchen units. Joe went to help unload the shopping and Olivia dived into the downstairs loo to splash cold water on her red eyes and comb her hair before facing her cheery stepmother.

As she entered the kitchen, Bridget was drying the little dog, who squirmed in circles as she rubbed his belly fur with a towel.

'I love what you've done to the kitchen, Bridget. So light! What does this do? Oh, it's an ice-cream maker, brilliant! However did you get the old range out? That was quite a museum piece. Where shall I put this?' Olivia extracted a tissue-wrapped loaf from the shopping bag and held it up interrogatively.

'That's Joe's special salt-free bread, it goes in that tin.'

'Why salt-free, Dad?' Olivia assessed her father from the corner of her eye. His springy red hair had thinned and faded to a sandy grey, and maybe he had put on a bit too much weight. He looked as though he had gone up several collar sizes, the angle of his jaw engulfed by new folds of neck.

'It's good for blood pressure, they say.'

'Why? Is yours high?'

'You don't want to know. The medico gave me pills, but they made me feel so awful I don't take them. Knocked the stuffing out of me. I must just be designed as a high-pressure system.'

Olivia wondered what to say. She remembered the gravely neutral face of the doctor in the Florence maternity hospital, as he undid the blood pressure cuff from her arm and rolled it up. And the morning several weeks later, when she'd woken with a sense of loss and then a quick, panicked realisation why. The baby had stopped moving. The absurd, exciting sense of a person squirming and kicking inside her had gone. Olivia had no need of doctors to tell her their son was dead. She switched the memory off with an effort.

'Maybe you should stick to the medicine, Daddy. I'm glad Bridget's taking good care of you.'

Just then, Anne put her head round the door. 'Bye Olivia—sorry to rush off, have to go and muck out before it's too dark to tell the dung from the straw. Please come again—we're sisters aren't we?'

'Of course we are. It's been great to meet you properly, Anne. Weddings and funerals aren't the best place to meet, are they?'

Anne laughed. 'Can I come and see your farm? I'm very jealous. And I'm looking for a field, I'd better warn you.' She kissed Olivia quickly and, seizing a handful of carrots from a vegetable rack by the back door, ran out. Soon they heard her car churning up gravel.

'She's a talented rider,' said Bridget. 'She'd love to help on the farm. You have only to say the word.'

'She's a terror,' said Joe indulgently. A little stab of jealousy pricked Olivia.

'I must be off, too. I'll get my coat, I know the hall cupboard.' She kissed Bridget and patted her father's shoulder. 'I feel so much happier, Daddy,' she said on the step, out of earshot of Bridget.

'Me too. So long, my love. See you soon?'

'Very soon.'

The business discussion would have to wait. Reconciliation with her father was worth more than anything.

'Damn!' Olivia dropped her paint roller into the tray. The landline phone in the passage rang. Sunday morning at Oxhide. Giles, doing the dining room ceiling, stood on a stool holding a full paint tray in his left hand.

'You better get it, Olivia, no way I can.'

The swish of the paintbrush stopped as she answered. 'Hello? Olivia Gabrieli, Oxhide.'

'Liv! How are you? It's only me. Okay if I come over today?'

'Oh, Anne. Hi, good to hear you. Well, when would you like to? I'm a little tied up at this moment.'

Anne was insistent. 'There's lots of things I want to talk to you about. Daddy's been on at me to phone you. In an hour or two?'

'Has anything happened, Anne?'

'No, don't worry. It's only I'm a bit desperate.'

'Oh Anne! Tell me.'

'I have to move the horses. Olivia, you couldn't?'

'Is it urgent? It's just, horses—I love them, but they aren't the best for my fields, you know? With winter coming on? Look, come over tomorrow and we'll think about it.'

'Oh, wow. Thanks Liv. About two?'

Doubtless Olivia herself had been equally insensitive at nineteen. It wouldn't take long. Bridget would want Anne to get home again to the Hollies before it was pitch dark, she was that sort of parent. Olivia agreed, and returned to the half-painted room.

'Sounds like you have a problem there,' said Giles. 'This Anne, she's trouble, is she?'

'No, not at all,' said Olivia. She picked up her gloves and moved the paint pot to the windowsill ready to go on with the work. 'She's my sister.'

'I thought you only had your twin brother, who passed away?' It was good to have Giles helping but sometimes he seemed almost too much at home in her house. It was a fine line between solicitous and nosy.

'Anne's my little half-sister. My father's second daughter. They live in Ilkley, I'll see quite a bit of them I expect.' No harm in Giles knowing she wasn't entirely on her own. 'Anne needs grazing for her horses apparently. It's not a good time of year, is it? Those horseshoes make an awful muddy mess of a field. She's coming over.'

Anne turned up at two thirty. They had finished the walls and

Giles was doing the windows with masking tape, going all round the mullions with dedication.

'Ooh, can I help?'

'We only have two paint rollers,' said Olivia.

'But you've got to do the woodwork still,' said Anne. 'Couldn't I do some sanding or something?'

'Don't you bother, Anne,' said Olivia. 'Giles is nearly finished for today, it's quicker when you've had plenty of practice. And the light goes so early, it's hardly worth starting now.'

'I've had practice,' said Anne. 'I helped Mum do all the bedrooms at The Hollies.'

'Really?' How hands-on of Bridget. Olivia couldn't imagine Isobel contemplating doing the decorating.

'Mum's an interior designer. She'd still be working, only Daddy won't let her. By the way, Olivia, did you know, *Brilliant White* isn't usually best for old houses. There's a Farrow and Ball colour called *Pointing* that's softer. Goes better with stone. Most people prefer it. Mum can get you some at a discount.'

Giles stopped painting with a snort of laughter. 'That's you told, Olivia.' He climbed from the stool and deposited the roller and paint tray on the floor. 'Did anybody say tea?'

Giles put out mugs proprietorially and offered Olivia's biscuits to Anne, who picked out two chocolate ones. There was more banter about paint. Afterwards, Anne said she wanted to see the farm. It was a late afternoon of low sun after rain. Olivia took her along the road a little way to view Oxhide and its land from relatively firm ground. Anne wore sensible horsey outdoor gear.

'It's not really horse country, I'm afraid,' said Olivia, before Anne could start on again, cadging grazing.

'The grass is still growing, isn't it?' said Anne.

The small fields along the road sloping up the valley side in parallel strips between massive limestone walls, glowed bright green, horse heaven.

'They're hayfields,' said Olivia. 'They wouldn't stand up to horses' feet, they'd poach the soil to mud in no time.'

'Oh, that's normal,' said Anne. 'They'll be green again in the spring.'

'Aye,' said Giles, who'd abandoned his painting to tag along. 'That's nature. Always comes up again, you won't stop grass growing with a few horses on.'

'Not so,' said Olivia. What did they know of invisible wildlife? 'You know what happens, Giles. All that dung and trampling, you get nettles and thistles and docks. Not cowslips and orchids. Of course, you don't have orchids at Skellside, do you?'

'We just have ordinary grass. A few weeds, but horses won't mind what weeds they're on, long as they're green,' said Giles, and Anne laughed, displaying those flawless white teeth. 'My Dad might have a bit of land for a horse or two, if they were quiet, like. He's used to horses, he used to have two. I can show you now, if you don't mind a bit further to walk.'

'Seriously?' Anne said. Olivia remained silent.

'Aye. You don't need to come, Olivia, our yard's mucky. I can see Anne's used to country ways.' He glanced approvingly at Anne's ordinary non-Hunter wellingtons.

'Is that okay, Olivia? I'll be back as soon as Giles's shown me the field.'

'Of course it's okay. You're not the one I'm paying.'

'Oof.'

'Sorry, that was so ungrateful of me, Giles. I'll go back and enjoy my beautiful newly-painted room. See you later, Anne. I'd like to see a horse or two around the place.'

'You won't have to worry about no orchids getting trampled at Skellside, any road,' Olivia heard Giles say, as she turned to head back to Oxhide.

Half an hour later Anne was back with Giles, beaming. 'Giles's Dad said I can have their field and a shelter for the winter. I'm over the moon! When can I bring them?' She turned to Giles.

Them? Surely Anne had only mentioned one, her rescue thoroughbred. Called Dreamcatcher, like something in a pony book.

'Soon's you want, Anne. Dad and I'll be in, we're not going anywhere. Want me to get you in some hay?'

The Yarkers obviously didn't make their own, from the look of their fields. He probably meant fetching a few bales from a friend, probably baled damp and mouldy inside.

'Ooh yes please,' said Anne. They arranged that she'd bring two horses the very next week.

The following Friday, as Olivia worked on her sheep course, the phone rang again. Anne with her horses, due to arrive within the hour at Skellside.

'I'll come over,' said Olivia, half resigned, half pleased at the distraction and the prospect of seeing horses. She too had a pony childhood, and found equine solace in her stormy teens. And she even had to admit she looked forward to Anne's cheerful face. She finished her paragraph and stacked her work away.

Giles was letting down the front ramp of Anne's trailer as Olivia picked her way into Skellside's quagmire of a yard. Knowing what to expect, she was in wellingtons. Mud threatened to seep over the tops of Anne's jodhpur boots as she went to untie the first horse's headcollar. He was a dark bay cob, already shaggy in his winter coat, who emerged calmly.

Anne handed the lead rope to Giles and went for the other horse. A white blaze on a long chestnut face appeared and with a bound and crash a tall skinny thoroughbred burst out.

'The cob is Comet,' said Anne, 'and this is my rescue horse. Dreamcatcher. My baby. She'll make a super brood mare. She's by a Scorpion stallion. Well, that's what they told me.'

'That's a big horse,' said Giles. But when they saw the shed he'd divided into two loose boxes it was clear why he worried. He'd obviously not been expecting what was virtually a racehorse. Dreamcatcher revolved uneasily in a tiny space only just large enough to contain her.

'We'll do what we can, Anne,' said Giles. 'Dad'n me'll have a think. They can go out for now.'

He led the way to the field behind the farm house. Perhaps two or three acres, it was fine as a pony paddock, but Olivia couldn't see Dreamcatcher settling there. The enterprise looked like trouble and she wished she'd repulsed Anne's horsey overtures. She wanted to please her father and make friends with Anne, but now the rhythmic banging of Dreamcatcher's hoof against the flimsy walls of the Yarkers' shed seemed to beat out the knell of that budding family reconciliation.

Anne put a waterproof rug on the clipped chestnut and they led both animals out to the field. Comet systematically tore at the long grass, avoiding clumps of dying thistles, but Dreamcatcher paced around staring at the unfamiliar surroundings with rolling eyes. Giles promised to keep an eye on them and Anne said she would call by on her way home to make sure all was well.

'That'll do for a bit,' said Anne, as they trudged back up to Oxhide in the November twilight, Anne throwing backward glances as though she expected to hear galloping hoofs on the road. 'She does tend to jump out. It's better than where I had them before. My field's been sold to developers. Sixteen five-bedroom houses. "For the family that lives life to the full",' she quoted bitterly. 'I have to move them. So now we'll be neighbours,' she added with chirpiness, turning to Olivia. 'I'll be here lots. We can go riding, I can help you gather your sheep.'

Olivia made no reply. Could she stand having Anne around, schmoozing the Yarkers and dictating paint colours? But back at the farmhouse she had to admit Anne's company was welcome. Her loud voice denied ghosts and chased shadows. Far better than a sensitive companion sharing her sorrow and offering hugs. The tawny owl started up in the clattering ash trees. 'Spookeee!' said Anne, and Olivia laughed.

Anne built an efficient girl guider's fire that caught and blazed. Olivia had crumpets in the freezer. They sat in new armchairs each side of the hearth warming their stockinged feet, wiping melted butter from their chins and talking about their father.

'Your Mum's good for Joe, I can see,' said Olivia.

'Daddy? It sounds so strange, you calling him Joe. It's like he's two different people. What was he like with you, Olivia?'

'Imposing. Very busy. The mill took all his time. Eventually, I mean. At first, when I was tiny, he was fun. We went skiing, he's a very good skier, almost professional standard.'

'Daddy? I can't see him on skis,' said Anne. 'Too crumbly. He gardens a lot.'

'He's changed so much from how I remember. Sometimes on a Saturday morning Mama and I would go see him at his office in the mill. The wages clerk would be there, Mrs. Kershaw. She knitted me a shawl when I was a baby. We would go up to the machine room with the enormous looms, the smell of oil and wool lanoline. It was so imposing those days. It's hard to imagine now. The place is derelict. He has to inspect it for the insurance and he always needs a stiff drink when he gets back.'

'I think that insolvency must have been very hard for him. A family firm. He must have felt he'd dropped the baton.'

'What?'

'I think inheriting the firm was like a sacred trust to him. And he felt he was the one who failed to keep it going. Did you ever see the chimney?'

'What chimney?'

'It had our name all the way up. You could see it across the valley from the train. Burbank.'

'Wow. You must have been proud.'

'I was. Insufferable. Though Freddie thought it was funny, to have your name on a palazzo, I mean it was built to imitate an Italian renaissance palace and Freddie's family had lived in the real thing.'

'What a grand pair you must have been.'

'Yes . . . yes, we were pretty grand.'

The farmhouse was oppressively quiet, folded into the silence of a late November dusk, after Anne's trailer had rattled down the track. Olivia ran a hot bath in her gorgeous new bathroom, en suite with her bedroom, and mused about the day. Why had she been so negative about Anne's horses? How well Anne had taken it, having them relegated to scruffy Skellside. This was no way to populate her homestead. Affection warmed in her as she soaped herself and replayed Anne's nineteen-year-old voice in her mind's ear. Anne was her sister, for goodness' sake. Horses weren't irreconcilable with sustainable management—Comet might turn out to be perfect for riding up on to the moor to check her sheep; better than quad bikes. And a little horsey stuff would be a draw for the holiday cottage tenants. As long as they didn't get in the way of the soil scientists. Adding more hot water with her toes on the tap, Olivia dreamed about Andrew Bamberg and *Invisible Wildlife* at Oxhide. He hadn't responded to her rather drunken email. Hopefully, it had disappeared into his spam folder. What had he meant, saying he'd be up north in two weeks? Why would he have said that if he hadn't wanted to keep in touch?

The door to the Doctor's House on Sheep Street had a columned portico and fanlight, and an iron boot scraper set into the stone doorstep. Pippa tugged the handsome door open and was quick to explain the apparent grandeur of the interior as Olivia stepped in. 'It really was the doctor's house once, but now the practice partners live out of town, it's too big and draughty, and there's no parking. It was empty several years before we took on the lease. To be honest we rattle about in it rather at the moment.'

The too-familiar new paint smell was here, too, in the high vaulted hall, as if new beginnings were everywhere. New houses, new terms, new lives. Pippa, too, was nesting—with a more plausible rationale than Olivia's, being pregnant. She tore open a parcel as big as a sheep, unfolded a length of cloth and held it for Olivia to see, beside a sash window at least six feet high. The plain dark blue looked distinguished against the pale grey walls. The fabric was a bargain, the end of a roll, Pippa said, rerolling the cloth and heaving the pile of material on to a chair. Then she hugged Olivia. 'Oh Liv, I'm sorry, you didn't come to admire my curtains. What have I become?' She looked at her watch. 'I'd no idea it was so late. Twelve o'clock. Lunch time. Look, the kitchen's hopeless. Let's go to the café.'

It was an old-style market town café a few doors away, vases of blue and red anemones in the steamed-up windows and a queue at the doorway. Twelve o'clock meant a late coffee for Olivia, here the café was already busy.

Pippa greeted several people. Olivia admired how she blended, neat and clean in her calfheight sheepskin-topped boots and straight skirt. A smart blue leather tote bag held her scarf and woolly gloves. Going to Skipton was a visit to town for people here. Olivia, unused to misreading the dress code, felt wrongfooted in her brown cord jeans and old Barbour. Was she even a little smelly?

A waitress greeted Pippa with a 'Hi' and went to wipe clean a table for two in the window. Eventually Pippa turned to the subject Oliva wanted to hear about. 'Have you heard from Andy? He was very interested in your plans. He mentioned you again when he phoned Mark last weekend.'

'Really? No, I've heard nothing since that amazing lecture. Tell me more.' Olivia leaned forward, elbows on the table.

'He was definitely excited. He was going on to Mark about how some unspoiled farmland soil was just what he needed. Apparently, to get your research funded, you have to fill in forms saying what practical use it might be. There's a box to fill called "likely end-users of the data". Andy's thinking of you as an end-user.' Pippa giggled. 'Nicole the end-user!'

How exciting if there was invisible wildlife in her fields. An international scientist interested in Oxhide—that would be something to boast to Jane about. She pictured Andrew Bamberg arriving. Might he want to see around the fields? Might he stay? He could have the guest room. She would do it up; it would certainly be a spur. Anne would help. Perhaps he would like to bring his family for a weekend break?

'Has he a wife?'

'Not now. He did marry, very young—but she died, a long time ago. A freak thing, a cross-channel ferry accident. She drowned but managed to throw their baby, Julian, to somebody. Julian loves to tell people that, little show-off. The mysteriously-preserved baby. Oh yes.'

'So Andrew's a single father?'

'In school term time, yes, he and Julian live in a small house that's handy for Andy's lab. Julian spends quite a bit of time with his grandma Vanessa at weekends and in the holidays.'

'What's she like?' Jane had seemed rather sniffy about Vanessa that day in St. James's Park, even though they were cousins.

'Mysterious, glamorous. Very rich, very elegant and a very pushy absent parent.'

What an extraordinary story. Worldly success was no proof against tragedy. Andrew had lost his love too, but picked himself up and got on with life. He was luckier than Olivia, though—at least he'd been left a little son.

'Mark calls Andy a man with a mission, he's so dedicated to his research. But apparently things aren't going so well with his university job, which he loves. He'll be devastated if he loses it. Julian lives with him during school terms. Andy'll probably want to sell their little house if they make him redundant, which they can, apparently, by restructuring. It'll mean finding a new place to live, a new school for Julian—that's not good, either, just as he's coming up to exams.'

'Andrew mentioned he was having trouble with his university boss.'

'He'll be okay, though,' said Pippa, 'Vanessa's behind him. She has powerful friends. It wouldn't be the same as Mark or me losing our jobs. Vanessa's keen on family. She's some kind of aristocrat and has piles of money.'

The young waitress came over and smiled at Pippa, pencil

poised, 'Hi Mrs. Foreman. All right?' Pippa refused the crayfish salad, chose soup and a roll, and drank only water. The waitress tore the top sheet off her pad and made for the kitchen.

'That's Debbie Robertshaw. A cousin of your Robertshaws, I think.'

Olivia took in Debbie Robertshaw, determined to recognise her when they next met, however unlikely the context. What a lot there was to learn about the interconnectedness of life in a rural area. She'd be seeing the Robertshaws tomorrow. It was time to draft the ewes, Mike explained, keep the best for lambing and send the others to fatten up for slaughter on better pasture, at a cousin's farm near Catterick.

'Let's have a pudding,' she said. 'Then I have to go back and do my course assignment.'

She hadn't thought about the accident today. She was still wondering what Andrew Bamberg had meant by coming north in two weeks' time.

This sheep assignment was about balance sheets and butchery. She'd created a study from a small downstairs room with a high window to the yard, which she'd make into a cloakroom but for now it held an Ikea desk over which were scattered her A4 lined pad, lever arch file, laptop and a pot of pens. She was entering figures of live and dead weights into an Excel spreadsheet, but her mind kept wandering to the animals grazing in the upper field, their busy jaws and watchfulness; their femininity; innocence, calmly inhabiting the present, mercifully unbothered by their horrific futures. Lucky she had the Robertshaws to keep her feet on the ground. The eldest boy was calmly expert when he came over, as he frequently did, to help her move the flock, managing the tricky balancing act of keeping both the grass and ewes in good shape. If only Freddie were here, and their boy.

A little bored and depressed, she allowed herself a Google-around and a coffee, and was soon scanning Andrew Bamberg's academic publications. It wasn't at all like Freddie's. Fred had written a monograph on Giorgione's iconography, apparently well received among Italian art historians. His name was set in solitary state, gold lettered up the spine. It was on the shelf by her bed.

Bamberg's publications were all articles in scientific journals, easily found online; over a hundred, mostly behind paywalls so all she could read were titles, lists of authors and brief summaries. But that was enough to show he worked with people of all nationalities, all over the world. He had, as they said, 'global reach,' and scores of collaborators. What a contrast to the lonely enterprise of farming. His life and hers were as different as those of the captain and crew of a well-found ocean-going yacht, compared to a solitary transatlantic oarswoman. Jane had told her that farmers were prone to suicide, that supporting them was a continual concern of rural clergy. She must get out more, make new connections—and not just local ones, but national, international.

After she had completed and sent off her work, she phoned Signora Gabrieli, Freddie's mum in Fiesole, a call she'd been putting off, and invited her to visit in the spring when things were fit to receive her, with some Torralba stuff retrieved and polished from its packing cases. She decided to make a bargain with Anne, too—help with interior design would be required in exchange for horse livery; it would be good to have Anne around, and help her to avoid incurring too many obligations to the too-willing Giles Yarker. And Jane had promised to stay soon. Perhaps even Andrew Bamberg himself?

5

Julian

Andrew loved to take his son into the lab at weekends. Julian was enjoying a preview of the microbiology practical class Andrew was preparing for Monday. It was about the middle of the University autumn term. Sun shone slanting into the teaching lab, through windows that were horizontal slits just above the exterior ground level, lighting the old teak benches and scuffed wood floor. Mark joined them and sat on a lab stool, in his suit because of the evening seminar he was going to give at the hospital.

Julian crouched to open the door of an incubator that held stacks of Petri dishes. Slime moulds were set up to grow along a glass slide from one piece of nutritious jelly to another. Instructed by Andrew, Julian removed the cover from a dish, carefully placed it on the stage of a microscope, positioned the lens above and adjusted the illumination from below. His squeak interrupted an amusing medical joke Mark was telling Andrew.

'It's moving!' Julian looked up at Mark and leaned away from the microscope so he could look. Mark, nearing his punch line, moved to the microscope talking to Andrew over his shoulder.

Julian looked again to check that the wonder was still visible. 'It's like a river— oh—it's stopped, you should've looked when I said.' Mark at last bent over the microscope.

'No, it's okay, it is moving! Uh-uh . . . oh, it's changing round, it's flowing back! What is this thing Andy?'

'A slime mould. We don't really know where it fits in the great scheme. It's not a real mould, more like an extremely big amoeba.'

Mark and Julian's delight was catching. Andrew took his turn to look. There was the familiar tidal flow. The organism seemed initially inert. Then, in each of the veins, the bubbly protoplasm would start, barely perceptibly, to move; then it became a flow, a river of blobs like oil in vinegar, moving faster and faster; then the stream decelerated, stopped, paused, and reversed. What was it doing? Why this apparently pointless back-and-forwards surging, rather than a purposeful forward movement, or a proper circulation like blood?

'Is it tropical?' asked Mark.

'No, no—they're everywhere on leaves and grass, just too small to see, normally.'

'You should show a video next time you give a public lecture. Loved your presentation last week, by the way.'

'It was fun, wasn't it? I love telling people about these things. Nice girl you brought along.'

'You have a fan there. She's been asking Pippa about you.'

'Weren't Pippa and she flatmates?'

'Not exactly, Olivia's mother hired Pippa to help nurse Olivia after a terrible accident she had a couple of years ago.'

'Oh? She looked fine to me.'

'There was a fatal car accident. Surely I told you? It was Pippa's job to be a nurse companion for her convalescence all the time we were courting. Olivia had been newly-married to an Italian, but soon after the wedding he was killed, and so was Olivia's brother, and she was very badly hurt. It took a year for her to get back on her feet.'

'I see. Please fill me in about her now. What made her decide to be a farmer?'

'The husband left her a lot of money, and she was so devastated to lose him and their life together that she decided to keep faith with the project they'd had to conserve cultural landscape through traditional local-scale farming. She didn't want to stay on in Italy—and then she realised she could do that in the Yorkshire Dales just as well as the Apennines. She comes from up there, like us. She came back to her roots to lick her wounds and get back on her feet, to mix a few metaphors. Pippa got to hear of this perfect unimproved farm for sale, her father helped with negotiations, and there she is.'

'All on her own?'

'Yes. She's never going to marry again, she says, the farm project is her life. I never thought she'd stick it, but she seems to be doing well. It must be lonely, though, and a bit boring. It cheered her up a lot to think about invisible wildlife. She's clever, did a degree in classics at Cambridge before marrying and becoming a Florentine countess.'

'Sounds rather interesting. Cultural landscape is the expression of local geology. Unimproved soils there could be worth a look. I wonder if she'd like a microscope? They're scrapping these teaching ones. Shall I bag one for her?'

'That's just the kind of thing to cheer her up,' said Mark. 'I bet she misses the life of the mind, up there at Oxhide. She could have done anything according to Pippa, but she chose Frederico and being Signora Gabrieli in her villa.'

'I'll choose a decent one and put her name on it.'

'I want to be a microbiologist,' said Julian. 'Can't I have the microscope?' Light blue eyes, the colour of cold sky, met Andrew's with an intensity that gave his words the character of a declaration. The boy was serious.

'We'll label another for you.' He burrowed in a cupboard and handed his son a roll of adhesive labels. 'Put "Oxhide Farm" on one.'

'The nice one, or the one with the worn focus wheel?'

'The nice one, of course. Don't you know how to treat a lady yet?'

Julian made a sulky noise but said no more.

'Microbiology's a dangerous job,' said Mark. 'Bacteriologists are heroes in their way. Handling plague, cholera, MRSA. I knew a fellow who dropped a plate . . .'

'Yes, in the old days we actually thought all microbes were out to get us,' said Andrew. 'How self-centred can you get!'

Mark slid off his stool and brushed down his suit. 'Oh yeah, yeah. Invisible Wildlife. D'you know, I think we should go and have our birthday lunch now.'

'Yes, put this microscope away, Jules, would you? And the dirty slides go in that bin.' He stacked Petri dishes back into the incubator, except for the one with its lid off, which he put in the special bucket for sterilising and disposal. It would now be contaminated by airborne spores; no longer the pure culture science required. Double-checking the incubators and fridge were switched on as everything else switched off, he locked the door behind them, put the key in his inside pocket, and followed the others out, up steps to ground level.

The pub Julian had chosen for his sixteenth birthday lunch had an outdoor area covered with wooden tables beside the river, where hired motor boats with inexpert crews continually navigated under a bridge. Here in its upper reaches the Thames was a mere ditch by comparison with the wide stretch that flowed past Vanessa's house. The biggest boats could only fit under the highest centre point of the main arch of the bridge, and the frequent failures to achieve this provided a gratifying spectacle for watching drinkers. Andrew guessed this was his son's main reason for choosing the pub.

When they were settled with their drinks at a table with the best view of the river, Andrew proposed Julian's health, and Mark produced his godfather's birthday present. The small rectangular box wrapped in blue tissue paper contained the most comprehensive Swiss army knife, like a multi-decker sandwich. It had everything, including a compass, toothpick, magnifying glass, memory stick and saw. Julian allowed himself to be thrilled, opening each tool in turn. His happiness was catching. All three relaxed in the late autumn sun. Julian handed round the knife for each of them to play with. Andrew inspected the wooden surface of the table with the magnifying glass. It was slightly lichened with a fuzzy dry crust. A minute beetle entered the lichen patch, struggling through it like somebody pressing through knee-high heather, to emerge on the bare wood on the other side; it approached a wet ring of beer from a slopped-over glass. It tried stepping into the liquid, but could neither wade through, nor walk on top—it seemed to struggle on a surface skin that dented under its feet, like the covers placed over swimming pools in winter. Andrew rescued it by offering the terra firma of a crisp.

While they basked, slowly enjoying their beer and sandwiches, a huge pastel-coloured plastic-hulled boat, manned by a family elaborately dressed in shorts, striped tee shirts, and deck shoes, jammed itself under the bridge. They watched, tactfully blank-faced, as the Dad gave orders and the crew struggled with boat hooks and pushed against the stone arch with their hands to free the jammed superstructure. Eventually they gave up and resorted to a mobile phone, presumably to summon help from the hire firm. It was delightfully amusing. Andrew and Mark sneaked glances. Julian was still juvenile enough to go over to the parapet and watch openly.

'Anyway, how are things going?' said Mark. 'Office politics still a pain?'

'I'm thinking of making a move,' Andrew said, watching the beetle climb off the platform of crisp to the sun-warmed table and make its way purposefully to a concealing crack in the wood. 'They're just not interested in my kind of thing anymore. Nigel's says he's not going to let me keep my lab if I can't get the grants. I might try and leave before I'm pushed.'

Mark looked thoughtfully at his clean doctor's fingernails, which he was filing with the file from the Swiss army knife. 'What'll you do?'

'I've got to keep on with soil microbiology. Not sure where. Luckily I don't need the money, thanks to Vanessa. But one likes to be paid even if only for the principle of the thing. If only I had a base somewhere, to apply for grants. Trouble is, the exciting stuff, DNA technology, needs a proper set-up, facilities, people.'

'Mmm.' Mark sipped his beer and tried to set fire to the crisp packet with the magnifying glass. They watched a thread of smoke break from the brilliant spot of light.

'What about you?'

'All going according to plan, thank goodness.' Mark relaxed the slight frown with which he'd considered Andrew's work-life dilemmas. 'Yes, I'm an embryonic rural GP.' He grinned. 'I'm planning to be the old-fashioned sort with a framed Ordnance Survey map on the surgery wall, rushing to deliver babies in remote farmhouses in the middle of the night, loved and respected by all, and the fathers will give me a whole ham at Christmas.'

'I wish we could live in the country.'

'We? Who's the woman? You dark horse!' He laughed but Andrew was serious.

No woman. Julian and me.'

'So that's working out? I'm glad. You're so good with him. He needed a father at his age. It was great to see you together just now. Sorry I put my foot in it about microbes. Can't you come and work somewhere in the frozen north with us? It's a perfectly civilized place. And there's space. Julian can run wild on the moors, be a feral child.'

'What?' said Julian, coming back into earshot as he returned to their table. The boat had moved off, freed to barge on up the tiny river.

'Your godfather's sorting out my life. Come on, Jules, it's time to get back.' Andrew picked up the three glasses and edged back to the bar with them between the crowded tables. 'You off now, Mark? Enjoy the talk. We'll expect you when we see you, there'll be some supper, nothing special. We'll go back to Stockholm Street and pick up some chops on our way.'

'See you later,' said Mark. 'Bye, Jules, and congratulations. Life begins at sixteen.'

'Thank you for the knife,' said Julian, meaning it, and giving Mark his rare but enchanting smile. Really, he was a remarkable-looking young man.

'Well then,' Andrew said, as Mark strode away to his medical seminar to discuss cardiomyopathies, 'back we go.'

Julian put the knife in its box, rewrapped it in the tissue paper and put it in his jeans pocket. 'I'm glad I'm living with you. I like it here, Dad.'

Andrew cleared his throat. 'Long may it last. We may have to take things as they come, Jules.'

Julian took his hand for just a second and squeezed it as he used to, then dropped it quickly. They decided to walk home. It was only a mile or so from the centre of town. They left the historic stone centre and crossed the bridge to the eastern end of the city, the narrow pavements acrid with traffic fumes.

With the possibility of having to leave the place at the back of his mind, Andrew took in the street afresh. Long terraces of nineteenth century artisans' brick cottages faced each other across a narrow road, a continuous line of small cars and vans parked down one side. Piles of battered bicycles in the tiny walled front gardens betokened shared student occupation. A few with lovingly tended hedges and inexpertly-painted front doors belonged to young couples running huge mortgages on post-doc stipends. Music came from an open window. It was a young person's street. By his age a successful professional ought to have moved on.

But Andrew was happy. In the seven years until Julian moved in he'd lived mainly alone or with girlfriends, cocooned in a perfect little machine for living that made few demands and left him free to concentrate on research. As he led the way into number 43 he relished its neatness. The bright sky-lit eating area adjoined an elegant galley kitchen with built-in Bosch equipment and blue-and-white china in glass-fronted cabinets. From the captain's dining table (sourced from Portsmouth) you saw a bushy but well organised back garden hung with bird feeders and bee hotels made of bundles of hollow bamboo stems. And Julian had fitted in well, both to the house and work, helping in the lab and getting on with his schooling.

'Couldn't we have an incubator at home, Dad?' As they entered the narrow hallway Julian gazed around as though expecting a Tardis-like microbiology lab to open up in the tiny house. Andrew had already installed a desk for Julian's homework. They toiled together in the evenings. It was a good arrangement and Julian was clever and ambitious.

'There's not really room, is there? You've got Grandad's microscope in the kitchen. I used to spend ages at your age examining mud and slime with it. You don't need to grow cultures. You know, there's no reason why you and I shouldn't write a paper together. You could be my lab assistant, if only I could get somewhere where I'm the boss.'

'You should be the boss, Dad. What about this medal you won? Doesn't that make you important?'

'I wish. Still, let's see. I don't think we'll be here for much longer, Jules. But things might change for the better. Eventually. We'll see. *Che sera, sera*.'

6

The Trojans

On Friday Andrew pressed 'Send' and finally submitted the paper on soil protozoa to the journal *Nature*. Thank goodness it was off his desk. The last few weeks the manuscript had gone from hand to hand among the team, returning each time to Andrew with new Track Changes comments. It was a good paper and if a journal as high-powered as *Nature* accepted it, all the contributors' careers would benefit, not to mention his own. And if they didn't take it there were lots of others who would jump at the chance to publish his team's new results.

Having sent his work winging into the ether, he sighed with a mixture of fatigue and elation and let his gaze wander to the sky outside. Olivia's smile hovered in his consciousness and woke an urge to action. Before he'd given the matter further thought he'd emailed her: *Hello Miss Kidman, It was good to meet you in the museum last week and hear about your interesting project. Good to hear you made it back to the Dales safely—do let me know if you are in London again—it would be nice to meet if you're free. Very best wishes . . . Andrew.* He let his work signature stand on the message and felt a little foolish after he'd pressed 'send' this time. How juvenile! But she was a lovely girl.

On Saturday, feeling the need for a day away from the lab and weekend housework, he went to see Vanessa in Docklands. Julian was away for the day playing football, for which Andrew had no use or inclination.

Coming up from the tube, crossing the hurtling main road and penetrating concrete blocks of utility flats with their pee-darkened corners and huddles of hooded children was like approaching a mediaeval palace through a wash of beggars. Vanessa lived in Docklands, right on the Thames east of the city of London. Her modern house was built on a historic Dickensian alley leading down to the river, which lapped its frontage at high tide. The road's name honoured its past. It was still called Mud Alley, and even that had been a euphemism for something worse, but since the development of the old docks it was a sought-after address. Buzzed in through an inconspicuous door in the wall, Andrew entered from the back.

Vanessa called down the stairs, 'Andy, is it you? Come on up.'

Antique maps, with fish frolicking among small waves, decorated the hall. On a rosewood chest stood a bronze of Aphrodite rising from her cockleshell. A renaissance scene of dolphins, gods and goddesses looked down on him from the high white wall of the stairwell as he went upstairs to Vanessa's sitting room. None of these were reproductions.

Vanessa rose from a white sofa under the window. Lists and writing things lay on a low table constructed for Vanessa by Lord Linley with his own hands. River light filled the room. Andrew's eyes, as always, went to the Canaletto-like panorama from the big windows: the Thames and the Greenwich skyline; the Naval college; Cutty Sark; the old observatory marking the Meridian—longitude zero, the navigator's starting line.

Vanessa hugged and inspected him like a lioness with a returning cub. How different from Mum and Dad's home in Highgate, where he'd grown up. Vanessa's house was less a cocoon, more a launch pad. She was often away. Thank goodness for Helen keeping house. She'd given Julian a little stability. Vanessa hadn't the faintest about children's needs and routines, and no time for anyone too young for conversation.

'Is there anybody we want to add to this list, Andy? The Trojans bar is so right for this party. I'm excited. Helen's booked the florist and the caterers.' She passed a pearl-varnished nail down the list, pointing. 'Those ones at the top are family I want to show you off to. And these are from the Commission for Conservation of Cultural Landscapes. I told the chair about you and she's madly keen to come. And, I thought perhaps Jane, too? If you can stand it. I know she's a bore, but bloody useful to know, you have to admit.'

Andrew took the A4 sheet his mother held out. It had about fifty names in Vanessa's royal blue scrawl. A few of his family—his mother and father and Susan. Jane because she'd helped him get an internship after he'd left school. Vanessa's extensive and formidable family, including her father, the mysterious powerful Max she occasionally mentioned.

'I asked the Genetics Society to send people in your field,' she added. 'And I've included all those brilliant people you work with, the names you gave Helen.'

Andrew thought of his research team. He imagined them at the party clustering in a corner, as immiscible with Vanessa's family and friends as oil in water. They begrudged time not spent on their research, and tended to damn most human interaction as mere small talk. Who could he ask who would sparkle for him?

'I met an interesting woman at the museum. She works on farm soils.' He didn't add that she could pass as Nicole Kidman and had hung on his every word at the Natural History Museum lecture.

'A lady biologist? Oh, all right,' said Vanessa. 'If you don't think she'd feel outclassed?'

Andrew didn't think so. He promised to get Olivia's address for Helen.

'I'll get Helen to send her an invitation when she gets back. I'm so proud of you, darling. I always knew you would do great things in life. And Julian, too. It's a great lineage and you are a credit to it.

Threading east parallel to the Thames, Olivia's taxi took her away from tourist London. They left the blocky fortresses of the Tower and the Bank of England and entered the regenerated old London docks. Whimsical monoliths of new power, toy-like from a distance, rose topless like cities within a city, their upper storeys lost in the sky above the former wharves and Dickensian streets of the East End. It didn't feel like any party venue Olivia had been to, and she'd been to a lot in her student days. She checked the invitation, which was unfortunately still marked with a muddy thumbprint.

It had arrived when she was helping Pete put up electric fences in the rain.

The Lady Vanessa Uphill
requests the pleasure of your company
at a reception to celebrate the award of
the Genetics Society Special Medal to
Dr. Andrew Bamberg
on Saturday November 21st 6-9pm
at the Trojans' Bar, Limehouse Road, London E4

Holding the gilt-edged card between a damp thumb and forefinger, Olivia felt her heart thump. A party, with Andrew Bamberg, hosted by the Genetics Society, in London! And there was a folded note around the card: *Do come! I want to hear more about your project. A.*

It was the kind of note that in the old days she would have read and re-read, with that old girlish thrill. She told herself firmly now that Andrew Bamberg would be a useful future ally for Freddie's project, and stuffed the card and note into the pocket of her waxed jacket.

That evening she placed the invitation card on old Mrs.

Robertshaw's fawn tiled 50s mantelpiece in the sitting room. The accompanying blue-biro scrawled note she filed in her study. An autograph from Andrew Bamberg of *Invisible Wildlife*! Not to be tossed in the waste paper bin. He had nice writing—confident vertical strokes, legible but with character. How sweet he'd signed himself with just an initial, as though they were already friends. The paper looked a page torn out of a small plain paper notebook—perhaps one he carried for field notes?

She phoned Jane to tell her about this terrific networking opportunity for Oxhide, and it turned out she'd been invited too; a real do for policy-makers and opinion-formers, she said, and Olivia should feel herself honoured to be asked. 'You must have made an impression. Andrew Bamberg could be a big help to you, Olivia. And how lovely for me to see you again. Would you like to stay the night?'

What a pity Olivia had already resigned herself to a night with her mother in Elizabeth Street. But she took the opportunity to make a pencilled-in date for Jane to stay at Oxhide in the spring.

As the taxi drew up to the kerb by the entrance to the Trojans' Bar in Limehouse, Olivia grew nervous and wished she hadn't come alone. She'd know nobody at this party except Jane. She'd probably only been asked on a kindly whim of Andrew Bamberg's, maybe prompted by Pippa. The cab drove away and she stood looking up at the brushed-steel and glass facade of the Trojans' Bar. She hadn't worn her Ted Baker dress in the end, even though she and Pippa had spent an afternoon seeking it out and accessorising it in the King's Road. Isobel had taken one look and whisked her off to Angela Negretti's, her own dressmaker in Bleeding Heart Yard.

'Yorkshire lady up in town for the weekend,' had been her comment on the Ted Baker, as Angela produced a grey-green silk top, the colour of olive leaves, knitted in a chunky rib to show off Olivia's shape.

'Perfect! We'll just run you up a little black skirt. A girl like you, Olivia, should look gorgeous without effort, without trying.'

With a consciously effortless flick of the hair, Olivia prepared to make her solitary entrance to the reception. Facing her was an inconspicuous glass revolving door inserted into the high blank wall of the building like a cave mouth at the base of a cliff. Inside, as she gave her coat to the attendant, and showed him her invitation (her thumb concealing the muddy mark) Olivia recognised the busy murmur of a party from a lower room. Descending a curve of shallow pine steps she entered a room full of river light, November sunset reflected from the glowing Thames that seemed almost to lap the floor-to-ceiling windows filling the opposite side of the space.

Twenty or thirty people had already arrived and others followed her in. There was a bar on her left, but most of the area stretched to her right, where low tables surrounded by leather chairs at the sides of the room were already occupied by dark-suited men and a few women conversing with lecturer-style gestures. She guessed they were members of the Genetics Society that was awarding the medal. A less earnest, younger and smarter group by the windows looked like family and friends, sharing jokes and already knocking back champagne offered by waiting staff from silver salvers. Directly opposite her, across the room from the entrance, was a low dais of the sort to accommodate a small band, rigged as a podium with microphone and water carafe. On it, Andrew Bamberg himself, slender in the tailored suit she remembered from his lecture, bent to plug in a lead. As he straightened, he glanced at the arriving guests, and—thank God—recognised her.

'Olivia! Olivia Gabrieli from Oxhide! I'm so glad you were able to come. How are you? Look, we must get together later. Vanessa's insisting on making a speech once everybody's here, and I'm afraid I'm going to be the centre of attention—but afterwards?'

Heads turned to see who had attracted the prize winner's delighted attention. Andrew Bamberg didn't look to Olivia like somebody likely to get the sack—or not in any really wounding way. Before Olivia, blushing, could reply adequately, Vanessa sailed up.

'Vanessa, I want to introduce Olivia Gabrieli. Olivia farms in Yorkshire.'

'Gabrieli? A name I haven't come across. Do you know the Fattorinis? My dear, how lovely to see you. Coming all this way! You must be exhausted.' Vanessa's light scent was different from anything Olivia was familiar with. It suggested luxurious exoticism, driving in an open Bentley through groves of frangipani.

Before Olivia could explain that she was staying with her mother in Belgravia as she usually did in town, Vanessa, with a hostess's touch on her elbow, steered her towards a stocky woman in dark grey descending the steps into the room, beadily scanning guests, like one expecting to be greeted. It was Jane. She and Vanessa bent towards each other and performed a ritual kiss, to which Vanessa added a light upper-arm squeeze, administered underhand—a curiously obvious power gesture.

'Jane, meet Olivia Gabrieli, a friend of Andrew's from Yorkshire,' Vanessa said; it sounded a touch dismissive. 'Olivia, this is Jane. We're sort of cousins. Jane wields immense power from Victoria Road. Civil service—staff of hundreds—oh excuse me, there's George. Dear George Monbiot. Now we're complete, I think this is the moment . . .'

She swept towards the flower-bedecked podium, where Andrew waited to fix her up to the microphone. Jane led Olivia to a table near the dais with two low armchairs, collecting drinks and a plate of canapés for them both.

'How're things?'

'Going well. We did very well at the ram sales. I mean, Mike Robertshaw did, on Oxhide's behalf.'

'Oh good. And will you make any money this year?'

'Some. Mike expects Oxhide to turn a profit next year.'

'That makes you an actual SME. A small or medium enterprise, that is. Business, but not big business. The kind of small firm the minister wants to help. There are rural schemes coming on stream.'

'For farming?' Olivia had read about subsidies for tourism and recreation, perhaps forestry and flood alleviation—but no mention of support for sheep farmers, whose gentle skill over so many centuries made the landscape she, and so many, loved. If they had to give up producing, so much would be lost that might never be put back. The Yorkshire Dales were a priceless asset, even if not one accountants could measure.

Jane leaned forward. 'That's interesting. The Minister says—'

Preparatory microphone noises alerted the guests and faces turned to Vanessa standing tall on the dais. Against the last glimmer of sunset across water, she almost glowed. Light haloed her golden curls and reflected from a close-draped sheath dress of cinnamon silk. Olivia thought of a Botticelli woman in the Uffizi, not a Madonna, more the impenetrable, pagan sort. Freddie would have been entranced. The background of darkening sky and an artful florist's creation of autumn crocuses, ferns, red rowan berries and moss, as well as the extra height conferred by the dais, contributed to the larger-than-life Olympian impression.

The goddess pinged a glass. 'Welcome, welcome, everybody. Wonderful to see so many old and new friends, and family, too, to celebrate this great recognition of Andy's work by such an eminent learned society. Just a few words, to say how much we admire what he's doing—not that I would understand any of it! This new DNA technology is a great gift to mankind! A powerful tool to understand the mind of Mother Nature! But some people plan to use that tool to exploit her. To change her for their ends. Maybe in ways that might not be for the best—selfishly, for gain, even in ways that could change her forever.' Her voice sank to a husky contralto. 'I think that's wrong!'

The party became quiet; Olivia sensed people were avoiding each other's eyes.

'In Andy's hands, nature is safe! For him, genetics is a route to understanding, not manipulation. I'm sure we agree that is the proper, honest use of what we have been given. In recent times, profit has become the measure—even in universities. Andy has the courage to plough his own furrow. How inspiring a learned society is still willing to support that noblest aim: Nature Study. Ladies and gentlemen, I give you Andy—and the Soil Association!'

There was instant applause and cries of "bravo" from the family and friends, but Olivia noticed the geneticists did not clap. They leaned towards each other exchanging comments in low tones, glancing across at Andrew and Vanessa. One of them pushed back his chair and stood. Granite-faced, brushing aside a waiter, he strode from the room.

'Well, that's put the cat among the pigeons,' observed Jane, putting down her empty glass with a bang. 'Mother Nature! Cultural Landscapes! That was Andrew's Head of Department. I'm not surprised he left.'

'Why? What did Vanessa say to upset him?'

'She was being political. Andy's day job's in a university. His biology department will lose industry funding if the agrichemical firms suspect he's anti-business. There's a man from Monsanto here, over there—with the red tie and glasses. Vanessa should have more sense. It's just reckless self-indulgence to sound off like that. I think the trouble is she doesn't live in the real world. She and her friends live in a bubble of money and don't need to make hard decisions and budget like the rest of us. Look at her Commission for Conservation of Cultural Landscapes. A Burlington House office, a Sloane ranger PA. Not exactly in touch with the NFU! Vanessa and her friends think the manpower to repair walls comes with the land. How much does a shepherd cost?'

'Forty thousand a year, my neighbour told me,' said Olivia. 'Exactly. You can't get the serfs these days.' They both laughed.

'But why is Andrew worried for his university job? His research is on genetics. Isn't that a help in engineering new crop plants?'

'He doesn't want to do that. He says it's technology, not science. He wants to explore the unknown. Soil biodiversity. His *Invisible Wildlife* might be important some day. Vanessa was right to push him in the direction of television. But the market's not interested in "might be". Business can't afford to gamble on long shots.'

Olivia nodded. 'Yes, he says the new techniques in DNA technology are turning out to be fantastic for nature study. Apparently there are all sorts of undiscovered creatures in ordinary soil. I'd no idea, it was all just earth to me before I saw his slides.'

'His wretched mother is his main problem. The university is right to be worried about the way people like Vanessa talk. Influential people with no scientific background. There's too much at stake. GM's a powerful technology in the hands of businesses placed to exploit it. Glyphosate is huge, the only answer to feeding our population and cutting agricultural carbon emissions. The UK needs to be in there exploiting those technologies. If we don't, others will. You're a businesswoman, Olivia—you must be aware of commercial competition? Fact of life.'

Olivia weighed the arguments, and tried Jane out with ideas she'd gathered from the *Guardian*.

'There are dangers, though, don't you think? Don't glyphosate-resistant crops mean farmers use glyphosate herbicide all over the fields and kill wild flowers and the rest of the food chain that depends on them, bees, birds? Herbicide resistance genes getting into wild plants and making superweeds? Insecticidal toxins in pollen, poisoning bees and butterflies?'

'The green lobby's noisy, I agree,' conceded Jane. 'But these special interest groups and NGOs are irresponsible, I'm afraid. Biotech can't afford to drag its feet to appease them. There's not one reputable study that supports their position. What we know is that food will run out if we don't look ahead.'

Andrew appeared at Olivia's shoulder, just in time to ride to her rescue. 'Hello cousin Jane! What're you telling Olivia? We'd certainly have world starvation pretty soon without bees!' He captured a chair and joined them. 'I agree with Olivia's point—with some of the biotech that's being done, the dangers to the environment haven't been properly examined. And some of goals we're chasing are wrong. Agritoxin-resistant crops—who needs them? We can use molecular technology to learn so much more, to do real science.'

'Oh, you mean as part of an aid programme,' agreed Jane grudgingly. 'Drought and salinity tolerance? People at DIFD do that.'

'I know, I worked there on my gap year.' Andrew attracted a waiter carrying a tray of tiny hot sausage rolls. 'Mmm. Why not?' Chewing, he went on, 'I believe we could use GM technology to breed crops that'll grow in the desert, in shallow sea. There are local varieties—land races—with useful genes that can be put into commercial varieties with CRISPR, and also, nobody's tried manipulating the soil bugs that help plants grow in nature. But first we have to find what the critical genes are, not make naïve guesses. Some of the experiments going on are so crude. They make me think of Martians arriving and trying to make cars go faster by adding more wheels.'

'Well, they would, wouldn't they?' said Jane.

'Not unless they had extra motors to match,' said Andrew, luckily forestalling Olivia who was about to say the same.

What a minefield. It all sounded so intellectual, and yet both Jane and Vanessa spoke with emotion, on opposing sides. It was far more than a mere personality clash. It was worrying that each of them seemed so influential in their spheres. Olivia decided on balance she preferred her godmother's sensible pragmatism to Vanessa's drama and hyperbole. Vanessa's noisy friends looked far less reliable than the geneticists in their conventional suits conversing in normal tones. She decided to find out more before leaping to judgement.

'What is GM, really,' she asked Andrew. 'How's it done?'

'It's been around for over thirty years now. It's only a technology for inserting a bit of DNA. Most sensible people see nothing amiss in that, bacteria do it all the time. But unfortunately the first people to monetise it, as they say, were the seed and chemical merchants who formed an unholy alliance back in the eighties. The chemists had a good weedkiller and the plant breeders made crop varieties resistant to it. Then the breeders and chemists sold the seeds alongside the weedkiller. All you had to do to keep the crop weed-free was drench the field in weedkiller. And so that farmers couldn't just produce more seed by collecting it from the crop, they introduced what they called "terminator technology" so the seeds of new generations weren't fertile and the famer had to go back and buy more GM seed every year from the merchant.'

'So they were messing with the fundamental way plants work, and exploiting farmers?'

Andrew's face lit up. 'That's exactly it. The merchants stealthily assumed power over both nature and the land. It caused revulsion at quite a deep level, that people couldn't articulate without sounding like nature worshippers. Then academics got caught in the crossfire. Protesters accused them of being Frankensteins and they accused reputable protesters like the Soil Association of being quasi-religious mystics. But I agree with Vanessa. Nature is our birthright as humans, I feel that, don't you? And crude business-driven GM threatened to wreck the economies of small farmers in developing countries. Local varieties of crops suited to local conditions, landraces, that generations of local small farmers have cultivated, might be displaced and lost. And it's those landraces now that could provide good plant genes for a more modern approach to genetic engineering, more intelligent, accurate gene editing.'

'Like what?'

'Now we know how to catalogue the whole genomes of plants, and test for what the genes do, we can be far cleverer, and engineer to accentuate the plant's natural abilities—genes that let species grow in dry and salty regions. I'm all for that—though it's not as money-making as selling Roundup Ready cereals to rich first-world arable farmers.'

At this point Vanessa floated over and touched Andrew's

elbow. He turned and smiled at his mother. 'Hello, Nessa. We were just talking about landraces.'

Vanessa gave Olivia a demure closed-mouth smile. Her barely-perceptible lipstick defined the perfect bow of her lips. 'I can always spot an academic huddle. I'm sorry to have to postpone the latest breakthrough, but I need to drag Andy away for a family chat.'

Olivia exchanged an acquiescent smile with Andrew. Unresisting, he moved away with his mother, only pausing to pull a card from an inner pocket, half turn, and catch her eye for a second. 'Mama wants me to say hello to Grampy. Let's keep in touch, Olivia, it's been interesting talking to you, may I contact you?'

Of course he could. She stowed the card in an inner pocket of the silver leather clutch bag Isobel had lent her for the party. This must be what people meant by networking. It was more exciting than she'd realized.

In Victoria Street, Jane composed a memo for the minister:

UK biotechnological research: the future

To optimise global competitiveness in agricultural biotechnology, UK bioscience research policy should be streamlined towards effective market outcomes.

- Funding structures. Urgent priority should be given to restructuring the funding model, to align the national research effort with the requirements of the global agriculture. With the advent of rapidly advancing exploitable technologies, current academic science funding models run the risk of diverting support into unproductive research remote from market outcomes and are no longer fit-for-purpose. An unhelpful deference to the poorly-defined concept of academic freedom appears counterproductive to UK advance in biotechnology at a time of resource constraint, and may seriously damage our country's competitiveness in world markets. There is a risk of diverting effort towards 'ivory tower' lines of enquiry remote from commercial reality.

- Public perception. We consider management of public perception of GM technology as a priority. Industry research has identified clear health benefits of genetically improved food plants (N.B 'Golden Rice'). However, development is currently under threat from NGO's with diverse agendas. Such interference has the potential to imperil UK innovation, competitiveness and food security. Discretion will be important in ensuring democratic outcomes to benefit the UK taxpayer, in the face of growing pressure from crowd-funded interest groups.

- That the three principal UK Science Research Councils be brought more explicitly within government control, to streamline the administration of science budgets. At the same time, channelling support towards themes agreed with Industry and leading to marketable outcomes will ensure that research lacking clear commercial relevance will be eliminated by a process of natural attrition, facilitating necessary University restructuring.

Jane Gray

7

A Fight

Monday morning, nearly the end of term. Students barged past, humped with backpacks, shouting to each other down corridors. Andrew loved the university buzz, being surrounded by another clever keen generation. And he loved the internationalism of science too, the conferences and research visits; in labs and libraries, deserts and jungles around the globe. In weekly seminars and corridors and coffee rooms there were always new projects to discuss and findings to report and learn about. The university was his window on the world and the view from it challenged and excited him. And the journal *Nature*, probably the most widely-read scientific magazine in the world, had accepted his paper reporting his team's discovery of a whole previously unknown tribe of soil microbes. He had to admit he'd like to see his rivals' faces when they read it. He smiled as he approached the lecture theatre, handouts in his case.

'Hi Andrew.'

'Morning Dr. Bamberg.'

'Dr. Bamberg, can I just ask you something before you begin?'

They trickled in and arranged themselves in the lecture theatre in gaggles of friends, keen front-row types toting tombstone files. Chatting groups near the back were augmented by carefree latecomers as he unpacked his laptop on the lectern, teased out cables from below and plugged in. At long last, after flickering and 'no signal' messages, an image of Julian plastered in mud and holding up a specimen tube appeared on the screen.

'It's what we do,' he told them, and got his laugh.

The amusement gave way to respectful attention from the rows of faces as he gave out his handouts and began. That was the great thing about students; they pretended to be zombies, careerist drudges animated only by pop culture. But then they would light up with enthusiasm, fun, and curiosity. As he laid out his topics and illustrated ideas with pictures, graphs and videos, the lecture sailed along; he felt he had everybody in the room on board.

Afterwards he looked forward to a cup of coffee and informal discussion of the lecture with students who wanted to ask questions. Often, among the would-be tiger conservationists and whale recorders there would be somebody inspired by Andrew's lectures on invisibly small organisms, who wanted to do a project with him. Some of these would become his research students and associates in the lab, a few would ultimately be professors, part of the intellectual succession. It was how ideas dispersed and took root in the future.

Unusually, there was no queue in the coffee room. He couldn't see any staff, only students and technicians. The chairs had been shifted from the usual railway carriage layout, assembled in random groups. Diet Coke was popular, and the noise more shrill than normal. Where were his coffee companions? Nobody he recognised was in the Prof's corner, where there was usually a research discussion among Nigel's senior associates and postdocs, which Andrew sometimes joined. He asked Jen, the tea lady.

'They're all out, aren't they? Gone off somewhere for the day. Chief told me to only make one pot today. Thought you'd be off out too, why aren't you?'

'Did I miss an email?' he asked at reception. 'Is there something

I ought to be at?' Barbara uniquely knew who stood where in the shifting dictatorship instituted by the new Professor, Nigel, and his cronies. She had been in the department for yonks, had signed Andrew on to the staff list when he'd first been appointed seven years back as a 'New Blood Lecturer', and always made his favourite lemon-flavoured biscuits for his lab birthday parties.

'I think there's some sort of away-day,' she said, as though the mass efflux that must have occurred while he'd been lecturing passed invisibly before her desk beside the main entrance. Andrew pictured Nigel and his acolytes bent double below the level of Barbara's counter, scuttling out on tiptoe. Looking up from the diary log on the desk Barbara gave him a kind look, reminding him of his mother Mary.

'Sue was booking the function room at the Cathedral Park Hotel. I think that's where they've gone.'

She might as well have said, *go on Andy, go there now, you have to stand up for yourself.* The beggar must have had his name taken off the email list.

There were spaces in the car park normally jam-packed with illegally parked late arrivals sticky-labelled across the windscreen by security. They really had all gone off to the Cathedral Park Hotel, obviously to plan a departmental strategy.

'Ah, Andrew.' Andrew queried Nigel next day in his big light office overlooking the park. 'It wasn't a meeting you'd be interested in.' He leaned back, twiddling a gold biro, and assumed his confiding manner; the tone Andrew associated with foisting a new manoeuvre on his staff. His pink face conveyed bland malevolence, like a school bully.

Andrew waited. He wasn't going to make it easier by feeding Nigel lines.

'I'm in an awkward position, you see,' said Nigel, with fake complicity. 'There's no money, as you know.'

'Yes.'

'Much as I'd like to retain a natural history sideline, we must reposition going forwards.'

'Ah,' said Andrew, his pulse accelerating.

'I am appointing a cadre of younger scientists to build our strategy.'

Meaning, not you. Was forty two, old? Andrew guessed how Nigel wanted to run the place. Several ambitious thrusters had come with him from his former post, including, as rumour had it, a mistress. They weren't much younger than he was, just pushier. Hungry, the corporate people called it.

'You'll be reporting to Andrea.'

'Reporting what?'

'She'll be your line manager. You will work for her.'

Andrea the female thruster. She was fresh to the department, seconded from a new private company, Trent-Delibes, to develop a maize plant genetically modified to be poisonous to insects. All insects. Andrea was a membrane biophysicist by training. She couldn't tell the difference between a bee and a boa constrictor. No way would Andrew involve himself in her project. Whatever it was, it would be a blind alley from his point of view, a digression. Did Nigel not read his publications? Anger boiled up.

'Sounds like constructive dismissal to me,' Andrew heard himself say. 'And I shall be glad to go. I regard what you have told me as a disreputable travesty of all a university stands for.'

'Say that again,' said Nigel, rising. This was just like school.

'A disreputable travesty,' said Andrew, hurling down the gauntlet. His heart thumped.

Hardly knowing what he did, he stepped forward a pace, briskly as he had last done at seventeen. His straight left caught Nigel on the jaw and he followed up with a right hook. Time stopped. His hand hurt like hell and he heard himself pant like a thug in a film. Nigel lay unmoving on the carpet. He had hit his head on the corner of the desk as he fell, Andrew remembered a cracking a moment before—that must have been it. He stared down, aghast, then crouched beside the body. Thank God, Nigel gave a gasp and blinked, then pushed himself up to a sitting position. Awareness dawned on his gobsmacked face. Ought Andrew to call for help? Or at least send for one of the registered first-aiders in the department?

Luckily the man was not badly injured, sitting up now on the Persian carpet with which he had equipped his corner office. From departmental funds, no doubt. 'You bastard!' he said.

As though watching himself in a film, Andrew heard the phrase, 'turned on his heel' as he walked out of the enormous office, momentarily elated. On his way out of the building, however, he mentioned to the chief technician who he met in the corridor that he'd heard funny noises from the Prof's office and it might be worth checking, in case anything was wrong. That evening, Andrew wrote a letter resigning his university post, and delivered it by hand to the central offices.

'You need to run your own show,' said Jenks. 'I'm glad I got out when I did.'

The Racehorse was a snug muzak-free one-room pub inhabited mainly by old men, hidden down an alley off the tourist beat. John Jenks sat in his usual corner behind a coat stand hung with the kind of dark woollen garments and rainproof hats favoured by the Racehorse's clientele. He was half way down his pint of Guinness, a book open among beer mats on the table in front. He wore the same sort of Donegal tweed jacket Andrew remembered from field trips, rainbow-flecked on badger brown. Perhaps the same actual jacket. How soothing to see his old friend and mentor.

'Ah, Andrew.' John looked up under eyebrows like rusty wirebrushes, 'would you be interested in a copy of Hooke's *Micrographia?*' The old boy's book business must really be taking off. 'Nobody knows how to do microscopy these days. Just come round and see it, Andrew. I'd like to give you first refusal before it disappears into some Philistine's bank vault. What can I get you?'

'No, let me.' Andrew seized Jenks's rapidly-drained glass and fetched another from the bar, with a pint of Black Sheep for himself. 'It's not a good moment for me to buy anything, unfortunately,' he said, setting down the two glasses. 'I've lost my job.'

'Oh. Mmm. Why? Your good health.' Jenks raised the glass to his lips.

'A new broom in the department. Restructuring. The new head's getting rid of ecology. *Just nature study*, he called it.' Andrew mimicked his boss's voice.

'It always happens. New boys, keen, throw their weight about. What'll you do for cash?'

'Not such a problem. I'm lucky there. Trouble is, my research is going very well. We have papers in press and I'm a keynote speaker at a big congress in California next spring. This means dispersing the team, losing the lab, all our equipment and so on, when we were making such good progress.' Andrew was aware of his whingey note. Jenks was rightly unsympathetic.

'*Lab work* ,' he said, like a tennis player dismissing ping pong. 'What has that to do with ecology? You have to work with real organisms in the field. Go out and get your hands dirty.' In his first year, Andrew had stood for endless hours under dripping trees as Jenks had truffled into saturated mud rootling out rare insects, moss and underground fungi, holding out slimy fragments on mud-caked fingers. A semicircle of students would watch him smelling, and even tasting, these objects before passing them round, and producing a Latin name which the keen ones wrote in their polythene-backed field notebooks. Some ancient bequest, ring-fenced against depredations by twentieth-century Vice Chancellors, had enabled Jenks to lead regular Saturday forays, redolent of a leisured age, over heaths, through forests, abandoned quarries and along distant sea shores, reached by subsidised coach. Even some of the rugger players had yielded to the enchantment of the unending plants and animals Jenks revealed.

Andrew had absorbed a surprising knowledge of what grew where. He could name the plants in a Constable painting, even if, close-up, the only clue was a smudge of blue or brown; the lie of the land, colour of the woods and water, evoked the names of living things. Jenks showed them how to identify finds using microscopic clues, features made out with a lens if you knew what to look for, details that distinguished species almost but not quite the same. The Latin name was like a secret code at first, but one Andrew was later to discover, was readable throughout the world by those who shared his interest. Each organism had only one Latin scientific name, which got over the confusion that happened with common things like ladybirds and dandelions, with multiple local names according to country and dialect. At home, it seemed abstruse. But what a thrill to find shared understanding of those Latin names across the world, even where you had barely the knowledge to ask the way.

But at eighteen he'd felt self-conscious about enjoying these nature walks. There was a quaintness, a whiff of the Edwardian undergraduate reading party, about these trips. A kind of innocence pervaded the group, who behaved with unaccustomed decorum; the girls were fresh-faced types lacking the wicked glamour of the English Lit and Modern Languages lot. They spent long afternoons poring over pickled insects and pressed plants. Meanwhile, geneticists made discoveries every week, genomic technology was a matter of everyday routine and the secret of life seemed within grasp.

The new DNA technology was not only glamorous but, Andrew soon realized, an Open Sesame to the world of soil organisms. As a child, with the *Observer's Book of Pond Life*, he'd found that amoebas came in three or four sorts. With a microscope and the traditional identification books at university, he reckoned there might be fifty more. But now, in a pinch of soil, you could find the DNA signatures of hundreds nobody had seen. Soil was teeming with creatures new to science. With his career ahead, Andrew had set himself to learn the world-changing new methods and launch into the unknown territory of hidden creatures.

But he continued to join the Saturday outings, and tried to atone for going over to the molecular biology side by acting as unpaid demonstrator and equipment carrier for Jenks. They had remained friends.

Jenks peered at him over the rim of his pint, an invisible smile crinkling the corners of his eyes. 'So why not go back to work with real organisms now? Go out and get your hands dirty, as I've always told you.'

'Yes. Maybe it is time to do that.'

'Come and do the microbes in Hattersley Pit,' invited Jenks. A row of bound student theses in the library, going back to the fifties, testified to Jenks's unwavering devotion to the complete description of this small gravel pit near his house on the outskirts.

'Well, I'd love to, but I have the offer of a site in Yorkshire, which is interesting for the varied bedrock,' Andrew replied with tact.

Jenks gave an approving h-hmm. He came from those parts, Andrew remembered. A lot of good men seemed to come from Yorkshire. Women too, look at Olivia Gabrieli going it alone on her farm in some remote fastness of the Yorkshire Dales. Maybe it wasn't only the effect of the three pints that made him cheerful for the first time since the away day.

8

News of the Hero

Olivia was shopping for essentials in Skipton when her phone buzzed.

'Liv, do come round. Now. Something extraordinary has happened. Don't worry, it's nothing bad. Well, not really bad. I think you might be interested. I'll put the percolator on.'

The main door from the small car park behind the Doctors' House was unlocked, as it always was during surgery hours when the annexe was busy with patients. Olivia made her way through the private section of the building. In Pippa and Mark's grand empty sitting room she found Mark, on a step ladder, putting up a long shelf. Olivia dropped her Boots bag on the bare boards and sat on the little red sofa.

'We'll be with you in a minute, Olivia,' Mark said. 'Only three more screws.' Pippa, supporting the shelf, grinned at Olivia over her shoulder. Mark backed down the step ladder. 'What do you think? Will it stand Pippa's Mum's wedding present crystal rose bowl?'

'Easily. What a good idea. Perfect for the room. Bridget would have charged a thousand pounds and have done no better. D 'you know, Pippa, my stepmother was an interior decorator before she snagged my father?'

Pippa laughed and put away Mark's tools in their box. 'A highly respectable calling.'

'So what's this news you promised? I bet I can guess.' Pippa hadn't yet made any announcement about her forthcoming baby.

Pippa straightened, hands on hips. 'You won't believe this, Olivia. Andrew Bamberg's got the sack.'

'Andrew Bamberg? That's ridiculous. He has to be their star person, he's so well known.'

'He hit his boss. Knocked him down and gave him a black eye.'

Olivia remembered Andrew Bamberg's tone when he'd tried to enthuse Jane about bees at the Trojans party. The evident enmity between his band of colleagues, and the opposing biotech suits, the cold fizz of barely-restrained anger. But how impressive to take this fight to a physical level, like some ancient hero. Wow, thought Olivia, more people ought to do that, stand up to bullying, stand for what they believed in, refuse to be victims.

'I can't understand it,' Pippa went on. 'He's such a gentleman. So kind to Julian, and always so polite and considerate in that old-fashioned way of his. He must be ill.'

'But Pippa, it's part of being a real gentleman to fight for what you believe in,' said Olivia. 'Duels, you know? You say, "pon my honour, Sir", and fling your glove on the ground, or something. You see it in cod period films. Oh, I wish I'd seen that. Good for him.'

'Darling, what do you think?' said Pippa, as Mark returned with a tray of coffee and placed it on the floorboards beside Olivia. There was no coffee table yet because they had determined only to acquire things they really liked.

He bent to pour their coffee, remembering Olivia liked hers white with one sugar. He stirred her mug then stood twirling the teaspoon in his hand. 'I don't know. He was a ball of fire at Cambridge. I can't help feeling impressed. It's not completely out of character, but not exactly adult, either. Grossly irresponsible and unprofessional, I suppose I ought to say. But won't.'

'Who'd have thought Andy would behave like a drunk footballer?' Pippa went on. 'He's a university professor. It doesn't make sense. Olivia thinks it's heroic, but it's so out of character.'

'I think Olivia's right.' Mark leaned proprietorially against the black marble mantelpiece, his back to the handsome iron fire basket somebody—surely Pippa—had filled with a bucket of bulrushes. 'He's dedicated his life to this idea of invisible wildlife. Gave up a promising medical career for it, remember, and took the risk to launch out. And it's beginning to bear fruit—a paper in *Nature*'s a major achievement. He realises he's on the track of a breakthrough in our fundamental understanding of nature, using genomics to understand the tiny stuff. And then he sees stupidity and greed standing in his way, in the shape of Nigel Socket. Damn lucky he didn't kill him, though.'

'But did he need to resort to violence? He behaved like one of those stupid bikers they get in A and E. We have to cut them out of their leathers. I always thought Andy was above that sort of thing. I still can't imagine it.'

'It's not the first time, love,' said Mark. 'There was a bit of a fuss when he was a research student. He attacked another student with a soil corer—a kind of giant's corkscrew. We laughed at the time. But that fight was about work too. The other fellow threw out a rack of samples Andy had got from a collaborator in India. Apparently that little rack held the results of a huge effort to get official permissions and organise drivers into the remote highlands. I think Andy saw it as a massive disrespect to the Indian's work. He had to defend the honour of his team and the enterprise of Science against an act of mindless vandalism.'

'Yes, that's it, I think. I'm sure he's not ill, Pippa,' Olivia said. 'Unless being passionate about a mission is an illness.'

'Like a two-year-old,' said Pippa. 'Nobody understands them, they can't speak properly. In the end they yell. Maybe a scientist feels like that when they are the only one who realises the importance of what they discover. I can imagine they feel lonely and misunderstood.'

'Yes, and not just selfishly. They know they have something good for humanity, but humanity won't listen. And yet—with *Invisible Wildlife* on the telly, articles in the *BBC Wildlife Magazine*, kids with crushes on him, that clever son who adores him—who'd guess Andrew could be lonely?'

Pippa refilled Olivia's mug. 'How can we help? He has us. How can we stick by him, Mark?'

'The problem isn't losing the salaried job, so much as losing the lab. He's financially independent thanks to Vanessa. But a life scientist like Andy can't just go off and freelance; he needs experiments, and molecular biology needs complicated technology, big machines like sequencers and all the new imaging technologies, technicians, enormous teams of specialists. And the chance to travel and work with colleagues around the world.'

'But don't you remember, Mark, how interested he was in Olivia's farm project? He said it was time to take the work into the real environment.' Pippa looked from Mark to Olivia.

'At Oxhide?' Olivia wasn't sure what they were suggesting.

'Yes, he's keen to see your place, Olivia,' Mark said. 'He's been trying to find farmland that's never been tilled or fertilised. He talked about looking for places with a range of soil types, under traditional management. Man-made landscapes, but semi-natural. It's Vanessa's influence, she's into cultural landscapes, indigenous knowledge, that stuff. He listens to her, God knows why. And he loves field work.'

They were both smiling at her. They knew how much she'd been hoping for this. She felt a rush of affection for them, and excitement at this evidence of their trust in her project. What an accolade, to host Andrew Bamberg at Oxhide. How thrilled Freddie would have been. At Trebbia they'd tried to learn about the geology and soils, and the scientific basis of good land management, but never managed to engage the interest of the scientific community. How interesting it would be, too, to have someone like Andrew Bamberg as a visitor. It was wonderful to live remotely, but one did feel a little cut off.

'Goodness, that would be terrific. Will you be seeing him? Do tell him he's more than welcome.'

'Don't feel you have to, Liv,' Pippa said. 'It's probably mad. It was just Andy was so impressed by what you said at the party.'

Andrew Bamberg? Impressed by what she'd said? 'I wonder what he'd need, to do work at Oxhide?'

'In the Western Ghats he said it was a lucky thing to find a level lit surface for a microscope,' said Mark. 'And he could help you, Olivia. He could give your farm publicity, advice, and put you in touch with an international network of environmental scientists. And even Vanessa might be useful. She wields huge influence in some quarters.'

Olivia stood and went to the window. Golden leaves swirled around the surgery car park, the sun lit a blue sky. What if Oxhide had a scientist on site, as well as sheep-counting pens? Somebody with global connections, to have conversations with as she'd had with Freddie, not the mundane banter of Anne and Giles.

But for now, duties called. She checked her watch. They'd be waiting for her back at the farm, to take ewes down to Catterick, to Mike Robertshaw's cousin's farm. Pippa came with her to the front door as Mark made off back to his two o'clock surgery. 'Tell Andrew that if Oxhide can be any use to him, it's all his.'

'That's generous, Liv. Mark'll tell him. We can't guarantee his good behaviour, though.'

'Good behaviour can go too far.' They laughed and Olivia strode back to where her new Land Rover was parked. Later, she would wonder what Pippa meant.

'Teeth and tits,' said Mike Robertshaw.

Anne giggled.

'It's what a ewe needs on the hill,' said Mike to Olivia. 'No teeth, she can't thrive on moor grass. No tits, she won't suckle lambs properly.'

Giles stood ready to release the ewes through the counting gate. Mike's keen eye was fixed on the stream, ready to switch the hurdle across the stream of sheep to separate possible draft ewes. Sheep who were too poor for market would go down to better grazing where they would put on weight, and hopefully bear twins instead of the singletons they had on the sparser grazing of the hills.

Finally they had about fifty allocated for the draft, which meant two more journeys down to Catterick with the trailers in convoy. This was Olivia's first involvement with her sheep, the first time she'd had her hands in their wool and stood among the pushing flock in the pens. She was on a high. The fells were indescribably beautiful, the sheep's voices gloriously archetypal, she was in Arcadia. The new Land Rover Defender, a pleasing cream, fitted as naturally into the romantic scene as a farm wagon. When the ewes had been loaded she climbed up into its rugged cab and felt the mistress of the land, with Mike, a well-heeled sheep farmer, beside her. Giles and Anne followed, closing the trailer ramp and jumping into Giles's borrowed pickup. As they drove, Mike shared sheep lore with her. He explained the sheep pyramid, the modern breeding system that had evolved to make sheep the perfect match to the northern landscape, linking hills and lowlands in a cycle of production to convert bare hill grass into protein, meat and wool. Her tedious sheep course came to life, explained this way. Her farm had a future, of course it had.

Mike's voice broke in on her reverie. 'They've got a new litter at Catterick. There might be a dog for you there, Olivia.'

Truly, this afternoon was like a dream.

9

Shipwreck in Academia

Mark felt his way cautiously down the steps of the Biological Sciences department. In the shade they were still icy at mid-morning, and the tower of empty cardboard boxes he carried obscured his view. Above, students came and went around the bicycle racks calling to each other with end-of-term excitement. Lectures were over and soon tomorrow's leaders would leave for home, these streets returned to sober natives.

As he reached the bottom of the steps and went into the big basement teaching lab, he saw Andrew in the far corner, putting books off a shelf into piles on the wooden bench. The room felt neglected, the grimy walls and ceiling needing redecoration, but there was beauty in a row of fine old nineteenth-century didactic coloured prints. Mark's favourite was the comparison of conifer life cycles, the cones, magnified pollen, and yes, The Larch, with its surprising pink flowers. He dumped the boxes.

'Hullo Mark. Thank you, this is so kind. How's Pippa? Is she with you?'

'Flourishing, thanks. She's at home, nest-building. It's just me.'
Mark gazed at the dark benches and dusty, nearly subterranean
windows. 'Well, you'll be glad to get out of this.'

'They've taken my office, too. I have to be out by Monday
morning to let the new people move in.'

'Okay, I'll get the stuff into these boxes. I'm parked at the top of
the steps. Shall I start with the books?'

'Yup. Thanks, Mark.'

Mark started to pack books, showing a good eye for optimal
spacing.

'These too?' He picked up a set of ancient models, each
beautifully painted and mounted on an ebony stand. He looked
closely to read the small brass plate. 'Berlin, 1815. *Puccinia graminis*.
For teaching agronomy I suppose. These must be worth a fortune.'

'Not so much now,' said Andrew. 'Too battered. I rescued them
from the skip.'

'No? Really? They're museum pieces.'

'You wouldn't believe what that fool's ordered to be thrown
out. There was a teak parquet floor in a seminar room. He had
the parquet blocks put in the skip. They disappeared overnight,
unsurprisingly. And library books. We found a copy of *The Origin
of Species*, an early edition, in a disposal bag.'

Mark had wondered if Andrew was mildly delusional in his
distrust of his manager. But on the evidence he was seeing, the
little department had fallen into totally unfit hands.

Andrew phoned his post-doc researchers Erik and Meera to
come down and decide where to put the equipment, incubators
and freezer. When they saw the empty room and full boxes
waiting to be removed, Andrew's books gone and the lab benches
denuded, they seemed nonplussed, downcast, like members of
a tribe whose leader had been toppled in battle. Meera asked
Andrew kindly if he wanted a tea or coffee. Erik seized a heavy
box and ran up the steps with it showing Scandinavian disregard
for black ice. They understood their prof had been ousted in a
coup, not disgraced.

Meera held out a card. 'The lab sent you this, and this.'

Mark looked over Andrew's shoulder as he opened the Good Luck card. There looked to be about twenty signatures. The parcel held a magnum of Veuve Clicquot. Andrew passed a hand across his forehead, momentarily speechless.

'What will you do now?' asked Erik, as they sat in the corner of the huge room, drinking Nescafé.

'Read and think. Work on my new series for next year. Do a bit of fieldwork maybe.'

'Oh? Where? Can we come and help?' said Erik.

At that moment there was the sound of somebody coming down the steps outside the window and Mark saw grey-trousered legs. The door opened with a draught of freezing air and Julian came in, looking as though he'd grown several inches in the weeks since the birthday lunch by the river. He slung a book bag on the bench. 'Hi, Dad. Hi.' He acknowledged Meera and Erik. 'Can I have some tea? Where are my cultures?' His eye fell on the packed-up boxes and general dereliction.

'I'll make you some,' said Meera, smiling at Julian.

'They're not in here.' Erik said from an incubator. It appeared empty. He went into a cubbyhole behind. 'Are these the ones?' his voice muffled.

Julian followed. 'They're in the bin!' his voice had the shrillness of childhood, so recently lost. Andrew joined him

'The bastards!' he said. 'Some of them look okay, Jules. Take these and we'll see if we can recover them at home. Those two boxes are the microscopes I've bought from the department, the ones you labelled, remember? One for you and one for Olivia Gabrieli.'

'Why is this all so sudden?' asked Mark. 'They could have left it until the end of the vacation surely. It seems almost vindictive.'

'The space is needed.' Andrew snorted. 'To reduce the departmental deficit they've let it out to Digital Humanities. Next term this place'll be all digital humanists doing Wordles on Wordsworth. The books are all gone.'

Meera cleared the mugs.

'The incubators,' said Erik. 'They were on our grant I think, Andrew.'

'They can go up to the labs with you,' Andrew decided. They had both been reassigned to other supervisors in vaguely-related disciplines. 'Keep in touch. We might even get back to doing something together in the future, who knows. The tide is turning. They'll have to realise they need living soil under their tractor wheels. We'll just have to hope it won't be too late.'

Half an hour later Mark's Volvo was parked outside the small terrace house in Stockholm Street. Andrew's boxes rose ceiling-high in the tiny hallway.

'We'll have to move eventually, of course,' said Andrew, looking at the towers of cardboard. 'I've no reason to stay. And Julian's not attached to this place, are you, Jules?'

'It's too small, compared to Nessa's house it's a slum.'

'You ought to come and live near us,' said Mark. 'It's nicer. Lovely country and no silly house prices. We love our huge house. Move to Yorkshire, read, write and do field work, nip down once a month to record in London. Sorted.'

Julian looked expectantly at his father. Andrew rubbed his chin.

'Go and have a chat with Olivia Gabrieli. Her farm's only half an hour from us. Pippa did sort of broach it with her, you using Oxhide for field work, and apparently you'd already given her your card? Olivia's tremendously keen you know—she hasn't forgotten that day at the museum. Sheep aren't all that intellectually stimulating. I bet she's waiting for you to call, nice old-fashioned girl that she is.'

'She's a brave woman. Good-looking, too, don't you think?'

The leopard didn't change his spots. 'You and Olivia would be a perfect match,' Mark said, 'as collaborators. You're both dedicated, obstinate beggars. Don't you see? You have the two halves of a worthwhile project between you. The invisible wildlife that sustains our cultural landscapes.'

'Okay,' Andrew agreed. Julian was paying silent attention. 'But we should meet on neutral ground, I think, before I barge in and offer to install myself. Mark, you and Pippa are coming to our Christmas party, aren't you? Will Pippa be up to it? Think I could invite Olivia?'

'Oh, do. Pippa was worried Olivia was going to be alone over Christmas. And she hasn't yet taken sole charge of her own sheep, so there's somebody in charge of the farm. Phone her—I'll give you her number. What fun. We'll all meet in Highgate, like the old days.'

'Reliving the Christmas vacation,' said Andrew, and smiled at his son. Julian smirked back in his patronising teenage way.

Olivia was helping Pete throw building rubbish into a skip in the farmyard, arbitrating over what to dump and save, when her phone rang. Pulling off a work glove, she sought it out of her inside pocket.

'Hi, is that Olivia Gabrieli?'

Holding the phone to her ear, Olivia walked quickly away towards the house. It was him, Andrew Bamberg. Covering the phone, she cleared her throat. 'Yes, hello, hi!'

'Is this a good time to call? It sounded as though you're busy.'

'No, it's just bricks hitting a skip.'

His deep laugh. 'You are busy, then. Look, I'm sure you're not free at Christmas. I know farmers work all the time. But just in case . . . I asked Pippa and she thought you wouldn't mind me phoning like this . . . my Mum and Dad throw a little party at their house on Christmas Eve. Mark and Pippa come, and I wondered . . . they'd be glad to give you a lift down to London if there was any chance you could make the time away from Oxhide?'

Her cold cheeks stretched in an involuntary grin. 'I'd absolutely love to. Thank you. Thank you very much. Thanks for phoning me.'

How gushing, but who cared. No dull Christmas lunch at Craiglands Hotel with Joe and Bridget, no lonely time alone at

Oxhide. Instead, a family party in London with the most exciting man in the world. It would be like Christmas with the Gabrielis in Fiesole. Fred would understand. He'd be alongside her, knocking back a festive glass in spirit.

'Sure you can leave the farm? It's maybe a bit much to ask?'

'Actually Anne, my sister, would love to have this house to herself over Christmas. Her horses are here and she could escape bridge with her mother.' Andrew laughed. 'She can take charge easily—just as well as me, if not better. Yes, please, Andrew.' There—she'd called him by his first name!

'It's on Christmas Eve, until late. You'd have to stay over.'

'I'll stay with my Mama. I want to go and pay her a Christmas visit. What sort of party? What should I wear?'

'Ask Pippa—I don't have a feel for these things. I usually wear trousers.'

She laughed. 'I'll very much look forward to it. Thank you so much, Andrew.'

He said goodbye and rang off, and she was left gobsmacked in the turnip field, Giles looking across the field to see what was keeping her.

That evening Anne was thrilled, as anticipated, by the idea of having sole charge over Christmas. Olivia hugged herself—Andrew! She'd said it twice. She said it again. Then wondered at herself. She was Freddie's wife; she would never forget that.

10

The Bambergs of N6

When Olivia arrived with Pippa and Mark at Highgate the place was full of talking and laughter, feet running up and down stairs, and somebody playing Christmas carols on the piano loudly and rather well, but the focus of the festive preparations was the kitchen. Instead of taking them to their room, Andrew led them there first. It was an enormous Edwardian space with few modern gadgets or even basic equipment.

'Mummy, look who's here. Just arrived, probably starving. Here, give me your things. Sit with Mum and Louisa and I'll get your cases from the car.' With Pippa's sheepskin jacket over his arm, he left them to Mary.

'Mark! Pippa!' They both got a kiss. 'And Olivia? I've been hearing all about you, my dear! Excuse me, I'm in the throes.' Mary held up flour-covered hands. 'All of you, sit, tell me your news while I cook. Can I get you a snack for now?'

They'd driven over 200 miles. Dazed, Olivia felt as though she'd stumbled on to a stage. Mary set out bread and cheese at the corner of the wooden table. The rest of its surface was covered with bowls of chestnuts, peeled potatoes, two kinds of stuffing for the turkey, tins of mincemeat and cranberries, a bottle of brandy, and several half-empty egg boxes. The kitchen had a celebratory smell, of spices, citrus fruit and rum. This was the kind of Christmas Olivia pictured some day at Oxhide.

'We do Christmas on Christmas Eve,' said Andrew, rejoining them. 'Dad's family always celebrated in the evening on Christmas Eve, in honour of the Erfurt Bambergs, German ancestors. They were clockmakers and Dad's grandfather was sent to London in the nineteenth century to set up a branch. Which he did, very well. That one in the hall is his and it's still going.'

A small old lady called Louisa sat on a stool, taking glasses out of a bowl of hot, vinegar-smelling water, polishing them and lining them in rows. The array of clean glasses spreading across the table was getting in Mary's way.

'David,' she called across the hallway to Andrew's Dad sheltering in his study. 'Can't you get Louisa to put her feet up and have a drink? She won't stop work.'

'When I have the glasses done. The glass must sparkle at Christmas! Look,' Louisa held a crystal tumbler to the light to show Olivia. 'This was my job when I was a little girl, always on Christmas Eve, wash the glasses.' She spoke with a German accent.

'And this is my job,' said David, 'a little drink for Louisa. Mary? A glass of Madeira for the cooks.' He poured out four. 'You boys'll have to wait, you haven't done any work yet.'

'Nor have you, Dad' said Andrew.

'No, but your mother and I always drink together' said David firmly, leaning across the kitchen table to give Mary a kiss. He pulled up three chairs to the table. 'Louisa, Happy Christmas!'

'This is the best time,' said Mary. She took a sip of Madeira and sighed. 'Everything almost done, the family at home, the house occupied and cheerful. Just the tree still to do.' She smiled at Andrew. 'Children's job!'

There was no sign of the huge tree Pippa had mentioned.

'I'll change my clothes,' said Andrew. So they did change for dinner here. And seriously—he looked smart enough already in pressed cords and a checked shirt.

'There are gloves in the shed, Andy,' said David. 'Don't give yourself urticaria like last year.'

Andrew disappeared, feet pounding up the stairs, and returned in frayed jeans and an old Guernsey. 'Where's Susan?' he asked. 'Susan,' he yelled up the stairs. 'Come and help, we need you.' No answer. 'My sister only does the easy bits. Okay, come on Mark, this is a hellish job. You've been warned.'

'Come and watch this, Liv,' said Pippa.

Andrew escorted them out of the hall at the back, where stone steps led down into the darkness of the garden. The glow of the London sky ringed around, but the garden was pitch dark, shaded by full-size trees, somehow remote from the city. Dense overhanging bushes shed drops as they brushed along a narrow path, slippery underfoot. At the end a shed was discernible in the gloom. It was locked and Andrew had to go back for the key.

Seen from the dark garden the house looked like a fairy tale castle, enhanced by a mock Gothic turret at one corner of the roof, silhouetted against the orange haze. Every window was lit. It looked foreign, Wagnerian, the Bamberg stronghold in London N6. When Andrew returned with the shed key they stood for a moment in the darkness, looking up at the pile.

'It's too big for the parents now. I love the house full of people. Great Gramp had six children and crowds of staff.'

Farm staff were a part of Olivia's private dream for Oxhide, but with shepherds at forty thousand a year? She needed a way to populate Oxhide, bring the place to life.

'Does Louisa live with you?'

'Yes, and Vanessa spends a lot of time here. You'll see Nessa tomorrow, with the crowd coming to dinner. She's been asking after you. You impressed her at that party.'

Olivia was surprised. She'd had a strong impression of a brush-off from Vanessa. It must just have been her naturally imperious manner.

'Is Julian here?'

'Singing. Once in Royal ... you know? Trying out his new tenor voice. He'll come later.' Andrew stopped by the shed, pushed open the door, feeling round the jamb for the switch, and turned on a cobwebbed bulwark light. He disappeared into the depths to emerge dragging a large iron thing with four feet and butterfly screws. He brushed at it with a yard brush, displacing flakes of rust that fluttered on to his feet.

'The stand. Here it is.'

They returned to the house. Andrew, carrying the heavy stand, led the way into the high- ceilinged sitting room. He hesitated in the act of setting it down on the red Turkey carpet.

'Oh, damn, we forgot the flag. Come and help me find it.'

They ran upstairs, the three of them like children, and Olivia followed. At the top of the house, Andrew dragged a leather suitcase off the top of a Narnia-style wardrobe, prised up the locks and drew out a vast and grubby rectangle of multi-coloured cloth. It was like one of the ancient regimental flags you occasionally still saw at military memorials in churches, at least six feet long. He held it up by two corners for Olivia, Pippa and Mark to admire.

'Erfurt flag. From great aunt Lottie. Goes under the stand.'

The ratty old flag, treated like the symbol of some old household god, seemed to Olivia a touching symbol of a family's loyalty to its roots. She decided to write to Signora Gabrieli and get a Florentine flag from Freddie's family for the future Oxhide Christmas parties. With a flourish, Andrew spread the flag on the carpet in one of the two tall window bays of the drawing room, and set the Christmas tree stand in the middle of it. Then he put on leather gauntlets from a cupboard in the porch, and they followed as he returned to the garden for the tree, lying on its side on the lawn. It was a proper spruce fir at least fifteen feet long, freshly-felled, giving off a resinous scent redolent of the boreal forest. Andrew trussed it with a clothes line, ordering

Mark to hold the branches in while he tied it into a manageable bundle. They manoeuvred towards the house in the wet darkness, shuffled it along the path, and hauled it up the porch steps into the hall. Branches snagged on the carpet and it was a job to turn the bundled tree so it fitted through the drawing room door. The bendy top had to be curved against the opposite wall of the hallway. They manhandled the tree upright and jammed the base, sticky with resin, into the stand. The sawn-off trunk was too thick and Andrew had get a bow saw to trim it. When he untied the clothes line, the tree sprang back into shape, spreading branches. Mark exclaimed when prickles raked his scalp through his hair, as he reached underneath the branches to screw in the butterfly nuts that held the trunk.

'What a palaver. Susan does the rest—my sister. She decorates it. We'll go out for a drink now and leave her to it.' Andrew removed the gauntlets and brushed cobwebby grime off his trousers. Olivia was charmed by his transformation from formal lecturer into boyish beloved son of this great house.

Pippa said she wanted to help in the kitchen, taking a pile of mixing bowls to the sink, but Mark was glad to escape the family frenzy and go with his old friend to the local round the corner. And Olivia was relieved to be invited; facing the huge close family of strangers in their big house was too much, tired as she was after the long drive. And she hoped to have a conversation about work, not cooking. Refreshingly, the pub decor paid only lip-service to the season. Electronic baubles flashed and an old silver paper 'Season's Greetings' banner was draped over a Father Christmas advertising the brewery. Pop music thumped vaguely.

There were queues three-deep at the bar. 'Ah. Lovely,' said Andrew, lowering his lips to his foaming pint. He too was soothed by the pub's anonymity and unpretentiousness.

'Well, how're things?' said Mark. 'It sounds as if you told Nigel where he got off. Quite right. Somebody should have dealt with him ages ago. Why are academics so weedy? They talk of academic freedom but never seem to fight for it.'

Olivia murmured agreement.

Andrew talked about not wanting to let down his team, the publishing and research successes. 'I could go off and do something different. But I want to go on with soil research. I need the stability and flexible hours to be a father to Julian. I'm a single parent, after all.'

'What brought it all to a head?' asked Mark. A drunken party started to exchange loud banter at the bar and they drew their chairs closer to hear Andrew's reply.

'One thing after another. The economic climate's changed. Money for research comes from industry. And universities can't be fastidious about where they get research funding in these hard times. Well, let them do contract work on the cheap for business. It's okay if all you want to do is engineer tomatoes with longer shelf life. I don't. I want to do science.'

'I know, I know. But tell us the story. What actually happened? Did you get a letter?'

'No. Nigel made a ridiculous proposal and I . . . I flipped.'

'Sometimes you just have to stand up to bullies,' Mark said. 'You did the right thing, Andy. Don't you think so, Olivia? Sometimes you need to knock your boss down.'

They all laughed. Mark went on, 'And it's no good, Andy, if they weren't going to support the research you want to do. Even I can see your discoveries are valuable. You'll be finding new antibiotics from strange soil bugs long after the biotech bubble has burst.'

'Yes. But I have the practicalities to deal with now. What next? What can I do for my research team? Where shall we live? There's no point in Julian and me keeping on our little house in Stockholm Street, but where should we move to?'

'You'll certainly get a job somewhere. That's only a matter of time. Why not just allow yourself a sabbatical? Let things evolve? Spend time with Julian?'

'Olivia, you made a very kind suggestion, that you might let us do field investigations on your farm.' Andrew gave her a direct look from under his level dark brow. 'It's something I'd be interested to pursue, if you really mean it?'

She could hardly believe the host of *Invisible Wildlife* was asking for a favour from her; in fact for a rescue. 'Pippa thought you might have time to have a look. I'd love you to do that, and see if Oxhide might be suitable for your work. It's just a farm, though—an ordinary hill farm with sheep and a farmyard. No special facilities.'

'But you did good work in India without technical support on the ground, didn't you?' said Mark, helping things along. So he was onside. She hadn't counted on it. He might have considered that being distracted by pootling around on a remote farm was beneath his best friend.

'It's the soil which is the interesting thing for us,' said Andrew. 'Not the buildings and facilities. The opportunity of looking at soils of traditionally managed non-intensive farmland. They're getting as rare as hens' teeth. And the range from meadows to moors with different geology—that could be interesting. Maybe we could come and see it? Not to make a nuisance of ourselves, just a walk about, you wouldn't even need to be there.'

'I'd be very interested indeed,' said Olivia. 'I would certainly want to be. I even have spare rooms, so you could stay if you and Julian would like to, and can face camping out in a half-empty house. Can I get this round?' She collected their glasses and made for the bar.

'Come on, come on, we're waiting for you,' said Susan when the three of them arrived back at the house. 'Come into the drawing room, quick. Time for presents!'

Olivia laughed. 'I just have to powder my nose.' It was her mother's phrase for needing a pee. Pippa and she had laughed at it in Elizabeth Street.

The family party of ten people was assembled, their faces pale in the light from dozens of real candles on the tree, drawing glints from glass icicles hung on the branches. It was the only light in the dark drawing room. It reminded Olivia of a childhood picture book illustration she'd loved, a fire in the forest, elves and squirrels sitting round. It was so beautiful, they were all silent a moment, watching the candles flicker and throw dancing fir twig shadows on the ceiling. That smell—forest and candle smoke—did something profound, brought up some archetypal response. Maybe there was a race memory in what the neurologists called the 'old brain', some nerve centre that remembered humans long ago feasting in forest clearings, hunks of venison roasting, firelight keeping wolves and hobgoblins away. Real Christmas trees still gave her a thrill—as well as bringing back those carefree days of childhood at the Hollies. And now, Olivia felt she had already been given the best Christmas present. Andrew Bamberg coming to stay.

The Bambergs' presents to each other were either deeply worthwhile or amusingly valueless. David soon sloped off into his study taking his present from Susan, the latest edition of *The Bach Reader*. Louisa's presents were small and beautifully wrapped.

'I have no money, but I have a lot of time, so I go to all the little sales they have for charities. This little thing is for you, dear Andreas.'

It was a dented but still-working clockwork silver pocket watch of the sort you could wear on a chain across your waistcoat. Andrew was delighted, hugging his old nanny and threading the watch's chain through a buttonhole. Watching this, something happened inside Olivia. Something that made everything all right. The family presents were soon distributed and there small parcels for all the guests as well.

Olivia held an Emma Bridgewater mug decorated with blackfaced sheep among flowers and grass. It must be Andrew's doing. It was—there was a little Christmas card: 'Happy Christmas and every success for Oxhide in the New Year', in that blue biro, signed 'A'.

Blushing, she caught his eyes on her. She hadn't been looked at like that since Frederico. 'For my gentle shepherdess,' Andrew said. 'Happy Christmas, dear Olivia.'

'Oh, Andy!' It was the first time she had used his pet name, the one the family used. It came out spontaneously.

'Think of me when you drink your well-earned cup of tea. Do you like Emma Bridgewater? I must bring you some more for your kitchen dresser.'

So he would come, Andrew Bamberg would come to Oxhide. The New Year brightened ahead of her. She reached out and brushed his hand with her fingers, feeling daring, and he took it and squeezed, like someone making a promise.

At about six o'clock, when it was completely dark, guests arrived for the Christmas dinner. The closest friends drifted in first, behaving as though at home. First was Vanessa, tall and soignée with carefully-dressed curls and her trademark tropical evening scent. Mary called to Andrew that she had arrived, and he came running down the stairs to meet her.

'Darling Andy, Happy Christmas! How are things?' The unmistakable silver tones came through to Olivia, standing in the kitchen with Louisa.

Vanessa looked Andrew up and down and patted his shoulder. 'I hear you've brought Mark and his beautiful Pippa? I have to see her, where is she?' Mark fetched Pippa. 'Congratulations Mark! You deserve a lovely wife.' Pippa accepted her kiss, both sides, without looking surprised. 'And this is—oh, it's Olivia, Mrs. Gabrieli, from Andy's party! How lovely to see you here, my dear. Well, well, what a big party we are this year.'

Olivia remembered Jane's explanation of Vanessa, Andy's extraordinary pop-up birth mother. What could it be like for Andrew, having two mothers, Mary, who'd raised him, and a birth mother he'd always been taught to treat as his glamorous godmother? Vanessa was almost part of the household, although she didn't offer to help, but took herself off with a magazine and cigarette to the study.

Jane arrived soon after, joining Vanessa in the study by the fire, taking typed papers out of her big square black leather handbag. They sat close but almost in silence, exchanging the occasional word, but not making conversation. Louisa took Olivia and Pippa to finish laying the table in the dining room. They learned how to fold a starched linen napkin into a mitre and spent a happy half hour doing one for each of the fifteen places at the table.

Julian came in from his school carol service, and last to arrive was an Indian colleague of David's, a cardiologist, and his two daughters aged about twelve and fourteen. He was doing a six months' internship at the hospital. His wife was at home in Mumbai, but the daughters were here, at school at St. Paul's. David ushered them in, and they all moved into the drawing room for drinks. The Indian daughters had brought bright silk animals to decorate the tree, and fastened them to its lower branches.

At dinner, Mary placed Olivia between Pippa and Mark, opposite Andrew and Vanessa. Susan, Mary and Louisa brought things from the kitchen and Julian cleared each course under Susan's direction. All through the meal Olivia felt Andrew's overpowering presence, almost as though he was giving out magnetic rays. David carved in proper paterfamilias manner, and Andrew drew corks, poured wine, told them when to pull crackers, set light to the pudding, and finally sat everybody in the drawing room as he made the coffee with Louisa's help.

After a while Susan's boyfriend Jonathan left for his nightly training run, and that might have been the moment for the other guests to start leaving, but Vanessa suggested they all play charades. Astonishingly, David and Andrew eagerly agreed, and everybody else was quite keen, except Jane, who said she didn't do party games and would rest in the study if people would excuse her. Olivia was up for it; she hadn't played charades since, at ten, she'd been the star turn at home at The Hollies.

The drawing room was separated into halves by pulling a brown velvet curtain across, and David and Andrew each formed a team. Andrew picked Olivia, Pippa and Mark and the Indian family, while David's team included Mary, Louisa, and Vanessa. Andrew's side won the toss and had to act first.

'I've got a word,' he said, taking charge. 'Physiotherapist! Then for the whole word, Pippa can just enter and bow, you know, a physiotherapist! Would you, Pippa?'

She laughed and agreed. 'But they'll never guess, they don't know what I do.'

'All the more mysterious.'

'You can do the first part, Sunetra—just come on drinking champagne, you know, fizzy.

Then what?—somebody swear an oath, Vijay, you do that, you do such a good serious manner, and Mark, you can make an error, and then ... uh ...'

'Then Shivani and Sunetra can come on and tell everybody to be quiet, you know: Psst!' Mark suggested quickly.

'No, better, we come on reeling about, pissed,' said Shivani, and she and Sunetra fell about in giggles.

They acted so well that the word was guessed immediately, and it was the turn of David's team. It was obviously a more difficult group to organise, because there was at least a ten minute wait until David appeared from behind the curtain to announce that they would act a well-known story. He had persuaded Mary, aunt Nessa and Louisa to be three bears, but only Nessa had any dramatic instinct. Her Father Bear moved like a bear, had proper whiskers and a black nose done apparently with eye makeup, and reared on his hind legs, fearsomely annoyed that somebody had slept in his bed and messed with his porridge. There was nothing bear-like about Mary, she just was not an actress, but it was clear she must be Mother Bear. Louisa made a passable Baby Bear. She had the former nanny's gift of joining obediently in children's games as required while retaining her adult dignity. Also, unlike the others, she possessed a fur coat. David in drag made a memorable Goldilocks, escaping the shrill cries of Baby Bear by leaping out of the drawing room window. It was surprising that these people passed for normal grown-ups with responsible jobs.

Olivia hadn't been this happy for a long time. About midnight everybody had collapsed into chairs and it was time to get back to Elizabeth Street where she was staying with Isobel. Andrew escorted her to the door and waited with her for the taxi he'd called.

'Thank you very much for coming tonight, Olivia. I hope my family weren't too much for you.'

'I don't know when I've enjoyed anything more. I do hope you have time to come up to Yorkshire and see over Oxhide.' The drink and conviviality must have made her add, 'It would mean a lot to me.'

'I will. To me, too. Goodnight, Olivia. We'll meet again in the New Year.' He kissed her cheek.

She looked back out of the cab window and he stood on the pavement under a street light, waving. Strangely, in spite of his huge warm family, there was something sad about him, as if he didn't belong. Was it that he'd abandoned the world of medicine everybody else at the party was so obviously part of? Or perhaps his strange position in that close family, a cuckoo in their nest in which Vanessa, the cuckoo mother, was on cordial visiting terms. It was sad he wasn't Mary's birth child, and might not even know his own father. You needed a role model for handling whatever mix of genes you'd inherited. Something about Andrew Bamberg touched off a deep fellow-feeling. The remote TV celebrity turned out to be human and rather like her, a changeling child, full of passion and ambition. She touched her cheek where he had kissed her. How long since that excitement of meeting an interesting man. It was not that she had serious romantic intent towards Andrew Bamberg . . . but how exciting life could be, after all. Even the feel and scent of a London cab had a lightly aphrodisiac effect.

Isobel was performing in Manchester. For the first time, Olivia had the Elizabeth Street house to herself. Her childhood bedroom in the attic, used for school exeats and then, for the months after the accident, her only refuge, somewhere to grieve. Now it seemed to have shrunk into a child's bedroom from a historical

reconstruction. Looking at the single divan, the little utilitaria
n desk and chair, Olivia savoured the thought of her home at
the head of the dale, her shaggy terrace lawn and the dome of
stars. Only the half-finished portrait of Ben on its easel beside
the door made her sad. What would he have been doing now?
She needed her twin, it would have made the future warmer to
have had her brother to talk to. He would have matured, probably
be properly grownup now, no longer the cocky boy the painter
depicted posing with a shotgun broken over his arm. She turned
the painting to face the wall. As she fell asleep she counted her
own sheep going through the gate of hurdles, with Mike watching
and sorting them. Their baa-ing drowned the cistern refilling and
jets from Heathrow.

Days later, her train drew in at Skipton, and Giles was there
again to collect her. They chatted about motors, building jobs,
and his mother who kept Skellside going with her B&B, Giles's
capable hands on the wheel, the scent of the moors coming off
him. But all the time her brain held the image of Andrew
Bamberg.

11

Taking Sides: Vanessa vs Jane

Andrew bounded up Vanessa's polished stairs. Her hug embraced them both in a halo of her otherworldly scent; her hair curled down to her shoulders.

'Lovely party,' she said. 'David and Mary are wearing well. And now, Andy, exciting times! Goodbye University, welcome—what next? New Year soon.'

'I'm in disgrace.'

She took his arm and stood beside him at the floor-to-ceiling windows, looking across the Thames. 'Not with me. I'm proud of you. You are your father's son.' He liked how she kept up this trope, that the father he'd never met had been a man of action, devastatingly powerful and impressive. A proud lineage. Well, if it made her feel better, he was happy to go along, although the Bambergs were more than good enough for him.

'Some situations are bad for the soul. You have the spirit, Andy, to recognise and reject the limitations of little men.' She squeezed his arm. 'The world is threatened by littleness at the moment.

It's more insidious than catastrophe, but with the same power of destruction. Turning life grey when it should be gold and blue.' A gleam of sunshine fell across the river on cue, and gilded the cupolas of the Royal Naval College under a patch of blue sky. 'You did well, Andy. You're free. What now?'

'No more lab work for a bit. Real nature, real landscape for me now. It's time for me to see if we're right that the invisible world is the mainspring of natural biodiversity. The variousness of plants and animals that makes nature beautiful. Darwin's Entangled Bank.'

He couldn't have talked like this to anyone else. Julian put on a retching act if he so much as used the word 'beauty'. Mary and David would make neutral 'hmm' noises and turn the conversation practical. A beautiful sunset? Time to take the dog out before dark, then.

'I'm thinking about Yorkshire.'

'That girl, Olivia? She scrubbed up well. It was nice to see her at Highgate.'

'Yes, Olivia Gabrieli. And Mark and Pippa are based there now, you know, in Skipton, fifteen miles from Oxhide. That's Olivia's place. It could be good for Julian to get out of London. She's offering me a field site. Cultural landscapes are her thing—her life's work, she says.'

'Oh, really? I thought she was one of Jane's people. Might she join the Committee for Conservation of Cultural Landscapes?'

'I'm sure, if she knew about it.'

'More to her than I thought, then,' said Vanessa. 'I'll get them to send her the bumf. A cultural landscape is the evidence of love. Love and loyalty. It evolves through work and faith. That's where the beauty lies. And it takes time. *Biodiversity off-setting*, pah! You can't pick up an ancient wood and put it down intact somewhere else.'

'Olivia would agree. But she's practical. Hates what's happening to farmland, as much as you and I do. But she's got her feet on the ground, I think. We have to live with the fact that people in England only take you seriously now if you make money. She's going to make traditional farming profitable and show the world how. The Yorkshire Dales as paradigm cultural landscape.'

'Oh, one of those. Money and beauty are polar opposites, Andy, like God and Mammon. Beware of her clutches.'

'She's not romantic like you, Ma. She's forsworn human love, don't worry for my virtue.'

'Bizarre. Is she all there?'

'I'll tell you that when I've been to see her land.' He heard strains of Helen's music from downstairs. 'That's a step up from Helen's usual folk music. Has she found new friends?'

'It's not a record, it's Julian practising. Had you forgotten? For his music scholarship competition. Not bad, is he?'

The violin sounded to Andrew like Izaak Perlman. 'That's amazing. He has come on, hasn't he?'

'Come with Helen and me this evening and hear him.'

'Yes. Yes, I've no lectures to prepare. Why not?'

Helen had set out soup and sandwiches on low tables in the room below. They watched the light fade on the river as they ate their pre-concert supper. Some passing boats had coloured lights, casting long rippled reflections. Greenwich came to life, lit against the navy sky.

Helen, Vanessa and Andrew chatted in the taxi to the concert.

'So you're moving, Andy? What about Julian?'

'He'll be back here as before for a while, at weekends and holidays, until I find somewhere else. Stockholm Street's on the market.'

'How much for?' asked Helen.

'Five hundred and forty K.'

'Oh, I was thinking I might have bought it. But no hope.'

'Thank goodness,' said Vanessa callously. 'Who'd look after me?'

Helen laughed with good humour. It wasn't a bad deal for her, being Vanessa's housekeeper and PA. A stylish house on the river and only light duties. The unambitious life had its attractions.

'So when are you going to Yorkshire?' Vanessa asked him, her face pale in the passing headlights as she peered at him in the half light of the cab.

'Oh, by and by. Olivia Gabrieli invited me to stay. But I want Julian to come too and be involved in any project,' said Andrew, looking past the driver at the unreconstructed muddle of the Old Kent Road, the bustle of little unsmart shops. 'I can't impose him on anyone at the moment, he can be so rude and unpredictable.'

'It's the age, a phase,' said Helen, with the authority of a nanny. 'He's a charmer when he wants.'

'We'll go and have a weekend up there in the spring, stay with Mark, go for a walk, maybe just phone and drop in.'

'Nearly there,' said Helen, before he had a chance to hear Vanessa's response. The taxi stopped behind the hall. 'I do hope he isn't nervous. He's such a star, I think he'll win.'

'Of course he will,' said Vanessa, 'he's my grandson.'

Thank god, whatever remote rural outpost he might get bogged down in, Vanessa would take care of Julian's future. Andrew put worries about his team to the back of his mind and prepared to enjoy the musical contest.

Her first New Year at Oxhide. Olivia felt for her slippers with bare feet in the dark. It was almost six in the morning. Half asleep still, she knew she was happy but not why. She explored her half-awake mind for the sources, and remembered last night, New Year's Eve. The entire Robertshaw family had arrived to first-foot her just after midnight.

'Your lights were on,' said Meg, in the front porch, swinging a traditional paraffin lantern from her hand. 'Can we come in?'

Olivia threw the door open wide, standing aside to let the family troop past down the narrow stone-flagged passage. The kitchen was warm from the new electric Aga, giving out its motherly stored heat, and in the sitting room the fire came easily to life again with a few sticks and some puffing. Olivia brought out a bottle of Scapa from her mother's glass-fronted tallboy, the single malt she'd laid in for her father, and poured them a dram, including Jack, who was about fourteen and almost full sized. Luckily there was Anne's Diet Coke for the younger two.

'We missed you over Christmas,' said Meg. 'Though Anne was here almost the whole time, and Giles too, they enjoyed it, didn't they Mike?'

'They did that.' Mike exchanged a knowing glance with his wife. 'Well, here's to you, Olivia. Were you kids going to sing anything?' And they all joined hands, Meg and Mike grasping Olivia's, and struck up with Auld Lang Syne. Olivia did her best without knowing all the words. Did anybody? At last, with their neighbourly purpose achieved, the kind Robertshaws left, and the gentle roar of the new central heating was audible again in the dark silence of the first day of the new year.

The alarm clock beeped as soon as she'd fallen asleep, and she stumbled into her piled-up clothes, stamped on boots and went out into the dark chill to check the ewes, accustomed now to take the steep path through the intake fields on to the moor, as she had that first week with Giles. Once fully awake, she loved the routine. Already, only a week after the solstice, there was a sense of lengthening days. The morning star shone in the navy blue eastern sky and there was a fresh pre-dawn breeze. Her leg hardly ever hurt now. Jane was coming to stay, and they would discuss plans and accounts, and perhaps she would mention to her godmother the potential of Oxhide as the perfect site for the scientific investigation of invisible wildlife. Scientists started the day early too, didn't they? A future vision of Andrew in a lamplit lab by the end of the cowshed swam into Olivia's mind.

By eight she was back for breakfast, scrambled egg and coffee on the scrubbed table. Sitting with her back to the warm life-changing Aga, she mulled over the party at Andrew's parents' house. It had been like a university party. Although so mixed in age and nationality, they were all similar somehow, with that confidence to act the fool. They behaved as if entitled to their status and security, as Olivia remembered feeling herself, long ago as a little girl at The Hollies. Jane and Vanessa had seemed best friends, closeted together by the fire in the Highgate study, in spite of the odd antipathy her godmother had let slip that time in St. James's Park. Their conversation at Christmas had sounded like the gentle sparring that was normal between cousins. Vanessa was the stunning one, Jane square and plain, but with a surprisingly warm smile and intelligent eyes that focussed on you. How had Vanessa ever given birth to Andrew, and why give him away? Jane must know; perhaps she could be induced to talk more about Vanessa.

Why, anyhow, Olivia asked herself, was she so nosy about Andrew Bamberg's antecedents? All she needed to know was whether his science was sound. What business of hers were his relatives? Funny, though, that his name and hers were so alike. Bamberg, Burbank. What were people like in Erfurt? Were his eyebrows a bit like those of J. S. Bach? But no, he was only Bamberg by name, not ancestry.

She pushed back her kitchen chair with a clatter, swept up her breakfast things into old Mrs. Robertshaw's massive sink, then ran upstairs and set about getting the spare room ready for Jane. Giles had done a good job with the Farrow and Ball, but there were still small brown pellets of some kind on the floorboards. Bat shit! She laughed. London seemed like somewhere the other side of the world. How surprising that in a little country like England the differences between town and country were still so deep. Long might it last, she thought, opening the cupboard off the landing that she had designated for linen, and taking a pair of sheets still wrapped in green and white John Lewis paper. She, at any rate, was going to do her best for the miraculous survival that was now her land, less than three hundred miles from that chaos of noise and glare and the Great Gatsby's *vast carelessness*.

She ripped off the cellophane and shook out the sharp-creased cotton. By the open window she paused as she always did to scan the high horizon of the opposite side of the valley, the misted top now just catching the sun. Another month and pre-spring colour would wash into the bare winter trees, alder along the river and birch on the lower fell side would turn that glowing pinkish brown, the first sign that winter was loosening its grip on the landscape. A wren hopped and chirred under the hedge at the edge of the terraced lawn under the rainy window.

The phone rang into the stillness, the landline downstairs. Her godmother was on her way.

12

Philosophy, Politics and Economics

'Give me your accounts to look over,' said Jane, looking up at Olivia from one of the two white sofas newly installed either side of the sitting room fire. 'Bring me a pot of tea and leave me in peace an hour or so. Then we'll have a think about your business plan. After that I'm standing you dinner. A surprise dinner.'

Olivia wished for a moment Jane was her real mother, rather than just a godmother. An older woman prepared to drop her own concerns, to turn her experience and energy on giving Olivia advice and practical help, showing her how to do accounts, gently setting an example of leadership with her own disciplined energy; what wouldn't Olivia give, even at 29, to have a mother like that. With Jane in the house, she felt less alone, more light-hearted. She speculated on how many godchildren Jane had. Probably dozens, all her younger staff would want to bag kind, important Jane for their babies. She must be equally devoted to lots of others. Jealously, Olivia hoped she was the favourite. To an extent that surprised her, she wanted Jane's approval. She wanted to talk to her about Andrew, to enlist her sympathetic support in inviting him to Oxhide.

The original business plan her father and his accountant had helped her to frame was in a box file in a small room next to her bedroom that Olivia had set aside for a temporary office. Next to the file was a pile of folders containing more recent documents, relating to the flock, the income from the sale of two rams and the draft ewes, outgoings including feed bills, insurance, the vet, the purchase of her Land Rover Defender, new files containing planning and architectural documents relating to renovation of the farm and its buildings, and some bumf for which she hadn't yet identified a category. It was all far from paperless, as she had inherited Mike Robertshaw's methods. But at least she had moved on from simply impaling the bills on a spike, as Mike's father had probably done. Transferring these data into the new desktop that stood ready was one of her New Year resolutions. Olivia carried the box file, topped with as-yet-unfiled papers, into the sitting room, followed by the puppy Moss, biting and chewing at her flapping trouser hems with her needle-like teeth. Pity the poor mother dog if these were milk teeth. Jane watched this with a carefully neutral expression. This system must be very different from the procedures of Jane's Whitehall office.

'I'm doing the module on farm accounts next term,' said Olivia defensively as Jane eyed these arrangements. 'I know the subsidy applications have to be done online. I need to play more with Excel in the long dark evenings.'

'Well, this is a more sociable approach,' said Jane, and smiled. 'It looks as though you've kept everything, at least. A good start. And don't worry too much about the online stuff you'll get from us. It's all going to be easier. It's good you're already signed up for ELMS. The Minister says we learned a lot from the early problems with single payment. The farm maps were part of the trouble. When people saw their farms were in the North Sea they rather lost faith in the software. The Devil's in the detail. It's all changing now. Maybe even for the better.'

Jane drew reading glasses from a metal case, opened Olivia's box file and arranged the contents on the coffee table. She opened her laptop, bringing up online forms. 'These make me so angry. Picture a lonely elderly farmer on an economic knife-edge, just getting by doing things the way he and his forbears always have, with a mortgage and a ridiculous vet's bill and not the faintest idea what computers are. There are suicides, you know.'

'I know. That's why I want to learn my way around subsidies and understand how the money side works. So I know what I'm talking about and can perhaps offer people a hand myself, eventually.' Olivia watched Jane scan the papers. It was like waiting for test results from the doctor.

'Well, you seem to be doing pretty well, as far as I can see from this.' Jane looked up over the top of her spectacles. 'What a lot people pay for a ram! Sixteen thousand pounds? Sheep look much the same to me. I suppose if it was easy to spot a ram worth sixteen K you'd have them stolen from the field.'

'I was surprised, too,' Olivia admitted. 'They're not all worth as much as that, but the Robertshaws' sheep are famous. They've been breeding Swaledales for a century. A good ram can be the pinnacle of a sort of cross-breeding pyramid. He becomes the great grandfather of whole fields full of expensive fat lambs down in the lowlands.'

'So a ram's just a package of good genes?'

'Yes, I'm afraid so. Well, that's what males are, aren't they? Though they're very much individuals to me.'

'Of course,' said Jane, with an amused smile, then focussing again: 'You're a shepherd. How does the cross-breeding thing work? I see you've been planning various crosses. But all the sheep I've seen here look the same.'

'Cross-breds are larger and faster-growing. They get produced on better grass, not up in the hills. Mike has relatives who farm down in Wensleydale near Leyburn and on the plain at Catterick, it's a family collaboration, Swaledales up here, cross-breds down there.'

'So they do it all in house, so to speak,' Jane said. She made a note with her fountain pen. 'That takes some of the uncertainty out of the system, I suppose. For them.'

'Yes, it's all very networked. I guess that's why the Robertshaws are so much richer than the Yarkers. I'm going to leave you in peace, Jane. More tea?'

'No thanks. Give me an hour or so, then we'll go out and have a launch party for Oxhide. I've booked.'

Olivia had been up since five, on the moor on the quad bike checking sheep and then preparing Jane's room. She left her mandarin godmother scrutinising Oxhide's crumpled accounts by the fire, and went to change out of her farm clothes.

Showered and lying on her bed in her dressing gown, Olivia relaxed into a reverie. Sheep and Excel spreadsheets revolved in her brain and a kind of vision came, an out-of-body sense she was just one more generation of wool merchants; setting out to make her own way, she had found herself on the same long path as centuries of forbears: sheep farmers, shearers, draymen, carders, spinners, weavers and exporters, with accountants like Jane in offices, reckoning the cash flows, trying to forecast the difference between fortune and disaster and buffer their families against ineluctable uncertainty; governments calculating taxes and tariffs on wool and woollens. Such a local matter, shepherding, and the manufacture of woollen cloth; and yet so vulnerable to global winds. As her father had found, and perhaps tried to warn her, that day ten and a half years ago, her penultimate sixth-form year.

In a flashback she pictured the shining copper and dark wood of Whitelocks, that day she had come from school to a Leeds University open day. In between sessions she had skipped canteen fare with the students; it had been a rare chance to see her father, who she missed. It was a shame she'd cold-shouldered him as a young teenager. Joe had taken her out for a business lunch: roast beef and Yorkshire pudding among the pub's famous mixture of merchants, artists and office workers. He had asked her about her plans, how she saw her future, what career had she in mind? Afterwards, while they collected their coats, he said there was time for them to go and check on the mill. It meant she would have had only a brief glance at the university. But keeping the lines open with her father came first, and Leeds had been her third choice.

The factory stood beside the river Aire, in a bowl rimmed by upland horizons, a landscape scarred with blackened industrial and agricultural remains. They drove past broken stone walls around minute fields. Rows of tiny houses, each with its cement backyard and stone privy, clustered near derelict Methodist and Baptist chapels used as warehouses. Garages selling Ford Fiestas and Vauxhall Corsas with five-year-old registration plates appeared at intervals. Then Joe turned off the main road and Olivia saw the mill from above, in its grand setting, in the depths of the valley, even more impressive than she remembered. She peered down through sycamores, their sticky late-summer leaves sooty-dark, at its gothic skeleton as they wound their way downhill. Her father parked on a cindered yard by a bank of ragwort and thistles.

Bright clouds silhouetted the derelict seven-storey-high building, and pigeons cooed from a high ledge. Most of the tall windows on the lower storey had lost their panes, and gaped black. Fly-by-night businesses had colonized bits of the ruin, like nomads camping in a rockhewn desert temple. Discordant signs painted here and there on the walls advertised their activities: 'Best Beds in Bradford'; 'Discount kitchens'. Two Asian men carried in cardboard boxes from a blue lorry. The chimney had born her own name, BURBANK, painted top to bottom like a school pencil. Mica sparkled in the sandstone setts of the mill yard, and in this late summer sunshine, the boastful Italianate architecture had a surreal beauty.

But as they approached, the reality of dereliction was overwhelming. Blackened by Bradford smoke, its eighty lintels rain-stained, and with willow herb and buddleia rampant in the gutters, the building looked as though it had been bombed in the war rather than succumbing to the winds of economic change. Burbanks had made serge, the cloth of grammar school uniforms, woven from tight narrow threads of twisted wool, made to last; not washable. Over the years sales had given way before the march of synthetics: terylene, crimplene, tercel, viscose. Inside, detritus of the mill's last years remained: a rusty filing cabinet backed against crumbling plasterboard, a scatter of torn yellowing file paper. Up stone stairs in the huge machine room, oil stains remained visible on the floor and the long room above held rails with jumbled metal garment hangers.

Olivia unhooked one, a memento, she told her father. He said they ought to be able to do better than that, but all they could find was a box containing a chaos of small machinery spare parts, even less collectable. Scavengers had been there before them. Surely something could be done? But recession had hit them all, said Joe. Burbanks weren't the only ones. He pointed out Drummonds in the distance; he thought there must be a score or more of these old mills. If only there was a market, he'd get rid of it. But for now, he was lumbered with it.

'I just make sure it doesn't fall on anybody, let it out as storage space, that's all we can do. I hate it. Let's go.'

'Aren't you proud of it at all?' asked Olivia, as they walked back to the car. These mills had made the country rich, fuelled an empire. Being a Burbank was important to her.

'It certainly made us comfortable. Your great grandfather built the Hollies with his wool fortune. But what about life in those squalid houses? The racket of the looms, it was awful, I couldn't bear it. And the smoke blotted half the sunlight, like a roof. I read somewhere that average life expectancy for the mill workers in the eighteen-forties was under twenty. Their children died working here.'

Back in the fragrant leather of the Jaguar's rear seat, she gazed at the landscape as they left the river valley. They passed streets of semi-derelict Victorian merchants' villas on the Bradford outskirts and drove uphill along an arterial road bordered by cloned post-war semis. Strata in the Anthropocene, she thought, pleased with the idea: these layers of habitations left by people doing their best with what was available. Buildings thinned out, followed by garden centres, a golf course and farm shops, until at last the car rattled over a cattle grid to open moor.

How had the years changed her father? In her mother's eyes, Joe as a handsome twenty five-year-old must have seemed the romantic heir to a great merchant dynasty. The decline and fall of Burbanks would have disappointed Isobel, but Olivia guessed that Joe might have welcomed an honourable escape from the responsibilities of a failing family firm. The ruined factory had filled her with sadness, but Joe was surprisingly unsentimental about it. And at least he had managed to hang on to The Hollies.

Then her father slowed as a pub came into view. Dick Hudson's, the old stopping place of her childhood: beer for her father and mother, ginger beer for Olivia and Ben.

The low bar was unchanged: crammed with people at closely-spaced tables. Most of the noise came not from conversation, but assiduous eating. Crouched low over plates, the diners prioritized feeding. Knives and forks clattered on plates, partly drowning out light music warbling in the background. The air smelt of chips and beer and face powder. Once notorious for nobody knew quite what, Dick Hudson's remained a honey-pot for coach trips. When they had finished and were leaving the pub, the wide view of hills was partly obscured by a coach; 'Executive Travel', it said on the back, and on the front, incongruously, 'Merlin's Mystery Tours'. A party of pensioners straggled back towards it across the car park, some leaning on sticks or on each other's' arms. 'Poor beggars,' Joe had remarked. It was indeed a poignant sight, bent figures outlined against the landscape like one of those monuments to the oppressed. Her father was a kind man.

Now she was late, and hurried to get ready for Jane's dinner treat. Usually, Olivia hated not to be in charge, but this evening she was happy to sit childlike in the passenger seat of Jane's car wondering where they were going and what the surprise was that Jane had mentioned.

The wipers swept away sleet with a cheerful two-beat rhythm and the headlights opened a winding path through the pitch darkness ahead, spotlighting rain-slick stone walls on each side, Jane's face dimly lit by the elaborate dashboard of red and blue fairy lights. It was certainly a surprise when Jane drew in to the forecourt of what Olivia remembered as a very ordinary pub by the road in Addingham. But that was twenty years ago when she'd been a nine-year old drinking lemonade in the garden. The Good Pub Guide had waved its wand. A wood smoke aroma hung in a reception area of low lighting and tartan armchairs, with a log fire and the glitter of a bar beyond. There was a huge arrangement of lilies on a polished oak chest, under a painting of Bolton Abbey. It was a Saturday and middle-aged couples thronged the bar, scented women who'd been at their hairdressers' that afternoon, men in blazers.

And here was Jane's surprise—Joe rose from a high-backed chair in the corner like the ghost of Christmas past. 'Olivia!' Joe hugged her, then holding her at arms' length, smiled, his eyes the same dark grey as her own. 'How good this is! Jane said we were celebrating. No one's birthday, is it?'

'It's an audit dinner,' Jane said. 'For Oxhide farm. You should be proud of this daughter of yours. Not every young woman could manage a start-up on her own, specially in these uncertain times. I've seen the accounts. There's potential there—she has your flair. Risk—of course. But I'm impressed how that's allowed for in the business plan. The holiday lets and residential field courses should provide counterbalancing income streams. Let's go straight in and eat, shall we?'

They had the best table and there was bottle of Champagne already beside it in an ice bucket. A waitress appeared and poured with a flourish of white napkin. Jane, as the driver, took only a small glass. But as they worked through starters and then grouse, Olivia allowed herself to get rather drunk, and so did Joe.

He became pink and his conversation lightened. 'It's like the old days. Didn't we have fun Jane? Have you never regretted the things we didn't do, eh?'

'There are always things to regret. Are you going to finish that, Joe, or can I have it?' She reached across the table to capture Joe's abandoned grouse leg in her fingers, gnawing it with a surprising lack of polite inhibition, as though at home. Olivia stared at them both.

Jane laughed and explained. 'Excuse us, Olivia. Your father and I go back a long way, from old times. Before you were born. Our grandfathers were part of the old Bradford wool mafia. We were Young Conservative kids.' She gave Joe a coy glance.

Joe leaned back in his chair and snorted. He looked as though he'd had a pint while waiting for them to turn up.

'Remember when we got lost on the car treasure hunt somewhere on Angram Moor? I had that MG midget. We were both still at school. Or had I gone to University?'

'It was at the end of the summer holidays after your first year. You'd just come back from a reading party with your new friends in Surrey.' She picked at her lemon meringue pie. 'Surrey?' Olivia pricked her ears.

'Yes,' said Joe. 'Jane, you were going out with that chap Rory.' He turned to Olivia. 'That's when I met your mother. She bowled me over.' He gazed into her eyes. 'You have such a look of Isobel tonight, love.'

Jane excused herself and headed off to the ladies.

There was a silence. Joe was chasing the last crumb of his apple pie round the plate. He up-ended the wine bottle into his glass.

'Poor Isobel. Ilkley Music Festival was one of her first public recitals. She was at the Wigmore Hall the next year, and now she's international of course. Right out of my league.'

Olivia could see Joe was happier at The Hollies than he would have been arriving at Holloway, Isobel's family home on the North

Downs, with its two-storey-high entrance hall with chandelier, and the stable yard at the back.

He went on, 'Isobel tried so hard to find musicians to play with in Ilkley. Two chaps used to come and play trios. But even I could see she outclassed them. And she hated outdoors. I'd imagined showing her my favourite places in the Dales; Buckden Pike, the Cam High Road over by Yockenthwaite. But Isobel hated mud. It revolted her, she didn't distinguish mud from dung. Open spaces bored her. She's a 'people person', as Anne says. Are you a people person, Olivia?'

'I'm too like you Dad.' She loved him at that moment. 'I'm a hill farmer, a sheep person.' Jane came back. They both grinned at her.

'What happy smiles! Wait, I must take a photo.' Jane pulled out a mobile—so she did have one—which made Joe and Olivia smile, and then handed the phone to Olivia. The two faces in the little square were similar: the wide smiles, the serious grey eyes. 'A chip off the old block,' Joe agreed, and she caught Jane giving her an almost motherly look. She felt loved and slightly tipsy. Nobody, after all, was closer to her than Joe, now Ben was gone; certainly not her mud-fearing mother. Her father would take to Andrew Bamberg, she was sure. Andrew liked mud, after all.

Poor Jane, poor Joe. Pennies clattered down in Olivia's mental slot machine. Here was Jane still bravely single, after Isobel the southern interloper had stolen her Joe Burbank. And now here was she, Olivia, daughter of a Surrey mother and widow of a Florentine Gabrieli, drinking too much and feeling like a gooseberry in this horrible little pub. What if Joe had married Jane? Who would Olivia have been then? Heiress to a Burbank firm, probably flourishing under Jane's direction.

'Liqueurs?' asked the waitress.

'Why not?' said Joe. 'Join me in a Green Chartreuse, Olivia?'

The atmosphere in the car home was maudlin. Thank goodness Jane drove. 'You know, 'Joe went on, 'I'm glad this family's going to make its mark again.'

'In spite of everything,' Jane said. 'Bradford's unrecognisable now, isn't it? No mills, no soot, nothing.'

'Have you seen our place recently?' said Joe, 'An insurance nightmare. At least the stack's down.'

'A landmark gone. No Burbank chimney any more.'

'I'll tell you a secret. I kept the B. It's behind the garage at the Hollies. It's metal, taller than me, it weighs a bit.'

'You can't face down global trends single-handed.' Jane patted his knee, beside her in the passenger seat. 'Bradford woollen mills thrived on an empire that's gone.'

'Grampy used to make the cloth for Ghurkha uniforms,' Joe remembered. '*Tempora mutantur.*'

'So Olivia,' said Jane, impatient with her old flame's Latin tags, 'I suppose you'll go back to being Olivia Burbank at Oxhide? Keep up the family tradition?'

'No. Oxhide is Freddie's as much as mine. More so. Nothing as important as marrying Freddie can happen to me again. I'm Olivia Gabrieli. I feel as though Olivia Burbank died in the same accident as Freddie and Ben.'

Olivia woke at four with a throbbing headache and when she got up to fetch a glass of water her lurching stomach told her she was extremely hungover. The spare room, from which Jane's snores could be heard, was next to the bathroom, so she staggered downstairs, balancing with a hand against the wall, to be sick in the musty lavatory off the kitchen passage. The night outside was quiet with no wind. Then her alarm went off and it was time to wake her guest with early morning tea.

Olivia always went outside as soon as she got up, to take the temperature of the day. A moist grassy breeze from the west erased traces of last night's sleet. Jane's lamp sent a golden beam across the wet garden from the guest-room window. For the first time this year Olivia noticed clumps of snowdrop spikes under the hawthorn hedge that edged the strip of lawn. Moss, released, bounded out into the morning and flurried around, already growing into a proper Collie, an eye on Olivia's every move, listening. A canine ally. And having her first guest to stay also felt like a milestone; she could be a host, and her farm a place of hospitality. Perhaps there should be a visitor's book, a gilt-embossed red leather affair on a hall stand, though with Moss around it might not last. Could she get one in Skipton? Imagine if, one day, she staged a Christmas here like the Bambergs, with Oxhide full of family, friends and colleagues, not just next door neighbours, but from all over the world, friends from Italy, scientists. Before going up to check the sheep she laid two places on the kitchen table with her new cutlery and the big red and gold porcelain breakfast cups from her mother's family, and called up to Jane she'd be back in an hour and a half.

Jane wasn't a breakfast talker but her silence was friendly.

'I thought of a tagline for marketing Oxhide Farm,' Olivia said, reaching for the coffee pot.

'Mm?' Jane was on the toast and marmalade. 'Sustainable, scenic, scientific?' Olivia suggested. 'Scientific? How so?'

'I've invited Andrew Bamberg to scope out Oxhide for a project. And he's accepted.'

'Andy? To do a programme? Good idea. That could raise your commercial profile very effectively. But remember, product placement can have snags. It can happen that the orders flood in faster than a firm can deliver, and that can damage your brand.'

'I want my brand to do more than sell produce. If I can get Andrew as resident scientist, it would make Oxhide's name as a model farm. We could have open days, and demonstrate science into practice. Think who would come—soil experts, hill famers, George Monbiot, policy-makers like you, ministers! Wouldn't that be great? Andrew Bamberg's research is so interesting. And he's looking for a field site.'

'I don't think so. Andrew's tied up with his university work and television.' It was disappointing flaw in Jane, that she persisted in talking down Andrew just because of an old jealousy of Vanessa.

'I know he *was*. But it's so strange, haven't you heard? His university has given him the sack. A man like that, with such interesting ideas.'

'The sack? No! Andrew? Vanessa's Andrew?' Jane put down her marmalade-burdened knife and stared at Olivia. 'He didn't mention that at Christmas.'

'I'm afraid so. Remember my friends Pippa and Mark at the Bambergs' Christmas party? Mark's Andy's old friend from way back, and he's a GP now, near here, in Skipton, I see them quite a lot. They told me about it. Andrew got into a fight with his boss and knocked him down, after they took away his lab and reassigned his research team.'

Jane's face changed. Olivia realised she was seeing someone's jaw drop. For a moment Jane was struck dumb. Then, 'Good God,' she said. 'I didn't expect them to go that far.'

Why was Jane so agitated? 'Really, some of these higher education administrators have got above themselves. Behave as if they're real CEO's. Giving Andrew Bamberg the sack! I never heard anything like it. The Minister had better call in the VC.'

It looked as if poor Jane was so shocked she had defaulted into civil service mode, forgetting she was here as Olivia's guest and godmother. Surely honourable Jane couldn't have . . . could she?

To get her back on course, Olivia elaborated her plans for helping Andrew; how after talking to Pippa and Mark he began to see the wreck of his university project as a spur to taking his research in a new direction, that he was looking for sites as near to natural as possible, and how Oxhide might be just the place. That he was planning to have a look.

'Maybe I can build him a little lab. A scientist on site! Rather like having a hermit somewhere on your estate, thinking wise thoughts in an elegant grotto.'

Jane leaned forward in her chair. 'Don't, Olivia. Just don't. Your business plan is fine, but it's early days. There's no fat on your business yet. The last thing Oxhide needs on the payroll is an out-of-work academic. He may well be the next big thing, but you are just not in a position to absorb that risk. Think of your father, the thought he's put into your balance sheets, the projected year-on-year returns. You owe far more to him than to that ridiculously spoiled young man. Build your new machinery shed, field studies barn and the holiday flats. No lab.'

Was it the godmother talking—or Vanessa's rival? It was dispiriting. Jane left the next day as planned, via probably the first Uber driver ever seen in Upper Wharfedale, and Olivia was alone, trying not to hear those words on repeat. *Don't. Just don't.*

Well, Olivia told herself, *she would. She just would.*

13

Cold Comfort at Oxhide

It was lonely after Jane's departure, as Christmas cheer receded with the old year. She'd hoped Andrew Bamberg would contact her, but when she rang Pippa it turned out the Foremans had heard nothing from him either, not since the party in London. Mark thought he might have gone abroad. Scientists travelled a lot for work.

Olivia was glad Giles had come over from Skellside this morning to help move the electric fence they used to release the ewes at intervals on to new areas of turnips. It was time to build them up, ready for lambing. They were collecting the loops of electric tape and moving the posts and heavy lead battery. Out behind the barn the field was muddy, pocked with small sheep's footprints. Bulging under their wool, the pregnant ewes stood in the low field where they'd been collected off the moor for lambing. Rain that had just held off since dawn started again, and the sky darkened, throwing the sleet-blanched moor top into dramatic relief. With each step mud sucked at Olivia's boots. Rain washed the tops of the turnips free of soil so they stuck out as purplish-white lumps. Even the puppy Moss looked despondent and had to be taken back to her bed on the quad bike. Giles turned up his jacket collar, bare-headed as usual, his curly hair impervious to the wet. Her own was soon slicked around her face.

'That work on t'house's going on grand.' Giles's usual cheerfulness was undimmed by the foggy silence hanging over Oxhide. In the fields, away from the need to act the cool car salesman in his part-time garage job, he would use the comforting native speech. 'You'll be a real lady of the manor, Olivia.' From his searching look, she realised how wet and bedraggled she must appear. Her complexion was her mother's, she didn't go rosy in cold, just pinched. He smiled at her.

'Get yourself back in the warm.' He laughed when she refused. 'My dad called you a soft southerner. She'll not stand it up here, he said. I told him you were different. Aye, Olivia, it'll all look better, come Easter.'

Olivia smiled back at him. 'I'll hang on to that thought. This is bloody awful, isn't it?' Giles got on so well with her father when Joe paid visits to see the farm work in progress.

His steadiness brought her down to earth with human work like this: moving an electric fence to give the sheep their fresh supply of turnips, doing what was needed, putting one foot in front of the other through the seasons. The fence finished, they returned to the yard in companionable silence.

There was plenty of room for just a small lab, it couldn't cost a lot, surely. Jane was such a bean counter. Civil servants were like that—blind to the bigger picture. Jane hadn't fully understood Olivia's vision for Oxhide, to be a beacon for twenty-first century hill farming.

Jane was too careful to dream. She was timid, like Joe, terrified of debt. Look at Vanessa, with her style, her principles, the way she'd taken on the learned geneticists at the Trojans' Bar. And there was Andrew, physically knocking down a biotechnologist bully. They were Olivia's sort. Obviously, Andrew Bamberg would need somewhere for equipment, a lab bench, and a bit of office space. As the RSPB said about encouraging nature—*give them a home and they will come.* Olivia smiled.

If only he rang. It was six weeks and four days since Christmas. Then, he had spoken as if he might turn up at Oxhide any time, had shaken her hand so firmly, not just a shake but a clasp, like a promise. He had kissed her cheek. How she longed for his presence. She would stand firm in her invitation, it was her duty to Science. And he was Mark's friend, and Mark was no fool, and nor was Pippa. And surely practical Giles would be impressed when Olivia imported a scientist, and Anne would be bowled over to have a tame TV celebrity on site.

At that moment, the hollow musical clatter of shod hoofs on wet tarmac came up from the road. She must have heard it subliminally. It sparked a line of music in her head: *Winterreise*—the hoofbeats of the mail coach, the abandoned lover's despairing song, hoping in vain for it to bring a letter from his love. Those ups and downs of love. Thank goodness she'd put those behind her. It freed you to make friends with men, to enjoy them as colleagues. She admired Giles's profile as he gazed down at the road.

'It's Anne. Don't they look lovely? She has to exercise them twice a day, now they have to be stabled. Oh, I wish the rain would stop, it's not fair.'

'She can ride, can your sister,' said Giles. They both watched the chestnut thoroughbred Dreamcatcher doing his floaty trot, with Anne riding, and leading the bay cob Comet, with his shorter legs and faster stride. 'She exercises them twice a day so they don't spend too long in the field messing up your wildlife.'

Every ten paces or so, the ringing hoofs came back into synchrony, as energetic as two hammering machines. Glancing up at the farmhouse as she passed, Anne saw them and waved. The rain stopped and a gleam of sun shone on the wet road. She loved them all.

'It makes me so happy, having so many people around now. You and Pete, and Anne and the horses, and the Robertshaws and the contractors at work, and your parents, and my Dad, and Pippa and Mark. Things are getting going, like a real place, a homestead. Do you remember that evening I first turned up at the Bell, Giles? I think I might have given up and gone home that night if it hadn't been for your kindness.'

'I doubt it.' Giles gazed after the horses on the road.

'And I think we might be getting a new person. Do you ever watch that programme *Invisible Wildlife* on TV?'

Giles stiffened. His attention swung back to her. 'Our Mum does sometimes. I don't watch those things much, it's more the football for me, and *Top Gear*.'

'Oh. Well, this scientist I know, who's on TV quite a bit, your Mum will tell you about him, he might be coming here. He might do some research on the soil.'

'Oh aye.' Giles was expressionless. 'Know him well, do you?'

'He might even have a small lab, perhaps. I was thinking there'd probably be room for one at the end of the new cowshed.'

'I never heard of a lab on a farm before.'

'It's not uncommon. You know, for testing. Milk and soil and so on.' 'No need for a scientist for that. You get test kits, send in the results.' 'Well, I meant not just for testing, I meant for scientific research as well.'

'You want a space-age building on your cowshed? What's he going to do, this scientist?' 'Work on how to keep the soil good. Specially the bugs in it. That's the invisible wildlife he works on. Everything that grows has its own friendly bugs in the soil. Not many people know that. Soil's alive.'

Giles laughed. 'Hello bugs, have a yoghurt,' he said, scraping mud from his boots with a plastic fence support. Olivia asked him to join her for a bite of lunch. But Giles had to go back to Skipton that afternoon.

She phoned Pippa later, ostensibly to fix a day for her and Mark to come. She worked the conversation to a casual question about Andrew Bamberg's plans. The last Pippa had heard, Andrew was talking with Mark about field experiments and how to get collaborations to handle something Pippa wasn't sure about—bioinformatics? It looked as though he had plans for fieldwork at Oxhide, Pippa said, but they hadn't heard from him for ages. He was like that. Anyway, Pippa was fine, not sick any more, looking forward to the baby. After that, Olivia couldn't decently press her further about her husband's old friend.

The days went on; January became February without word from Andrew Bamberg. And any moment they would start lambing. It was early for lambing, but they had indoor pens and Oxhide was on the sheltered side of the hill. Now she'd be able to use that hands-on practice with a model ewe, the normal birth position of the lamb, and once the two little forefeet and nose had emerged everything should be okay. There was that scary business of feeling inside to release the lamb if a foot had got tucked up or the presentation was otherwise atypical.

Would she manage? Giles would be there, a comfort, and Mike if things got urgent, although he had his own flock. Olivia kept visiting the new barn to admire the lambing pens she and Giles had prepared under Mike Robertshaw's direction, and the new roof that would keep them safe and dry. She imagined the space filled with urgent sheep voices, mothers and lambs, like on *Countryfile*.

As the days slowly lengthened it got colder. An East wind challenged every crack of the house and turned the surroundings hills monochrome; a mean dry wind that sought every weakness and niggled at loose window panes and the dead stems of summer's roses. 'Wind from the feet of the dead', the Welsh called it, but she loved the Roman names best: Aquilo, Boreas, Auster and Zephyr; to ancient Roman farmers they would have been like familiar neighbours; mean, dangerous, generous, kind. Snow that fell soon after Jane left had now been banked against the moor walls for weeks, the drifts turning brown and yellow with mud and sheep pee, and she was bored with it. Everything so quiet, birds moving as little as possible, the beck silenced under a white blanket that filled the ghyll. It was a poor lookout for her pregnant ewes who stood despondent, waiting, in the low field. No time to bring lambs into the world.

For two days she'd been marooned until Giles came with his tractor and ploughed her out. Now she could get down to the shops, the bank and the pub. But from four to eight, from tea to breakfast, she was alone in the dark. The Bell drew her to its warmth and companionship and she changed from a tentative visitor to a regular, drinking with the boys. 'Miss G.' they called her now, and sometimes 'boffin'—Giles had evidently shared his reservations about science on the farm.

The pub was a slippery slope, but you couldn't watch television non-stop, and she had never had Bridget's capacity for sitting, and even Pippa, these days, reading about the stages of pregnancy and studying books about babies. Once or twice she'd been to Women's Institute meetings, enjoyed the company, and convivial female solidarity, although most members were married, and older than her. She must have seemed a little strange to them. Felicity, an ebullient type in her fifties, who tended to wear quilted gilets and tall suede boots, was the wife of a farmer Olivia first got to know from taking sheep to market. These new circles joined a network of acquaintances. She felt increasingly at home in the valley as she came to know the occupants of most houses dotted about the landscape.

But evenings were still long. Even *Invisible Wildlife* failed to grip. Andrew had done a series on life in extreme conditions. The Australian Outback was unreal compared to the cold realities of Oxhide, and Andrew appeared little, ceding the chief role as commentator to an Australian. There had been no more news. Her heart sank at the idea that his coming to Oxhide had been a fantasy—a whimsy between friends. She tried to make herself believe he owed her nothing. But what had happened at Christmas? He had felt it too, she knew. But evidently not as she had, viscerally. He was Mark and Pippa's old friend. But to her, what was Andrew Bamberg but a charming TV expert? She wouldn't stoop to stalking, not even to advance science. First thing in the morning she went inspect her ewes, surely overdue! Giles had set up the lambing pens with lights and power, even laying on hot water for handwashing with a geyser and basin. He'd run a new cable to the mains, bypassing the generator. Giles knew all about voltages and the right kind of cables and transformers. They'd been in touch with the vet and got in all the mass of supplies, medicines and antiseptics required.

From above the ash trees came the appalling intermittent whine of his chainsaw. He kept her log pile stacked, bringing in fallen branches on the trailer, sawing them into sections on a saw-horse, chopping each cylinder into three or four sectors like long slices of cake, which he arranged against the back wall of the house in the lee of the porch. Their ends made a pattern of triangles reminding her of Switzerland and childhood skiing holidays with Ben and their parents, helmeted Ben slaloming in his show-off way and crashing yelling into bushes. For a moment she smiled, then cut the mental videotape and brought in logs from Giles's pile.

They were damp ash and sappy slow-burning sycamore. Creepy crawlies fell out of them on the stone flags as she carried an armful to her sitting room and tumbled them into the inglenook for a fire that would make her damp socks steam, when dusk came and it was time to relax in front of the hearth. Next year she would have a log store and give the wood time to dry.

In the snug evenings when physical work exhausted her, just changing out of wet clothes and having tea-cakes by the fire was enough for happiness. She loved the mornings, too, dawn a little earlier every day, the bare, wind-trimmed trees looming into sight through grey mist, the herb-scented hay as she forked it out for the ewes; the way they hurried up and set to, their breath fog-on-fog.

Was she becoming a hermit, alone, never leaving her remote farm? The routines of the place gave her purpose and energy. The farmhouse was now triple-glazed, smart as paint, carpeted upstairs, properly lit, and centrally heated with a state-of-the-art straw-burner. Every morning started with heaving straw bales into its huge iron maw, barrowing out the ash and doing the rounds of the sheep.

Even so, her resolve sometimes faltered, when she would let herself daydream. What if the accident had never happened? Fred on the lawn at Torralba, leaning on the iron parapet in the evening surveying their terraced gardens below and the wide reach of the valley opposite.

Then the spirit Freddie would turn to her, her body remembered the magnetism that pulled them together, the warmth and fire of coalescing bodies. Could you do without that? This morning the weeping thing had stolen up on her again; she had collapsed on her new sofa in the sitting room, tired by the early start, and dreamed of their honeymoon.

In the Italian dawn she peered at the conifer-clad ridge rising behind Torralba, then down at the back garden under the window. Behind her in the villa's high bedroom Freddie slept, his handsome nose burrowed into the pillow. She shrugged on his huge soft bathrobe and crept barefooted out of the room and down the front staircase, drifting through the stone porch with its maps, umbrellas and walking sticks, and down balustraded steps into the garden. A yellow rambler rose hung over the sagging summerhouse. Smoke from the chimney of a villa further up the hill rose like a vertical vapour trail pale against dark cyprus and juniper. On the gravel court, the polished windscreen and bonnet of their wedding present Jaguar reflected leaves and sky. Cream leather seats invited her to climb in and luxuriate in soft upholstery. Then they were on the Florence-Pisa autostrada under driving rain near the Abbetone junction, Ben showing off at the wheel. The silly argument Ben started with Freddie. Ben taking his eye off the road to glare at Fred.

The chainsaw stopped. Through the passage snatches of

birdsong filtered in, not just the harsh cawing of rooks in the ash trees. Olivia went to look out of the door, and finally—signs of spring: small local twitterings and chirpings from hedge sparrows, great tits and chaffinches exploring unfrozen earth along her straggly hedge; a trio of blue tits making their way up the big sycamore, new plumage bright blue and yellow against smoky grey lichen. Celandines glittered, and coltsfoot like leafless dandelions opened into coronas of fuzzy gold reflecting the sun's image back from the ground. And here was Giles, her Oxhide Lanfranco, with news of her flock.

'This is what we want. Looking well, the ewes. Lambing won't be long now.'

Giles stood in the doorway clapping sawdust off his work gloves. The wind that made her shrink inside her layers of wool seemed to cause Giles to expand. 'Bit o sunshine's what we need. A lamb'll do in t'cold, but he'll not thole the wet.'

But the first lambs arrived as in a sleeting wind. It was all tougher than Olivia expected, the continuous work and anxiety, the cold and wet, the tragedies and triumphs of birth over and over again. At the first opportunity she drove to Skipton and bought woollen liners for her wellingtons, and thermal underwear, long johns and vests with sleeves, the kind of things you saw advertised in the *Sunday Telegraph* for pensioners. She had a headscarf to keep her hair from lashing, with a waxed cotton trilby pulled down over the top of it. Wet gloves hung permanently to dry from the saucepan rack above her Aga.

Then for days, they took turns to patrol the low field checking for newborns and herding them into straw-lined pens out of the rain. Lambing pens filled the new and old barns with an overflow in the old stable too. Sam Robertshaw went home for a meal about seven. Every night new mothers were added to the ones suckling their lambs under the barn roof. Rain beat on the corrugated iron and the ewes bleated. Giles was deft and confident with them. At the first problem birth, it appalled Olivia to watch him with his hand inside the struggling mother doing God knew what, blood seeping around his wrist. Then the nose and minute front hoofs appeared, Giles holding them together, arranging the lamb like a tiny diver aiming out into life, and almost immediately it lay on the straw, amazingly in one piece. And then the mother took over, knowing what to do, and the licked lamb knew it had to try and try until the rubber legs raised the tiny body for long enough for it to find the teat. Giles was looking at her with a smile as she smiled back, sharing the ewe's small but gigantic achievement. They hurried back and forth between stable and barn through rods of rain illuminated by make-shift floodlights slung up on the barn gables on extension cables. It was a massive ongoing nativity scene with every birth a new triumph. It was lovely to see each new lamb, safe and warm in the straw, stagger to its feet and suck, while the storm slammed bursts of rain on the iron roof of the lamp-lit barn. It was like a rainbow, the promise of a better future taking form in present darkness and chaos. Olivia felt lightheaded with amazement and fatigue.

'Come in for a warm-up?' she said at last. 'Everything looks under control here for a bit.'

'Aye, don't mind,' said Giles, hollow-eyed in the lamplight. Following her into the porch, he grabbed her arm above the elbow to steady himself as he levered off each muddy boot with the toe of the opposite foot. Somehow, even when he was standing again on his own two woollen socked feet, his hand remained on her arm. She looked at him and their eyes met.

Gently disengaging her arm, she patted his shoulder. 'I'll get the tea.'

Dead lambs pervaded Olivia's night thoughts. *Coom on, yer little booger*—Giles swearing at a tiny scraggy body, rubbing at the blood and mucus coating the thin beginnings of wool, then holding the little creature up, both willing the folding legs to stiffen, and raise the half-alive creature to its mother's udder. Death took nightmarish shape in the lamb who didn't get it, who begged them to give up, to let it escape into the dark. You had to get them to taste milk. It was as if milk infused them with the lust for life; gave them a vital foretaste of sunlight and grass and play. Some chemicals in our bodies, she'd read, could tell cells to die; mightn't some molecule in milk say, *live*?

These exhausted nights, when she fell into bed and deep sleep, were the first at Oxhide she had not conjured Freddie into the room as she drifted off.

She would remember the first secret clasp of his hand over hers at the Cambridge party; how from that instant the fuse lit and there was only one outcome. Their dinner at the Garden House Hotel had been merely Freddie's observance of the rituals of polite seduction; one of the fastest dinners she'd eaten. Telling the waiter they had a train to catch, they'd abandoned their half-finished main course and made for his hotel. Her first time—but Olivia had always known what she wanted, and gone for it. This story was the first of their marital myth-making, one they would tell each other ever after, a prelude to re-enacting the occasion.

But now, nativity scenes from the lambing shed overlaid other images in her dream vision.

In pre-dawn reverie, before her alarm went off, or rainy light glimmered in her uncurtained window, Freddie's face no longer appeared so complete. The shape of his nose, the arch of his eyebrow, remained—but for these she had the daily reminder of his portrait hanging by her bed. And they were only stills—the changing expressions of his mobile face, which had once turned her on so gloriously, now refused to play in her memory.

Resolving to face the day, she dragged on last night's jersey woollen socks and stained cords. Then opened the green velvet lined box on her dressing table to gaze at the emerald ring. Square-cut, the stone glinted even by the thin light of her bedside lamp. She slid the gold on her finger. It would fit under her gloves. She needed her talisman to survive these days.

Two more weeks, and they reached relief, with most of the ewes tending healthy lambs. Calm maternity replaced the drama of birth in the lambing shed, and Olivia and Giles spent cosy breakfasts in the kitchen, bacon and eggs one end of the table and the lambing record book open at the other.

The peace was broken abruptly. Olivia was sweeping mud from the kitchen floor after lunch, when her mobile buzzed. She snatched it from her jacket pocket.

It was Anne, distressed, phoning from home. 'Oh, Liv, I don't understand what's going on with the Yarkers.'

'Giles? What's he done?'

'Not Giles. It's his father, Harry, messing around with the horses. He's moved them into Low Field, he says.'

'Low Field?' Olivia felt a flush of anger. 'Low Field's where the primulas are. The horses are meant to be on Skellside land only, we agreed. Didn't we?'

'That's what I said. Liv, I can't get over until this afternoon. Can you do something?' Damn, damn and blast. 'Did he say why?'

'He said they were poaching his ground too much. All the rain we've had.'

'*His* ground? Bloody man! Can't you get him to stable them until the ground dries a bit? Anne, I don't want to get into a fight with my neighbours. D'you mind just telling him to get them in for a bit? I'll call in socially, go and buy some of Mrs. Yarker's eggs or something, but if I go straight down there I don't think it would work out well. I think he's a bit crazy, to tell you the truth. Offer to pay him, I'm sure that'll do the trick.'

'Okay, Liv, I'll phone him now. I do understand. But if you could find out what he's thinking? Oh crikey, how difficult it all is.' Poor Anne was near to tears.

'I can be scary if I must. I'll drop in on her this afternoon when he's out. They tell me Harry spends a lot of his time at the Black Bull in Skipton. I can see their yard from here, I'll go down there when his car's out.'

Olivia stopped at the ramshackle entrance to Skellside, its splashy sign advertising fresh eggs for sale. Sure enough, Dreamcatcher and Comet stood fetlock-deep in Low Field, sheltering, heads to the hedge, tails to the wind. She approached the back door up a pebbled path lined by white painted stones. Over the wall in the muddy yard, Red Maran hens clucked and pecked, scanning the ground for grain with jerky robotic glances.

'Come in, my love.'

Mrs. Yarker towelled her hands on a flowered apron, which she untied and flung on top of a nearby cardboard box of dusters, dog collars, seed packets and other detritus. She led Olivia past the kitchen door through a dark passage to the front parlour, standing aside to usher her in. The air smelt still, as though it had been closed up long ago. Pottery puppies with huge eyes regarded Olivia from the beige-tiled mantelpiece.

Mrs. Yarker plumped a brown velvet cushion, releasing a smell of elderly upholstery. 'Will you have a cup of tea, love? Take the weight off your feet, there.'

As soon as Olivia sat, Mrs. Yarker darted into the kitchen, where she rattled crockery and ran water into a kettle.

'One spoon or two?' she called down a passageway. 'I've some Earl Grey. Do you prefer Earl Grey? Harry won't touch it, but I think it's ever so refreshing. In the afternoon, like. But it does come out pale. Like dishwater. Men like their tea strong, don't they?'

'Oh—just ordinary tea's fine, honestly.' Olivia rose from the smelly embrace of the armchair, to show she didn't need to be waited on. 'I mustn't disturb your afternoon; I know you were working in the kitchen. I only called by for some eggs, if you have any to spare?'

'It's no trouble at all for you, lovey. You just sit like the lady you are. I'll bring it through. Make ourselves comfy, just us two. It's ever so nice to have a woman to talk to. I get lonely, with just Harry all day, and Giles and Pete with their muddy boots, in and out. Ah, we'll be girls together, you and me.'

'Well, just a quick cup, thank you, Mrs. Yarker. I really mustn't keep you, though. I have to be in Skipton by five.'

Olivia stood in the kitchen doorway while Mrs. Yarker poured boiling water into a rococo gilded and flowered tea pot she had to fetch from a high shelf, standing on a chair. She assembled tea things on a tray covered with an embroidered cloth. When everything was complete she swept Olivia back into the airless parlour holding the tea tray in front of her like the cow-catcher on a locomotive. She set it on a fifties coffee table with spindly splayed legs on a beige shag-pile rug. 'It needs a minute to mash. I'll just leave it a while. Help yourself, my love. Have anything you like. There's Bourbons, and cake. Giles's favourite, that is, Battenberg.'

A Yorkshire farmhouse tea should have hot buttered tea-cakes, and fruitcake accompanied by moist white Wensleydale cheese, thought Olivia. But perhaps this was the new authenticity in the Dales: Bourbon biscuits and Mr. Kipling cakes were staples in the village shop. She waited for Mrs. Yarker to broach the subject of Low Field, but she went off on a different tack.

'Giles is a good boy.' Mrs. Yarker poured pallid tea into two flowered china cups and added an equivalent volume of milk. 'He looks after his old Mam. He made me that book stand. Only twelve, he was. Carved those cheeky kittens with his penknife. Pick it up if you like—it's strongly made.'

Olivia turned over the bookstand carefully, and inspected the kittens fixed to each end, painted artfully like Siamese, cream shaded to brown paws and nose, with green eyes, though the young Giles had given them round, human pupils in place of feline slits. It gave them a knowing, anthropomorphic look.

'It's beautiful,' she lied. 'Only twelve? That's amazing.'

'He's spending a good bit of time up at Oxhide.' Mrs. Yarker had taken back the book stand and spoke with her back to Olivia, replacing it on a tiny glass-fronted book case, beside three matching Rexine-bound Reader's Digest volumes.

'I've been so grateful for his help.' Olivia crossed her legs and sipped. 'Without him and Pete doing all that work on my fencing we'd never have managed to get Oxhide straight so soon.'

'Aye, well,' Mrs. Yarborough, still standing, turned and looked down at her, hands on wide hips. 'We all need to help each other. That's right and proper. Fair exchange is no robbery.'

'I hope he's happy with the rates we agreed,' said Olivia.

'It's up to you, young lady, whether my boy's happy or not,' said Mrs. Yarker, with a sudden forcefulness beyond anything appropriate to a discussion of farm wages. The parlour was hot, but Olivia felt a chill. These boys and their mothers. Surely Giles didn't discuss her at home with his mother? He was thirty-five if he was a day.

A pause ensued, broken by the squeak of the back door hinges.

'Am I interrupting summat?'

Mr. Yarker looked half the weight of his wife, though about the same height. With his pale eyes behind brown-tinted glasses, wearing a leather jacket, his appearance was far from the stereotype of a hill farmer. His Datsun Outlaw shone outside the parlour window. Olivia hadn't been expecting that. The old collie, Tess, slunk into the room keeping a low profile, like a dog trying to avoid a scolding, and quickly sank herself into the shag-pile at his feet.

'Here's Miss Gabrieli, Harry,' Mrs. Yarker spoke in appeasing tones, as though to an unpredictable child. 'She's come to visit. We were just talking about Giles. The time he spends at Oxhide. With Miss Gabrieli. He worships the ground you tread on, doesn't he, dear?'

'Oh, surely not. By the way, I'm a Mrs. But please just call me Olivia.'

'It must be awkward for you, having a foreign name,' said Mrs. Yarker. 'Mustn't it, Harry? It sounds foreign, doesn't it? Where's it from?'

'Italy. My late husband was Italian.'

'Bessie goes to Italy,' Mr. Yarker spoke at last. 'My Cousin Bessie, you know, Dot? Cousin Bessie always goes to Capri. She likes Italian food, she says. Spaghetti. She likes that, doesn't she, Dot? Can't fancy it myself. Gets on your clothes. Not the rings, though. I like spaghetti rings.'

'Our Giles has done wonders for Oxhide.' Mrs. Yarker was back on track. 'Pete, too. Miss Gab . . . Olivia's lucky to have strong young men at her beck and call. They want to work for her, on the farm. We don't grudge the help, do we Harry? After all, she's like family, isn't she? Now? Like I was saying when you came in, it's right for family to help one another.'

'Aye, it's time Low Field come back to Skellside,' said Mr. Yarker. 'It's good you and Giles are close, like, Olivia.' She couldn't believe her ears. He seemed to be predicting a dynastic alliance, with the aim of recovering scruffy little Low Field for Skellside.

Mrs. Yarker poured tea for her husband; Olivia gazed at the ceiling. Round the room, a yard below the cornice, ran a shelf on which, she observed, a magnificent collection of antique pewter was ranged. Ten great trenchers glimmered in a row each side of the room, and a pair of ewers, bearing the patina and dents of centuries, faced each other above the empty fireplace. They spoke to Olivia of past prosperity, and the wool-based wealth that had built those solid stone barns and the striding walls dimly visible through lace curtains.

'You're admiring my pewter, then.' Mr. Yarker brightened. 'My hobby. It's worth a bit, mind. Keep my eyes open, I do. Those ewers came from the church—made them an offer they couldn't refuse. Seventeenth century. Not making any more o' them, they aren't.'

'You had 'em valued, didn't you, Harry?' prompted Mrs. Yarker.

'Aye, I got a valuation from Sotheby's. They come up here, tha knaws. Even those London chaps, know where there's value, they do. What d'you reckon they're worth, Olivia?'

Enthusiasm overcame his reserve. 'Twenty five thousand pounds, that's what. Twenty five K. Something to fall back on, eh? Not that we're short, not us. We've none of those mortgages here. My family's been at Skellside longer than anybody knows, haven't we, Dot? Not like some of them grand folks, big houses. Banks own 'em. Mortgaged, they are. Those folks an't got nowt after all. You'll be paying a mortgage on Oxhide, I reckon?'

'I'm not sure quite why you would assume that,' Olivia said. 'And I really don't think this is the moment to discuss my affairs. I just dropped in for eggs. If you have any, Mrs.Yarker?'

'Ain't got any to spare, not today,' Mrs. Yarker said. 'Don't lay much in t'winter, tha knows, Olivia.'

Anne would have to sort out her own grazing problems. And more importantly, Olivia needed to assert her ownership of Low Field. She'd have to give the lawyers a call.

At Oxhide she phoned Anne to admit defeat. Anne promised to come over and bring the horses in. Turning over her conversation with the Yarkers, Olivia was tempted to cry. How could she not have been clearer with Giles? Why should she assume he would project-manage for her, work all day in the rain, for practically nothing? How could she have assumed he knew of her vow to stay faithful to Freddie's memory? She should have made her non-availability clear from the outset. What on earth could she do now to clear up this embarrassing mess? She phoned Pippa.

'Oh, how awful,' said Pippa. 'But I'm sure it's not your fault, Liv. The Yarkers are trying it on, to get Low Field back. Everybody knows what they're like. Giles is lovely. I'm sure he's just being neighbourly, remember how kind he was that night you arrived. Can you come over, Liv? This evening, share our spag bol? We have some news about Andy.'

Pippa stood at the cooker stirring the ragu, unmistakeably pregnant. Surely this wasn't still news? Soon, Mark came in from surgery, kissed Olivia hello and took the wooden spoon from his wife. Pippa subsided on a chair and put her feet up on another. She and Mark together, smiling, looked so normal, so much like the first two cards in a happy family of four, Mr. Rabbit and Mrs.

Rabbit, that Olivia very nearly giggled. Instead she gave a cough and asked the usual question.

'When's it due?'

'From the scans, mid-May. When the lambs are out in the fields.'

Pippa couldn't be a better person to receive these gifts, nobody could deserve happiness more. And Pippa was her friend. Yet, momentarily, a cold wave of envy washed over her. Olivia drew a deep breath, recollected herself and took enthusiastic part in the baby conversation. It was a boy, he would be born in Skipton Hospital, Pippa would opt for an epidural. Mark liked the name Ross, but that had been the name of Pippa's family's dog—it seemed inappropriate to her. Olivia stifled a yawn.

Mark changed the subject. 'You may be getting a visit soon, Olivia. Andy's back.'

That was proper news. The blood drained from Olivia's head. She leaned a hand on a chair back. 'Back? From where?'

Mark looked her up and down, doctor-faced. 'Sit down, Olivia. Here—' He poured her a small neat whisky from the new sideboard. 'Didn't Pippa tell you? After the fight he resigned immediately, before they fired him, and took off. Not a word to anybody, just fixed for Julian to board full time, and vanished.'

'Even Julian didn't know where his father had gone,' Pippa said. 'He asked me. He was quite upset, poor kid.'

Mark took up the tale. 'Between leaving the UK and last week he was out of contact for weeks. D'you know, I think maybe he was in some fugue state. That fight, not like Andy at all, on top of his history of identity confusion in early adulthood, that stupid woman Vanessa playing her mind games, coming and going like the Cheshire Cat. What a mother—or rather, a non-mother.' Mark poured himself a nip from the bottle he was still holding. 'But we knew he was due to speak at a big meeting in California last week, and sure enough, last night he finally phoned, asking to stay here—he didn't say how long.'

'Not indefinitely, I sincerely hope,' Pippa put in.

'He'd been for a wander in the Rockies, apparently. Always been liable to disappear for long periods. But we knew he had a big meeting to go to in San Francisco with his team. He's surfaced there, he phoned us at five this morning, about to leave for San Francisco airport to fly home. He didn't say much but he sounded mad keen to come up here.'

'Even though some of us are going to be rather busy,' put in Pippa with uncharacteristic acerbity, moving a cushion to the small of her back.

'I'm glad things are turning out better for him.' Olivia's voice sounded odd to her. That breathlessness—she wasn't used to neat whisky.

'He'll be with us in Skipton next week, Liv. Would it be okay for us to bring him over to see Oxhide? He keeps asking how you are. And what you're doing.'

All the way back to the farm, the words, 'mad keen to come up here' ran in Olivia's brain, replacing replays of Mrs. Yarker's recriminating voice. Repeatedly she parsed Mark's words.

Did 'up here' mean a stay with the Foremans, convalescing from that strange-sounding 'fugue state'? Or might it mean 'up here in Upper Wharfedale', getting down to soil research at Oxhide? Anne's horsebox parked at Skellside brought her back to the present with a thump. It turned out Anne's solution to the endless late-winter mud was to take her horses from the Yarkers' to a livery yard ten miles away. Giles was helping her load them, looking grim. He had only a brusque '*all right?*' for Olivia, as he fastened the rear ramp of the lorry and prepared to get into the cab alongside Anne. Olivia would have to attend to her ewes herself, and it would be dark in an hour.

14

Californian
Sunshine

Newly arrived in California and still jet-lagged, Andrew strode to the conference centre. It was not yet six, too early for his hotel breakfast, but the IHOP by a gas station provided him with coffee, porridge ('oatmeal') and fruit. When he arrived at the place where the posters were to be shown, he found Meera, the most intelligent and devoted post-doc he had ever had, alone in a still-deserted seminar room, fixing their display, making free with the usual miserly supply of sticky-backed Velcro. She gave him her wide smile. Erik, never an early bird, was nowhere to be seen.

Andrew took in their eye-catching posters again with pride. It had been worth sending Meera on the MapInfo course. Familiar as he was with every detail they'd argued over in weekly lab meetings, the display still looked super-cool. He loved the teasing title, 'How Loyal is Invisible Wildlife?' and how it was flanked by bright research council logos, plus the banner of a house building firm, *Durian*, that had sponsored their presentation as a greenwashing opportunity. Inset on landscape maps were two big pie charts of microbial variation between sites, the message clear: a field could have its own microbiome, its signature community of soil microbes, just as much as a human gut. The underground flora was as distinctive as the vegetation above. He looked forward to hanging around at coffee breaks to chat with the crowd it would attract. With luck he would hook a job for Erik.

Placing his team with good groups would be crucial, if he really did decide to go it alone for a bit in the wilds of Yorkshire. He hoped he wouldn't lose any of them to *Durian*.

How loyal *was* invisible wildlife? Although microbiologists trotted out the mantra, '*Everything is Everywhere*', meaning all bacteria were cosmopolitan and had no unique local habitats, people were beginning to accept that this just wasn't true. Soil bugs only lived in places that suited them. More to the point, they only grew where the chemistry, the climate, the roots of local plants and grazing habits of local animals, suited them. And now it was likely they remained a long time: decades, centuries, even millennia.

Everything about this project excited him: the evidence, the wonder, the new techniques of geostatistics and bioinformatics, the tramping across lovely wild places, talking with local farmers. And also, undeniably, the possibility of fame. Some day, not far off, a local metagenome list (a catalogue of indigenous bugs) would be the first thing a land manager would ask for, and Andrew's group would supply it. An irreplaceable soil community would become a thousand times more powerful an argument for conserving a prospective greenfield building site than a crested newt, a unique family of bats or an Anglo-Saxon hoard. That was why *Durian* were sniffing around his group. More than ever, now, he would need a wide network of international collaborators to collect data from soils in all conditions, from arctic to tropical, desert to swamp, poisoned to pristine.

Perhaps the shipwreck of his university career had been a blessing. The opium of academic routine, the annual cycle of teaching and research, examinations and committees, following each other as predictably as the agricultural calendar, let you sleepwalk on. Decades could vanish as fast as years. Decades when you might have made a difference.

Vanessa was right that he'd been in a rut, though he couldn't get excited about the new directions she urged on him. She kept hinting it was time he went after a professorial chair, made a splash in the news, ran the BBC, stood for parliament. But maybe, with Oxhide as a launch pad, if Olivia Gabrieli was serious about offering him a research facility, he could found a scientific institute, even a dynasty. Olivia.

Standing there, he pictured her, and a whisper of excitement ran like an undercurrent through his body. He imagined that plausible and eager Nicole Kidman among the noisy kids at the museum. His lips were even forming her name. Steady on. He checked his watch for the date: 14th February. St. Valentine's day, when the birds mated. Spring. How ridiculous, he was past that—as far as any pre-senescent man could be. Boys would be boys, it was biology. Collecting himself, he glanced around for his team.

The hum of conversation and morning greetings rose in the atrium, people put down coffee cups and moved in groups to the main lecture theatre where the important plenary sessions were due to start.

By nine, Erik, in his Uppsala sweatshirt, was positioned at the lectern, the room packed, with late arrivals having to sit on the stairs. Andrew focussed and looked forward to watching his team's work played back by this classy Scandinavian in his precise English, their ground-breaking findings unrolled in Erik's smart-themed slides. It was so cool the way brief references to publication in top journals—*Nature, Science, Molecular Ecology*—were all you needed to send people searching out the data online, revealing to those in the know, the sheer sweat and man-hours behind the stunning results. With flicks of his green laser pointer Erik transported the audience from prairies and rainforests to the genes that programmed the microbial work going on in their soils. Prolonged applause followed as Erik showed the final slide of credits. Well-aimed questions from influential elders and keen students had finally to be stopped by the chair. After, streams of people headed towards the posters, and soon carried off all the fifty A4 handouts Meera had stacked in a pocket envelope beside the display.

In the gardens at the coffee break, watching a humming bird poised at a huge hibiscus-like flower and listening to lively groups talking in variously-accented English, Andrew felt more at ease than he did at any of the northern European meetings he regularly attended. Away from local petty rivalries and infighting, people talked as though better understanding the wonders of nature was a sufficient goal for science. The main competition here seemed to be to excel in pure research; people weren't pressured to justify their work in terms of immediate commercial benefits, and if there were struggles for funding and promotion, he wasn't part of them. Olivia would have enjoyed that humming bird.

At the end of the day he had a notebook of scribbles to write up, and stacks of business cards from old friends with new jobs, including potential collaborators around the world. He found Erik in the bar, extracted him from a circle of Chinese academics and suggested a stroll to the beach to see the sun set over the Pacific Ocean. Down on the board walk over the low dunes they strolled barefoot, beside a calm sea gently swishing its wavelets on to the beach. How far Asilomar felt from March in England, how much larger with possibilities.

'They accepted your proof of concept,' Andrew said. 'now we can extend high throughput metagenomic soil analysis to all sorts of questions. The possibilities are huge.'

Erik agreed. He had approaches from groups in Alberta, Finland and Tamil Nadu. Some wanted to explore pure science and restore natural ecosystems, others approached with specific applications for environmental problems such as salinity, drought and pollutant problems: mine tailings permanently poisoned with arsenic and mercury; rain fouled with nitrate from diesel fumes;

the resulting eutrophication that smothered sticklebacks, caddis flies and crayfish in streams. Analysing a soil microbiome could bear on so many urgent questions.

'It's tempting to make it an excuse for lots of exotic travel,' Andrew mused. 'But I quite like the idea of a focus, at home. A single place described exhaustively, with changes followed over time from a baseline. Like Rothamsted's Broadbalk data, a kind of information bank of soil bugs' preferences. But in more natural, long-term ecosystems, not arable—ancient plant communities on different underlying geology.'

Erik made non-committal noises. He wanted to travel. He was only twenty-eight. Andrew persisted. 'Look, can you come see a place with me when we're back? We can do it in a day or two. It's in the north of England, we could have long term access. I can show you.'

He sat on the board walk and pulled out his iPad. Shading the screen from the brilliant sunlight, he brought up the OS map of Upper Wharfedale, in the North of England.

'It's a little glacial valley, look how the brown contours cluster. There's a small paradise of old hay meadows along the valley floor, primaeval ash woodland clinging to the valley sides, and peatland on the millstone grit. It's already well known for the range of geology and land use, it even comes in a famous old children's book, *The Water Babies*. And the place is in the news now too; some call it 'sheepwrecked' and advocate turning it all over to nature: rewilding. Imagine what the local hill farmers think of that—families have been there for generations. For them, shepherding is like a divine right to Arcadia.'

Erik objected that the British were peculiar about access. There was no *allemansratt*, permissions would be difficult.

'You Swedes are so sensible. I know, there's none of your *everyman's right* with us. But it is a National Park, and I have an invitation from a farmer there who's just started up.'

What would elegant Olivia look like, dressed for farming?

After the expansive Californian scene, Stockholm Street looked smaller than ever and felt freezing to Andrew. His boxed-up lab equipment and books piled in the cramped, narrow hall were unbearably sad. With Julian a weekly boarder now, in London from Monday to Friday, and ever more inclined to spend time with his friends at weekends, Andrew had no company except the regulars at the corner pub. Fine in their way, their phatic remarks, soothing at times, weren't the responses he needed for the questions now roiling in his mind. He couldn't stop thinking about Oxhide Farm. Luckily Mark, at home and enjoying a free moment between surgery hours in Skipton, answered his phone call at once. Yes, of course, they would love to see him. And his post-doc too. Yes, of course Mark remembered Erik. Pippa would be so pleased, it could be a dinner party like old times in London, their first at the Doctor's house. Then—was there anything up? Of all the people he knew, Mark was the most attuned to his wavelength. A pause for electronic calendars to wake up, and a date was fixed.

Weeks later, he and Erik set off for their weekend stay with Pippa and Mark, to size up Oxhide as a potential study site. Andrew wanted to survey it before raising expectations or making commitments to Olivia. The warmth of the Christmas party had changed things.

She'd obviously taken to him, as they always did, unfortunately. In a way he wished Oxhide Farm belonged to a man, or at least a company. What male could negotiate a business arrangement with a pretty girl in terms of purely intellectual and economic goods? He was afraid for her, and a little for himself. He knew himself too susceptible; with women, too mercurial, too capable of heartbreak.

He told Erik simply that they would reconnoitre the Dales National Park with a view to an ecological collaboration with the University of Lancaster, which was within easy driving distance from Oxhide, across the Pennine ridge. They would include a visit to the farm in an itinerary taking in the contrasting soils and vegetation of limestone and millstone grit, and consider their options before making overtures to Olivia.

A blustery afternoon in late March found them nearing the head of Wharfedale. 'This can't be it,' Andrew said, as Erik, with the large-scale Ordnance Survey map on his knee, indicated a slight widening of the lane, the nearest place to Oxhide it was possible to leave the car.

Beyond, the high stone walls on both sides allowed only a foot or two of grass verge each side of the tarmac. They had already had to reverse a hundred yards for an early tour bus. A group of bullocks knee-deep in mud raised their heads gloomily and came over to stamp and snort inquisitively, blowing mist into the cold air. This style of land management was not what he would have expected of Olivia Gabrieli.

Erik checked his map. 'That house is called Skellside. Oxhide is the next house up the valley. Up there is Skellside Moor,' he said, leaning across from the passenger seat and craning to see the horizon through the window on the driver's side. 'There's a bridleway marked that leads to the top of the hill. Look, there. If we walk to the top and then half a mile west, we get a heliview of Oxhide farm. Andy, is that actual woodland over there? The slope's vertical, yet the trees aren't conifers, they look mostly bare. I want to get up there.'

'They've been there a few thousand years,' Andrew said. 'Pennine ash woodland. There are ancient woodland plants in there—lily of the valley, juniper, bird cherry. Neolithic remains too. Can't you just imagine their mycorrhiza mining the limestone? You have to have the right friends to flourish up here. The rewilding people think the grazed land up on top could be re-wooded and filled with of all sorts of beasts and birds if sheep farming was controlled. My mother Vanessa's very excited by the idea.'

Erik strode ahead up the steep fields, Andrew pretending to be just as fit, trying not to pant. Soon they reached the moor-edge wall, scrambled over a broken gate, and were on the heathery plateau between dales. Turning left towards the head of the dale, they proceeded along gritty little sheep paths between peat hags, keeping parallel with the silver thread of the river below. A curlew called. It felt wild and almost Nordic. Erik, consulting his map again, pointed downhill to a farmstead overlooked by bare ash trees, beside a deep cleft in the hill. It was full of activity, conspicuously in this otherwise almost silent landscape. The sounds of demolition came up to them from the yard, men's shouts and machinery, while from the fields, the cries of new-born lambs and their mothers' deeper responses evoked a timeless pastoral. A chimney sent up blue woodsmoke. It was almost mythically like a human habitation in wild country. Andrew was terribly tempted to abort his cold plan of observing from a distance, and instead slither down there through the steep little fields, knock on the back door of Oxhide farm and enjoy the welcome he was sure Olivia would offer him.

'It is a beautiful place,' Erik said. 'A glaciated valley, yes. Look at that distinctive stratigraphy, and the changes in vegetation, clearly associated with it. These farms—how long have they been here? And a native relict flora, you say. The farmer, he is in favour of science?'

'It's a she,' Andrew said. 'A girl—woman I mean. She runs the place on her own—came here quite recently. She's renamed her farm, it's been split off from a larger holding up the dale. The new name's not on the paper map. It's called Oxhide now. I think she would be keen to help us.'

'Then, for what are you waiting?' said Erik. 'The others will be interested, too. We will see the underground wildlife that makes this beautiful landscape. We can make a website and blog. Live-stream data.'

They talked global soil microbiology all the way back to Skipton.

'So, what did you think?' Mark asked, looking from Andrew to Erik. 'Interesting site? Worth investigating? Come on in.'

Andrew and Erik started to speak at once.

'Undoubtedly interesting—' Erik thought aloud. 'You know how it is,' Andrew said. 'When you go house-hunting, see plenty of possible but boring places, and feel easy about it, no pressure. Then one day somewhere strikes you as perfect, a once-in-a-way opportunity, and you're faced with a decision. We could actually do this. I've got to decide. It's like the *Road Not Taken*. Accepting this chance that Olivia Gabrieli's offering could be the start of something tremendous. Taking microbiome research into real landscapes. People are starting to piddle about with small investigations, but we could build a global network from there. It's timely—scientifically and politically. There's no end to the ramifications.'

He noticed Pippa catch Mark's eye, and their suppressed smiles. He realised he had been talking like an excited nerdy student, the way he and Mark used to in college. 'Of course, it's not a choice just for me,' he went on, as soon as he could. 'I'd want to see what Vanessa thinks. And Julian. We'd have to move up here, at least for part of the time, and it might not be the best time for him to be stuck in the wilds.'

Mark laughed. 'Leeds is only two and half hours from London, and he's weekly boarding anyway, isn't he?'

'Well, Vanessa,' Andrew went on. 'She'll think I've turned into a local agronomist. I'm supposed to be heading for world fame. She'll think I'm abandoning her.'

'Well, *she* abandoned *you*,' Mark said. 'Anyway, the upper classes can live anywhere. She'll be impressed. You'd hardly be slumming it with Olivia Gabrieli at Oxhide. Pippa, love, show Vanessa that piece about Olivia in *Tatler*.'

Erik spoke in his slow, clear voice, hooking everyone's attention. 'It is a very good field site.' Then, wryly, added, 'And I think perhaps you should marry this lady, Andrew.'

'What the fuck, Erik!'

Pippa giggled, and again exchanged glances with Mark, the conspiratorial tendency of the long-married.

'She isn't available, Erik,' Andrew said. This was the moment to lay it on the line. He knew what Pippa and Mark were thinking, but he wasn't intending another of his old amorous adventures. 'Olivia is in mourning for her husband who died quite recently. Remarriage isn't on the cards, nothing like that, she is dedicating her life to Oxhide.'

Pippa backed him up. 'Liv'll love to have you there. She misses her clever friends. She's brainy, not like me. She reads your work, Andy. I saw the printouts on her coffee table. But she's not dating any more, that's definite.'

Andrew told himself to say nothing. He shouldn't feel insulted at Pippa's implication that he was some Casanova. Pregnancy affected women's minds, that was it. A beat passed. 'I'll bring Julian and see what he feels about it.'

Later, on the landing by the Foremans' as-yet minimally furnished guest bedrooms, Andrew and Erik conferred and agreed. Given the choices available to the team, it was a huge opportunity. As Erik summarised, inverting the Greens' catchphrase; they would think locally and act globally. Oxhide would become as important as Rothamsted, Andrew said. As important as the Galapagos, said Erik.

Andrew couldn't sleep. He didn't want to foray downstairs to make tea, as he would at home when anxieties kept him awake. He'd been familiar with Mark and Pippa's domestic arrangements in their Elizabeth Street basement, but here nothing yet had its fixed place and he probably wouldn't find their tea making things even if he could get down to the kitchen without waking the household. He had nothing to read. The heating came on with clicks and gurgles and the radiator beside his bed started to grill him like the martyred St. Lawrence. At last he heard an alarm clock go off somewhere below, and pale dawn light shone through the thin curtains. He padded down two flights of stairs to find Mark in his dressing gown preparing a tea tray for his wife. Being a good doctor, Mark recognised signs of strain and set a steaming pint mug of strong tea down on the work top for Andrew, before leaving for upstairs with the tray. Then he returned, and sat waiting for Andrew to speak. They were such old friends, Andrew didn't need to explain. He cradled the warm mug in his hands.

'Thanks, Mark.'

Pippa's waxed terracotta tiles gave a warm glow to the bare kitchen. Mark's graduation tankard, a present from his parents, had been installed on the pale oak sideboard, the beginnings of a new household.

'This is a lovely house. Pippa makes everything feel so good. Lucky you.' Andrew sipped tea, watching the steam rising. Mark said nothing, just stood there giving off kindly-doctor vibes, waiting. It was cold. Although the boiler roared, down here it hadn't dispersed the chill of the March night. 'What shall I do, Mark? What would you do?'

'What do you *want* to do?' Mark sounded as if he had been on a counselling course.

'Eliminate Nigel and get back to where we were.'

'You weren't happy.'

'I suppose not, no. But things took care of themselves, somehow.

'Where do you want to be by the end of the year? Still in Stockholm Street? Scratching a living teaching in between TV shoots?'

'Of course not.'

'And you don't have to, Andy. Build on your reputation. You owe it to us all. You're a national celebrity on telly. What were you doing last month? Only giving keynotes in California! You're also well-connected and probably extremely rich. Come on, man!'

Mark started to lay the table for breakfast, taking plates from a rack above the dresser. He gazed down at Andrew. 'Also, you have a brilliant young son, you don't have a home worth the name, and you need to get yourself together. Seize the day.'

It was true, Julian and he wouldn't have a home once Stockholm Street was sold. At the end of this summer they would be—where? In Vanessa's house? With David and Mary? Or successful, with a new project and a fresh start? It didn't look too certain.

'I could come over to Oxhide with you and spend the day with you and Olivia if you like. Pippa would like to come too, I know,' Mark said.

'How do you mean? You're too busy.'

'Well—I suppose your first step would be looking for your field sites and all that. I'm due a morning off today to go and help Dad cut down a tree, but he would understand me having an urgent call. He needn't know it's to buck up some drip who can't make up his own mind.'

Andrew smiled in spite of himself. 'Suppose so.' He looked up from staring into his tea. 'Field sites, yes. That's the idea, isn't it?'

'A bloody good one. I have a feeling about this project.' It was the sort of thing Mark likely said to seriously ill patients, when everyone was only too well aware that the outcome of whatever treatment was unknowable. 'What's to lose? What are you afraid of?'

'You're an optimist. Thank you, Mark. You're a good friend. I'd be glad of your company tomorrow.'

'You'll look back on today and realize this moment was the start of something fantastic.' Mark had reverted to a trace of a northern accent he had in the first year at Cambridge. 'My grandpa had a Latin wartime saying—*forsan et haec olim meminisse iuvabit*—one day you will rejoice to remember even this. He made me learn it when I failed maths.'

It was persuasive from Mark. Everything about him gave off integrity, authority and human sympathy. What must it feel like to be so grounded, so *grown-up*?

Andrew agreed that good could come out of disaster. They would see Olivia. He would phone her to fix it. He would be friendly and appropriately business-like, as if she were a man.

Olivia, discussing planning consents with the architect in the barn, gasped and excused herself when she saw Andrew, Mark, and a tall blonde man she didn't know getting out of Mark's car down in the yard. They were looking around, preparing to approach the house. Andrew was gazing about as though newly arrived in a foreign country. A breeze ruffled the dark hair across his forehead.

'I can see why you don't stay long when you come to London,' Andrew said, greeting her with a warm handclasp and a kiss, a peck on the cheek. It fell within normal social kissing rules, but the blood surged to her face, making her too self-conscious to return it in the conventional manner. 'This is picture book stuff, Olivia. Hard work, too, I expect.'

'It's good up north,' said Mark. 'I think we're going to convert you, Andy, aren't we Olivia?'

'Mind you, it's damn cold, you have to admit,' said Andrew.

Mark laughed. 'If you come up to Yorkshire in March dressed for California.'

Andrew looked tanned and wore only a cotton jacket over his blue open-necked shirt and denim jeans. He was thinner than she remembered. He must be freezing in this frosty wind. Erik looked snug in his enviable Nordic anorak. She invited them for coffee and put a match to the ready-laid fire. Warming those elegant hands at the flames, Andrew told them of the meeting he and his team had been to, and the trip down the Pacific coast he'd made after; Monterey, Cannery Row; the narrow strip of productive land with the desert of Death Valley inland, real Steinbeck country. He wasn't as devastated about losing his job as she'd expected. It was as if he was glad to have got the sack. Of course, she remembered, money was not a problem. Like herself, Andrew had an inheritance and could do what he liked. 'An independence,' they called it in Victorian novels. It gave you freedom from everyday money constraints. But freedom to do what? That could be a problem too, she knew.

'Pippa told me you're thinking of a new project?' she ventured.

'I got the sack,' he admitted, cheerfully. 'It's a stroke of luck, in a way, that business. Now I can concentrate on soil bugs one hundred per-cent—my first love. The research and the message. No teaching, not much admin. We brought back good footage from Australia for *IW*, and more important, a good collection of samples.'

IW? *Invisible Wildlife*, of course. But what did you do with samples if you had no lab? 'Luckily my team are still in place, for now, at any rate. Erik here is keen to stay with the project. That's why he's come along today. We can surely carry on here. It's such a transferable question. We can work all over the world.'

All over the world? But she wanted him here. She must have let it show, for he quickly went on, 'But one problem is to find a proper base. Mark and Pippa tell me you might still be up for an analysis of your soil? It might help you with management, and it's a rare opportunity for us, to find a documented unimproved site in an iconic location. Everybody's interested in the Yorkshire Dales.'

'I thought all farms in England are arable.' Erik spoke at last, helping things along. 'This is postglacial country. I am homesick already.' He gave Olivia a brotherly smile. He was tall, young and nice-looking in a healthy, straightforward way.

'Please make Oxhide your base. I would like that more than anything. Anything you and your team need, let me know.' Her delight had made Olivia solemn. This was a formal invitation, appropriate to the status of her prospective guest.

'I could give you a lift over here tomorrow,' Pippa offered, turning to Mark. 'Or you can have the car, can't they, love? We won't need it.' How like Pippa to help things along so unselfishly. The Foremans needed their car. Pippa must have been less than eight weeks from her due date in May.

By Sunday morning Andrew and Erik returned in a hired car, in waterproofs, wellingtons and carrying rucksacks. Olivia would have liked to tag along if the new lambs hadn't had first call on her attention. She noticed the striding figures going up to the moors about midday, and by late afternoon they were busy in the beck, putting mud and water into little bottles, making notes on a tablet. Only when the light faded was there a knock on the back door. Both looked sodden, the canvas bag bulging. She invited them in, offered refreshments.

'I could do with a cup of your excellent coffee,' said Andrew. 'We'll just pack this lot up. Is there somewhere cool we can store them until Pippa comes? I've had such a wonderful day, Olivia. What a place. And all yours. You must be proud of it.'

'Yes, I am. And proud that you're here.'

The samples were in screw-top bottles, mostly looking like ordinary mud or muddy water, and a little muddy on the outside. Olivia found a corner of the fridge for them and made coffee. 'Will you look at them down the microscope?'

'No, we'll take them back tomorrow to my postgraduate students, and they'll extract DNA and send it off to the Joint Genome Institute in California.'

'What, DNA from each of the microbes in there?' Olivia was impressed by such diligence.

'No, DNA from the whole samples. These days you can look for species markers and genes in mud like that, it tells you what's there, you don't need to separate the organisms first. No culturing involved. In fact, we find lots of new bugs that were missed before because they can't grow in culture. Things that depend on each other, rather than dead remains.'

'Really? I need to learn about that. There was nothing in school biology about it.' Olivia sounded fatuous to herself.

'I'll send you articles. I've some favourite links, they're on my web page.' He pulled a tiny notebook from a pocket, wrote the link and handed it to her. She stowed it carefully in a pocket of the file she kept on the dresser for vital phone numbers, as if she hadn't already examined his impressive website that listed masses of publications, microbe videos and interactive maps.

'You have to send samples all the way to California?'

'Just the DNA. That's quite easy to extract, and surprisingly tough. You can send it in the post. There's this institute with huge facilities there, the Joint Genome Institute, and if the Americans agree that your project is interesting, you can have the work done for nothing. It's a public service, because it's such a powerful way to find new exploitable bugs. High-throughput—thousands of samples a week. I couldn't afford to have that done in the UK, not for my sort of ecological research. Blue-skies, business people call it—useless, they mean.'

Olivia hung their wet jackets to steam over the Aga, and produced tea and cake. They chatted about the Christmas party that seemed so long ago. Olivia asked after Julian and Vanessa, Mary and David, Louisa, then about the California meeting, hoping that something might come out about where he had disappeared for the six weeks afterwards. But Andrew had other matters on his mind. He was touchingly proud of his son; he told her how Julian had won an important music scholarship and was excited about starting work for A-levels. With the sale of the little house in Stockholm Street, Andrew would miss him.

'He's got used to spending a lot of time with school friends in London, and he can't stand not being able to practise. He's spoilt, Vanessa has a Steinway.'

Olivia threw another log on the fire. 'But you could work in the north of England?'

'I'd like to. Lancaster University can rent me lab space, which could be convenient. We'll see what emerges from the samples I collected today. They may all be the same old same old set of moulds and bacteria, but nobody's looked and if they are interesting Oxhide could be an ideal site for a pilot investigation. If you were willing,'

She was willing. They fetched her diary, and fixed for Andrew and Julian to stay for a week the following month. April. A month to prepare. It was high time anyway to get a proper surface on the potholed track up the road, and rehang the gates.

Indoors was another matter. The main guest room ought to be *en suite*. She would get a proper craftsman to restore the windows, and the oak floor would look lovely professionally sanded and polished. In the evenings she studied magazines with pictures of the latest authentic 'farmhouse' finishes, expensive mattresses and vanity units with concealed shaver sockets. She neglected her week's sheep assignment.

Getting the piano up the track to the house was a complicated undertaking involving professional packing and the hire of a lorry with a crane. Giles contributed another of his Sundays. But finally the handsome Broadwood upright was installed at the end of the sitting room and the house rang to the tuner's scales and arpeggios and repeated interrogations of single notes. When he'd gone, Olivia washed the mud and sheep dirt off her hands and trimmed her nails before sitting down and opening the book with the 48 Preludes and Fugues, inscribed to her from Isobel, a fourteenth birthday present. The sitting room with its low ceiling was a hundredth the size of Torralba's music room, with a homely acoustic, but how glorious to make music again. She turned the pages and settled on the lovely and not too difficult Prelude IX as the one she would start practising again. Sudden energy loosened her stiff fingers and fired her spirits as the familiar alleluia of its opening major arpeggio filled her house.

Damn. The phone. But not a cold-caller selling double glazing. 'Hello—oh! Pippa.'

'Hi Liv. How're things?' 'I've got a piano.'

'That's lovely. You've inherited your mother's talent.'

'I mean, I think I'm all ready to invite Andrew Bamberg to work here at Oxhide. There are two decent guest bedrooms now, so he can bring Julian if he wants. Or that nice Swede.'

'This is all working out so well. It's lovely, isn't it? Mark's Andy's old friend, and you and I are old friends. It's amazing luck, isn't it, Liv?'

They fixed for Olivia to go over to the Doctor's house the next afternoon. There was so much to talk about, so much to learn about her prospective house guests.

15

A Hero's Welcome

Olivia put a glass of jewel-coloured anemones on the chest of drawers in the guest bedroom. She opened the window a fraction and cool moor-scented air washed in. Polished oak had been such a good choice for the window frames, and checked wool curtains were perfect—as well as showing off the modern design coming out of the renascent Yorkshire wool industry. It was a wild and brilliant morning, the top of the moor opposite still white with shining snow, a smell of sunshine on the freezing air. 'Should I put a fan heater on?'

'Yes, it's icy,' Anne said. 'You keep your house much colder than Mum. She says she's a chilly soul. It's more welcoming to have a guest bedroom nice and cosy, she says. They'll have had a long journey, won't they, they'll be tired and it'll probably be dark when they get here. Giles brought some dry logs into the sitting room. I'll vacuum the moss and stuff that fell on the carpet. There are nibbles on the silver tray.'

She padded out and downstairs. Anne only ever wore socks indoors, spending most of her time in wellington boots and seeing no need for indoor shoes. She was helping Olivia prepare for her guests as though they were horses: fresh bedding, warm rugs, suitable food were uppermost in mind. Olivia wondered if there should be books in the room, but didn't dare expose her choices of reading to an eminent person she hardly knew yet.

With everything upstairs prepared, they went down to cook and lay an elegant table. Andrew Bamberg's impending arrival warranted the Torralba silver and cut glass from the boxes sitting in the understairs cupboard since she had arrived at Oxhide. Time slowed.

Mark phoned: they were leaving Skipton. Plenty of time. Mooching round the damp lawn, she saw nothing suitable to grace Isobel's white linen damask cloth until she noticed the crocuses, almost too small to pick. She recalled Vanessa's party at the Trojans and the florist's mossy creation. She fetched a trowel and dug a clump that fitted an old terracotta bowl from Mrs. Robertshaw's larder. She scrabbled some moss shining emerald green on the limestone rocks edging the terrace lawn, and tucked it round the purple and gold buds.

'You are so artistic, Liv,' said Anne, when Olivia placed this mini-garden in the middle of the table. Surrounded by white napery, silver and shining glass, it looked good, biodiverse. There was even a little slug, Olivia noticed. Then the rumble of a car coming up the track electrified them both.

'Oh God, I'd hoped to have a shower. How could they have been so quick? That's them, I'm sure.' Olivia hurried downstairs to switch on the yard lights, snatching a glance in the mirror on her way to open the door. A pale face stared back, framed in dark hair and the darker passage behind, Freddie's diamonds glinting at her throat. The image was arresting, like a late Rembrandt, a classical lady, perhaps Dido about to welcome Aeneas to Carthage. She smiled and Dido smiled back with an inappropriately modern grin, half triumphant at landing her hero scientist, a woman-of-the-world amused at her girlish excitement. The next moment Mark's loud double knock sounded at the back door. Andrew Bamberg's first view of her house would be the damp dark passage to the kitchen. If only they'd got the front door accessible so visitors could arrive in style, without being drenched by wet shrubbery and snagged in thorns.

Mark's big estate car shone in the dark yard, the light coming on in the packed interior as its doors opened. She heard his voice first, the far side of the car. 'Here we are, I'll go and tell Liv we're here.'

'We heard the engine,' Olivia said, stooping to smile through the car window at the arrivals.

Andrew was uncoiling his long frame from the passenger seat, but Julian was already standing behind Mark, stretching and looking blindly around. 'Ugh,' he said, 'it's dark.'

Mark's laugh came from the murk. 'Welcome to proper country, Julian. Oh, look at the stars. And the clouds sailing along in the moonlight. We get real dark sky up here.'

They all looked up. A satellite moved across the northern hemisphere. The only sounds the tick of the cooling car engine, a faint wind in the ash trees and the beck's gurgle and splash beyond the yard, loud with April meltwater coming off the moor. A tawny owl hooted.

'It's creepy,' said Julian,' I don't like it.' He backed towards the car, like a doubtful calf edging close to its mother.

'But it's lovely,' said Andrew. Olivia hadn't noticed his voice before, but the surrounding darkness closing them in, lent it an intimacy. 'Doesn't the air smell fantastic? It's geosmin. Greek for "earth smell"—from soil actinomycetes.' He spoke precisely, sounding the t's like an old-style BBC announcer, then laughed, as if hearing himself lecturing.

Mark pulled two suitcases out of the car and handed a box of books to Anne. Andrew and Olivia hauled bags from the boot, and Julian slung a rucksack over one shoulder and carefully lifted a violin case from the back seat. They processed into the house, Olivia leading the way. In the passageway, Andrew handed her a wooden box he carried by a handle on the top. 'We didn't bring any After Eights. But I thought you might find room for this microscope. It's only second-hand I'm afraid. But a microscope is a fun thing to have. I find them essential myself.' He didn't give her time to express her delight. He set the box under the coat hooks and walked on into the sitting room, shooing Julian in front of him.

'I'll show you your rooms,' Olivia said, taking coats to hang. 'Mind your heads.' Andrew and Julian followed her upstairs, stooping. Throwing open the doors of the transformed bedrooms, and relishing exclamations of pleasure from Andrew and a teenage grunt of appreciation from Julian, she was reminded strangely of the autumn day she and Mike had brought back new tups from the ram sales and released them on the soft green grass of Low Field after their long day in pens and in the trailer. She showed Andrew and Julian where things were, and told them to take their time and come down whenever they were ready. The scent of toast and wood smoke drifted up from downstairs. Mark called up that he was just off home again to fetch Pippa for dinner and they'd both be back by half past seven. Olivia slipped into her own room, where she brushed and brushed her hair. Standing at her mirror she adjusted the low cowl neck of the dark green silk top and slid Freddie's emerald ring on her ring finger. What heaven this is, she thought, turning her hand under the lamp to watch the stone glint green. My house, my guests. Out there in the dark my land, my first year's lambs, my future. This is the real beginning of Oxhide, at last.

She went down to the sitting room. Anne could be heard clattering saucepans in the kitchen. The dinner was her contribution, she'd told Olivia, refusing help. To her surprise, as he'd seemed shy and likely to wait for his father, Julian appeared first, his short black hair slicked. She stood. 'Come in, Julian, you're the first. Did you find everything you needed?'

'Thank you,' said Julian, coiling his thin body neatly onto a small chair. 'This's a very nice room, Mrs. Gabrieli.' He still wore the black leather bomber jacket he'd arrived in, and sat stiffly as though trying to be a good boy.

'Call me Olivia, do. I'm going to call you Julian.' The boy remained silent. 'If that's okay?' she added.

He unnerved her. It wasn't that he was staring, but that pale blue of the irises was odd, somehow otherworldly. He had Andrew's dark hair but where his father's eyes were deep set, Julian's were slightly protuberant, offset by girlishly arched eyebrows and long dark eyelashes. He smelt faintly of aftershave, not a common sort, but citrusy and spicy reminding Olivia of a dapper Gabrieli uncle Eduardo from her wedding in Torralba.

'Yeah, of course,' he said, in a normal north London teenager's voice, demotic but cultured. He replied politely but tersely to Olivia's conversational overtures.

When Anne appeared with a question about food, Olivia needlessly followed her to the kitchen. 'I hope Mark and Pippa get back soon. I feel shy. He makes me feel so old. Ah, there's Andrew now.' They heard feet on the wooden stairs, and father and son greeting each other.

'Let's have drinks straight away. That's how Mum deals with awkward visitors.' Anne rattled glasses on to a silver tray. 'Let's use these cheesy crisps, all the kids like them. Even snotty teenagers. Should I get him my Diet Coke?'

Andrew was thankfully full of everyday conversation and bonhomie. Julian ate crisps, not silently, but without speaking.

'I'm so excited to see you for real, Dr. Bamberg,' said Anne, doing her bubbly thing. 'I love your programme. Almost as much as Liv, though I wouldn't stay in just to watch you like she does.' Andrew grinned at Olivia. Bloody Anne!

Anne burbled on untroubled. 'It's fab to meet a telly star who appreciates the countryside. Isn't Oxhide brilliant? I think it's very clever of Olivia to buy it. My clever older sister.' Anne swigged her whiskey. Clearly, she had been exercising the cook's right to an encouraging glass or three while whipping the cream and reducing the *jus*.

Andrew gave Anne an amused smile. 'It's unique. We've been

looking at the map. You can almost picture the glacier that carved this dale, with the stream meandering around the valley floor.'

'Are you a geography lecturer at the university?' asked Anne.

'No, I just have a bad habit of telling people things,' Andrew said, with that smile. 'So, you're Olivia's sister?'

Olivia explained. 'Half-sister. Same father. Anne belongs here, she's the native, I've kind of washed up back here, I expect Pippa's told you.'

'It sounds almost as complicated as my family,' said Andrew. 'So are you at college, Anne?'

'No, I'm not at all brainy.' Anne's cheeks had gone attractively pink. She giggled. 'I'm a horsey girl, me. I have two horses here, Comet, who's a cob, and Dreamcatcher, that's my thoroughbred I'm bringing on. She's by Scorpion. Do you ride, Dr. Bamberg?'

Surprisingly, Andrew smiled and said yes, he did. 'As Mark will tell you, I became a country gent unexpectedly in my first year at college, and learning to ride was part of the metamorphosis. All sensible people love horses. It's such an honour to be liked by a horse.'

Anne beamed. 'Come and see mine tomorrow. They're stuck in stables, bored to bits. Olivia won't let them graze on her meadow. She's a dog-in-the-manger, the grass looks delicious.'

'It's not that I don't like horses,' said Olivia. 'It's just that I put my old turf first.'

'That's good to hear,' said Andrew, cutting the banter. 'An old grass pasture takes some replacing. If it ever *can* be replaced. There's a lot to discover about turf.'

'I thought perhaps we could—' The sound of Mark's diesel returning interrupted Olivia, and the next moment Pippa and he were coming in, tugging boots off their feet in the passage and stepping on to the white carpet in their socks with typical considerateness. Both kissed Olivia. Pippa, who was short, stood on tiptoe to kiss Julian, saying, 'a kiss for your Auntie Pip? You're so tall now. Welcome to the Dales, Julian.'

Mark went over to Andrew and laid an arm across his shoulder, smiling at Julian. 'Well, father and son! You both look very much at home.' Then, turning to the cooks, 'What a very good smell, Anne. I'm extremely hungry. We couldn't face motorway burgers.' Anne hovered, holding an oven cloth.

'Let's have dinner, then,' said Olivia. 'Are we all ready?' Her mother's words, she realised, smiling. She must be conjuring old times at the Hollies, the first dinner parties she'd been allowed to stay up for.

'I just need a hand wash,' said Mark. 'Always wash your hands before meals.'

Andrew raised an eyebrow at Olivia as though amused by Mark's fastidiousness. As she smiled back, drawn into his good humour, she caught an oddly hostile glance from Julian's strange ice-blue eyes.

As soon as they were seated, Olivia taking the head of her table, Anne carried in a long rack of lamb, browned and sprinkled with rosemary, standing to attention like an honour guard at a wedding. Piles of sprouts and roast potatoes steamed on the table. Olivia lit candles and Mark turned off the light after she had carved the meat, so that the silver shone. A Champagne cork popped and Mark poured the fizzing bubbles. He raised his glass. 'Here's to friendship. Friendship and fresh starts.'

Moved, Olivia sipped the heady wine, mentally saluting Freddie. She angled her ring to spark the emerald's green fire and it was as though he hovered in the shadows at her shoulder. The crocuses opened wide in the warmth, showing gold saffron stamens like a promise of arriving spring. Olivia felt complete.

After, by the fire, Pippa asked Julian how things were going at school, congratulating him on his music scholarship. She would have known him from a baby, Olivia realised. They had been close, Andrew and Mark, and Pippa had been assimilated easily into their circle. Julian visibly relaxed and chatted about his subjects and friends, his pose of angsty cool thawing in the warmth of Pippa's interest. What a good mother Pippa would be. When a silence fell, all of them relaxed and full, Andrew suggested Julian might play them something.

'If you do, too, Dad,' said Julian.

'Let's do them the *Lalo*,' said Andrew. 'I see you have a piano, Olivia. May we?' 'Prepare to be wowed,' said Mark. 'This is some double act, Olivia. Your piano won't know what's happened.'

They got up and hauled the sofas and chairs into a semicircle round the piano. Andrew screwed the piano stool down about a foot and pushed himself back to give play to his long forearms, shooting white cuffs and running up and down scales and arpeggios. Then he sounded an A for Julian, and the E, G and D. The tuning sounds gave Olivia the usual anticipatory shiver. When Julian swung the violin to his chin the silence was as profound as in a concert hall, and even the logs in the fire seemed to settle more softly than normal.

'Lalo's *Symphonie Espagnole*,' announced Julian.

The piece started with big declarative piano chords, filling the room with a stamping Spanish show of masculinity. Then Julian's violin took over, trailing Lalo's melting melody above the piano's murmured accompaniment. Soon, the piano asserted again, leading the violin back into the dance, urging it on so it strode and fluttered and shook its plumage.

Julian's mastery was bewitching, his chin clamped on the instrument, the fingers of his left hand dancing on the fingerboard, bow flashing seamlessly up and down. At one point his eyes caught and held Olivia's. They spoke something helpless, ancient, and shameless. There was no denying what the music was about. At last the violin flew up in a virtuoso flourish before subsiding again into the opening melody, and Andrew brought the first movement to its triumphant finish with another series of crashing chords.

There was a silence and then they all clapped.

'I told you so,' Mark said to Olivia. 'They're pretty good. What a piece, though. X- certificate. It shouldn't be allowed.'

Olivia found her voice. 'Thank you, thank you.'

'Well, go on then,' said Mark, breaking some kind of spell.
'Next movement please.' 'We haven't done that,' said Andrew,
smiling.

'I only have to play the first movement for the exam,' said Julian,
looking pleased. He loosened bowstrings and put the violin away
in its red velvet-lined wooden case.

Olivia declined a suggestion she play. She'd feel like Mary
Bennet, working earnestly through Prelude Nine after that
bravado and virtuosity. But Anne had no qualms and offered to
play old Irish songs they could sing to. By eleven they'd moved
on to *Ilkla Moor baht 'at*, that coarse Yorkshire *liebestod*, at which
Pippa and Mark said goodnight. Julian went to bed and Anne said
she wanted a hot bath.

Olivia made coffee for Andrew and herself, bringing out the
tiny gilt Torralba cups, and they sat on each side of the subsiding
fire. Andrew leaned back and crossed one leg over the other at
the knee. 'Do you know, I haven't felt as relaxed for ages. It's
so peaceful. It's kind of you to have me. I'm afraid Julian's at an
awkward age.'

'We've all been through it,' said Olivia. 'His playing is
phenomenal. What a gift.'

'Yes, he changes when he plays. He's not a country boy.'
Andrew smiled. 'He's scared of sheep, but he'd die rather than
admit it.'

'My brother was like that.'

'You have a brother as well as a sister? Somehow I had the
impression from Mark you were all alone in the world.'

'My brother died.'

'I'm so sorry. It was crass of me to ask. I apologise.'

'You weren't to know. It was in the same accident as my
husband, Freddie. Fred Gabrieli. It's two years ago now. It was
a car crash on a motorway near Florence. Ben, my brother, was
driving. He was offended in some way with Fred. He was driving
too fast, in a sulk. It was snowing a little—do you know

Abbetone? They even ski there, in the Apennines. It does snow a little. And then a red lorry came up out of a slip road . . .'

'Olivia, don't. I'm sorry. Here, I'll get you some water.' Andrew did a strangely old-fashioned thing: he felt in his trouser pocket and drew out a spotless white handkerchief. He gave it to her and then went to the kitchen to fetch the water.'

'I'm so sorry.' She dabbed her face, but didn't like to blow her nose on the perfect white cotton, so she sniffed.

'I'll tell you my story,' said Andrew. 'My wife died too. Cressida. It was a stupid accident. She took our baby, Julian, to see her parents in Bordeaux. There was an accident on the ferry coming back. She fell between the gangway and the quay. Another passenger rescued Julian.'

There was a pause.

'It worries people, doesn't it?' she said. 'To be bereaved so young. Did you find that? I lost touch with all my university friends. Being widowed is for old people.'

'It's true. Though Mark has always been there for me, ever since Cambridge. I don't know how I would have coped without him. And Pippa too, of course. Being a single father's difficult. It helped I have two mothers, one does glamour and the other is kind.' He laughed and Olivia smiled, remembering the Bamberg Christmas party, with silk-clad Vanessa politicking with Jane in the Highgate study while Mary did her mummy thing.

'Well, so do I too, in a way,' said Olivia, smiling too. 'Have two mothers, I mean. My actual birth mother lives in London, you've been in Pippa's old flat in her house. She's not mummyish at all, Isobel, she's the pianist Isobel Burbank—did you hear her play when you and Mark visited Pippa's flat in London? And I've recently got to know my step-mum, Anne's mother Bridget. My father remarried after divorcing my Mama. Well, she left him, really. Bridget's certainly kinder than Isobel.'

'Pippa told me a bit about you when she entertained us in her little flat. Not often, but once or twice, when Mark was around, back at Guy's from his GP placements round the country, and

I was still at Cambridge turning myself from a medic into a soil ecologist. Happy days. I remember hearing piano practice from upstairs. So that was your mother?'

'Yes. She practised all the time. Very different from Bridget. Bridget doesn't suffer from ambitions at all. But I mustn't be rude about her. She's good with my father, that's what matters, isn't it?'

'And here we both are like two shipwrecked sailors come to land,' said Andrew. 'It's a funny old life, isn't it? But it looks as though you've found home, Olivia.' He stood. 'I'm off to my gorgeous comfortable bed. We have work tomorrow'. He bent his six-foot-something under the door lintel. 'Goodnight, Olivia, and thank you again for today.'

For a moment she thought he might kiss her goodnight. Luckily, he didn't—she might have passed out.

She woke before dawn elated, as if somebody had given her a marvellous present, something life-changing—what? As consciousness returned, the evening came back; the music, the magic. And then the awful knowledge that she stood on the cliff edge of falling in love again. Even though nothing outward had happened, something inside had shifted, something she thought she had locked firmly in some vault of the heart. Like the Craven Fault, she thought. That line of weakness not far from here, where a movement of rock strata deep underground caused surface quakes that could send crockery crashing from kitchen dressers. Folklorists had uncovered a local cluster of legends about poltergeists and Nibelungen. Oh, for goodness' sake! She clicked the bedside light on, as if to chase away fantasy, to assert her loyalty to Frederico, but a voice in her head still said, *Andrew. Andrew Bamberg.*

It wasn't an exaggeration, that word, *falling*. Even as you tell yourself, *you're riding for a fall*, a part of you wants to rejoice in your abandon, to let the force take you like a bolting horse. Even if you know it might be the end of you, you can't help revelling in it, amazed at the power of your self-immolating will. Sensible people,

people like Bridget and Pippa, were proof against such upheaval, so grounded, their marriages so calmly enjoyable.

She dressed in the first old clothes at hand, not pausing to hang her silk shirt from yesterday evening, and went out as usual before dawn to check the sheep and lambs, so as to be free later in the morning when Andrew and Julian would begin their first day's work.

Skirting the rock fall below a small limestone cliff, she climbed over the moor stile to the open heather. In the lee of the wall, groups of sheep regarded her as she walked slowly past. They had capable feminine faces, watching warily but standing their ground. This was their spot: hefted ewes, who would come back here, year after year, with their grown lambs. She felt a little better. All was well with her flock. The sun lit the tops of the ash trees with a russet-red glow as she strode home down the inbye. And there below was her beloved house, smoke rising from its chimney, containing her rescued hero.

No, enough with the myth-making. Not hers, not rescued, not a hero. Andrew Bamberg was a well-known scientist, a possible future asset to the Oxhide enterprise.

Somebody had already made tea in the large pot she had left out with milk and cereal on the dresser, and drunk most of it, too. There was no sound upstairs. On the lawn at the front of the house she scanned the valley. Father and son were out already, down on the flat valley floor by the river. Julian had the rucksack over his shoulder and Andrew, in wellingtons, stood in the marshy place by the river where monkey flowers grew in summer, passing things from the ground to Julian who did something to each one—perhaps writing a label—before putting them in the rucksack. Julian carried something white that flapped, probably an open map.

Olivia drank lukewarm stewed tea, scanning Farmer's Weekly. Anne must have gone down to Skellside to do the horses. She cleared and wiped the table and spread the architect's plans.

There would be a field lab. No, there wouldn't, these were the plans Jane and her father had worked out. These foundations would never bear the imaginary weight of castles in the air.

An out-of-tune rendition of some pop song about love, and boots being flung down on the stone floor, made Olivia startle and fold the plan guiltily, as if Anne would spot the ghostly footprint of her imaginary microbiology lab and tease her, in that coarse teenage way. Where was this guilt from? Fred wouldn't have disapproved of pursuing science to improve farm management. Joe and Jane would surely understand such diversification. But last night's events had left a strange atmosphere in the house.

Anne padded in and beamed at her sister.

'Morning, Liv. Wasn't that a success? I loved your new friends. Specially Dr. Bamberg. He can sample me anytime.' Anne giggled and put on the warm kettle to reboil. 'You're looking at the plans.'

Olivia had to explain about Oxhide's new scientific role.

'So, it'll be a lab, like a research station? The Oxhide Institute—of what? Compost? Slurry? Giles was being funny about it.'

'Oh, just a little building to prepare samples, maybe at the end of the old cowshed. Just a small lean-to, with a tap and lighting. All the high-tech things would be somewhere else.'

'Will he be here often? Oh, how exciting. Even Julian's quite cool in his way, though he is young. Perhaps you'll become Mrs. Bamberg!'

'Don't be bloody stupid. Honestly, Anne!' Olivia seized the Jaycloth and mopped the clean draining board with pointless vigour. 'I'm off now to see Mike Robertshaw. I expect you'll be gone by the time I'm back. Give Dad my love.'

'Okay, I'll give them both your love. Such as it is,' said Anne, to Olivia's retreating back.

Now was a peaceful moment to look at the present they'd brought, the microscope. She was a little in awe of it—she'd last twiddled the knobs on a microscope at school, taking turns, and never getting the hang of it, although when the teacher had set it all up it was amazing to see that wood was made of cells. She'd never seen human cells or microbes.

Perhaps if she got the microscope out on the table Andrew and Julian would just come in and use it, and she'd be able to see what they did, to learn without looking too ignorant. Carefully placing its heavy wooden box on the wiped table, she drew it out and plugged it into the kettle socket with an extension lead. The light shone obediently up through the little hole where the slide went. But she had no slides, she would just have to wait until they returned.

She was still daydreaming when she heard Andrew's voice in the yard, talking to Julian, the man's and boy's voices alternating. Her pulse missed a beat. 'How did you get on?' Forcing a breezy outdoor tone like Anne's.

'Pretty well, I think. Time will tell. Julian'll do a short report for you.'

Andrew stamped off his boots, but Julian walked straight into the kitchen, spotting the microscope and gravitating to it. 'Hey, what're you looking at? Haven't you got any slides?' He pulled out a little drawer inside the top of the microscope box that Olivia hadn't noticed, and grinned at her. 'Ever used one of these things?'

She had to admit she hadn't, really.

'Moss is good,' Andrew said. 'Down by the stream, get a few different ones.'

Julian came back in minutes with a green tuft in each hand, and Andrew peeled off a few minute leaves with forceps and put them in a drop of water on a slide. 'Look, Olivia—here, let me—low power first, let's raise the condenser—so—' He stood aside.

Cells! Like little green boxes. Olivia exclaimed with delight. She'd remembered this all taking a whole afternoon, taking turns to peer at dusty slides labelled 'cork cells' Miss somebody had produced with great ceremony from the biology cupboard.

'Julian, why don't you run Olivia through the use of the microscope?' Andrew said, and turning to Olivia, 'He's a good demonstrator, my boy. If we get you set up now, you'll be able to play with it, get to know your way around in the long evenings.'

Julian sat beside her and explained what the beams of light did, and how to align the beam from the condenser below on to the specimen above. It was true he was a good demonstrator.

It was all clear, she felt empowered, as if he'd given her the keys to the microscopic kingdom. She couldn't wait for him to let her explore Oxhide's invisible wildlife for herself. She would buy herself a lab notebook at the art shop in Skipton.

'Just make sure you don't get mascara on the eyepiece,' Julian said as he got up from the table to help his father. Olivia never wore mascara. However keen and clever Julian might be, she sensed something a trifle nasty about him. It was probably just a touch of adolescent misogyny he'd grow out of. He reminded her a little bit of Ben that way—although Julian was thin and dark and sly, rather than blonde and bumptious and annoying. It was reassuring that he appeared to notice her change of expression now, and quickly offered more constructive advice. She should use the low power lens to begin, and try looking at different kinds of moss—she would be amazed how different their cells were.

Andrew smiled approvingly at his son and turned to her. 'You'll want to hear what came out of the DNA from those samples Erik and I collected last month. There were interesting sequences, not matched by anything in the databases, meaning we don't know what they are, just that they are fungi. And others that did give matches—they were interesting, too.'

'Oh?' This was all so much more real, so much less mad, than last night—this straightforward shared delight at the thought of learning of the unknown life around her.

'So you might really think of an investigation here? How terrific!'

'Yeah.' He nodded. 'Yes, I think it could be worthwhile. And doable.'

'What's the next step?'

'Getting funded,' said Andrew. 'We'll need equipment, services like sequencing and bioinformatics and imaging. Lancaster will help, but they'll need paying. And salaries for an assistant and maybe a studentship.'

'My godmother Jane seemed to think we'd need to apply to UK research councils or the EU for a grant.'

'Yes, eventually. For now, we'll collect enough samples over this visit to do a pilot study and show them what we're capable of. And I might get start-up money to fund that.'

'Where from? Who decides?'

'Supposedly, committees. Which can include your friends, or, unfortunately, your enemies. I'm afraid I've made a few. And then the science budget's tight and a lot of it is allocated to particular lines of research.'

'Who allocates it?'

Andrew laughed. '*The Powers that Be.*'

'Who are?'

Andrew broke into a smile. She raised her eyebrows in a question. 'What about my mother and your godmother?'

16

The Powers That Be

'That was very good, thank you.' Vanessa handed her tray up for the cabin crew to take. 'Ambrosia. I'd never travel any way but Olympian.' The woman smiled, took the tray and then bent and murmured.

'No—if you have no objection I will keep my blind open,' Vanessa said in a clear voice. The woman backed off and trundled along the aisle to mutter to a colleague.

Jane, sitting next to her, had taken out a tablet and was peering at a spreadsheet. 'It's so bright at this height. Blinding. I have work to do' she complained.

'Before you get completely stuck in,' said Vanessa, 'There's something we need to discuss. Not to put too fine a point on it, I've a bit of a bone to pick with you, J.'

'Which is?' Jane did not lift her eyes from the screen.

'Andy's out of a job. You and I both know why. What are you going to do about it?'

Jane looked up at Vanessa sitting opposite in Olympian's spacious business class, her ageless yellow curls shining in the five-mile-high sunshine. 'I'm sorry if he's upset. There was bound to be collateral damage, it's nothing personal. Anyway, he seems to have found his métier in the media now, hasn't he?'

'Only as a way of spreading the word. He needs to pursue his exploration. He's at a new scientific frontier, but he can't progress without a lab.'

'But who's to pay for nature study, just for its own sake? Where's the return? It's all too vague, he's just indulging his curiosity. Fine if that's what he wants to do, let him be a gentleman scientist like Robert Boyle or Peter Mitchell, but I can't condone the use of taxpayers' cash for projects that are merely curiosity-driven.'

'So, we pay for a moon shot but can't afford to catalogue the living things on the planet. Just when, as Andy says, the tools are to hand with gene technology. Jane, you owe it to him to find something. You have the power. Family must count for something.'

'I wish you'd lower that blind. You're giving me a headache.'

'But look at the sea ice. So beautiful. That's taiga—see the little fir trees, like on a Christmas cake—it must be Ellesmere.' Vanessa half-lowered the blind and continued to squint at the mountains of ice like rows of white pimples that came and went through drifts of far-down cirrus. Then she withdrew her gaze and focused again on her half-sister.

'Studying nature is noble. Part of being human. We've been doing it since Lucretius, since before. It's not all about economic competition, whatever your paymasters may say.'

Jane gave a small *ufff*. 'Well then, Andrew needs to find private venture capital. Some enterprise with an aspirational brand that matches his values. A not-for-profit. A philanthropist! They do exist.'

Vanessa lowered her blind all the way down.

In the calm gloom of the cabin Jane closed the file, put away her tablet and straightened her back. 'Ah. Mm. I wonder. No, it wouldn't be fair.'

'What?'

'Remember my God-daughter Olivia? You invited her to Andrew's celebration at The Trojans.'

'I remember. Little farmer. Always seems to be hanging around Andy. She was even at our Christmas party.'

'He'd invited her, actually.'

'Really?'

'She's starting up a farm business.'

'More power to her,' said Vanessa, glancing at her flawless nails. 'She has lots of money.'

'No!'

'Yes. She's an heiress. But she's serious about using her inheritance well. She's starting up a model hill farm. And she wants to do scientific research there, on soil. I don't support that, it's mission creep and I've told her so. But if Andrew wants a study site—well . . .'

'So, you're suggesting I sell my son to this little empire-builder?'

'Don't be ridiculous, Vanessa. Olivia Gabrieli might very well want to put venture capital into a joint project with Andrew. Their personal aims are entirely complementary as far as I can see. Soil is very *in*, now. Carbon sequestration technology, antibiotic resistance—that could be supported.'

'I don't want him stuck on a *farm*.'

'Why should he be? There's no onus on the co-directors of a company to cohabit as far as I'm aware. She wouldn't have any matrimonial designs on him, if that's what you're afraid of. She's done with all that, she told me. The love of her life was killed. Tragic widow. Her whole enterprise is a sort of shrine to her dead husband. It's a perfect fit.'

'Ah. That's different. And you think there might be a fundable project Andy could do on this farm, something to further his career?'

'I'd have to ask. But there is a proposal in the office for a little seed-corn grant aimed at scientists who want to make interdisciplinary moves into themes the department favours. And the minister is into peat moors for flood alleviation.'

'Seed-corn?'

'Small grants for pilot projects. The point is, they come through faster than full proposals. We could move quite fast.'

Vanessa's perfect eyes narrowed. 'That would be helpful. Yes, do that, Jane.' Vanessa fished a tiny flask from a maroon suede clutch bag and, raising her chin, spritzed her long white neck with a light spray. 'The air gets so dry on these long flights. Like some?'

'No thanks.'

'Let's get them together and discuss it. I could hold a small do at Uphill.'

'Oh really, V! No, hold an exploratory meeting with Olivia and Andy and me, and you too if you like. I'll explain the funding options, Andy can explain the science he'd do, and Olivia could decide if she wants to contribute in kind, by providing the site, and maybe helping with the work as well. She's clever, you know.'

'All right. But in the country, please. Not in Victoria Street for God's sake. Can't we do it at Uphill?'

'Yes, of course,' said Jane, with one of her rare smiles. 'Why not?'

'Okay, good. It'll be fun. Soon as we get back. Then we can let them know right away. The funds are there.'

Both the cousins reclined their seats and slept away the last thousand miles of their flight, Jane heading for the US Department of Agriculture, Vanessa for the Metropolitan Museum in New York.

A week after Easter, Olivia's computer pinged with Andrew's forwarded message. With dawning understanding and a surge of delight she read that they had been awarded a seed-corn grant from the Commission for Conservation of Cultural Landscape for '*a pilot investigation on the soil flora of a traditionally managed hill farm in the North Yorkshire National Park* '. According to the award letter, funds would be provided '*to develop a genomic approach to characterise the composition and function of microbial communities associated with semi-natural vegetation, with a view to identifying possible roles in plant resilience to intensification and climate change.'*

Fred's vision would be realised. Oxhide could become a model farm. All this beauty, the earth beneath her feet, would be valued and understood, as never before. Scientists, as well as farm workers, friends and relatives would come from across the globe, and she would carry on the great tradition of European uplands, her sheep turning tough moor grass into food and clothing, Oxhide flying the flag for human-scale life and landscape.

Funding for a scientific collaboration meant more than a budget for salaries, equipment and consumables. It promised new relationships, a shared purpose. At the outset, the team were chosen only for their varied individual insight, expertise and knowledge; all clever, ambitious and with their own loyalties. Who knew what problems lay ahead—Jane had told her about business analysis of group dynamics and the cycle of Forming, Storming, Norming and Performing—but for now the grant meant a wide open future, personal and collective validation. She and Andrew Bamberg would be joint captains of the enterprise. Oxhide would be a scientific centre and Olivia Gabrieli a scientific collaborator—well, a research assistant—with Andrew Bamberg of *Invisible Wildlife*. He would be working at Oxhide Farm, in buildings she would provide. If only Freddie could have shared this.

17

Longings

Olivia twisted Fred's ring on her finger as if to invoke his spirit. But it was physical reality she craved. If only there was a medicine to silence desire; then, how she would now be looking forward to working calmly alongside Andrew Bamberg, with Fred's invisible blessing from wherever, whatever, he now was. Excitement fought with foreboding. She needed to see down-to-earth Anne.

It was a cold morning and Anne's breath steamed on the air as she barrowed muck energetically up a ramp to the top of the heap. Olivia was glad she didn't have to do this. Herbivores were so amazingly productive. An energetic routine activity was good for the soul, perhaps that explained Anne's even temper and unfailingly sunny mood, about to be interrupted.

'Oh Anne!' Olivia hadn't meant to crumple like this, to collapse on a straw bale and bawl. Anne put down the barrow and ran to her.

'Sorry. It's okay, I don't know why I'm so upset. There's nothing wrong really.' 'Never mind. Come and look at my horse.'

Dreamcatcher was sheltering by the wall, but whickered and came over towards them as they approached. Anne felt in her jeans pocket and brought out a handful of feed. There was something calm about the animal's soft champing.

'She's enormous, isn't she?' Olivia said. The mare's back was level with the top of her head. She reached to scratch the chestnut flank. Dreamcatcher snaked her head round and made a face, ears back, a flash of massive teeth.

'So big and still spooky,' Anne said. 'She's been badly handled, poor thing. She's a pussycat in the stable.'

Olivia didn't reply but absentmindedly rubbed the horse's side. 'Tell me what's eating you, Liv,' Anne said.

'Anne, d'you think I'm mad? I mean, deluded? With this lab thing?'

Anne was silent as though weighing the proposition. 'I don't really understand the lab. But it's what you want? To have Andrew Bamberg there?'

'Yes, it is. It is. Last week I was on a high. It was like a new life for me.'

'So that's good, isn't it? It's lucky he was free to come here.'

'But building this lab in the yard—it's not exactly farming, is it? What was I thinking? Exactly the opposite of what Oxhide's meant to be.' Olivia heard a catch in her own voice. 'I like him. But Giles doesn't, much. Daddy hates the idea. But it's a kind of life-line for me. He's on my wavelength.'

Anne thought for a moment. Then she laughed, Bridget's laugh. 'Don't beat yourself up, Olivia. We all have silly ideas. Look at me buying this racehorse. Crazy. But fun. You deserve some fun, Livvy.'

'I know I'm being disloyal to Dad. I ought to ask him, when he put so much work into our business plan. I meant to, but . . . and with Andrew, and Jane and Vanessa all being so encouraging . . .'

'Andrew's started to mean rather a lot to you, doesn't he? It's not just about doing science here, is it? Be honest, Liv.'

'I admire him.'

'You're blushing!'

'Well, yes, I've got a thing about him. I can't concentrate, it's obsessive. I wish I hadn't. I wish it would go away. If only things were simpler! Don't you think he's attractive?'

'Me? Andrew Bamberg?' Anne broke into a grin. 'No way! With that southern la-di-dah accent? He says everything in a roundabout way, as if he's taking the piss. Giles can't understand what you see in him.'

'Giles? What's it got to do with him?' Olivia felt a flush at the thought of this disloyal gossip, in her own backyard.

'Search me.'

Anne could have taken the whole thing more seriously. Now she picked up a stone and scratched some words on a flat stone in the wall. 'O heart A'.

'It's true. Anne, it's true. Oh God, what shall I do?'

'Tell Andrew. Why ever not? It's the twenty-first century. Go for it, Liv. I dare you.'

Giles loved driving the massive digger, carrying on until into the early evening, turning Olivia's yard to a Goya-esque chiaroscuro as headlights, mounted high on the machine, moved backwards and forwards in the dark. Sometimes his friends would spectate, attracted by moving lights as they passed the road below on their way home from work. Perhaps he even invited them.

Annoying as these local hangers-on might be, standing around exchanging banter in her yard, they were a welcome bulwark in the face of the demolition team hired by the builder, mercenaries over whom she had no authority. And who was she to criticise Giles, her indispensable rock, on hand in the filthiest weather, quad-biking hay and silage to the moor flock through the worst of winter snow, when she'd had a cold? He was ever ready with ways to move great piles of stuff, a part of farming she'd never appreciated before.

However, in under two weeks the site-clearing was done, the yard stripped to rutted mud, salvageable stone and bricks piled in builder's bags, scrap metal in a skip, shards of ancient asbestos safely bagged. Only the old stone dairy and a small stable remained, up behind the house, beside the unmade track that led across the inbye fields to the Robertshaws' farm. The site seemed bigger than when the ground had been concealed under broken-roofed buildings, leaning cart sheds and abandoned objects hosting mounds of creeping grass and nettles.

Today, Giles had been clearing a terrible old slurry pit leaking brownly into the beck below the farm, probably for years. Olivia stopped him from dumping the fouled soil on the fields. Giles agreed reluctantly and she arranged for it to be transported expensively by lorry. So much of the damage farms did to the landscape got done out of misguided thrift. Regulations said you had to clear up—but how much easier to let liquid manure seep into a nearby stream, and tip bulky rubbish into a hidden limestone scar or remote mine shaft. Poor old planet, ulcerated with spent nuclear fuel, undecomposable landfill, and the ammoniacal slurry of intensive production.

With the first signs of recovering grass, Anne let her horses out at Skellside for a little longer each day, and her rides extended up on to the moor tracks. It was good to have her cheerful company, somebody to give the moral support needed to enjoy a ploughman's at The Bell. A good thing to do, Olivia realised, if you wanted a feel for what your neighbours were saying about you. Sitting in the window seat with their soup, unfreezing their hands after a morning moving bales of horse bedding in a grey East wind, they were chatting about Olivia maybe having a ride on Comet some time, about Bridget wanting to see Olivia's refurbished guest rooms, and Joe's health, which was a worry, when, in one of those odd pauses in conversation, Olivia overheard someone at the bar make a pointed remark about *that foreign woman*, her needless extravagance and hobby farming.

She couldn't see the speaker without turning her head too obviously, but caught Anne's eye and raised an eyebrow. *Nick*, Anne told her in a stage whisper. Sitting opposite her, Anne had a clear view of the group at the bar. Olivia knew Nick—one of those spectating young men who'd made themselves at home around

Giles's digger. He was a disaffected layabout from Grassington, who sometimes helped the Robertshaws. Giles must have been sounding off to his audience, and Nick had picked up nuggets of insider gossip about the new owner of the farm and her nefarious intentions. On their way back to the yard, Anne elaborated; there'd been chat among The Bell's regulars, not all of it approving. Word had got around that something scientific would be going on at Oxhide. There were lights up there in the dark.

Strange men too, and a car with foreign plates. They'd been seen with test tubes near the river, by someone who'd wondered if the police needed to know. It was all owned by one woman now, a foreigner nobody knew.

In farming, reputation was everything, especially in remote uplands with their vicissitudes of weather and shepherding. The kind of life she was living depended on the kindness of the collective. And there was friendly rivalry too, in the judicious making of decisions—when to lamb, the husbandry of grass, managing through lean times. Olivia knew they all had a good look at each other's land as they drove by. There had been sympathy and approval for her work at Oxhide so far, but now it looked as though it was time for some damage limitation.

She must reassert her Yorkshire credentials, and reassure everybody that the young woman with an odd name, who'd taken over old Mrs. Robertshaw's place, wasn't up to anything sinister. Olivia needed her father's Yorkshire antennae, their solid English name.

Joe and Bridget were quick to accept her invitation to Sunday lunch at The Bell, followed by a viewing of the cleared Oxhide site and maybe a stroll if the weather was fine. To make it more of a party, and let her father see how well she was getting on with her well-established neighbours, she phoned Meg Robertshaw and invited her and Mike to join them.

Sunday was like summer, the first time this year Olivia had noticed the sun's warmth on her back, and the day seemed lovelier when her father emerged from the car with Bridget and they approached the back door, still the only jungle-free way into the house. This was a proper Ilkley couple, well-heeled in Sunday best. Smiling, she hugged Bridget and then Joe.

'I hope we look the part?' Joe said. He was on her side, always had been. This arrival reminded her of his occasional parental visits to her at school; her mildly amused, ironical, proud father. She could rely on him to shore up her credibility with the other girls and staff. How much friendlier the world seemed, with Joe Burbank to define her to herself as a loved daughter. *Daddy.* He caught her approving gaze, and returned it with a wink.

They decided to walk straight to The Bell and return for coffee and a look around after. A good thing the track was decently surfaced now—both wore shiny brogues. Olivia knew this get-up well; her father's smart tweed suit with checked flannel shirt and no tie, navy raincoat on top; Bridget, in pink roll-neck jumper with indigo velvet jeans and three-quarter length wool jacket, had done her bit too. Joe took a red and white golfing umbrella out of the car boot and they set off, before some small but fast-moving grey clouds could catch them out.

Mike and Meg Robertshaw were already at the pub. It was crowded, warm with conversation and wood smoke. The first sunny Sunday for weeks must have encouraged people out. Olivia recognised a few of the pub's regulars now; farmers and various farm workers and their spouses, a couple with a weekend cottage in Grassington, the postman in mufti. There was only a short lowering of the conversational noise as their entrance was clocked. But her association with the respected Robertshaws, and the evidence that she had proper family, had not gone unnoticed, she knew.

Joe and Mike shook, in the way rural lawyers greet big farmers, and Joe introduced Bridget. 'Well, we're putting another winter behind us now. How's it been up here?'

'Can't grumble. This Oxhide place of Olivia's had a good first lambing, even though we went for it a bit early this time. Some nice ones in there. She'll make a right Dales farmer, your daughter.'

'I don't know how you did it,' Meg said to Olivia. 'Out there in all weathers, up at crack of dawn. It made me shiver to see you when I went by in the car. And now, all this new building work.'

'Bye, it's all change up there,' Mike said. 'Not before time, mind. I reckon you'll have new ideas for the old place? Grandma would've been pleased to see old shippon still standing.'

They chatted on about farm matters, upland-lowland partnerships, the sheep pyramid and traceable mutton, like an educational episode of *The Archers*, until any listeners would surely have lost interest. Joe regaled them with a long anecdote about the history of his negotiations with the Robertshaws, which had originally enabled Olivia to buy the land. Once their table in the window was ready, beautifully laid with white cloth and sparkly glasses, and they'd all five opted for the roast lamb, Olivia felt that any fears about sinister non-farm-related activities at Oxhide had been well and truly laid to rest. Not only that, but her mission, as re-affirmed by her father, was clearly viable, sensible—and above all, a worthwhile way to spend a life. She shouldn't let herself be so easily swayed by Jane's hard-nosed corporate pose or Vanessa's absurd Arcadian fantasies. She was the boss, after all. Joe and Mike were her appropriate role models, not those power-hungry poseurs.

After, Bridget wanted to go and see Anne and the horses down at Skellside, and Joe told her to take the car to save her shoes—he'd done his bit at Pony Club duties, he would stay with Olivia and see over her building plans and progress. Olivia had her father to herself.

Over coffee, Joe asked to see the latest version of the plans, and Olivia fetched the ground plans and elevations as far as they'd gone and spread them on the kitchen table. There'd been changes—arrangements for school visits and holiday catering were included in the new footprint, with a larger car park at the end of the track behind the farmhouse. Joe wanted to know if

Olivia had taken Jane's advice and omitted laboratories. Olivia quickly said she had; she told herself that, after all, a biology class room for visiting 'A'-level students needed to hold a class of thirty, and its fittings could be flexible supposing anyone wanted to undertake more technically sophisticated science projects. Similarly, holiday flats could surely accommodate visitors other than holiday makers, specially out of season. She hadn't really lied—had she? It was important Joe shouldn't be worried—Bridget had said so.

Folding the plans and returning them to their drawer, she suggested they should go out to see the cleared site. In its Sunday afternoon silence, the yard now looked full of possibility, more like her own again, free of Giles's garish JCB, his friends and the demolition men. Joe picked round the drier edges, and Olivia led them to the ghyll to show him the violets. The beck was calmer now, but still deep with winter rain. The pool below had cleared and you could see what looked like a paved bottom to its lower end, where the flow was dammed by a low wall.

'I think I remember this place,' said Joe. 'In fact, I think it might be where we once . . . er.'

He paused, Olivia looked at him and he chuckled. 'It's so private, you could bathe here in the summer. It's very nice, I can tell you.' When her father's face lit like that she could envisage him as a young man.

'Did you . . .'

Joe changed the subject. 'It must be an old sheep wash,' he went on, reverting to local historian, so she would never know if he—and even Jane—had once skinny-dipped here on a long-ago August hike over the moors. How she loved his mix of romance and practicality.

On the way back, they admired the old dairy, revealed in its vernacular elegance now the rubbish was cleared from around it; long and low, with a stone-flagged roof and what must have been a little stable at one end. Joe pointed out the long flat stone shelf that he said would have been where the milk was left to stand in big shallow pans for settling, letting the cream rise so it could be skimmed off. This was the stone Andrew had pointed out to her, saying it would be perfect as a balance shelf—a perfectly level stable surface for weighing minute quantities of chemicals or tiny dried samples.

She had to come clean with her father. Leaning against the stone shelf, she told him how Andrew Bamberg of *Invisible Wildlife* had been here, brought along by Pippa Illingworth and her husband. 'Remember the Illingworths I used to play with?'

'Yes,' Joe said. 'A nice girl. What happened to her?'

Walking back to the house they had a catch-up about Pippa and Mark, who Joe showed interested in. Olivia lit the fire in the sitting room and settled him on the sofa as there was no sign of Bridget yet. Joe thought she and Anne must be playing My Little Pony—Bridget had been a keen pony child herself, and supported Anne's equestrian ambitions.

'Funny,' Joe remarked, strolling to the window, now much more at home. 'Funny, how ponies were such a girls' thing.' Not funny at all, thought Olivia, obvious. A pony was freedom, transport to wild places, and gentle company on the way.

As she brought in coffee and mints, Joe was opening her piano. 'This is nice. What are you playing? Lalo?' He inspected the music lying on top of the Broadwood. 'But this is for violin and piano—you don't say Anne's showing musical inclinations!'

Olivia quickly set down the tea tray. 'Well—no—we had a dinner for them—Anne and I, a special dinner for Pippa and Mark and . . .' She stalled, flustered. Joe waited. 'They brought Andrew Bamberg, he was staying with them. He has a very musical son—they played for us.'

'Goodness, Liv! Not just a farm, a salon!'

'It was a lovely evening. I'd been a bit lonely, you know, and it was extraordinary. Andrew's a fantastic pianist as well as a soil ecologist.'

'Anne never said anything about it. What dark horses you women are! I'm glad you're finding worthy company, love. I've been worrying about you, all alone with the labourers, dwelling on Frederico's memory as you have been. It's not right for a good-looking girl like you.' He sat in the window seat and she joined him.

Gazing across at the shadowed fell side opposite, as she had last autumn at the Hollies, she confessed. 'I've offered Andrew Bamberg the run of the farm for his work. He's contributing his expertise free, and has a special grant to install a little lab—it won't interfere with the business plan.'

'This isn't that idea you had to get him here, that Jane advised against? Isn't that slight mission creep?' A note of nervousness tightened his voice. 'Olivia, do be careful. I don't mean money-wise, that sounds all above-board. But this Bamberg? . . . I think you're a bit like me. I want you happy, love. Lalo and alcohol, it sounds a powerful mixture. Don't do anything irrevocable. There's a legal phrase I always remember, it's from the law of contract, but I've found it's useful in life, too, with sex and so on, you know. Aim for *consensus ad idem*, agreement on the same thing. Make sure you know what you're agreeing to with this chap. And there's a good English phrase too, *don't mix business with pleasure*.'

It was a shock that her deepest feelings were so patent. It was hard to know how to reply to a warning so well deserved and sensitively offered. Her mind churned like the overfilled beck. There was a silence. Her father, larger somehow, watched her with benign understanding. Not too soon, they heard the car returning and the back door opening. Bridget stood in the doorway ready to start their drive home to Ilkley.

Joe rose and hugged Olivia. She hugged him back. Then he went quickly from the room to join his wife, grabbing his raincoat from the hook in the passage. Olivia followed, held open the car door, waved to Bridget at the wheel, and watched as the dark Jaguar slalomed elegantly down the hairpins of the farm track and turned out on to the road below, its lights coming on in the late dusk. She wished she'd had time to thank him.

18

'You Have to Be the Boss'

For the first time this year, Olivia had the chance of a long weekend break. Andrew, back at Stockholm Street, was writing a review, with Julian locked in A-level revision in London. At Oxhide, everything was under control, as far as it could be, with the farmyard site levelled and the builder booked to start the new footings in a fortnight. Olivia decided to spend a few days with the Gabrielis in Florence, to reconnect with Fred's brothers and sisters and cousins—people who, in a counterfactual life, she would now have been getting to know as in-laws. In Italian, there was probably a word for those relationships. They deserved to know how she was using Frederico's inheritance, how she was carrying on his work, and Fred's mother had pressed her to come. Being at Torralba would help refresh the good memories, to keep Fred real in her thoughts. Visiting the places they'd been together—the hills around Trebbia, and that meadow, green as the emerald in her ring, might help her feel whole again, even cure her of these weird feelings around Andrew Bamberg and his son. The destruction of the old farmyard, though necessary, had disturbed her in a way she hadn't expected.

Change had to happen. But must things you loved be lost?

Wanting not to feel a tourist, she took the number 7 bus from the Piazza San Marco to the villa. It was as if she'd never been away, and as she entered the familiar portico with its umbrellas, walking sticks and wellingtons, the stab of sorrow was the sharper for knowing where their bedroom had been on the first floor. They had stood on its balcony the day she'd become Frederico's wife, the newest member of this ancient family, looking across the roofs of Florence towards the opposite hill, the city's famous landmarks sparkling as night fell, with the beautiful four-poster bed in the room behind.

But now old Gino appeared as she stood in the entrance hall, and seized her suitcase, Maria came upstairs from the kitchen, and there was Giulia, Signora Gabrieli, Fred's mother, and her old sister, his aunt Francesca. A tide of loving greetings and exclamations engulfed her. They didn't blame her for Freddie's death, why should they? And what had she feared, why hadn't she come here sooner and often? They made her so at home, it was like the prodigal's return, and once they had seen her settled in her room, gave her space to rest before dinner, which would be at seven, Giulia said—'but of course, you know that, dear Livia.' Dinner was simple but ceremonious in a domestic way, with several more of the family and their friends gathered to celebrate her return. It was good to fall asleep knowing that the big quiet house was filled with other sleepers. Outdoors didn't impinge on the inhabitants of this solid place. There was no north wind worrying at the windows, no roaring water or wild animal barks and screeches. A fountain played at a steady pace, unlike the changeable temperament of her beck. Civilisation had a lot going for it. When Olivia woke it was after eight and she had no memories of dreams.

Giulia took her shopping after breakfast. She had errands on the outskirts and then they decided to enjoy the Lungarno like tourists, lunching by the Ponte Vecchio and spending time in clothes shops. Fred's mother, in her sixties, cut an elegant figure. Olivia hoped she would age as well herself, but doubted it. You had to concentrate on *la bella figura*, not take your eye off the fat ball. That sculpted hair and expensive heels were inconsistent with almost everything she most liked to do. It was a relief when, at the villa that afternoon, Giulia put on boots and gardening gloves and invited Olivia to give her a hand in the vegetable garden that stepped downhill in green terraces below the house. Head down, weeding with her busy fork between prickly globe artichoke plants, Giulia drew Olivia out on her life in Yorkshire, praised her loyalty to Fred's mission, her enterprise and courage. She spoke of Fred's childhood, sharing anecdotes of his babyhood and schooldays, and Olivia related stories of their meeting at the Archaeological Society lecture, their subsequent courtship, even how she'd fallen in love with Frederico—though she didn't mention that abandoned first dinner. She told her one-time mother-in-law of her plan to revisit Trebbia to remember the time she'd been there with Freddie.

Giulia made no reply but gathered the weeds she'd dug out into a bucket, stood, and looked down at Olivia still diligently rooting in the artichoke bed. 'I try not to think about him at all, Olivia. I have accepted our Frederico is dead. He won't come back, we have our lives to live and enjoy. How old are you now?'

Next September would be the big birthday. Olivia didn't like to think about it. Thirty, she admitted.

'We have biological clocks, we women. Don't throw your life away. We have both grieved, you and I, but we are alive, we have feelings, possibilities to be happy. After a year, do you not sometimes forget and feel happy?'

'Perhaps I won't go to visit Trebbia after all.' Something lightened inside Olivia. 'Frederico gave me the inspiration to start out at Oxhide. And the means. Perhaps I have got things wrong, got a bit morbid. You're right, Giulia. I should remember Frederico as spirit rather than ghost.'

'You are just lonely, Livia. I'm going to come and stay with you, and you will hold a party for me. Don't tell me you have no admirers. The mysterious queen, alone on her hill, in her stone house like a castle—you must be a legend, the boys of Yorkshire must think of no one else!'

'They do gossip about me, I know. And I have someone coming to see me—a famous TV presenter, a scientist, interested in the farm.'

Giulia had a searching gaze. Olivia flushed, then laughed it off. She explained all about Andrew's visit, the dinner, Julian, their scientific plans and their luck in winning funding for research. Immersed in Oxhide's future, they tidied the weeding things and went for a stroll round the garden. Spring was much further on here than in the north of England. A pair of goldfinches chirped in the olive trees and the orchard grass was full of wild plants in flower, yellow and white and blue. When they returned to the villa, Giulia fetched Olivia a pile of books about Italian Renaissance gardens to imitate in Wharfedale, and Olivia promised to send Giulia a link to a podcast of Andrew Bamberg's *Invisible Wildlife*. Olivia even shared with her mother-in-law the difficulties she'd had with unfriendly local gossip, the gangs of demolition men and cheeky builders.

'You have to be the boss,' was Giulia's advice. 'It is you who must tell them what to do. Be there. Have you got a site office? You must have a site office. Make visitors report to you. Check the accounts—and keep back five percent until the job is finished to your satisfaction. That's what we do. They will, as you say, take liberties. Livia, have you a yellow hat?' And, laughing at Olivia's blank look. 'A hard hat. A hard yellow hat and labourer's boots. In between, elegance, a trouser suit, but feminine. Then you will look like the captain. Do that, I tell you it will make a difference. Remember who you are, Livia. When I come to see you, it will be a royal visit.'

As the plane descended towards Stansted, Olivia craned across the window at the farmland of Essex appearing through its veil of cloud. Soon you could make out the pattern of fields and often the ancient boundary of a holding, with its farmhouse in the middle. Then the field colours developed as the plane came closer to land—the nitrate-glutted blue-green monotone of wheat drilled in big rectangular fields, where only a paler stain in the crop showed the lost networks of cart tracks and footpaths. Around the big houses stood cars, paddocks with horses and jumps, sometimes swimming pools. As the plane lost height, fields gave to the purplish-grey of toy houses, close-packed in lines and crescents, and finally the familiar car parks. Then they were bouncing along the runway. Her country, the United Kingdom, surely deserved better; woods and pastures, cattle and sheep, public paths and hay-filled barns; the lost country of children's books, that had all but vanished in these southern arable lands under subsidised industrial chemicals and contractors' cash crops. There was a better way. She and Andrew would lead the green counter-revolution.

Olivia felt renewed and empowered by her days at Torralba with Giulia. Admittedly some of that holiday energy drained away at the terminal, and in the crowded delayed train to Leeds, but the conversation with Freddie's mother had freed her from an imaginary haunting that she now realised had come, not from any lingering ghost Freddie, but inside her troubled brain. She was regaining her libido, mojo, vim—whatever made life worthwhile. Excitement, not misgiving, stirred at the thought of the work ahead.

She had the Site Office set up at the rear entrance to the farm yard, where the track from the Robertshaws' farm reached Oxhide. This had a gentler gradient than the track from the road, and no stone gateposts to impede large loads. The Site Office had a prominent notice on its door telling visitors to report here. Inside were the components of an office: electrical and Ethernet connection, LED lighting, filing cabinets, a shelf of lever arch binders; a year-at-a glance laminated calendar, a week-to-view A4 desk diary and desktop computer with heavy duty printer. Two office chairs faced each other across a grey metal desk, the bigger one hers. Her new yellow hard hat and hi-vis waterproof hung on a hook on the back of the door.

Twice a week, they would have a site meeting, she told the builder, and copied in the quantity surveyor in a confirming email. Perhaps she should include Giles—she was still thinking about how to be fairer to him after that embarrassing scene with Mrs. Yarker—but decided on balance to find another way to provide him with a more formal job. She set up a meeting with a representative of the Dales National Park to get updated on regulations. The plans were displayed on a cork pinboard with copies in wide flat drawers under the desk. Only the stone dairy and the newish Dutch barn Mike had put up three years ago, would remain in the new scheme of farm buildings. The collapsing cart shed beside the track to Robertshaws' would provide the footprint for two rentable cottages.

She let Joe and Jane know the start date for building, hoping to see them as soon as they were free to visit and advise. Jane had recommended extra accommodation, and after a chat to the architect Olivia was excited by the idea of building into an old lime quarry behind the farm, to produce two deceptively large but unobtrusive apartments with a view across the dale over the farm roof. The old cowshed would make a communal space for teaching environmental science and geography A-level students, and might also include lab space for the *Invisible Wildlife* project, as she now called her planned work with Andrew. She jotted a further list of 'nice-to-have' additions as the years went on: 'hospitality (pods in the stone field barns), riding and walking trails, parking; education (schools lab., dormitory, small conference and display room, video theatre). Display space for products—wool, traceable mutton; Belties??? (keep old cowshed, storage freezer, place for packing; feed stores, barn). Eco credentials; (small wind turbines, satellite communications, solar

panels on house roof. NO Archimedes screw in the beck).
NB—Sight lines from the road uncluttered.'

Then she thought about the road signage. Some farms had cut-
out iron signs, and others, business-like notices—these usually
announced partnerships between farms. Alone in the as-yet-
empty site, Olivia doodled on the first page of her building
journal. 'Olivia Gabrieli: Oxhide Farm. XXX Swaledales'—she
would need a name for her herd as her reputation grew. Gabrieli
and Bamberg Farm Partnership. Oxhide Swaledales: Olivia and
Andrew Bamberg. The fantasy perceptibly raised her pulse. She
turned on the lights, tore the page from the diary and stuffed it
into her pocket to dispose of safely in the farmhouse range.

Two weeks later work was underway and the bare ground
marked with orange-topped pegs and string, ready to pour the
slabs for the footings. Olivia added photographs to her journal for
posterity, and patrolled the area each afternoon as soon as work
stopped.

She was wrestling with a desire to phone Andrew; not about
anything, just to hear his voice. His image kept popping up in her
mind; she was almost verging on the obsessive. This was no start
to an objective scientific collaboration. It was what her father had
seen coming. She tried to focus on his warnings. A *consensus ad
idem*. She could not say that Andrew Bamberg had shown any
sign of passion towards her. He had kissed her on the cheek,
held her hand, because he was naturally charming, enthusiastic,
appreciative; it wasn't his fault he was handsome, a celebrity with
an impressive record and moving history. She must not embarrass
him. She must not embarrass herself. Officially she was in
permanent mourning for her dead husband. That was the myth of
the mysterious lady of Oxhide.

If only there was a pill to suppress desire. An emotional
contraceptive. Maybe there were calming herbs? Pippa was the
nearest to a wise woman Olivia knew. It was embarrassing,
shaming even, to bother her when Pippa had her own

preoccupations, being only a week from her due date. But that afternoon Olivia drove to the Doctors' House.

Pippa was in bed. Not ill, she insisted, but obeying orders. She lay among pillows and bright blankets with magazines strewn around, her knitting on the bedside table, TV set at the end of the bed. High blood pressure, she explained. Olivia knew about that. She suppressed the old ache, the imagined toddler with Fred's dark eyes, who should now have been playing round her feet. Pippa said she'd have been shoved into the hospital if she hadn't had Mark on hand and the surgery next door. Nothing to do but lie here being monitored, hopefully not for more than a few days. They'd probably induce labour soon and she'd be a free woman again, a mobile mummy complete with pram and car seat. Olivia put her bunch of budding red and purple anemones into a vase. She made tea as Pippa requested, brought the tray into the bedroom, poured them each a cup, and obeyed Pippa's invitation to sit in a big orange armchair under the window.

Everything was so bright and new, Pippa so calm and cheerful and grounded. Olivia felt restored to escape here from her febrile isolation at Oxhide, holding court with architects and builders, amid the roar and churn of diggers, skips, demolition lorries, cement lorries, bricklayers, scaffolders, roofers; all the while keeping track of accounts, orders and deliveries. She had set the whole thing in motion, but events still occasionally threatened to engulf her.

Olivia rebuked herself for selfishness. Why should she expect Pippa, who lay there quietly achieving the greatest project of all, to take seriously her self-indulgent recital of an imaginary problem. But Pippa was bored, she told Olivia, and eager for news. How were things with Andrew? It was obvious she meant personally, she wasn't asking about advances in microbiology.

'I bet you're pleased we went to his lecture last autumn! It was killing the way he pretended he thought you were Nicole

Kidman!' Pippa burst into such giggles she had to quickly put down her full mug.

Tears started to Olivia's eyes, spilled down her cheeks. Pippa's expression switched from hilarity to concern. 'Dear Liv! Oh no! Tell me, quickly, what's happened?' Pippa pulled a tissue from a box beside the bed and proffered it.

'Andrew . . .' She couldn't go on. Pippa waited. 'He brought me a microscope!'

Pippa held out her arms. 'Nothing's this bad. Tell me.'

'I've got a thing about him. I can't seem to shake it. I keep thinking about him in a stupid obsessive sort of way.'

Pippa's blue eyes stared at her, then the corners of her mouth curled. 'Haven't we all? You've been overdoing it, Liv. These things pass. You must have had these feelings for people. You keep them under wraps, they pass.'

'It stops me sleeping, I can't concentrate, I don't seem to be able to think of anything else. I'm supposed to be in charge of a building project and I keep forgetting what's supposed to be happening next.' Olivia appealed to Pippa's professional knowledge. 'Is there some pill? I feel I'm losing my grip.'

'What's Andrew done?'

'Nothing. That's the problem. It's just me. I wish he *would* do something, but I'm afraid it's all me deluding myself. Remember how I worshipped him from afar, when we watched *Invisible Wildlife*, before we'd even met? I hate feeling this way, I swore I never would fall in love again, that I'd focus on Oxhide. If I can't stay true to my own mission, who am I?'

Pippa propped herself up against the headboard, folded her hands on her bump and considered. 'I don't understand. Why don't *you* do something? Phone him, pay a visit. Is this about honouring Freddie's memory? Freddie's gone, Liv.'

Olivia knew her sense of Freddie was fading. Giulia Gabrieli, Fred's own mother, had given her permission to love again. It was as if Freddie had become a shadow, moving steadily away, into the dark. A Christian like Jane, with faith in an afterlife, would say he existed, but somewhere else where there was no giving in marriage.

Pippa's friendly grin had firmed into a neutral professional expression. 'Look, Liv, it's not an illness, falling for people. We've all been there. You're overwrought, upset. Freshen the pot, would you? The chap in here is kicking me in an odd place.'

So it was a chap, a boy. Lucky Pippa.

Nurses don't deal in existential terror. Their power lies in *'the kind of love called maintenance'*. Smooth sheets, calm attention to disgusting wounds and private functions, unflappability, confident application of simple remedies. Life, normal life, was worth living. The simple pleasure of tea. The morning star, the wind in your hair. Pippa smiled at her over her cup. Anguish relaxed its grip on Olivia's wits.

'Don't let this craziness spoil your life, Liv. Mark and I were really pleased you and Andy hit it off. Anybody else would see it's a fairy tale come true. You two meeting, at just this time, right for both of you. And now! To be able to work with him! You told us your dream was running a scientific model farm—though actually Mark told me in confidence he thought your castles in the air were impossible. But then this money comes along, so Andy can do boffiny stuff with you in your farmyard—it's like a godsend!'

'Does he talk to you and Mark about me?'

'You fascinate him, Liv. He says how he admires you. If you saw more of each other, who knows what might happen. The ball's in your court, you have to admit you're available, let yourself off this vow of chastity or whatever. He's probably respecting that. Oh Liv, don't throw your life away. Go for it!'

On the drive home Olivia stopped the car on the moor edge by Embsay to get out and enjoy the May evening. A pee-wit screamed from a field, urgently distracting her from its nest. Everything smelt of new life and hope, Nature was on her side now. Surely it was wrong to call this the pathetic fallacy. We are all one breath; of course, we have empathy with other creatures. She smiled; she'd been in love with Andrew Bamberg since last autumn, and now spring was here.

Later that same evening, as she made herself bacon and eggs for supper, Mark phoned to say that labour had started and they were on their way to hospital in Skipton.

19

Up and Running

Olivia paid to park the car at the station, so she could wait for Andrew by the ticket barrier. There he was, walking fast, looking around. As soon as she caught sight of him, her heart stopped and restarted with a thump. He put his rucksack on the concourse and kissed her on both cheeks, quickly, one and then the other. His smell was fresh and familiar. She stepped back and he hoicked the rucksack over one shoulder and urged her to go first with a hand placed lightly between her shoulder blades. It seemed to her that with these social gestures he gently suggested more.

Because he planned to come to work at Oxhide regularly through the summer, bringing the awkward Julian along, Andrew had rented a flat in Grassington, complete with bicycle. The cowshed lab had been completed to schedule on the last day of April, and now it was time to receive and install equipment that had been on order since news of the grant. Soon they'd be ready to work in earnest. Andrew asked her to put him down at his lodgings, gave her the address, and they arranged for him come to Oxhide the next morning. He insisted on cycling—he would enjoy it, he said. He had decided to go with Mark to collect second-hand equipment from a former colleague who worked at Lancaster, the far side of the Pennine ridge.

They chose a day when Mark and his big car would be available. Olivia was happy to sit in the back while Andrew and Mark chatted, mainly about their sons: Julian, about to start sixth form, and Mark's baby son now already weighing over nine pounds. Julian was going to work on bioinformatics in America, if he didn't decide on music. The baby would be the third generation of Foremans to practise medicine. Olivia noticed how the curl of dark hair lay on Andrew's neck, just above his shirt collar; it was endearing and distinguished, far more refined than Mark's mouse-coloured mop. Staring at it did funny things to her breathing and pulse. Imagine having a little boy with a dark curl like that. *Oh, stop it!*

Built during the sixties expansion of higher education and sited to regenerate a former industrial town, the Lancaster University campus lay draped over a windswept hill, low-rise functional buildings, dominated by the bulk of a sympathetically-restored nineteenth century warehouse. They circled the campus with its duckpond, small copses of birch and alder penetrated by informal paths, desire-lines made by hurrying students. Prickly thickets only partly concealed refuse bins and utility service points. It looked confusing, but Andrew soon homed in on the Applied Sciences block.

'It's easy. Biology buildings always have glasshouses on the roof,' he said, and sure enough a greenish light shone against the grey sky.

Andrew explained that Russell, whom he'd known since student days, had started up his molecular genetics department twenty years previously. He met them in the reception area, greeting Andrew as an old friend, and smilingly shaking hands. Stocky and ponytailed, with a midlands accent and frequent loud laugh, he was more like a gang leader than the head of a University department and Fellow of the Royal Society. He offered them coffee but Olivia wanted to go straight to the lab to see what went on there. The terse technical descriptions in Andrew's papers had meant nothing to her in terms of the hands-on work. Russell understood. His technician was standing ready to show them the serviceable equipment he'd lately replaced with more state-of-the-art stuff.

Russell's lab was like the kitchen of a hygiene-obsessed chef, with white worktops and rows of sparkling blue and red-stoppered bottles on shelves, expensively streamlined appliances and washable flooring.

'Okay, Jilly, show them the car boot sale.'

Jilly, his technician, a girl of about eighteen, had lined everything for them, in the order it would be used. Andrew explained each one to Olivia. First, a small vortex mixer, a water bath and a microcentrifuge for extracting DNA from soil. Then PCR machines, to purify the parts of the DNA needed to identify them. There were also two gel tanks with electrical power supplies, for separating DNA fragments of different lengths on gels, and a system for photographing the gels under ultraviolet light to make the DNA show up.

'You must have a test-drive. We're all above-board here,' said Russell with his bark of laughter. 'No damaged goods. Jilly'll stick a gel in, run it for you, you can see it fizz. Do a demo, Jilly, will you. Okay, Jill?'

Jilly giggled. 'The students used it all last year. You can see it running, then I'll pack it up for you.' She seemed more like a student herself, inexplicably confident about such complicated manoeuvres. While she got things set up, Russell toured them round his department. He had a role rather like a ship's captain, jollying the crew but keeping them in line; bringing home the prizes—significant discoveries, big research grants, international fame celebrated in smartly presented posters along the corridor walls. He had started in the Merchant Navy, Andrew told her. Just the right experience, she supposed, for such teamwork, every member with a different job, but the enterprise going nowhere without a captain. And, like the crew of a ship, they jointly faced unpredictable forces: politicians, global economics, research councils, vice-chancellors, journal editors, even the climate of popular opinion, making the weather in which they voyaged to discoveries, or foundered.

Jilly had everything on the bench and switched the power on. Andrew carefully looked over each bit of apparatus and got Jilly to go over details of their operation for Olivia. He outlined the Oxhide plan to Russell.

'No shit!' said Russell with his reflex bark of laughter. 'Molecular diagnostics in the wilds? Crazy! Crazy, but cool. Count us in!'

When the demonstration was finished, Jilly switched off the power, tipped the water out of the gel tank, got the instruction manuals out of a labelled file and handed them to Andrew in a large envelope.

'Yeah, crazy but cool is right,' Andrew said, grinning at Jilly who responded with a cheerful giggle. Olivia wondered if she had been one of the occasional girlfriends Pippa mentioned, who sometimes stayed over at Stockholm Street. Jilly made her feel a bit ill. She was glad when they were on the road back to her Oxhide. Andrew drove, with Mark beside him, while Olivia sat steadying the boxes of apparatus beside her on the back seat, watching for curlew and trying to close her ears to their banter about old college friends and girlfriends, commenting on Jilly's attractiveness, and other matters that pre-dated Olivia's acquaintance with either of them. It was unfair to feel so jealous. Sharing the back seat with the boxes of stuff brought back childhood memories; family trips up the Dales in the back of the Jaguar, sick with envy of sporty Ben for being their parents' favourite.

The landscape scrolled by as she mentally went over all she'd need to learn, trying to remember the point of each of the elaborate procedures that bloody Jilly knew so well. Really, it was just cooking, but with invisible ingredients in dolls-house mixing bowls. You had to have faith that the molecules you hoped you isolated were still there, while you mixed and blended and separated them in tubes that appeared empty throughout. All you were doing, she realised, was extracting the invisible DNA molecules from a sample of soil, snipping out the particular sequence that was basically a barcode of the species it came from, and bulking just up that bit and no other, until there was enough of the one identifying DNA sequence, to be sieved out on a gel to give a DNA fingerprint, or analysed in Russell's DNA sequencing machine. And all that Russell's clever sequencer did was give you a read-out of the sequences in the sample. You could then identify them against the databases of what had already been found and named. It was exciting if there was no known match. It could mean you'd discovered something new. But also that the databases might be wrong. This was the sciency stuff they'd be doing in the Oxhide lab, and it was so simple, Andrew said, that she could offer molecular ecology projects for A-level students, if she wanted to earn educational kudos for Oxhide.

The challenging bit would be later—analysing and comparing sequences with complex computer programmes that told you why your organism grew where you'd found it, how it had evolved to live there, what it fed on, how its activities affected others, for better or worse. This was the part Andrew said he hoped Julian would do, being mathematically gifted; it would be a chance for him to learn on the job, fantastic work experience to help him with university admissions. With luck, Julian would have his name on a paper before his eighteenth birthday.

They crested the moorland ridge above Ramsgill, as rain clouds thinned and the top of Wharfedale came into view, snaking away below. When she opened the window to smell the air, the tyres swished on the wet road, and tormentil shone golden-green along the sheep-cropped verges. The next day would be exciting.

In the course of the following weeks, results emerged: the DNA fingerprints of the invisible wildlife underfoot in the moors and meadows of Oxhide. The force of their shared purpose generated a strange electricity around them as they pipetted and centrifuged and labelled the rows and rows of tubes. Things had changed, there was trust and excitement. They discovered not only uncommon species, but evidence for a major group of ancient microbes from deep peat samples. Andrew said they should go beyond simple identification and see what kind of metabolic apparatus there was in these unknown bugs. They seemed to manage without oxygen—where did they get their energy from?

Sitting out in the evenings after work, gazing unfocussed at the ash woods across the valley, and the pale limestone scree above, became a special moment in Olivia's day, a moment for exploring the events that brought each of their lives to meet. For the first time since the accident, Olivia found it possible to talk about Freddie without breaking down. She talked about Torralba and the Gabrielis, about Freddie speaking in Cambridge and sweeping her off her feet, and it was okay to laugh. Andrew told the story of Cressida, how news of her death had reached him, and Mark had helped him then, making arrangements to look after baby Julian, and later Pippa too, when she and Mark became a couple.

One effect of the new activity at Oxhide was that communications with the outside world became routine. Even snail mail arrived regularly, the postman's red van managing the resurfaced track once or twice a week. And one day an email message made him yelp. It was from his American collaborators in San Francisco, he told her, printing the letter. They wanted to add Oxhide to their worldwide list of sites for *a microbial community audit, using new computational tools for symbiotic network analysis.* Oxhide would be even better for this, apparently, than the Amish lands in Indiana they were using. Their research needed traditionally farmed soil with well documented management, and no intensive interventions. Not only had Upper Wharfedale been farmed for thousands of years, it had the added attraction of two sharply-contrasted types of bedrock, alkaline limestone and its cap of acid millstone grit.

'It's amazing how the people have been here so long,' They were working side by side at the bench. 'Right back to that neolithic woman in her cave. They thought she'd probably been growing some kind of cereal, too, her teeth were worn down, they thought it must be with grit from milling corn. Poor woman, in a cave, eating gritty porridge year after year.'

'Though some of them went on long journeys,' Olivia said. The long-distance path, the Saltergate, had been a packhorse trail, the equivalent of a motorway in mediaeval Yorkshire. A cattle drover the original Eddie Stobart driver.

'I'd have been one of those long-distance men. I'm a footloose sort of beggar, Olivia.'

'Me too. Look at me, turning myself into an Italian.'

'But you're rooted here now. You come from deep-rooting stock. I bet you'd have stuck it out in the Neolithic. I'm just a blow-in clockmaker from the Teutonic forests. Here today, gone tomorrow. It takes all sorts, you know?'

She laughed. Without knowing why she was so sure, she knew he'd stay.

'Moment of truth,' said Andrew the following week. 'Click there, there, now on that.'

Olivia sat at the keyboard, Andrew stood behind, directing the BLAST search to identify sequences.

'Which first?'

'Low Field samples.'

She cut and pasted the first sequence into the GenBank search box and pressed 'submit'. 'Your job is being processed,' said the computer.

He leaned to peer at rows of text on the monitor, giving off a faint scent of laundered cotton with herbal undertones, his cheek temptingly close to her shoulder.

'Ha—here come your matches.'

She read out the name from the screen. '*Hygrophorus psittacinus*? What's that? The parrot-like water carrier?'

'You're a classicist! Yes, the Parrot Waxcap. Great, that figures.

At least it's not palm trees or salmon. Must look out for them in the field, lovely little bright-coloured toadstools.'

'I haven't noticed them.'

'The fungus could be helping your grass without sending up any toadstools. That's the joy of identifying DNA in the soil, you can find important things that don't show.'

An extraordinary idea, the earth underfoot a hive of activity, if only you knew how to look. Humans were so prejudiced, size-ist. It was wrong, how people stereotyped microbes as mere bugs or critters.

'It's good news,' said Andrew. Waxcap fungi only survive in old pasture. They're a sign that the soil's alive, full of mycorrhiza to scavenge nutrients for their plant friends. And, even better, some waxcap grassland's protected under law, so nobody's allowed to plough up that pasture. Tell that to your Yarker neighbours. Next?'

He leaned forward again to watch the screen, as she cut and pasted in another sequence. How odd to think of their data winging their way across the world, interpreted in San Francisco for the two of them here in Upper Wharfedale. In minutes, the details of Oxhide's invisible wildlife skimmed like Ariel across an ocean and a continent.

20

The Shake Hole

Next morning they were out soil sampling again and Giles was coming to help. It was a relief to have this buy-in from him. He was all energy and good cheer, loading up the Land Rover for their work on the moor.

The new lab had a separate 'dirty' section, a separate lean-to at the back of the main building, which Olivia had had thrown up from rendered breeze-block when Andrew explained you couldn't bring field samples straight to a sterile environment. It would be like going into an operating theatre in muddy boots. Just one spore drifting on to one of his sterile tubes could wreck days of work. There had to be this sort of garden shed to keep those not particularly scientific-looking things for taking samples of soil from around the area: spades and trugs and buckets and flagged poles and hundred-metre tape measures and coulter counters and screw-top tins and bottles and racks to hold them, sticky-backed labels and magic markers and string and scissors and a shelf of grubby notebooks in which irreplaceable primary data had been scrawled in all kinds of weather by muddy hands. There was a cold tap, a big sink and bins for discarded mud and vegetation. A chest freezer was for multiple soil samples in labelled polythene bags and even the occasional dead animal.

She'd entrusted the care of this room to Giles, who now stood at its open door, leaning against the wall in the sun and lighting up. She was sure she'd asked nobody to smoke around the farm but Giles had decided it was okay in this straw-free place out of sight of the main house and yard. He had her gorgeous new Land Rover drawn up ready in the sunshine with the top off.

'Morning, Olivia. All ready for the great man?'

Olivia threw two picnic cool bags she'd carried into the back of the vehicle and covered them with a tartan rug. It was an outing, and Anne and Giles deserved a day like this on the open moor. They'd been days sampling dull fields, wet stream-sides, bogs, the slurry pit, the turnip field, the Yarkers' bullock pen. They'd travelled fifty miles to various depressing places in the pesticide deserts of arable land beyond the A1, predicted by Andrew to be free of anything interesting and therefore a useful comparison. Anne had made a special picnic, and Giles, in a white shirt and leather work boots, looked dressed for a day out.

Olivia powered off up the moor track with Andrew at her side, and Giles and Anne, with the puppy Moss and old Tess in the back, cracking jokes. A cuckoo called, quite close. She bounced deliberately over rocks and potholes. Anne, clinging to the thin-cushioned metal bench seats, gave little shrieks and clutched Giles to save herself from falling into the foot well.

'So where do we go first?' Andrew shouted.

'Let's go up on the top,' said Olivia. 'Right up beyond Foxup on to the heather. I want to hear curlews.'

'Aye, by Churn Milk Holes,' said Giles. 'Those shake holes, by old Cam High Road.'

'Yes,' said Anne, 'grand place, those shake holes.' She and Giles laughed.

They drove on for another half mile or so and reached the top of the Pennine watershed from where the sea of dark heather spread out. The long-distance path to Carlisle ran away to the horizon but no other route, path or road was visible. There were no walls. In the middle distance some remains of one of the abandoned lead mines showed as a bare patch, a small pile of mine tailings and a partly collapsed ventilation shaft like a squat factory chimney. Otherwise there was no sign of human buildings or activity. Two sheep with nearly full- grown lambs raised their heads to take a calm look at the Land Rover. To their right a line of recently-repaired shooting butts stretched away and a grouse rose from the heather clucked *g'back g'back g'back*.

When Andrew cut the engine and their ears became accustomed to the relative silence Olivia realized the air was full of the twitter of meadow pipits. She looked around.

Andrew wasted no time on birdwatching but cut to the microbiological chase. He jumped out holding the white rolled-up sheet of a map and unrolled it on the hot bonnet of the vehicle. 'We'll do the usual hundred-metre random transects in this area. See, this is that little hill, and there are three sink holes there. Let's say transects here and here and here.' He drew five spaced-out lines in pencil on the map and lettered them A, B, C, D and E. 'Olivia and I will do A and B, and Giles, will you and Anne do C, D and E?'

'Why more for us?' said Giles.

'You're younger.' Andrew counted the necessary sample bottles, markers and clipboard into his old alpine rucksack, quickly, like a seasoned player dealing cards. Picking up the long steel soil corer from the back of the car he waited for Olivia to collect her stuff. 'I wonder what we'll find. Peat's so ignored. People think it's just an inert preservative for pollen grains and wizened Neolithic corpses. It looks as though it may have the most amazing life—protozoa, acid-adapted, anaerobic ones, and fungi, forced into all sorts of weird symbioses, who knows?' He smiled his smile again, dark hair blowing across his eyes, his rucksack slung by one strap over a lean shoulder.

He reminded Olivia of Freddie, on Barden Moor the summer

before her wedding. The *déjà vu* was so strong, something within stirred and she almost reached out to touch him.

He picked up a bundle of short canes with orange pennants from the back of the car and they set off to lay out the line of the first transect, accompanied by the chinking of collecting tins in the rucksack, occasional gritty footsteps as a boot ground into the sandy soil between the heather bushes and, yes, there it was—the lonely cry of a curlew.

Andrew anchored one end of the hundred-metre tape with a big stone and walked away unrolling the tape to its full extent and fixing the other end with another stone. He came back and handed her a bundle of ten of the flagged poles he'd been carrying, for her to stick in at ten metre intervals. The ground was spongy and yielding and the job was soon done. Then he gave her a bag full of tins and picked up the steel corer.

They worked together for about an hour, collecting ten peat cores at each flag.

The peat was black and sticky, difficult to sample because it had to be pushed out through the corer and bits of it stuck and crumbled so that Andrew couldn't always get a nice clean cylinder to fall neatly into every tin. Olivia, feeling cold despite the April sunshine, held the labelled tins as Andrew plunged the corer in ten times at each flagged sample site and extruded the black cylinders of peat into each one.

'Pretty much the same, aren't they?' Andrew stretched his back and smiled at her. 'It's worth it, though, doing all these replicates. So tantalizing when you know there's a trend but it's lost in the noise.'

'Mmmm,' said Olivia, unsure how more samples would lessen the noise. His meaning was lost on her; she had been listening to his voice rather than the words. She pictured the tins jostling in the rucksack, clamouring to be noticed. She labelled another.

They worked on for a further three quarters of an hour.

'That's it,' he said, when finally they reached the end of line B. 'Let's take a break. Show me one of these shake hole things.'

He picked up the corer and his rucksack to move on across the sampling area. Tramping through the scratchy heather, still winter-dark, with last summers' flowers hanging on, dry and grey, they came on a bowl-shaped hollow about fifty yards in diameter, like a gigantic shallow-sided pudding basin. Tormentil and eyebright shone from its bright green grass floor like a foretaste of summer.

'Rather like a nest,' said Andrew. 'Is this it?'

'Yes. The limestone underneath gets dissolved away and the surface falls in.' 'It hasn't fallen far. We ought to sample this I think, don't you?'

'Yes, maybe.' She looked into the hollow. Her heart felt as though its beating must show.

Andrew ran down the short slope to a patch of short grass at the bottom of the sinkhole and looked up at her, smiling. 'How many samples should we take here do you think? A hundred? Two hundred. No, say two hundred and fifty.'

As she ran down the slope into the little amphitheatre, the distant view disappeared and it felt as though they were held there with the sky an infinite lid, pale at the edges but deep blue above. The sun was warm out of the wind. Andrew flopped on the grass bank and lay gazing up at the sky as if exhausted. He was older, she should have thought about that. Forty two. She bent to unpack the equipment again in preparation for yet more soil coring. She was scuffling for still-empty tins in the rucksack and had laid a dozen on a patch of sheep-nibbled grass when she heard Andrew snort with suppressed laughter.

'You believed me! Two hundred and fifty? You didn't really?'

Lying there, he reached a hand and drew her down. She resisted slightly, until she realised he wasn't laughing any more. Then she gave way and their lips met. The longed-for moment expanded, the outside world fell away, and it was as though the sink hole was the portal to another dimension. It could have lasted seconds or minutes, she couldn't remember.

'I've been wanting to do that for a long time. Ah, Olivia!'

'Oh Andrew!'

It was like being a teenager again. But they weren't teenagers. They walked hand in hand back to where the Land Rover waited and Anne and Giles were unpacking for lunch. Appearing as a couple didn't disturb the dynamic of the group—if anything had changed, it was that Olivia's open endorsement made Andrew one of them, accessible, no longer the awe-inspiring scientist from London. Only Giles seemed a bit silent on the drive home.

'I love those shake holes,' Anne said that evening, as she and Olivia washed and put away the picnic things in the kitchen. 'I had my first kiss in one. You go for a hike over the moors, you can see for miles, and then there's that little private space where nobody can see you. *Ilkla Moor bah't 'at.* The trouble is everyone knows what happens, they run up and peep in.'

'You are a witch, Anne.'

21

Wild Swimming

Olivia woke at first light, about four, on fire with expectation, wondering what the new day would bring. Things between Andrew and her had changed—but how?

At six, the sun already up, but before he had pedalled up from Grassington on his bike, she took the lab key from its hook on the dresser and went into the side office where he did his writing and they kept a steadily-accumulating shelf of field and lab notebooks. Yesterday's notebook was on the desk beside the computer, her neat columns of pencilled numbers and notes, the irreplaceable first-hand dated records of every sample they'd collected together; over more than four weeks' work; the raw data for their first publication. The work that might be published under their joint names, together with a British University and an American Institute; that would also bear the name Oxhide. There were famous examples of husband and wife teams in science, weren't there?

She brought herself back to earth by focussing on the huge pinned-up OS map now covered in coloured pins marking every site they'd sampled.

The last entry was dated yesterday and brought back the sensation of scribbling on the pressed-open page, bending over to lean it on one knee, or crouched over the pages flattened on a rock. Earthy smudges reminded her of that first gold-edged invitation to the momentous party at The Trojans Bar, opening it in the field under Giles's eye, the postman's van paused in the lane below Oxhide. Here and there Andrew had added an annotation to her numbers in his fluent spidery hand.

Olivia sat at the desk, switched on the computer and placed their notebook beside it. There'd be time to type some of the data into a spreadsheet before he arrived at nine. But her mind was still exploding with yesterday, however hard she stared at the notebook and told herself to get to work. The way he formed his letters was somehow of more interest, the distinctive looped capital P. Schoolgirl-like, she tried imitating it. Then there was a lovely line of birdsong outside that might be a black cap, so she had to look out the window to see.

Concentration was impossible. Mechanically, she forced herself to transcribe figures from the notebook into the top row, one row per sample, a column for each site. She stuck at it, like a camp-follower knitting socks for her absent soldier, all the rows complete and no dropped stitches. At last she could back up the file and close the machine.

As she left the little building the beck seemed to call her. Had her Dad really bathed there in his youth? She smiled at the absurd thought of Joe and Jane as daring teenagers. The limestone basin looked like a wild bath, replenished from a cold tap of moor water falling in from the top of the stone ledge above. It looked terribly cold, but some people did wild swimming all year round; the shock of cold couldn't be dangerous. A dip in that clear pool would be refreshing after the Excel files, and a chance to try those enormous stripy towels she'd got for the guest room. Olivia ran across the yard, inside and upstairs, and ripped one from its packaging. There was still nobody around and the birds sang harder than ever.

The towel over her arm, she swung down by a tree branch until she stood on the edge of the deep pool, overhung by tufts of grass and newly-unfurling spring fronds of royal fern. Quickly, before she could think better, Olivia took off her clothes and stood on the mossy bank, soft and cold under her bare feet, shivering as the air moved slightly over her bare white skin, turning the dark nipples pointy with surprise. She couldn't give up now. At least, once submerged in the beck, she'd be out of the wind. A shelf of limestone about a foot wide under shallow water, looked a good place from which to enter the deep pool. As she stepped on to it, her toes disappeared in a thin layer of mud with some kind of small blue-flowered plant growing in it. She crouched, hands braced on the shelf, self-consciously pre-Raphaelite, and then slid into the pool feet first. It was deeper than she'd thought, and for a panicked moment it felt as if she were sinking into some abyss; some hidden cleft in the rock would suck her into one of those underground labyrinths of potholes to churn out her remains years hence somewhere like Malham Cove; but then her foot touched a sloping rock, and then another, and after briefly submerging again she gained a foothold, kicked herself upwards and was treading water and grabbing at plants that overhung the edge. The submersion left her spluttering and breathless, but then, grabbing an overhanging branch she let herself float Ophelia-like in the rushing stream. Her body adjusted to the cold, and it was joyful to lie back in the pool, her winter-white legs glimmering, and to turn her face to the sunlit roof of budding ash tree branches and the blue. It was one of those moments you knew you'd remember forever, the second in only two days.

Then came a third.

A face appeared at the top of the bank. It was looking down at her, eyes shadowed under thick brows, a pale forehead and flop of dark hair. She shrieked and then recognised Andrew.

'Good idea!' he called. 'Don't get out, Olivia, you look beautiful in there among the ferns, like a water nymph. Can I come in?'

He was already descending the bank. 'It's freezing,' she warned.

He took that for permission, stripped, climbed a tree branch and let go. He sank at first as she had, then bobbed up laughing and spluttering, standing knee deep on a rock. He was hairy, lean. He had good legs. You noticed these things.

'Enough, we'll get hypothermia,' she said through chattering teeth. 'Come on, come into the house, quick.'

Wrapping herself in the towel, she held out a hand. He snatched up his shirt and trousers and tugged them on to his wet body, shuffling into shoes. *He either fears his fate too much, or his desserts are small, who dares not put it to the touch, to win, or lose it all.* It had been her mantra from childhood Pony Club days. There was nobody in the house. The builders had gone. It was Giles's day for being with his parents; Anne, too, was at the Hollies with Joe and Bridget. Only Moss would see them, and Moss liked Andrew.

She heard her own voice—almost in spite of herself. 'I think we need a nice warm bed. Don't you Andy?'

Still nobody around, as they emerged from the ghyll. Hand in hand they ran to the house and upstairs, and laughed and hugged under the new sheets and blankets until the effect of the cold bath wore off. Andrew was considerate, expert and enthusiastic. Everything worked perfectly. Afterwards they found themselves grinning like idiots.

Later that morning they enjoyed a large breakfast, and Olivia attended the sheep while Andrew went to the lab. But that evening he cycled back to his digs. They had decided not to wait to be discovered by Anne and Giles in the morning, like students having a fling. Dignity must be preserved. There might be new arrangements at Oxhide, they agreed. But people would need to be told properly.

In the late dusk, a thrush sang in the tops of the ash trees. *Kiss me, kiss me; be quick, be quick, be quick.* He sang every evening, but during the day he and his mate worked constantly, smashing snails on their anvil by the hedge, flying to and fro from the hedge with full beaks. Olivia opened her bedroom windows as far as the casements would go. It was so quiet you could hear the beck. Light was fading from the sky, the room just dark enough to need the bedside lamp. In its glow she opened a drawer and took out the little box with Freddie's emerald ring. She gazed at the green glow for a long moment, then shut the box and stowed it at the back of the drawer, together with the wedding photo at Torralba, which she took down from beside her mirror. Then she spent a long ten minutes sitting by the open window, looking out from her bedroom over her land, at the beginnings of the river down below, and the darkening ridge of moor high above it.

This changed everything. There was no pretending nothing had happened. The absolute, overwhelming joy of their act had welded her irrevocably to her new love and reset the future. If she had ever allowed herself the thought that one day her vow to Freddie might run its course, that she might even marry again, she hadn't imagined she would jump naked into a freezing beck and immediately into bed with Andrew Bamberg.

The evening was colder, frost had been forecast. She went down to take Moss for her customary evening sniff around the inbye. 'We're going to be a family now. You like Andy, don't you? Of course you do, you're a good dog.' She ruffled the soft black and white head and Moss licked her hand and gave a discreet wag of the tail, sheepdog-style. Telling the humans that she and Andrew were together now wouldn't be so easy. She'd have to tell her father before he heard from Anne. That meant phoning first thing tomorrow—or sooner; in a heart-sink moment she realised it wasn't yet too late to ring; Joe and Bridget would be watching the ten o'clock news over a cup of tea.

'Oh my love . . . (*long pause*) . . . are you sure? Of course you are. Oh, I hope . . . (*second long pause*) . . . ah well, it's none of my business, to tell you what to do, I mean. Olivia, congratulations. On finding happiness. We must all find happiness where we can...' and the line went dead, and nobody answered when she rang back. She would try again in the morning. Perhaps that hadn't been the best way to tell him. It was upsetting that her news had shocked him so badly. What did he fear for her? It must just have been that her news reminded her Joe of his own ill-fated romance with Isobel, the youthful impulse that had swept him up, but ended with both her parents making each other miserable enough to break up their family and to send Olivia and Ben away to be educated by strangers.

She told Pippa the next day, driving over to Skipton ostensibly to get antiseptic flystrike treatment from the farm supplier. Pippa looked exhausted. Philip the baby cried all the time he wasn't feeding, she said. They sat outside on a bench at the edge of the carpark, the only outdoor space now the Doctors' House was converted for surgery purposes, and Olivia fetched coffee and biscuits. At least there was a hedge, and pots of multicolour polyanthus. Pippa settled Philip to suckle, and the baby's calmness created a small cloud of content around them. Nothing was said for a minute, while Olivia took in the baby's gentle sucking, cars on the High Street the far side of the house, and the rustle of small birds, dunnocks, hopping inside the yew hedge. Pippa divined her news before she'd framed an opening.

'Liv,' she said, 'where's your ring?'

'In my jewellery box, of course. I don't usually wear my tiara to shop for anti-maggot ointment.'

'I was being tactful,' said Pippa, 'I meant, do you still feel the same about Freddie? Still eternally faithful to his memory?'

Olivia let her gaze slide out of focus. The baby made small sounds and waved closed fists.

He looked absurdly like Mark. Pippa changed sides, fussing with her shirt, waiting for Olivia's reply.

'No, I've decided to change.' There—she had said it.

Pippa looked up from nursing and stared. She and Philip looked so sweet with their matching blue eyes.

Olivia smiled back at the baby, and went on, more easily. 'I realised something when I went to see Frederico's mother, Giulia. She was so kind, but down-to-earth. She laid down the law a bit, told me that my staying faithful to Freddie was a way of keeping hold, refusing to accept the reality of his death. I never thought of it like that. But Giulia was so sensible, so unsentimental. Freddie was her son and she has as much right to grieve as I do. More. And she more or less ordered me to move on. She said you can't cuckold a ghost. She's funny, I like her. I realised that swearing everlasting allegiance to Freddie was a self-indulgence, it would make no difference to him.'

'That's right. But it wasn't self-indulgent, Liv, it was normal. Denial is a recognised stage in grieving. And anger, too. Do you think Frederico would have approved of Andrew?' Olivia blushed. 'Yes.'

'So?'

'I don't know.'

'Marry Andy, Liv. It's the best thing for you both, I'm certain of it. Tell him.'

'We have all we want, Pippa. We are married already, in every way that matters. I'd like Andy to move in with me, I think he wants to, too. It would be just as if we were married. Second time for both of us.'

Pippa said nothing, but turned her gaze from Philip to Olivia and raised an eyebrow.

'Andy's been widowed for sixteen years, though, Liv. Don't do anything too quickly.'

'I've made my mind up.'

'Oh Liv—I'm so, so happy for you, and for him, lucky old Andrew. How did it happen? I mean. Did he propose moving in with you?' Pippa's voice betrayed her concern.

'No, I did. It seemed silly, him cycling off every evening after work. I wanted him around. It felt better.'

She went on with an edited account, starting her narrative from the day with Russell and Jilly, her feelings in the lab, reciprocated; the day on the moor, taking the plunge in the beck. And finally, about her father's dismay when she'd broached the idea of living with Andy.

'Your father is an old curmudgeon.' Pippa had listened open-mouthed to Olivia's account of falling for Andrew, with *mms* and *oohs* of sympathetic appreciation, but Joe's reaction clearly left her baffled.

But Olivia understood her father. To accept love on this scale was a risk, and for some, like Joe, too great a risk. Loss could destroy you. Nobody could understand what divorce was like, nobody who hadn't witnessed a romance turned septic, watched powerless and unnoticed from the sidelines, as love curdled to hatred and lives fell apart, overseen by the cold eyes of lawyers. Where Olivia now foresaw an island of joy, Joe imagined a tornado, torn sails, the shattered hull dismasted. But she would prove him wrong, she and Andy. On the drive back to Oxhide she put Bach's *Magnificat* on the CD player, that most beautiful affirmation of female gratitude.

'I wish that hadn't happened,' Mark said to his wife that evening, from the bath where he soaped himself and played with the plastic duck Philip had been given but wasn't yet old enough to appreciate. Pippa was towelling her hair. 'It's not a good idea. What did you say to Olivia?'

'I said, congratulations. She'd been pining for weeks. I encouraged her, it is such a shame she should keep being faithful to a memory of Frederico when she'd fallen for Andy. It is unnecessary, deliberately refusing happiness like that—I could understand it at first, but I thought she was making grieving over Frederico an excuse to retire from life. So, yes, I did encourage her to go with her feelings for Andy, once he had fallen for her too.'

'Oh he loves her all right.' Mark submerged the duck and let it bounce to the surface. 'He's always been a romantic. I am a little surprised this time, though. Olivia's been through a lot. I don't know, he may finally have found the one. Perhaps I'm inventing problems for them. I know, Pip. Why don't you have a talk with Olivia and see if she mightn't after all consider announcing her engagement and fixing a date for getting married? I don't like this "above all that" pose.'

Pippa pulled a comb through her wet hair, tugging at a knot. It was a depressing thought. And now Mark put it this way, it did seem rash for Olivia and Andrew to make such a big deal out of what should have happened lightly—a cheerful summer flirtation, not this big secret deal. It was too soon for Olivia, she could see that now. But could she, Pippa Illingworth, admonish Olivia, her posh friend who'd always been the risk-taker? Olivia and Andrew seemed to her to be the perfect couple—but maybe she'd read too many romances.

'Why don't *you* talk to Andy? He's your friend. And you know him much better than I do, or Liv. Is he really such a horrible philanderer? He and Liv seem good.'

'It's tricky. I think he's always made sure his girlfriends knew where they stood. He would love them passionately. Never for more than a year. Then he'd hear the call. It wasn't just itchy feet. It was always an idea, a new quest he couldn't refuse. He's not ordinary, Andy. Girls used to ask me, the best friend, what I thought was going on.' Mark heaved himself out of the water in a shower of splashes, seizing a towel Pippa held out. 'Okay, love, I'll do it. I'll ask my oldest friend about his intentions. I don't want to, but I will. Just for you.'

'Thank goodness I've got you. Are you really doing the two o'clock feed?'

At the Top Ladies' Tea Club in Tufton Street, Jane and Vanessa wrangled amiably about work matters and discussed where to go for the holiday they usually took together in June. Jane was for sun and sand in Cyprus, but Vanessa wanted to try Costa Rica. Cyprus was full of bird murderers and anyway she'd grown up there and knew it too well.

Jane's heart wasn't really in office gossip or holiday plans, though. She was preoccupied with a phone call she'd received from Joe Burbank yesterday evening. Somehow she had to come out with it now, or Vanessa would accuse her of concealing the inflammatory news. How to broach the unwelcome fact that her god-daughter Olivia, 'the little farmer from Yorkshire', had captured Andrew, Vanessa's greatest hope and joy? And worse, that the pair were firmly ensconced at Oxhide, and that Vanessa's son, the apple of her eye and future of her line, looked likely to end his glittering career on a remote hill farm in frozen North Yorkshire? Vanessa ought to be delighted. She was always going on about the supremacy of love and joy in that annoying way. Surely she'd be happy that her Superman Andrew had fallen for a girl as lovely and resourceful as Olivia? But Vanessa wasn't like that. 'By the way, V, have you heard? It seems our plans for the young have turned out rather well. I have to congratulate on your son's good taste.'

Vanessa, applying strawberry jam to a tiny scone, paused, knife halfway to the jam pot, and stared at her. 'What d'you mean? Andy? Of course he has good taste.'

'My *little farmer*, as you called her. My god-daughter Olivia Gabrieli. Her father phoned me, Joe Burbank—my old flame, you know—in a terrible state, last night. Olivia had rung to tell him she and Andrew were living together from now on, at that farm. She's building Andrew a lab there, for God's sake. It's not my fault. I told her in so many words, her business plan wouldn't run to rescuing sacked university lecturers.'

'So you knew it was in the wind?' Vanessa's fury showed through her elegantly made-up mask. 'Jane, Andy only left my house last weekend. He said nothing to Julian or me. How *could* he be so treacherous to me, his proper mother? And the boy—my own grandson Julian—will be devastated. He hates being cooped in that dirty little farmyard, wasting his time doing baby sums on tiny data sets, when he has his revision. *Invisible Wildlife* indeed! I've got to go, Jane, can you pay, please? That girl's not going to get away with this. *Honouring the memory of her dead husband* indeed! Spare me!'

Not much work was getting done at Oxhide this morning. Andrew carried on at his microscope, but Olivia was perplexed. How did you announce you were married without a wedding? The main question was how to tell the world about the new regime at Oxhide. Joe must have told Jane, who'd pass the news to Vanessa. Pippa would tell Mark. But what about Anne, who'd supported and encouraged her to go for it, Anne who had scratched 'O heart A' on a stone? Olivia left Andrew at the bench and walked down to Skellside.

As she expected, Anne was busy with horse work in the little run-down stable, grooming the mud-encrusted Comet. How like the Yarkers, to still have a patch of mud in May. The cob was moulting the last of his dark winter coat, showing the bright bay of summer.

'I'm keeping him here for you, Liv. You ought to get on him, you used to be such a Pony Club whizz, Daddy said. Comet's a nice little horse, better for your shepherding than a quad bike. Dreamcatcher's away getting educated, this poor chap'll be lonely if he hasn't got enough to do.' Anne picked up Moss and gently introduced him to the horse, nose to nose. 'Imagine, you with your hair loose, up on the moor, calling *come by* from the saddle! It'd make great TV.'

'Anne?'

Checked by her sister's portentous tone, Anne paused her merry banter, put the puppy down and straightened to look up over the cob's back, a hand on the muscly hind quarters. She stared at Olivia.

'Andrew and I are together.' Anne looked past her, as if for a second visitor coming through the stable door. 'Not here. I mean . . .'

'Together? Oh—as in, an *item*?' Anne lobbed the brush into a bucket of grooming stuff and flung her arms round Olivia. 'Thank goodness! We thought you never would. Oh, wow. *Wow*. Exciting!'

Uncomplicated joy lit the stable. Thank goodness for younger sisters.

22

Midsummer

It is seven o'clock on a June morning, there's a cuckoo in the trees behind the house, and Olivia is scrubbing her hands under the kitchen tap to get rid of the smell of antiseptic while Andrew at the Aga prepares three full English breakfasts. This is having it all. Giles is still in the fields, finishing the job, dagging sheepshit off woolly hindquarters and sploshing on the anti-flystrike solution. But Olivia has a job in the lab today, she and Andy are going to run gels, so they'll have to leave Giles's breakfast to keep warm for later.

'There you are, Madame Curie!' He placed a plate of bacon and eggs with a sausage and tomato in front of her on the scrubbed table. Andrew's joke is that they are doing science as a couple, like the Curies. It was sad Marie Curie died of radiation effects, but probably worth it.

'It's Julian's first maths paper today.' Andrew took his place opposite her. 'Shall I phone and wish him good luck? Maybe better not. He likes to think he'll walk it. Such confidence! I suppose I was the same.'

'When does he finish exams?'

Would Julian turn up here? That might be a problem. Presumably Andrew had told his son they were living together? Selfishly, Olivia hoped Julian would have gap year plans that wouldn't include Oxhide.

'A-level results come out on the fifteenth of August. He's predicted five starred As. Vanessa's been on at me to arrange next steps. She's a wonderful granny, he loves her. I think she's making up for neglecting me. She sees him as her second shot at parenthood.'

'Has Jules anything in mind for what to do next?'

'He wants to do an American first degree. I might ask Erik's advice—remember, that tall Scandinavian who came along when we first came here in March? He's been doing stuff in California, with people I know at UCLA.'

'That's adventurous of Julian. More coffee?'

Ashamed of feeling relieved Julian would be far from Oxhide, Olivia cleared their plates into the sink, dropped four slices of bread into the toaster and topped up Andrew's cup. Then, not wanting to be mean, she added despite herself, 'perhaps he'll come here first for a break?'

After all, if she and Andrew were as good as married, she was effectively Julian's sole aunt. 'By then we'll have finished the holiday cottages, he can try one out.'

Andrew stood, put his breakfast things in the dishwasher, and kissed her. 'You are angelic, love. I know he's an awkward beggar. It wouldn't be for long.'

They went out across the farmyard hand-in-hand, to set gels going, a now familiar routine.

It was surreal. You set out to be brave and independent, and then something wonderful happens and turns your life around. Sometimes Olivia stopped whatever she was doing— breakfast, laying out apparatus on the lab bench, moving sheep, relaxing in the evening in the sitting room—just to gaze at Andrew. When he looked up and caught her eye, they tended to end in bed. She liked to buy him little presents. He had a sweater of wiry grey Herdwick wool with an Aran pattern, which she'd seen in a shop in Skipton, and he wore on cool evenings.

One day he'd presented her with his own treasure, the facsimile of Hooke's *Micrographia*, with engravings of the remarkable microbes the pioneering microscopist had recorded in detail even three hundred years ago. Andrew said people had forgotten about these creatures, which were neither bacteria nor fungi, but had more in common with us humans. Olivia found this hard to believe, looking at the tardigrade figure. Could such weird things exist on Earth? But some of these beasts' DNA was showing up from their heather moor samples.

She came to a stage when the gels could be left to run on their own, and went back to the house for a break.

Giles was finishing his breakfast, the fried egg crinkly and dried-up. He looked slightly fed-up, too, fastidiously scraping the brown bits to the side of his plate. She sat beside him.

'Sorry to go off like that, Giles. Did you do them all, the ewes?'

'Of course I did all, Olivia. It'd be a poor do if I just swanned off and left them to it. Those sheep don't dag themselves, mind.'

She made him fresh coffee, forgetting he always drank tea.

'I don't count for much around here now, do I? Time I moved on, I reckon.'

Giles's remark was unexpected, but perfectly justified, true, and a blow to the gut. Poor old Giles, her rock, who'd smoothed her acceptance among her northern neighbours, who'd stood beside her moving electric fencing in sleeting rain, that morning among the turnips when Anne had gone trotting along the road below. At such times, when the horizons around Oxhide contained her entire world, she'd almost wondered how they would fare as life partners, him outdoors, her indoors. And now how he must feel relegated, the farm help, dagging her sheep on the hill while she dallied with Andrew in the warmth of her house. She flushed, her eyes blurred.

'Ah, come now, Olivia. I didn't mean to make you cry. I'm just a bit put out, like. I hope you know what you're doing, is all.'

'Please don't move on, Giles. I need you. Things have happened so fast, things I never expected. I've been terribly thoughtless.'

'Never mind. It's like the movies here these days, all too romantic for me. You won't forget the show, will you?'

She had forgotten the high point of the shepherd's year. Kilnsey Show, and the Swaledale Breeders' classes, where Oxhide would make its mark, and hopefully her herd would win recognition to earn a place in the breeders' book.

'Of course not, Giles, how could I?' How, indeed. She phoned the show secretary and it was not too late to make her entries. She phoned Mike Robertshaw for advice of picking out her best beasts and went along to Ramsgill with Giles, where together in the big farm office Mike helped her fill the entry forms and helped them plan the special preparation to make the best of her ram lambs and gimmer lambs.

Going back to Oxhide, she and Giles discussed the likely competition Mike had identified, farmers she knew from their trips to market. For the first time, it was an authentic ambition, as if she belonged here, not an imposter. She told Giles how much, as a child, she'd looked forward to the Kilnsey show as a family day out, how much she enjoyed the trotting races and the fell runners coming down beside the crag on their apparently indestructible legs. She'd never dreamt of being a participant, an insider, with her own business to conduct.

'I rather hoped you and I might be together, once,' Giles said. 'When you first came. I had hopes, Olivia, unrealistic though they were. But it wasn't to be. I knew that for sure, as soon as I saw his majesty strutting around, in that fancy sweater of yours.'

She touched his arm. 'I'm sorry, Giles. I've behaved badly to you, and I'm very sorry. Really. Can we still be friends? You're still my rock. It could have been different, I know. It's just turned out this way. I understand how all this must make you feel.'

'Not to worry love. I never really thought you were for me. I've mi plans, tha knaws.' Stage-Yorkshire phrases were Giles's way of passing off embarrassment.

And they walked on back to Oxhide, where Olivia and Andrew and Giles sat out in the June sunshine for coffee on the new bench on the shaggy front lawn, not saying anything, just letting things change and settle.

It was the best sort of honeymoon to stay here, with Andrew at Oxhide. Thank goodness they hadn't accepted Joe's generous offer of a honeymoon in the Caribbean. They'd have been pining for all they had now, the excitement of each other in the high summer moorland, the unfolding of its ever more extraordinary microbes in their little laboratory.

Olivia knew this new married life was for good, when one morning Andrew placed a brown paper parcel in front of her, with a curiously ceremonial gesture, holding it in both hands as he approached and placed it directly before her at the breakfast table. She undid the ribbon. It was fabric, with a slight museum-ish smell. Some sort of gaudy Bohemian smock from a vintage shop? No—a plain rectangle of cloth about five feet by two, red and black and green on a grey-white background; she had to stand to let it unfold completely.

'Remember? Under the Christmas tree?' A puzzle. He was willing her to get it, focussing intently on her face, like Moss when she got out the dog bowl. Olivia almost laughed, but the penny dropped in time. Andrew had brought her his family's heirloom flag from Erfurt. The significance dawned on her. Andrew Bamberg had brought her his household gods! When she embraced him, the musty flag dangling from her hand down his back, his face at last lit. It was like a declaration.

'Can we fly it? When did it last fly properly in the wind, not just lie under a Christmas tree?'

Andrew couldn't remember.

'Can we fly it on my birthday? Over the house?'

That would help with the frightfulness of being thirty, evidence of something accomplished. Giles would know how to put up a flagpole.

'Or when our paper's accepted,' Andrew said. 'Whichever is the sooner. Come, time for work.'

They made their way to the lab hand-in-hand, passing Anne heading towards the holiday pods with an armful of bedlinen. The first two glamping families were due to arrive that Saturday.

Andrew's only time away from the soil project was in the evenings, when he used the long late light to realise Giulia Gabrieli's plan for an Italian Renaissance garden in front of the house. The farm building work had finished a week ahead of schedule and it had made sense to do final groundwork while the machinery remained on site, to produce a stone-buttressed lower terrace with stone steps into the field below, a small grotto with ferny fountain, and a patch for growing the more aesthetically pleasing fruit and vegetables. Now he was doing the biological part, populating the spaces with local plants he knew would thrive best in each area: Actaea, lily of the valley, juniper, Mimulus and fountain-apple moss. From the bedroom window Olivia would listen to the snip-snip of pruning shears as he trained the yellow rambler over the front porch, and the chirring hand-mower he liked, going to and fro, taming the grass into a strip of lawn like a look-out, where on warmer nights they sometimes lay on the aromatic grass, watching the constellations slowly arc the sky.

Giulia must be invited to see this reincarnation of her garden at Torralba that Olivia had so admired. After all, her present happiness was the result of Giulia's wise advice, without which Olivia might still be mooning about to her image of a husband who no longer existed on Earth. And she would invite Jane, too—her other reliable life coach and business mentor. Giulia and Jane had hit it off at Torralba at Fred and Olivia's wedding; they'd enjoy meeting again. And, hooray, it turned out both women were keen, and now Olivia decided on a weekend, soon. It happened that the soonest they could both get away was on a date Andrew would be in London with Julian and Vanessa, which somehow made things simpler.

Olivia was glad she had vacuumed the Land Rover and cleaned her shoes, as her two city visitors approached the ticket barrier. Negotiating the Leeds traffic system she half-listened in as her two guests made conscientious conversation, still feeling for common ground; travel, budget airlines, the changing faces of London and Florence, the North and South divides in Italy and England; dealing with tourists. But once installed in the guest rooms that Olivia and Anne had taken trouble to get ready, both were gratifyingly delighted and became more at ease; and when they strolled out together, drawn by the terrace with its deck chairs and unbeatable Wharfedale view, Olivia found it heart-warming to see how happy they were to be here, and how interested they each were in the other.

'I see what you meant when you told me the Dales were like the Apennines,' Jane remarked, as they stood in the cool shade of the grotto in the lower garden. The morning turning to a hot June day. 'Pastoral.'

'It's a farmhouse, but positioned like a palace,' Giulia observed. 'It is appropriate for you, Livia. Now I see why you decided not to have statues here. The water fountains up so naturally from the rock, it's beautiful without dryads and naiads.' She took out a small sketchbook.

Jane and Olivia left Giulia busy drawing, seated on a well-placed stone, and retreated to make coffee.

'Your father's well, isn't he?'

'I hope so. Did he say anything about me?'

Jane reached for a shortbread biscuit. 'Poor old Joe, always was a worrier.' 'What did he say?'

'Really, I couldn't understand. You know how he gets anxious, the old fusspot. He wanted me to tell you something, but I wasn't quite sure what it was. Could it have been a Latin tag of some sort?'

'I think it might be. He likes legal phrases.' Olivia knew, but she was not going to tell Jane about *consensus ad idem*, Joe's idea of a lovers' contract.

But Jane, nobody's fool, had picked up Olivia's unease. 'He's concerned about you, Olivia. I don't see why—you look to have things impressively under control here. Is Andrew a fixture now? Where is he today?'

'Oh, he has lots of meetings. The work is going so well. He's about to submit another big paper, on discoveries he's made here. I should say, *we've made*—he's taught me techniques, and I've done a lot of the lab work myself.'

'Anything the innovation people would be interested in?' Thank goodness, Jane had moved from Joe's state of mind, tempted by the lure of exploitable science.

'It might be. Did you know peat grabs on to metal ions? All living things need trace elements, like zinc. Andy thinks moorland bugs help, they capture scarce metal atoms for their plant hosts.' A eureka moment struck her. 'Gosh, those might interest renewables researchers—you could use it to retrieve rare earths like lithium from old batteries!'

'I can put you in touch with Technology Transfer. Are you and Andrew in formal partnership, or just living together?'

Thank goodness, before Olivia had to answer, Giulia appeared, beaming and pocketing her sketchbook, and eagerly accepted coffee. The topic was dropped. It wasn't until they were standing on Leeds station concourse on Sunday afternoon waiting for Jane's London train that her godmother said her goodbyes.

'It was lovely, dear Olivia. But I do implore you, for my peace of mind if not yours and Andy's, talk reality together. And, by the way, whatever you do, don't make him a director.'

The platform number for the London train clicked up on the departures board. Jane hugged her. 'Arrivederci!' With a quick grin her mentor vanished through the barrier.

Jane was so bracing and on-the-ball. It was interesting, that idea about lithium recovery. She knew her stuff on industrial innovation—not so much on human romance. It would be silly to worry over Jane's old-womanish words about signing some legalese contract with Andrew. Their love had no need of being declared by the exchange of crappy trinkets. That was for ordinary types. Poor Jane had never experienced the extraordinary, almost transcendental bond that joined her to Andrew more profoundly than mere words on paper.

23

Lammas

At eleven the roast was in the oven and Olivia, aproned, was tidying in readiness for Sunday lunch. She'd invited Joe and Bridget. It was Andrew's idea; but Olivia was nervous. Was it fair to put her father in the position of having to treat the imposter with courtesy? But she couldn't think of a better way to demonstrate herself and Andrew as a committed couple. It might even be that, face-to-face, her father and her husband (as Andy was now, in every way that counted) would get along excellently. They had so much in common; Joe would surely understand why Andy meant everything to her now.

Then Bridget phoned: breathless, barely coherent. 'Olivia? It's Joe. Something's happened. He's had a funny turn. He's not making sense. The ambulance is coming, it's not here yet, I'm on my own, Anne's away. Olivia?'

Anne was at the Hawes Sales with Giles, they had taken the draft ewes to market.

'Call the doctor, too. Bridget, hang on, I'm coming over, I'll be there in under an hour.' Olivia, a horsewoman, never normally drove fast round blind corners, but she did now. At The Hollies the front door stood open. She ran up the steps and into the sitting room. Joe was in an armchair. He muttered something that sounded like, *It's happened.* The corners of his upper lip were white. With terror? His right hand and arm lay flopped on the chair arm. A whisky tumbler lay on its side on the white carpet, the brown tongue of spilt liquor only half-absorbed into the pile. Thank God, almost immediately a loud knock. Two paramedics ran in through the hall into the sitting room. Then again, the brisk knowledgeable hands, the tilted stretcher slid into its place in the ambulance, Bridget ushered in beside Joe, one of the two ambulance women following; the other shut the rear door and ran to the driver's seat and they were off. Olivia ran for her car keys, did a lightning three-point turn in the drive and zoomed after, crashing up through the gears.

She was panting. The blue light had disappeared towards the ambulance entrance and there were no free parking spaces. Then one at the far end of the car park. She slammed the car door and ran uphill to the main entrance, got directions from the reception desk and ran along the warren of corridors, past the signs for different departments.

Eventually she reached the waiting area where a nurse with a clipboard took notes from Bridget, who answered her questions with a stunned matter-of-factness, but paused to squeeze Olivia's hand. 'Hello, dear. They've taken Joe for scans. Sit down, you're all flustered.' Then to the nurse, 'This is his daughter.'

It would take a little while, the nurse said; she would report back as soon as the medics had seen Joe, studied the scans and decided what they needed to do.

Then it was waiting time. Olivia and Bridget settled on stacking chairs as the sun faded from the high corridor window and evening slowly arrived. From time to time Bridget reached out a hand and Olivia held it. Everything looked unreal, as if seen through scratched plastic, while inside she tried to face the truth that her father might be about to die; her father, who loved her and whose warnings she'd ignored. What had she been thinking of, to demand he meet Andrew face-to-face, as if mounting a challenge? She hadn't intended it that way, but now realised he might have thought she was squaring up to him, presenting her capture of Andrew as a proud *fait accompli*. Even though she'd known he was ill, known stress might kill him. He had seemed so monumental and until recently, remote; but also, so reliable, and as kind to her as he knew how. Her getting Oxhide wouldn't have happened without Joe Burbank's local networks and love. What kind of gratitude was it to defy him? Was this August Sunday the day that she would become fatherless?

The grey plastic composite covering the corridor was stiletto-dented like muddy sheep paths in winter. With panicky humour, Olivia fancied her feet would wear a trod into the floor as she went back and forth fetching Bridget tea, biscuits and sickly-sweet flapjacks from the League of Friends café. The business of the hospital went by, other traumas, other people doing their jobs. Olivia went over and over the gaudy picture on the opposite wall, child art, meant to be cheering, infantile splashes of primary colours, not a lot of help at the crux of life and death. She counted stripes on the curtains and divided the number by two, three, four and so on.

'I do love Joe,' Bridget said.

Olivia laid a hand on her arm. 'I know.'

'I'm glad you're here,' Bridget went on. 'It's kind of you, Olivia.' She picked at a loose thread in her tweed skirt. 'I'm glad you made the first move like that, love. Coming to the Hollies as you did. I expect you wondered why I didn't get in touch myself?'

Olivia couldn't deny she'd felt cold-shouldered when her father was helping her buy Oxhide and there was no contact from Bridget. She made a kind of 'not at all' noise.

'I felt bad about taking your Dad from you,' Bridget went on. 'It wasn't for a long time, you do realise, don't you, Olivia? It was three years after your mother left him, he asked me out.'

Olivia had assumed Bridget had made a beeline for Joe as soon as the coast was clear. Three years was plenty long enough to grieve a lost partner. She said so to Bridget, who looked brighter. 'Do you really think so?' Olivia said, yes, life is too short to give up years to melancholy.

'But you don't get to choose, do you?' Bridget said. 'Melancholy comes, whatever you think you decide.'

At long last a nurse came up, smiled and asked Bridget to hear the consultant's verdict.

When Bridget returned she was smiling. It was going to be all right. Joe had suffered a TIA, a Transient Ischaemic Attack. They would keep him in for now, but didn't think there would be long-term effects. It was a warning. Somebody would explain to Bridget about the medication he would need.

It was dark by the time they were back at the Hollies.

'Shall I make you a scrambled egg? Will you be all right, Bridget?

'Yes, please, dear.' Poor Bridget dropped on to a kitchen chair and watched Olivia lay plates, stick slices of bread in the toaster and beat eggs. 'We were just setting out. I think your Dad was nervous about meeting Andrew. I'm afraid he was bothered for you, he kept saying, "This will bring her down," again and again. I told him not to be silly, he was making a drama, being doomy like that. I said I would go and cut a bouquet for you and he should fetch a bottle from his cellar as a present. To celebrate. And Oh! I'm afraid I gave him a glass of whisky, just a little tot, thinking to cheer him up, we didn't want to arrive at yours with him being like that. Then it happened.' Poor Bridget's powdered face crumpled again.

Olivia rang Oxhide to let them know she was staying overnight at The Hollies. Bridget was alone and she knew what a lonely night could be like. Andrew answered.

'My darling, I'm so sorry. I could come over?' It was the first time he'd called her that.

No, she told him, everything was under control and the best way he could help was to be nice to Giles. She switched on Bridget's bedroom television and they watched *Question Time*, then a soap Bridget liked. Gradually something like normal returned. A *transient ischaemic attack*, Bridget repeated. Olivia brought her cocoa and drew the curtains.

Alone in Olivia's sitting room, Andrew worked late, laptop on his knee in front of the fire, thinking about their data. Only a log settling or a bit of the rose bush blowing against the window disturbed the silence. He let the Excel programme present pie charts and response surfaces and little landscapes of columns like the Giant's causeway, a single malt at his elbow. He daydreamed of the soil, alive out there in the dark; the processes he was trying to disentangle working away beyond sight. Intellect and imagination whirred in sync. A line of poetry came back to him from school: 'the drunkenness of things being various'; by Louis McNeice, Google told him, and he filed it mentally to share with Olivia. She'd be back tomorrow afternoon, she'd said, once she'd taken care of things for her stepmother.

A little after midnight he shut down the computer and luxuriated in the firelight and silence, thinking about Olivia, full of wonder such a girl should exist, and gratitude to fate or whatever that brought them together. Individual lives were threads, strung through time, twining and untwining, knotted or woven. And all those fates or norns or whatever, were always women, of course; spinning the long warp of our lives. Men shuttling away, planning their next job move, looking after their families, were nothing but weft, the short back-and-forth of everyday that built the material, but didn't change the fundamental shape of things. Olivia was the centre of his life, and he was transformed by her. Whatever he did, he would be the planet to her sun, always within her field of gravity, impelled and guided by her energy. A tawny owl called. Andrew put up the fireguard, washed his whisky glass and supper remains, and went upstairs to bed.

Shaving next morning, looking out of the bathroom window, Andrew observed Giles's car turning into the yard and Giles approaching the back door, followed by his footsteps in the passage. So he had a key. Of course he had, Olivia treated him like a brother, or rather, a working partner. From below came the sound of kettle-filling and fridge-opening. Andrew dried his face, applied a dash of the special oil he used on his sensitive skin, put on his shirt and corduroys, and padded downstairs.

He surprised Giles, who was reaching to get a huge mug from the top of the dresser, and turned quickly at the sound of the door.

'Uh? Bye, you gave me a shock. I weren't expecting no one. Liv's usually up on moor by this time.'

'She's over in Ilkley—her father's been taken ill.'

'Aye, Anne said. Is he okay? Tell her not to worry, we can do the sheep, she's not to hurry back.'

The kettle whistled. Andrew made tea and waved the pot towards Giles in invitation. 'Olivia's lucky to have you two around. That's a good sized mug you have there. A proper man-mug.'

'Oh aye, 'twas a present from her. But I reckon you're the man here now, isn't that so? You can't have my mug, though.' Giles's expression reminded Andrew of the skew-wise grin cartoonists used to show mixed feelings. *Let the best man win*, Giles implied. It was a generous, man-to-man response. Andrew doubted he would have been so decent if their places had been reversed.

'That was a great day up on the moor. I've just been analysing the data. You might be interested. It's quite exciting, the life underground round here. Once you get down to a microscopic size-range. Very different from that arable land down south, which is almost an underground desert. Pretty interesting stuff here.'

'Seemed like ordinary muck to me. D'you mean if I looked at it with a microscope I'd see weird creatures too?'

'Not directly. We've been separating the interesting DNA. The DNA that doesn't match existing records, but goes with certain plants. Minute creatures on particular living roots.'

'Liv was cooking up microbe food, putting it in Petri dishes.'

'That was just at first. That's the traditional way, and it's okay for finding bacteria that give you diseases. But these wild free-living things that are part of the moor soil—they'd not survive that treatment. You have to give them what they like, what they know how to deal with—living plants—and then, oh, it's extraordinary what's turning up, Giles.'

'You don't say.' Giles took down a saucepan. 'Want some breakfast?'

It was easy to be nice to Giles. He was a decent man. Over scrambled eggs they got on to the subject of Low Field, by way of local oddities, naturalists, National Park regulations, and conserving rare flora. It was extraordinary no one from Defra had explained to people like the Yarkers why some places were so strictly protected, or why one plant was more valuable, more irreplaceable, than another, like the Birdseye primrose, the little flower that grew in Low Field. Andrew explained about the rare flora that had survived the ice age in tiny scattered groups.

'I like that name, *Primula farinosa*,' Giles said.

'I think it's Latin for floury primrose.'

'Aye, leaves do look floury.'

'Olivia tells me Low Field wasn't always part of Oxhide.' An idea was taking shape. Giles seemed so amenable. What would it take for the Yarkers to surrender it? He pictured himself presenting the title deeds to Olivia, like one of those sea-birds that did their courting by bringing bits of interesting stuff to add to the nest.

'My Dad's always on about it,' Giles said. 'I'd've never known it otherwise. But Dad's getting a bit funny. His health. Mum wants him to give up, she wants them to retire, there's a place in Grassington near her sister. It's not realistic, though. Not with how house prices are hereabouts, what with the second home owners, doing all right on pensions.'

'Ah well,' Andrew said, getting up and putting plates in the dishwasher. 'Strange times.'

'Sure are.'

Birds sang as he went to start the day's work in his converted dairy. Oxhide was starting to feel like home, his own base. Giles's car disappeared in the direction of his part-time garage job in Skipton. It didn't seem fair.

Andrew wondered if there was anything he could do to help. Passing a house agent's window in Grassington that evening he was startled by Dales house prices. All the same, why not? Vanessa would approve. Beauty must be preserved, even if it took money.

The next week Joe was declared ready to go home. Olivia offered to go with Bridget to the hospital, but was refused.

'Better you don't come, dear,' said Bridget, her bounce partly recovered, hair and makeup in order. 'Anne wants to be with her Dad.'

Olivia understood the implied rebuke, but that didn't lessen its sting. Lucky they were speaking on the phone and Bridget couldn't see her tears. Worrying about his crazy elder daughter and her rash marital and business ventures had probably contributed to Joe's stroke. Anne, the normal one, would cheer him up better than she could. Olivia was free to go back to Oxhide alone.

24

Julian's Ride

Nearly the end of August, and now the mornings came later and cooler, with dew on the grass. Traffic down on the road was at its busiest, caravanners, cyclists and coaches, nose to tail, frequently backing up to pass. Up on the moors, though, everything was peaceful, baking in afternoon sunshine, purple with heather and honey-scented. Olivia's Swaledale flock grazed the high plateau between dales. The old farmhouse below was surrounded by its restored and new outbuildings, built of (or faced with) local millstone grit. Her gimmer lambs triumphed at Kilnsey Show; she was (effectively) a married lady, and the first scientific paper from the Oxhide Institute was nearly ready to submit.

Of the two holiday pods cleverly built into the limestone cliff behind the farm, one had been inhabited, since yesterday, by Julian, her sort-of stepson, triumphant with his predicted five starred A-levels, but now seemingly at a loss, impatient for new trails. Because the Oxhide communications satellite system worked so well, Julian was busy with his laptop; annoyingly, at the lip of the ghyll where Olivia would have liked a dip. There he sat, an urban figure in skinny jeans and biker jacket, Diet Coke at hand, refusing the spiritual balm of wild nature. Olivia found this harder and harder to bear. It does not sit well with the Oxhide brand.

'Hey, Jules!'

'Mornin', Olivia. All right?'

'Yeah. You busy?'

'Nah, killing time. Hardly thrillsville, the north, is it? I fixed you a zipwire, might be good for the punters' kids. Look!'

He unfolded his skinny six and half foot from the bank, latched on to the handle she'd just noticed hooked into the tall ash tree, and launched himself with a whoop across the ghyll, grabbing a branch on the far side. It was the kind of thing she'd have done at his age. He was happy for her to have a go. It was terrifying, in a good way. When had she last felt the wind in her hair? The poor kid was missing his teenage thrills.

She had an idea. That evening she phoned Anne, and the next day asked Julian if he'd be willing to give her little sister a hand with her skittish horse, and when he guardedly agreed, pointed him in the direction of Skellside.

Julian realised his walk had been worthwhile when he found Anne alone, mucking out in breeches and a minimal top. Surely there must be at least ten years between Olivia and this blonde stunner. She was expecting him, and showed him around dingy sheds and then invited him in for a Coke, which, on seeing the grubby kitchen, he refused.

The troublesome horse Olivia had mentioned was in his stable, apparently. Anne opened the door. In the gloom, the animal looked enormous. It rolled an eye at him.

'You know, you could give Comet a hack out for me, then. Poor boy, stuck in his box on a day like this. It's the flies, I keep him in on hot days, they drive him mad outside.'

'You're joking. Olivia said he'd bucked you off. You trying to kill me or something?'

'We didn't realise he had a thing about spurs. I had them on 'cause I'd been schooling a horse for a client. I only just touched him—it must have brought back bad memories. The man we got him from was a nasty piece of work. Comet's a real gentleman normally. A complete pussycat.'

'But how will he know *I'm* not wearing spurs?'

'Just have a go, Jules,' said Anne. She rubbed Comet's forehead, the way he liked. 'You're not all togged up in riding clothes, he won't suspect you. You've ridden before, haven't you?'

'Of course,' lied Julian. Those kids trotting round in circles, little girls delivered on Saturday mornings by their mothers. It wasn't real riding, not like Napoleon on his grey Arab mare at Austerlitz.

'I'll be holding him, you can slip off if he does anything.'

'I don't do dressage,' said Julian, trying to sound as if prancing around a riding arena was beneath him, as if he used to hunt twice a week with the Quorn as a boy, before bioinformatics and the violin had claimed his valuable time.

'All the better. He'll look after you—as long as he senses you're not going to boss him about.'

Driving past with his father, Julian had seen Comet in the field, a little bay horse, heraldic against green grass. Close up he was surprisingly massive and masculine, not at all like the ponies in Hyde Park. Gingerly, Julian touched the great solid hindquarters and Comet gave him a stare, his sensitive-looking head held high on a shortish arched neck, like the sort of horse you saw on equestrian statues with some popular hero on top—Paul Revere, Garibaldi, Ataturk. Comet fluttered his nostrils and focussed on Julian with pricked ears and a penetrating dark eye. Julian wondered why he so much wanted Comet to like him. A horse was a powerful ally, of course.

'There,' said Anne. 'He's taken to you. He's a good sort. A fantastic ride. Jumps for fun. It's a shame he's not been out for a week. He's not the type you can put just anybody on.'

'You get on him first, then.'

'No, I told you, he doesn't like me. He's clever and too proud to forget my spurs. Make friends with him, Julian. Look, he wants you to.'

Comet reached out and took hold of Julian's sweater gently with his lips as though gathering a grass tuft. They both laughed. Anne's teeth were amazing. Julian put out a hand and Comet let him rub his neck behind his ears, pressing against Julian's hand. Anne slipped on the bridle and draped the reins ready over Comet's withers. 'Let's leg you up.'

'Bareback?' Julian couldn't believe this. He wasn't even wearing a hat. 'Just try. Slip off if he does anything. I've got him.'

They crossed the yard to the fenced arena Giles had installed for Anne at the back of the Skellside farmhouse. Riding felt higher up than Julian had expected. The warm back moved beneath him. It was like being a baby again, being carried by a hairy parent. They entered the fenced area. Anne let go the lead rein.

'Just let him carry you. Only a light feel on the reins, you couldn't stop him anyway if he wanted to go.'

The cob set off at a gentle trot down the long side of the arena. Julian felt himself tossed six inches into the air at every stride. At the corner he slid hopelessly to one side and clutching the mane didn't help. The horse stopped dead and with a gentle hitch of his right shoulder set Julian back in position again.

'They help you, these clever native horses. Look why don't you try him for a ride up the lane? Balance like on a bicycle, wrap your legs round him to hold on, the mane's no use as a handle.' Anne opened the arena gate to let them out.

Comet set off at a trot up the lane. Julian steered him out on to the green track towards the moor. Comet trotted briskly through the August morning. Flower-scented air tickled Julian's nose and the wind of their progress lifted his hair. Every muscle was stretched, every bone jolted, but he was riding, proper riding. They came out on to a soft peaty path over the moor side, clothed in green-smelling bracken. Without any conscious signal from him, Comet seemed to sense Julian's confidence and they were cantering with soft hoof beats, hair and mane lifting in time with the wind of their progress, smooth as a fairground carousel horse, but a million times more exciting.

'Hello! Olivia?'

The voice came to Olivia, reading in her sitting room, as if from the front door. Nobody arrived that way. But there Vanessa stood, in the rose-hung porch, confident as a Women's Institute bossy boots. She wore burgundy suede sandals and a floaty sea-green scarf twisted over her gold hair. Had she landed from a balloon? Olivia had heard no car, and Vanessa's bandbox appearance made it seem as if she had materialised from nowhere.

'Oh! Er—yes. Hello Vanessa! How amazing! You surprised me. Excuse me, I was miles away. Do come in.'

Vanessa gazed past her toward the dark passage to the kitchen. 'Is Andrew Bamberg here?'

'Yes, he would be here, but he's out today.'

'I need to see him.' Vanessa had such an imperious tone, as though she expected Olivia to run out across the fields. 'He mentioned . . .' Vanessa's voice trailed. 'Can I wait for him? I believe my grandson is here too, Julian?'

'Well—Andrew's out for the day at a meeting. I think Julian is around, though. What a tremendous set of A-levels he's got! You must be very proud.' It was while staying at Mud Alley that Julian had done the work now crowned with five stars. Vanessa would have urged him on—no cosy distractions there. It was hard to imagine anybody less like a lovely old Grandma.

'Oh. Would you be kind enough to find him, then, and tell him I'm here?'

'Certainly. Do sit while I go and look for him. May I get you a drink first? A cup of tea?' Vanessa declined.

'Well, do take a seat,' said Olivia. 'Please excuse me a moment.' She'd have to get Andy on his phone. She couldn't cope with his mother alone.

A moment of silence from Vanessa. 'Oh what a heavenly view!

All the little farmhouses! And the wild moor above. You can picture Heathcliff striding over the hills there, can't you?'

Not on limestone, you couldn't. Haworth was on the millstone grit, Heathcliff and his creator belonged to that dark rock, not the steely-pale lunar landscape of stepped limestone across the valley. Vanessa paced across the room.

'Did Julian paint this?'

'No, I don't think so.' The watercolour was one Andrew had done of the Skirfare in flood, given to Olivia after a picnic they'd had on its banks.

'Do you have children? It's good for Julian to be here. Toughen him up. Boys should be tough. Helen mollycoddles him. I say, you're a bit like Helen, you know. Good with housekeeping and so forth. Come to Mud Alley, I'll introduce you.'

Olivia stood in the doorway waiting for a pause in Vanessa's talk to make a polite exit.

Vanessa ran on. 'Is the project here going well? It's an important initiative. There'd be no point otherwise, would there, being hidden away up here?'

'I'm very pleased Andrew can work at Oxhide.'

'Is that a cave over there?' said Vanessa, still at the window. 'There are lead mines, aren't there? Landscape's only skin deep, isn't it? What if you fell through—down one of those mines—you'd be in an underworld, wouldn't you? Right down there underneath all the high teas and weekend coach trips.'

'Are you sure you wouldn't like tea? I'll go and look for Julian. He can't be far.' Vanessa was more than bossy, she was odd.

Olivia phoned Anne, stepping out on to the lawn in case Vanessa was listening. 'Out for a ride? Who with?'

'Comet.'

'What, alone? I didn't know he could ride already.'

'You don't need any experience for Comet,' Anne said, 'he's done pony trekking, he'd bring a sack of potatoes safe home.'

'Where have they gone? Vanessa's turned up, she wants to see Julian now.'

Holding the phone, Olivia went out on to the front lawn and gazed up and down the valley.

The landscape stretched glorious and green in an August doze. All the little roads and lands were draped over the hillside, like a page from *The Dalesman* calendar, and there was Skellside, but nowhere could she catch sight of a black horse.

'It wouldn't be like Julian to ride slowly for long. He's too adventurous,' said Olivia. 'Oh, Anne, what have you done? What can have happened?'

'If he'd fallen off, the horse would have turned up in the yard by now.'

Then Olivia heard hoofs approaching Oxhide from side of the yard that faced the moor, and ran round to the back of the house to see Julian and Comet coming down the track from Ramsgill. The tableau reminded Olivia of the Roman mosaic she'd seen with Freddie on their honeymoon. The black horse clopped decorously in through the gate with arched neck and pricked ears. And Vanessa, trailing silky chiffon, was leading him in. Olivia could imagine a garland of flowers round his neck.

How had Vanessa gone out up the yard without Olivia noticing? She must have floated silently out at the back while Olivia was on the phone at the front.

'Oh, wow, Olivia, we had such a ride,' said Julian. 'Olivia, I jumped him. I jumped Comet. Over a stone wall. We've been all over the moor, places I hadn't seen. I can gallop!'

'You'll be stiff tomorrow!'

'I don't care. Nessa, did you see me jump the wall?'

'You're a chip off the old block,' said Vanessa. 'Come up to the house and tell me all about yourself. You've grown! You're taller than me.' She turned to Olivia. 'We'll leave the horse with your man, if you would, thanks, Olivia. Time for that tea now, I think. I take Earl Grey, no milk.'

Olivia told Julian to make tea for his grandmother, and led Comet into the barn, where she untacked him, gave him a drink at the trough and tied him up. Dark sweat marks on the horse's black coat almost made her believe in Julian's wild ride, but it was a hot afternoon.

Anne appeared. 'Oof.' She dug out a packet of cigarettes from a jacket pocket, took one and repocketed them.

'But I left her in the sitting room.' Olivia looked shaken.

'Seems your as-if mother-in-law gets around,' said Anne, lighting up. 'Oops. What did I just say? I meant Andy's mother.'

'I'd better go and keep an eye on the pair of them. Vanessa certainly makes herself at home. Where did she materialize from? Those odd clothes. Purple sandals.'

'I think she's creepy.'

Stranger still, Vanessa carried off Julian in her sportscar when she left half an hour later. 'I'm heading down the M1,' she told Olivia; 'It's a chance to talk to my grandson.'

'Oh, well,' Anne said, 'It's their business. Are you okay, Liv?'

'That certainly messed up my literature survey for the day. Vanessa's exhausting. She just doesn't seem to behave like a normal human being. But thank you for giving Julian that riding lesson. He was completely thrilled, wasn't he? What on earth possessed you to take such a risk, I mean spin that absurd yarn?'

'A book Daddy read to me once. About a man who makes friends with the Romani he meets – studies their language.'

So Joe had read Lavengro to Anne as well. In a way she and Anne had experienced the same childhood; though serially, not in parallel.

Where had Andrew been? She felt miffed that Vanessa had turned up unannounced. He ought to have warned her. He was back that evening; she saw the lights come on in the lab about nine. He didn't even come into the house first.

The computer screen lit his face, intent on emails. He'd been meeting with his former team, planning the next stage, he said; they urgently needed to get a move on now their first paper was in press, it was vital to follow up ahead of rivals. There'd been a select meeting in Cambridge, apparently, which Erik and Meera had attended. Julian was there too. He'd had the firm offer of an internship at the University of California in Berkeley, starting September, the day after the American Labour Day. Andrew paused and glanced up at the closed lab window. Olivia followed his gaze, expecting a trapped butterfly or that robin that tended to get in and flap about. But there was nothing to see but the grey sky. He was missing his colleagues, missing being in the mainstream, fearing others were making crucial decisions. Was he feeling like a trapped bird? Resentment choked her. Those rescued are supposed to be grateful; fished out of a roaring sea, they shouldn't struggle to escape the rescuer's hook.

Too proud to confess her unworthy feelings, and at a loss for what wouldn't sound like whingeing, she brooded over the days he spent away with his group—and his mother, for God's sake.

Fearing she'd go mad if she didn't share all this, she took an hour of the afternoon to drive to Pippa. But it was Mark she encountered on the doorstep of the Doctors' House, unlocking his car, about to head off. At the sight of his kind, sensible figure, she broke down.

'Whoa, hey,' Mark said, momentarily confounded. He relocked the car and led her into the house, sitting beside her on the little red sofa, silently handing her a tissue and waiting in sympathetic silence.

'I'm sorry, Mark. Thank you. It's nothing serious, really.'

'It's Andy, isn't it? What's the silly beggar been up to?'

That was enough for her to relate everything. Mark listened, making 'go on' noises over his shoulder even as he made tea. They sipped in silence after she'd finished explaining her feelings of shock and betrayal, while Mark considered.

'Why is it so bad for him to travel, to spend time abroad with colleagues, Olivia? Mightn't he be doing that even if you were officially hitched?'

'I thought we had something real together, here. I thought we were going to base our joint project at Oxhide. Like founding a firm.'

'Are you pregnant, Olivia?'

'Not yet, I don't think.'

'Why don't you go with him?'

'And leave Oxhide? But this is where I live, run a farm, a business. The whole place is just getting going. I thought Andrew wanted to be part of that. That's why we decided to live together permanently. Exactly the same as being married.'

'But Olivia—did Andrew say that? That he wanted to live together all the time, for ever?'

Mark waited with quiet attention.

She explored her memory of the morning at the ghyll, in May. Had they spoken? Mark's eyes were on her, steady, neutral. It had been so obvious that they were made for each other, it hadn't needed saying. She resorted to checking Mark's memories of their first encounter at Oxhide. 'He really did want to come here to work, didn't he? Last spring? And now he's here and we came together in the summer, when I left Fred's memory behind, and it's as if we are one person. I couldn't ever live without Andrew.' She faltered.

Mark crossed an ankle over his knee and stared at his foot, stirring it round in its shiny black shoe. He looked up. 'Andy doesn't know how lucky he is. Pippa's right, you make a grand couple. But he's a complicated bloke, you know. Not every girl would take him on.'

'But I love him.' She'd said it again, realising that for her being in love with Andrew was a permanent state, whatever happened.

'He's worth loving. But, Olivia, I know him. I've known him a long time. It won't be easy. Remember, Pippa and I are here for you if there are ups and downs. As there always are, aren't there? Thing is, he's not a completely free agent. Oh, I'm not talking about employment. But he means everything to Vanessa, and everything to Julian. You've got competition. If you decide to really marry Andy, he won't always be sitting there the other side of the fire. But he won't let you down, either. You need to talk, decide what you want and what you can put up with. Even Pippa and I did that, and we're boring, normal types.'

Then he said he had to go. She'd already made him late for an appointment, she realised.

She trusted Mark, felt sure she could meet his challenge. If Vanessa and Julian were competition, she could see them off. Before starting back, she walked around Skipton nosing into book and dress shops. Mark was so sane. Thinking about early days living with Freddie, a new marriage was a strange, priceless, fragile object, which made you supersensitive to any tiny flaws. She would try to be more accepting. It was Andrew's global glamour that had first attracted her; she still hardly knew this new magnetic character in her life.

25

Storm Warning

Andrew looked forward to Julian's stay at Oxhide and progress report from Berkeley. Julian didn't communicate much ordinarily, and Andrew was wary of being a helicopter father and bothering him with calls or messages at school. Also, he had missed not only his son's company, but also Julian's bioinformatics skills. The results of microbiome investigations of Oxhide's varied soils was exceeding expectations. Julian handled the ever-updated software fearlessly, making the results accessible. Only an expert could interpret columns and columns of figures and Latin names, but Julian's infographics were instantly graspable.

Olivia worked alongside the Robertshaws today, so he took the Defender to meet his son at Leeds station. Julian had grown another inch or two, surely. He looked more like an undergraduate than a schoolboy, and gave Andrew a hug with none of his former adolescent embarrassment. American confidence infused his bearing; noticeably fatter, and with hair practically crew-cut, Julian was his own man.

'Olivia's making her special trifle,' said Andrew, as they sped through Roundhay.

'Oh Dad, I'm not ten,' said Julian, in a tone that damped Andrew's pleasure. 'Don't worry, I'll be polite.' What was eating the boy?

'Better than polite, I hope,' Andrew said, then wished he hadn't.

'I won't break up your idyll, if that's what you mean.'

Julian had never been hostile like this. It was like a chill in the air. 'What have you against Olivia, Julian?'

'She's okay. I haven't anything against her as such. I just wish you hadn't got yourself stuck away in that hole. Here we are driving along ridiculous little roads through quaint nothingness. How can you do real work tucked away? More to the point, how do you expect me to?'

'I wasn't expecting you to work, Jules—it'll be a holiday, a break from work. It's a super place. And it is interesting to me, workwise. You can ride! Go hunting perhaps? And I'm hoping there'll be things we can do jointly.'

'Vanessa wants you to get back to real life. She says you're heading for a dead-end. It depresses her, she says, you winning a medal and all that, and then dropping out to a cosy farm nobody's heard of, in the few acres they call a National Park over here.'

'It's motherly concern, Jules. Don't worry, she'll come around when we start publishing this new work together.'

But would she? Both of them knew Vanessa's impulsiveness could undermine their best plans for this Yorkshire adventure. Her wealthy Commission for Cultural Landscapes people had been their first funders, but what if she changed her mind? What if her ambition for him and Julian turned her against the Oxhide project? Andrew mentally crossed his fingers that their big Oxhide paper would be accepted, soon. That could win over his mother and his son.

As if his guardian angel had woken, it happened on a Monday morning in the first week in November, when Julian was on one of his visits. As he cast an eye down his inbox, Andrew's gaze came to a stop. He read—and read again. Then leapt up and shouted to his son.

'Jules! It's from *Science*! They're accepting our paper!'

The boy took in the thrilling message with one glance at the screen. Andrew embraced him. His heart thumped and his body filled with warmth. 'Where's Liv?'

Julian followed, laughing, as he ran across the farmyard shouting her name, forgetting she was somewhere up on Buckden Pike. The sun had come out, and the autumn robins' song was no longer sad. He could look forward to all that Winter would bring, they seemed to sing. That evening he and Olivia dined at the best restaurant in Harrogate, and drank so much they decided to stay the night at the Imperial Hotel.

The journal issued a press release, and social media were full of reactions and congratulations, as ripples of interest spread from specialist publications into the public domain and through the blogs of the conservation NGOs. Jane whipped up interest from industry, and appointments with patent agents were arranged. Even the *Yorkshire Post* ran a human-interest piece, with glamorous photos of Olivia cantering over the moor on Comet. #InvisibleWildlife went viral on Twitter. Vanessa insisted on a party for the Commission for the Conservation of Cultural Landscapes, importing a caterer and marquee. And all this did not go unnoticed by Andrew's American colleagues and their funders. A message from America was on its way.

The FedEx courier looked cross. He had driven his van up the track and puzzled out the gate catches, and now he'd had to step round a manure-brown puddle to reach the path to the rarely-used front door. He was standing under the porch, batting away rose thorns, hand raised to the door knocker, when Andrew, who had followed him round to the front of the house hailed him from behind.

'Sign here, please, sir.'

Sir? It was rare now for Andrew's letters to be addressed to

Professor A. J. D. Bamberg followed by the letters of all his three degrees and two fellowships. He took the thick cardboard envelope back to the lab, flipped it on his desk in the little side office and returned to the assays he had been doing when the courier arrived. He finished setting up his assay, racked the Eppendorfs in the water bath and set the timer. Peeling off his purple gloves, he took a scalpel from the lab into the office to slit open the purple- and orange-labelled FedEx package.

They weren't just inviting him to apply. They *requested* him to sign a contract, enclosed. The US Department of Agriculture. Sole charge of a whole new programme, *The Peatland Microbiome and Climate Change Resilience*. Andrew gazed unfocussed at the flying autumnal clouds, feeling a strange sensation; the corners of his mouth, curling in a small unconscious smile. Three years in the USA! What would it mean for them?

It was Thursday. He would give himself until next Monday, space to reflect on how he could put this to Olivia. He put the envelope and its contents into his desk drawer.

On Sunday, Olivia, about to dish up lunch at Oxhide, thought to herself that this busy, peaceful moment was the fulfilment of her dream. Things were working all right. She smiled at Anne and Giles, Bridget and Joe, her Burbank family united in happy domesticity. This was what farmhouses were for. There were voices in the passage and Andrew and Julian came into the kitchen. Side-by-side in the doorway, Julian was half a head taller than Andrew these days. Olivia was struck again by their family likeness; the same angle of brows and nose, the same wide bony shoulders.

She flicked twelve perfect Yorkshire puddings into a warmed dish, dropped the empty baking tray in the sink and handed Andrew the bottle of Montepulciano along with a corkscrew.

'This is the life!' Andrew drew the cork and filled her glass, set the bottle on the table and drew up a chair next to hers. A blackbird sang on the apple tree outside, where a few half-pecked away apples still hung. The sun had just come through after a morning of rain. It was called a St. Martin's summer, wasn't it—this last gasp of summer in November? A smell of wet vegetation from the open window mingled with the roasting and wine. Julian flopped beside his father, folding ungainly legs. He had not taken off his wet shoes, those high-top trainers he affected. Andrew didn't seem to notice.

Anne and Bridget placed a pile of five hot plates in front of Olivia. Bridget, wiping her hands on a dishcloth, was the last to sit. Proper Sunday lunch was one of the rituals Olivia had set up to create the feeling of a family. They talked about their plans for the rest of the day. Anne announced she was going into the town after lunch, and Julian spoke for the first time since he had come in.

'Give me a lift? I'm off to stay with Nick for the week.'

'Nick?' Andrew paused, holding the broccoli he was about to pass to Anne.

'You know, Nick. From school. Working in computation.'

'All the way to London?' asked Olivia.

Julian looked about to talk back at her, but his father quickly defused the moment. 'Okay, why not? When?'

'Now. Go with Anne, catch the train.' Julian picked up a fork and inspected it.

Olivia finished carving beef. She sat and pushed the horseradish sauce to Andrew. 'Why rush off this afternoon, Jules? Wait till Monday, I'll run you to Leeds. Enjoy your weekend. Relax.'

Julian flushed. He piled roast potatoes on his plate and set to, head bowed over his food.

'Quite nice, this Italian red.' Andrew touched his glass to Olivia's. 'Cheers!' He gave her a private half-smile.

She smiled back.

'You go when you want to, Jules. You've got stuff to do, I know,' said Andrew. He was the parent, after all, Olivia thought. Let him be indulgent if he wants.

'Thanks, Dad.' Andrew seemed the only person Julian would look at when he spoke.

Julian returned from his few days in London brightened, standing straighter. He even smelt smarter, somehow. Olivia realised that these days she was rarely completely clean.

Today she was working in the farm office, the cleanest place, but something about the forms she had open on the computer screen she was packing made her queasy. Saving and closing the windows on the screen, she went out into the fresh air. She leaned against the house wall and gazed across the valley, scanning the wide, detailed view, the farmhouses with their families that she knew, the indentations in the valley sides where becks drained water off the peaty moor, the small level green fields along the valley floor. The barn at Moss Dyke was missing. She looked away and it came back. Looked back and it disappeared again. That fragmentation of vision that precedes a migraine. No point in fighting it. She crossed the yard and went into the kitchen to make strong tea. She would take it into the quiet sitting room where nobody would disturb her, and lie on the sofa until the aura passed. The Defra forms could wait until the afternoon.

The door opened. Julian.

'Hi.' He flopped into an armchair and hiked his long legs over the arm.

'Hello, Jules. I was just lying down. Got a damn migraine.'

'Oh, tough. Can I get you anything?' He flipped his feet back to the floor, ready to do her wishes. The fireplace was behind him, reminding her of the evening the year before when he'd still been a boy, a marvellous young boy playing his violin, and they had listened in silence by the firelight, enchanted.

'No, thanks all the same. I just need half an hour or so. I thought you were finishing your project? How's it going? Did going to stay with Nick help?'

'Fed up with programming.'

'But it sounded really useful. It's so great to be working with Nick and his father. An LSE prof! Your Dad was impressed.'

'It's boring.'

'Lots of work is boring.'

'Oh, please!' Julian collapsed into the armchair again and stretched his arms with a histrionic yawn.

'Of course it is. Anything worth doing has boring bits. I get sick to death of processing all Andrew's samples.'

'You don't look sick of it. You look keen to me. You and Dad both.' His voice, his man's voice, had taken on a nasty edge. She drained the dregs of the teapot into her cup, not offering any to Julian.

'All the pipetting's boring, was all I meant. The results are exciting.'

'Yeah, yeah, I can see you're excited. That's obvious actually.'

He stalked out. Half her visual field was now filled with sparkling zigzags. She lay back on the white sofa and closed her eyes.

In the lab Andrew read out figures to Julian who sat at the computer: '1.2, 3.4, 5.3, 4.5'

Julian, at the keyboard, typed fast. 'Next?'

'27.1, 38.2, 35.4, 46.6.'

'Okay ... so ...'

The Principal Component Analysis graphic materialised on the screen.

'Wow. Fabulosa!' Delighted surprise made Andrew a schoolboy again.

Julian responded with fatherly gravitas. 'Is that clear enough?'

'Just no doubt about it at all,' Andrew agreed. 'A massive effect.'

Julian grinned and pressed the print button. 'Anything else you need, Dad?'

'No, I'll start on a draft this evening with Olivia. Letter to *Nature*, I think, this one.'

'Write it yourself, Dad. You don't need Olivia.'

'Oh, come on, Jules. It's her idea, her land, she funded it and she writes brilliantly. We do need her, Julian.'

'She's not as keen as you think.' He half turned to face his father. 'She told me she's sick of the work.'

'What do you mean? Why do you say that?'

'What I said. Bored with the lab. She's a farmer, Dad. A conservation nut. Not a scientist.'

'Maybe I'm asking too much of her? Making assumptions.'

'She's going out tonight, anyway. Heard her fixing to go to the cinema with Anne and Giles. You draft it, Dad.'

'If she's not going to be here, I suppose I may as well get on with it,' Andrew picked up the print-out and looked at the figures, but without taking them in.

How carelessly he had accepted Olivia's kindness; that invitation nearly two years ago, her love, her dedication to his project, her willingness to spend all day on repetitive tasks, making sure their results were sound and repeatable. He had allowed her to give too much, be too selfless. Why should he assume she would want to spend her life being his lab assistant? He had behaved like a typical male chauvinist, he realised. Just what they always seemed to be complaining about in the *Guardian*.

26

Catastrophe

How happy she was, Olivia thought. She had fulfilled her vow to Freddie's memory, and continued to remember him as she moved on with the living man she loved. Andrew Bamberg's scattered team were already reassembling around the Oxhide project. Erik the microscopist was now a regular visitor, his skill revealing that the organism they'd initially discovered only as a strange length of protozoan DNA, was a real and extraordinary micro-creature, a new Tardigrade, never before described, with a unique extracellular metabolism, intimately connected to the health of moorland peat. And here she was at the heart of it all, this morning in the bright little office that opened off the lab, a wild November gale rattling the ash twigs above the ghyll, while her screensaver offered a scrolling gallery of delicious landscapes from across the world.

Well, there was the problem of Julian. But Julian was going through a phase. He was nearly eighteen. It would pass. Adolescent men were like that. Like Ben, her mind offered; her brother's crazy resentment of Fred, that stupid error on the autostrada. She stood to banish the shadow of memory. A good book, that would help. On the high shelf in Andrew's office, among the equipment catalogues, stacks of blue and white boxed molecular biology kits, and the neat shelf of lab notebooks filled with all their data, was the priceless copy of Hooke's *Micrographia*. She reached it down, wiping her hands over her jeans before touching the precious pages. The detail of the microscopic drawings drew her in, as they always did. Nothing so beautiful and accurate had been produced since, even with electron microscopes. She was reading the Latin captions when she heard Andrew's voice in the lab beyond the little office. He was speaking to Erik, who had been at a microscope all afternoon.

'Hi, Erik. Can we have a photo of those ciliate thingies, the odd ones showing the anchor structures? Ideally with a root as well, to show them clinging on.'

'Sure, they are on now, take a look.'

There was the sound of standing up. 'It is top right, next to a bit of gunk.'

'Nothing. Some little clumps. Oh! There he goes! Dynamic, aren't they? How do we capture an image?'

'It will have to be a video still. Olivia got some yesterday. I will ask her.'

Olivia's heart thumped at this mention of her name. She listened.

'No, don't, this's okay,' said Andrew. 'One high mag, another low for the context. Black and white half-tones, we can't afford colour charges.'

'I think we do not need them anyway. These DIC images are the business, Andrew.'

'Yes, and with those path traces it'll make a nice composite figure. I'm writing a draft paper tonight.'

Olivia felt her face flush.

'Okay,' Erik said. 'Will you repeat the assays, Andrew? Wasn't Olivia wanting to do that?'

'No, I don't think so.'

There was a diminuendo of footsteps as Andrew left the lab,

and after an agonising twenty minutes Erik followed, with a click of the outer door. Of course she wanted to do the work. Even Erik knew that. What had Andy meant? She must have misinterpreted.

Later, she was making up feed orders in the farm office. Julian came in and leant against the wall watching her.

'Hallo, Julian,' she said neutrally.

'Hi. What're you doing?'

'Just feed orders. Like I do on Monday mornings.'

'We may be going to San Francisco,' said Julian, watching her face.

'Great. How exciting.' She managed an animated smile in his direction.

'Dad's fixed for me to do alignments.' Julian sounded determined to get a rise.

'Oh? What's that?'

'You know. Gene alignments. Synteny. Tree-building.'

'Sounds fun.'

'It's interesting. Quite tough, the Bayesian equations are non-trivial. We'll be staying on campus.' He had lost her.

'Non-trivial, yes. On campus?'

'Dad and me. And Erik and Stefan. Writing a phylogenetic tree-building programme for the sequences we got here.'

Olivia collected the feed orders and inserted them slowly into a used A4 envelope. She scrawled the merchant's name on the outside. Slowly, breathing deeply to keep an even voice, she asked, 'When are you going?'

'The 25th. No, 26th. Don't know. Dad knows. He did all the bookings and stuff.'

'Oh.'

'I need to get back to Berkeley, anyway. They say Burkley, did you know? Not Barkley.'

'Yes, I know.'

'You can do anything there. They do audio technology.

Apparently, I might be able to combine courses in performance and software development.'

She couldn't listen to any more. 'I've got to get these sent off now, Julian. See you later.'

She had to have it out with Andrew. He was packing his apparatus, about to take a lunch break.

'Come for a quick sandwich?'

'Yes. Olivia?' Something was coming, it was implied by his face, his tone. He opened a drawer. 'Look at this. What do you think?'

She took the cardboard FedEx envelope, drew out the package of papers and scanned to the top sheet, the contract letter. Frowning, she read it again and started on the second sheet.

'It's quite something, isn't it?' Hands in trouser pockets, eyes on the ground, he waited.

'Well done! They really do want you, don't they?' She grinned, stretching her mouth wide, but somehow the rest of her face wouldn't follow. Yes, it was great to think that she had what the USA wanted. But they couldn't have Andy. Could they? They'd have to do their own peatland research, she had the world expert here already.

She wasn't really surprised at his next words. 'I can't turn it down, can I?'

Keep cool, she told herself. 'Of course you can.'

He stared at her.

'I need some air,' she said. 'Come on.'

They climbed into the Defender. She glanced sideways at Andy's face, so familiar, the face she thought she knew. 'You're really going to California? For three years?'

'Yes. It will be good for us, Olivia. For making Oxhide a global base, part of a global soil research network. The USA's the future. They have the resources.'

'You're taking Julian.'

'Yes, he's done very well, he's a promising mathematician. Just the right moment to expose him to what's current, not just school maths. He'll be useful soon.'

'But what about us? Here?'

He was silent for such a long moment; she repeated, 'Andy?'

'Let's have a walk. It can be done. There must be a way.'

Panting, and not only from the climb, they reached a gate on to the moor, a deserted plateau five miles from Oxhide. The long-distance path stretched from its finger post through miles of heather, November-brown, like the night-time side of a globe, compared to the sunlit pasture this side of the high stone wall bordering the moor. Olivia sank on the sun-warmed grass bank at the sheltered base of the wall, her back to the moor, the old signal for Andrew to slide down beside her. He looked down, still standing, and she felt diminished, like a dog that rolls over offering itself for tickling, ignored, its master not unkind—just detached—but therefore even more wounding. Andrew was listening to other, internal voices, she understood with a lurch. Were they two separate people now?

'We never did go for that long walk, Liv,' he said, gazing not at her, but over the wall at the moor and the pale line of the Salt Path, almost overgrown by heather, carving a connection to the horizon, a curving line, like an animal's tracks, holding to its purpose: to carry the traveller to a distant place, with his pack animals, salt, sheep flock, to travel on by Oxhide into the world.

'I'm going to come back, and we'll do it together.'

'Come back?'

So this was it. She felt sick. Her premonitions had been right. The end was now, at this wall, at the top of this intake field. A sheep looked at her, chewing, unconcerned. The breeze fluted through the drystone wall, clouds changed shape and moved on, daisies nodded in the wind. Icarus can fall, and nobody notices.

'I've got to go, Liv. It's time. I've been thinking about it, worrying about you—but you've got so many friends here now, haven't you? There are planes. People commute across the pond, lots of academics have long-distance partnerships these days.'

'I suppose,' was all she could say.

But this was not what she had surrendered her loyalty to Freddie for. Nothing like the long-imagined goal of her odyssey since leaving Elizabeth Street. She pictured Oxhide's trim new stone buildings, the woodsmoke rising through ash trees as they'd first viewed it from above, the perfect Wharfedale homestead with its satellite dish and little wind turbine, so local and yet so infinitely connected. He seemed to think she was just another of his fleeting pick-ups: Olivia Gabrieli of Oxhide, inheritor and current guardian of a great mercantile tradition and lineage. What would they say at The Bell, if the foreign woman abandoned the project they'd all now adopted as their own, and boasted about. What about her own family and friends? Pippa and Mark, Jane and Vanessa, Joe and Bridget, Anne and Giles (oh, specially Anne and Giles, so rooted), Meg and Mike Robertshaw, Jane, Isobel, Giulia? And Julian—even Julian, she realized now, she didn't want to lose.

Julian would leave with his father. The day seemed to darken. She couldn't look at Andrew, but picked at a muddy mark on her boot. 'I don't understand. What's changed?'

'Liv, I could be a Dales farmer all my life. God knows that's what I'd like. Live here with you, work the land for forty years, be buried in Buckden churchyard. I'm just not made that way. I've got to play my part in the world. There're things for me to do. I thought two years ago I couldn't do them, that there was no way forward. But things have changed, haven't they? An invitation. An institute, in California. It's big, Liv, and it's getting bigger. I can't ignore this, it's Julian's future as well and mine and the group's. Molecular soil ecology is taking off. Now they want me. I know it's crazy—but you see, don't you Liv?'

She saw. Vanessa was behind it. 'You bloody, *bloody* traitor! I hate you. I wish I'd never met you!' She jumped up and ran away down the track, not looking where she put her feet, tears blinding, stones slipping beneath her wellingtons.

Andrew ran after Olivia. She was fitter, but he gained on her, calling, *wait, wait, Liv, wait!*, until his right foot slipped on a big fresh cowpat. He crumpled awkwardly on his back, his momentum carrying his body downhill over wet grass, right knee agonizingly bent up behind him. Wincing, he hauled himself upright, leaning against the wall, as Olivia, at the bottom of the hill, slammed the door of the Land Rover and roared down the lane.

He roused a faint phone signal and got through to Pippa. Then the battery ran out, and he was stranded until at last, three hours later, a passing mother on the school run gave him a lift back to Oxhide. It was five o'clock. The house was dark and quiet.

Mark came round that evening. Olivia had experienced a breakdown. She was being looked after. He didn't ask questions, but said he and Pippa were on hand if needed. Then he went away again.

Nightmares plagued her. The worst were the recurrent dreams of loss. Would it stop?

The plank bridge arced slowly to and fro on its flimsy central prop, and shivered at her every move. Olivia edged forward on all fours, reaching a single hand or knee at a time, transferring her weight by fractions. The timbers were weather worn and riddled with beetle holes and rotten patches. Splinters dug into her tensed palms. A calf muscle cramped and jerked her foot, loosening a slither of slate shards that cracked free from the timber skeleton, fell and vanished into the mist. No clatter or splash came back. She clutched the gappy framework harder. Cold fog filled her mouth and nostrils, the air was muffled, thick. At the next sway of the tottering structure, the timber under her right hand groaned, split, and broke. Her left hand clamped a pole, but the plank she knelt on hinged down. She hung a moment from her wrenched left arm, then fell into the clammy air. Something elastic slowed her inexorable descent and finally held her static in the gloom above the surface of black water. Black for lack of light, but not opaque. Clear water, with things in it, lamprey flesh, writhing tubes with toothless mouths glimmered near the surface and vanished again. She hovered, staring down. Something half-human, bloodied?—Freddie? You can't go there, Olivia, you're not allowed, Isobel's voice told her. The Freddie thing showed her its blind face, darkened, dissolved. Olivia reached down towards the darkness, but the elastic pinned her, bound her, wound her round. Arms and legs paralysed she hung mummified in the dark.

Scene two—she ran, ran, along a street of terraced brick houses, sunshine cold on deserted pavements. The street was strange but familiar. It was Cambridge but not as she knew it. How did she know? They said so but there was nobody there. Andrew, Andrew, Andrew; please could you direct me to Andrew Bamberg's laboratory she asked a person, a person on the pavement, what person? Round the back, hurry, it said. She ran, ran, ran round the corner, another long brick terrace. The doors were green, the walls red, the windows dark. Still the cold sun in a blue sky and nothing moved. Running and panting she woke, saw light on the white ceiling, lay still as the nightmare faded and she waited to remember who she was, and where.

27

Rescue

Noises of life came up to her, crockery and cutlery, the washing machine humming and churning, people moving in the kitchen below. The air from the open window smelt of rain. Voices chattered outside, and a car started and drove away. A dog gave a 'stuck outside a closed door' bark, plaintive but knowing somebody would open it. Normal life. None of it had anything to do with her any more. She turned and buried her head in the pillow. She sensed somebody open the door and stand inside the room, but in a minute or ten the door closed gently and the footsteps went away again.

Life crystallised and settled. Phantoms evaporated and Olivia's routine became that of a convalescent invalid. People visited and left flowers and grapes. Her wits reassembled and she began to face the everyday again. With it came the reality of her new, empty life alone. Each day she spent indoors, in the warm and quiet house. Somebody was always there; Pippa with Philip, Anne or Giles, Bridget; even one week her mother. Isobel lacked the capacity for calm, her comings and goings exhausting. Moss, always at her feet or lying on her bed except when out with Anne or Giles, was the lynchpin of her confined life. Day by short day plodded, each a few hours of light between breakfast and high tea, short remissions in one continuous night.

One morning Anne put up a Christmas tree in the sitting room. The fairy lights were cheering. Resin scented the air. Olivia remembered Highgate, and the relentless train of too-vivid memories started up again. She put on boots, an anorak. Zombie-like, she found her car key, hanging on the board in the passageway. She left Moss shut in the kitchen, hardening her ears to her whines and scratchings at the door.

Her Land Rover was left under cover in the barn. It started first time. She headed for Grimwith, up and up narrow roads slippery with recent snowfall, and stopped in the small turning space where the lane ended by water. Small snow drifts lay banked against each tussock of grass, and the east wind crepitated in clumps of purple-stalked nettles by the roadside. Olivia's toes clenched with cold inside her shoes as she scrunched over moss towards the edge of the reservoir. By the beached and sheeted dinghies of the sailing club someone had put up a notice: *No swimming at any time; beware of strong currents.* A skull and crossbones was painted below lettering. Tap-tap-tap went the rigging against the masts.

Catspaws ruffled the steel-grey water under an aluminium sky. A band of ice rimmed the lake, forming a ledge slightly above the water level. Olivia climbed stone steps to the grassy top of the dam and looked over the wall at the maggot-sized sheep grazing below, on a green strip alongside the culvert that channelled the outflow. Water gushed from the base of the dam, rushing past sheep towards the washtubs and sewers of Bradford.

The lake behind the dam glinted gunmetal grey. The reservoir was low, water locked in the frozen hills. On the far side a ruined farm house was exposed, its stables and middens long-submerged. It shone clean as bare rock. How welcoming the inorganic world was, free of human mess; clear and sharp. How appealing to rejoin the elemental cycles, she thought; to return your borrowed atoms of carbon, nitrogen, oxygen and hydrogen to be remade into new unspoilt beings.

The outfall tower, a crenelated fantasy of gothic waterworks, rose from the water fifty yards from the dam. From its base water was sucked into the outfall tunnel, down which it would fall the height of the dam, drawing currents across the depths of the reservoir like bathwater swirling towards a plughole.

The building was connected to the shore by a grey-painted iron walkway with hand rails each side, supported on piers twelve feet above the water. It was barred by a padlocked chain at the shore end. Taking care not to slip on the iced metal, she stepped over the chain, one foot and then the other, and walked towards the tower. From a decorative ledge, seamed with black moss, drops seeped from the stonework and fell into peat-brown water below with a syncopated plink-plink . . . plink, periodically drowned by gusts. She followed the walkway round the curve of the building and stared across the length of the lake. The rail froze her fingers as she gripped it and climbed over. With nothing between her body and the water below, she braced, holding on by the freezing railing, for a second . . . two . . . the water pulled at her, took her like an underwater river. She opened her eyes and the water was the most beautiful blue-green. She wanted to go on seeing the colour, but the river was going faster . . . then something caught her wrist, tugged as though fighting the river and she was the rope, her wrist burned . . .

'How did you know to go to the reservoir?' It was Mark's voice penetrating her dream. Through closed eyelids she became aware of being in her room, her bed, sunlight shining in. A conversation was going on nearby. She didn't feel up to waking up enough to join in, but she couldn't help listening.

'I saw Olivia go off in her Land Rover.' Julian's voice this time. 'It wasn't hard to follow the tracks once it left on the lane up to the reservoir, some snow had just fallen and there was only one set of tyre tracks. We'd been there before, sampling water for coliforms. I remembered the place depressed her that day, she said it was a place for suicides. I thought at the time it was just her dark humour. But I thought that might be where she'd gone, she might have been planning to do something. As soon as I came to the edge of the lake, there she was on the walkway above the outfall. I ran, and she jumped just as I got to the end of the walkway. The current near the dam almost took us both. It sucks at you, she was going down in the current, accelerating, but I grabbed her and hung to the ironwork under the walkway.'

Olivia opened her eyes. Pippa was sitting beside her bed. Across the room Mark sat in Olivia's little bedroom chair, Julian at the window leant on the sill.

She sat up.

'Hello,' Pippa said. 'You're back with us, oh, Liv, thank God.' She came over to arrange pillows behind Olivia's head. Her kind eyes inspected Olivia's. 'You've been somewhere else for almost a week.'

'We'll go,' said Mark. 'Come on, Julian.' They tiptoed out. They had been talking in the belief that she was unconscious. But she had heard every word. And now everything flooded back, and with it, the knowledge Andrew was lost to her, her castle of dreams had come crashing down and lay in ruins beyond the window of her room. Hot tears filled her eyes.

Later, at Pippa's urging, she got up, had a bath and came downstairs in her dressing gown. The stone flags chilled her feet. The sky was grey and the only green the algae on the wet ash tree trunks. Kind Pippa made parsnip soup, which they ate with a home-made loaf she'd brought from Skipton. The soup was good. She felt human again; unhappy, devastated even; but not mad, not out of it. The baby fretted and then set to cry seriously. He needed changing and feeding, Pippa said, standing. Olivia must stay awake until she got back. Obviously, Pippa was aware of her drugged state. Time to emerge from it, then. Waiting until

Pippa was audibly engaged in nappy changing in the downstairs cloakroom, Olivia climbed the stairs to her bedroom and for the first time since the rescue, put on proper clothes: tan cord jeans and a silk shirt, tan socks, a cream coloured Aran sweater. It felt good. Then she took the box with Freddie's emerald ring out of her top drawer. The ring slid easily back on, and her jeans felt loose. Good to be thinner—but she wouldn't look in the mirror just yet; her face didn't feel from inside as though looking at it would cheer her up.

'Wow!' Pippa exclaimed, when Olivia reappeared in the kitchen. 'You're viable again.' And she set the glass she was putting away on the dresser and hugged Olivia, sideways so as not to crush baby Philip, in his sling across his mother's chest.

'Oh Pippa. I know I'm a bore, but I'm okay.'

'Let's go out. Even if you're an invalid, I can drive you, we'll go for a little carriage exercise. That'd be nice, wouldn't it?' She made goo-goo noises to the baby, and proposed an outing. She wanted Olivia's advice on clothes for her return to work, a new get-up to inspire confidence in clients. Her baby-proof shapeless washable stuff wouldn't do, but it would have to be a local shop in Skipton because of Philip, whose presence cut the range and time available for the search.

Soon, Pippa was arranging him expertly in the baby seat that graced the Foremans' estate car, and they were bouncing down the track, the car heater blasting warm air and the wipers thrashing, Pippa in the driver's seat talking about her work plans. How capable she was; and this was the second time her friend had unselfishly devoted time to saving Olivia's sanity. On top of that, she'd been so good, devoting herself to sewing and decorating and baby production and helping Mark and everybody else; but now, aware of a cheerfulness in Pippa's demeanour, Olivia realised Mark and Philip and the Doctors' House didn't represent the sum of her friend's ambition, and in spite of her gift for maternity, she still looked forward to living her own independent life just as much as Olivia herself.

Within the hour they were in the coffee shop and she found herself the third at a window table in a corner where Pippa could feed Philip discreetly. How strange to be among the normal café bustle, the Yorkshire voices of elderly patrons overlaid by the louder more soap-opera chatter of young mothers in a circle of big pushchairs. It was super-alive, loud and technicolour. Reality. And it was only just over a year ago she and Pippa had been here, shopping for curtain material, Philip barely present, an embryo, and Oxhide a castle in the air. Such a short time in which to be so derailed. Pippa must be thinking the same.

'Poor old Liv.'

'I'm a fool, Pippa.'

'Yes, a complete clot.'

How good to be able to laugh again. Maybe one day she would feel happy again, maybe not. But she was alive, she was here with Pippa and Philip.

'Has Andrew gone?'

'Yes. Some time ago, actually. He has been calling regularly to know how you are.'

'Has he?' She didn't know what to think.

'Of course. Why not? We've all been very worried, didn't you know?' Pippa looked amused but there was an edge in her voice. 'But Erik's been working in your lab. He's lovely. Mark and he get on well. They're talking about fishing. I bet you forgot you owned fishing rights, didn't you?'

What else had been going on? Pippa chatted easily. Giles was planning for lambing and Anne helped. They had been discussing reducing sheep numbers and were waiting for Olivia to recover to discuss the possibility of going to upland cattle instead. The Yarkers had left Skellside to live in their dream home, a new bungalow on its own plot at Grassington. Giles was living at Skellside, a temporary arrangement until Olivia decided what to do with it now it was hers. She thought about a while, it didn't make sense, but at last she remembered why it was hers. And still it didn't make sense.

'Did Andrew buy it? Was it for me? Why did he do that, Pippa? When he went and bought Skellside for me, I thought he was showing me he meant to stay with me.'

Pippa looked up from stroking Philip's minute head. 'Andy's not like that. He wouldn't give a coded message. I think he just saw it as the obvious thing to save Low Field. The Yarkers really wanted to retire, and he has pots of money because of Vanessa. And he loves you, we all do, and you were kind to him.'

'I thought we were as good as married.' The café swam in and out of focus in Olivia's vision. Scenes from the last year montaged as she grappled to make sense of them from different perspectives. Pippa eyed her as one might an animal placed in new surroundings.

'We did try and tell you about him, Liv; he's always been a free spirit with women.'

But Olivia was different. Wasn't she? 'He's been emailing? I thought he'd gone for good. Erik's still at Oxhide?'

'Yes. Why not? Nobody's died. Liv, it's not a tragedy. He'll be back. He's just not the marrying kind, you know? This is the twenty-first century.'

Motherhood had made Pippa more assertive. Olivia wasn't used to this degree of authority from somebody she'd always thought of as a follower. It was nature, probably; think how dangerous newly-calved cows could be. She liked the new Pippa, it was restful to be driven around and told what to do. The future felt more open, more welcoming; the past, on the other hand, more mortifying.

After Philip had been changed again (how incredibly labour-intensive babies were) they were fingering garments in Pippa's favourite shop. Olivia held Philip. He felt real in her arms, and didn't cry, even though his mother was out of sight in the fitting room. The ladies who ran the shop did what they did, and they seemed real, too. Pippa emerged and twirled in the new season's clothes. Calf-length A-line skirts? Who'd have guessed?

And after Pippa had dropped her back at Oxhide, Olivia

walked to the shaggy winter lawn, treading carefully on the flat stones that made a rough path from the front door to the edge of the terrace, and surveyed the fields below; her territory that now included Skellside away to the left. Low Field was empty and a tractor was at work in the yard; probably Giles clearing relics of his father's neglect, the derelict slurry pit, the nettle-enfolded outbuildings and discarded rolls of sheep wire. It reminded her of arriving at Oxhide, phoning Isobel for comfort on that lonely Hallowe'en. Phoning her mother for comfort! When Isobel had lost Ben, her only son. Isobel who had been so courageously faithful to her career. Olivia had never acknowledged her mother's heroism, her hours of practice on the baby Steinway, her determined gaiety with her old less-than-perfect suitors whom Olivia had so despised; and all the effort and thought that had gone into finding Pippa to take care of convalescent Olivia, while she kept her musical livelihood going. A horrible shame assailed Olivia. She climbed behind the yard where there was usually a signal and tapped Isobel's number into her phone.

Once unpacked, Isobel was eager to be shown round. Her 'Oh' and 'Ah' at the domestic arrangements, including the big warm kitchen, the soft white sofas and view from the sitting room and the piles of logs stacked by the fireplace ('like winters at home, Cara') delighted Olivia. She felt an old affection for her mother welling and basked in Isobel's faint aroma of *Amazone* which brought back those early childhood days before the split, the evenings playing Bézique, the endless mornings with Isobel holding the saddle, helping Olivia to ride her little blue bicycle, or turning the pages when Olivia took her turn at *Für Elise*, thinking she must be the first-ever eight-year-old girl to play Beethoven.

It was a new phase in Olivia's daily life at Oxhide. Wearing her emerald ring every day, even on the quad bike sheep-checking round, was a way of being Olivia Gabrieli, faithful to her people and land. She kept clear of the lab, except to exchange a friendly word with Erik. She gave him the copy of *Micrographia*, later. Also, later, she promised herself to drop the antidepressants, but not until spring. She practised piano, simple Bach, and folk songs with Anne and Giles occasionally; it made them laugh. Pippa encouraged her to have people over, and helped to cater. She was back on track with her original dream of self-sufficiency.

In February, as Giles and Anne prepared for lambing and another year got underway, Olivia turned to the economics she had neglected. It was arranged that Jane and her father would help review the accounts. As Jane said, decide what you want; then cost the milestones, arranging funds accordingly. Andrew was no longer in the equation. But Olivia had never really considered Andrew in terms of budgets. Round the fire with Jane and Joe, she admitted to her father that he had been right in his misgivings about the lab. Rescuing her hero had not been in the farm budget. She had made a loss in her first year.

'The thing is,' Jane said, 'what do *you* want, Olivia? You've got your lab, and the grant to run your science project. You even seem to have a scientist at work there this morning.'

She was right. Erik's car stood in the yard and from time to time he emerged and strolled around, presumably while thinking or waiting for a reaction to complete. Joe had met Erik and they discussed fishing. The objections to the lab had fizzled out; it was no longer an occasion for shame and guilt, but an asset. Perhaps she was not such a fool.

'What about you, love?' Joe said. 'It's a lonely life you've chosen. You don't have to go with it, you know. We all make mistakes, false steps.'

Another week or two passed in sheep routine, then Vanessa turned up one afternoon unannounced; snooping, although she pretended to be dropping by as a friend. However, the goddess act was tamed. Grey was visible at the roots of the golden curls, and she arrived in a hire car from Skipton, not her oyster coupé. Olivia led them to the front door by way of the terrace. Giles had painted the park-style railings round the terrace white, and a rococo seat with pergola overlooked the fellside opposite. Watery sounds from below, from the splashing fountain and dripping grotto, cast a calming spell on the place. Vanessa cast inquisitive sidelong glances at the buildings where the lab was.

'How good to see you looking so well, my dear,' she said. 'We were so worried. Julian wanted to know how you were.'

Anne came out and suggested she make tea for them all inside, it was so chilly. Olivia knelt on the hearthrug in the sitting room and felt Vanessa's eyes on her back as she built a little tent of sticks, inserted a firelighter and added a roof of slender dry logs.

'You still have your piano,' observed Vanessa. 'I didn't know you played.'

Olivia struck a match that broke on the side of the box. At her second attempt the flame flared and the sticks caught. 'Oh yes. In the evenings, with friends. Television is such a bore, isn't it?'

'Well, of course, if there's nobody on one knows.' There was a chink of a teaspoon on porcelain as she added a sugar lump. 'Isn't it good about Andy?' Vanessa went on.

'Vanessa, do you know if Andrew is still working on the Oxhide results?'

'Oh, I'm sorry Olivia, I just wouldn't know. Science isn't my thing at all, I'm afraid.' There was no point, Olivia realised. Instead she asked about the Commission for the Conservation of Cultural Landscapes. Vanessa moved on from her son, and expanded on how cultural landscapes were now recognised as having economic value, quoting Dieter Helm. Olivia pushed aside her misgivings—she'd had a nightmare recently about Wharfedale being sold to a Shanghai corporation—and joined in discussion of UNESCO sites and national parks worldwide. Eventually, as the fire burned down and Olivia failed to add further logs, Vanessa said she must be on her way to see other people on her journey north.

As Olivia helped her with her coat, Vanessa said over her shoulder, 'Andy'll be back next month, I expect he'll be coming here.'

'That'll be nice,' Olivia managed to say, hopefully in a normal voice, her heart jumping against her ribs. She escorted Olivia through the front door; these days departing guests didn't have to leave by the kitchen passage and step over yard puddles. After all, Vanessa was a goddess—even if the magic was a bit flat today, and there was no sign of the burgundy Hunter boots or flying gold hair. She noticed Julian was driving. Everything moved on, whatever catastrophes might from time to time snarl up one's own little life.

Olivia had heard nothing from David and Mary in Highgate, although she'd found a chatty round-robin Mary had enclosed with her Christmas card, which had lain unread on a windowsill all the time she'd been ill. One morning Mary phoned, saying she'd just learned fragments about Olivia's illness from Julian via Vanessa, and wanted news. There was no need to go into detail, and soon they were talking about everyday plans. It ended with Olivia offering to source local cheese for Mary's upcoming lunch, for overseas medical students newly arrived in London. Andrew's name was conspicuously missing from Mary's news.

Olivia couldn't leave the healing wound alone. Mary would know where Andy was. She offered to take a load of Dales cheeses down to Highgate.

28

Realities

The Bambergs' house must be one of the last in Highgate N6 to have an 'in' and 'out' drive. It was good after the 400-mile journey not to have to cruise for a parking place. Mary's office—who knew that she had such a thing, nice mumsy Mary?—had its own entrance at the side, on the ground floor. None of the doors were locked and Olivia walked in with a light touch on the bell to announce her arrival.

Mary appeared and went into motherly mode. But there were signs that in her office, where she welcomed Olivia, she might have a different persona—her innate warmth and friendly smile as kind as ever, but the room was set up for consulting. Four small velvet-covered chairs stood around a low table with glasses and a water jug. Olivia's gaze took in agreeable small landscapes, a small piano, and a bird feeder on a winter-flowering small tree outside the window.

'I appreciate this, Olivia,' Mary said. 'Such a long way for you to come! But it will really make our party; delicious to eat, and a conversation starter too, for the new registrars. A lot of them are still improving their English and there's sometimes not much in common at first— but everybody understands cheese, and the idea of it coming in from the country to the city. Perhaps you'd better bring it into the larder now, and then we'll have a bite of lunch?'

While Mary did things in the kitchen, Olivia fetched her cheeses from the Defender parked under the overgrown laurels outside. She made several trips for the separate cardboard boxes, from different small family farms in the Dales: soft curd cheeses in pots, cylinders of a blue one, and delicious mountainy sheep cheeses, the traditional cheese shape designed to be rolled down to farms from upland grazings; stored summer milk, hard and dry to last the winter. Each time she went to the Land Rover, the massive vehicle struck her as more and more pretentious, less and less like the battered little trailer-draggers Dales farms had. It was embarrassing Mary could see its creamy bulk from the kitchen window, but Mary made no remarks except to show delight with the cheeses and carefully put them away for the party, labelling them with coloured post-it notes on which she pencilled Olivia's details of type and origin, ranging them on shelves in her cool north-facing larder.

Lunch was cauliflower cheese. It was good to sit at the kitchen table eating such sustaining nursery food, and Mary's company was calming as she chatted about David's work and they discussed the news, wondering mildly why the government seemed completely mad. Olivia asked if Mary had seen Jane lately, and what she thought, and Mary told her Jane was fed up, and even Vanessa a bit pissed off with the undignified behaviour of those who ought to know better. On this cordial note, Mary said it would be more comfortable to have coffee in her room with softer chairs, away from the racket of the elderly dishwasher.

In her office, Mary took the seat with its back to the window, and held out a plate of chocolate biscuits to go with coffee. They were coated both side with dark chocolate, and the middle was ginger shortbread. Mary took one too, and smiled quietly at Olivia across the low table. Discreet crunching the only sound.

Unspoken thoughts hung in the still air. It reminded Olivia of a scene from a favourite book of her childhood: little Lucy on a Lakeland hillside sharing a calm moment with the capable hedgehog Mrs. Tiggywinkle, after that animal had completed her arduous day of washing and they sat side by side in front of the fire, before returning laundered garments to her customers. Only then had Lucy noticed that her hostess had 'prickles, like hairpins sticking wrong way out'. Mary evidently had a professional side, beyond her family life. Mary had spine.

'That robin's there again,' she said, following Olivia's gaze at the bird feeder. 'I think he, or she, must be nesting in the laurels. Do birds nest in laurels? They don't look cosy, do they? Those big leathery leaves.'

'It's good to be here again,' Olivia gave in and offered a way in to what they both knew they were here to discuss. 'I'll never forget your Christmas party. It was wonderful. Literally. The smell of the Christmas tree. Magical. All your different guests, and the charades.'

'Andrew was here last week.' Mary's remark was a depth-charge in a fishpond. 'I found him crying. I hadn't heard him cry since Cressida drowned. An awful sound. I wanted to tell you that, my dear.' She poured more coffee. Olivia watched the tilting chrome cafetière catch the light, the steam rise from her blue and white porcelain mug. When she looked up again, Mary was observing her. 'I wanted you to know that. I thought perhaps you might not have realised how much you mean in his life, you know. I'm not advocating any particular course of action.'

Olivia took another biscuit without thinking. There was a buzzing in her ears. She must ask Mary where she bought her biscuits. Eventually words returned, bitter words. 'He told me he couldn't bear to stay with me. He'd been planning to leave, Julian told me. All it took was the money—he got offered a three year job—just three years—and off he went.'

Mary's expression changed. She was silent, twirling a teaspoon and looking down. At last she looked up and met Olivia's stare.

'You are both wrong. I can see why, and I think I can see what happened. In fact, the whole thing would make an interesting study.' She smiled a more private smile, a smile Olivia recognised as that of an intelligent person to whom an exciting idea had occurred. 'But I didn't summon you here to pretend to analyse your psyche or be your agony aunt, my dear. Nor—dare I confess—because we're short of cheese merchants. No, I just wanted to say, please trust Andy. And yourself.'

'It's no good. He won't stay with me at Oxhide, he doesn't want to settle there, and I've made it my mission in life to take care of it. I owe Oxhide my loyalty.'

'Are you sure you never want to travel?' said Mary. 'I adore travelling, specially with David. Home is your solid base for going out from, not to hide in all of the time. You can be loyal without clinging to the spot, surely?'

'But I have two hundred sheep. The land is my job. It is succeeding.'

'Olivia, I don't think you are a farmer. It's a nonsense. I see a lot of people reinvent themselves, as they call it. You've done a remarkable bit of self-invention. So has Andy. But underneath it you are real people who love each other. Honestly, dear Olivia, call off this ideal farm idea. Stay at your beautiful Oxhide, but don't make it a millstone. You and Andy would enjoy a while abroad, and I've heard you have a lovely sister who'd manage your farm. Better than you, by the sound of it.'

'Who told you that, Mary?'

'Julian, of course. He's a bright lad. Very fond of you, too, though he'd die rather than let on. In fact I blame him for a lot of what's happened. Julian, and silly old Vanessa, and even your esteemed godmother Jane, seem to have stirred the pot. You and Andy have listened to everybody but each other.'

29

Resolution

In March, Anne and Giles announced their engagement. Olivia didn't feign surprise, but her delight was genuine. Giles hadn't been up at Oxhide. He'd spent his spare time from the garage renovating Skellside. Anne's car was a permanent feature in the yard for most of the winter and the stables were the first of Giles's building projects, although he was now at work on the walls. Anne broke the news while she and Olivia hung over the door of Dreamcatcher's box, watching the thoroughbred pick at her hay net, her foal looking on.

'We're planning a June wedding. In the church at Hubberholme, and a reception here. You'll be my matron of honour, won't you, Liv? Mummy wanted to do it at The Hollies but I so wanted it to be an Oxhide affair. I'm family, aren't I?'

Olivia flung an arm around her sister.

'Shall we invite Andy?' Anne said. 'You are friends still, aren't you? He didn't do anything wrong to you, did he, Liv?'

Olivia had gone over the history of the love affair, again and again. As time went by, it dawned on her Andrew Bamberg had not intentionally done her wrong. Reflecting on Joe's warning, she realised how unjust she'd been. There was no agreement on the same thing, no conversation about how their separate aims in life might be aligned; and no marriage, real or imagined. It had been a glorious, unbelievably romantic *Midsummer Night's Dream*, and almost entirely her idea. All that remained was a longing to see him again, a longing for his bodily presence. And to talk, ordinary talk.

'Yes. Invite Andrew. Do, it would be lovely, I'd very much like to see him again.'

'And make up?' Anne pressed her point. 'Send him the invite. And I'll speak to him first, before he gets it.'

Pippa played the organ at Anne's wedding. She played a Bach toccata and fugue, some brisk hymns, and finally a medley weaving in horsey references. Who knew? She brushed aside Olivia's amazed compliments: it had been all in a day's work, she'd taken Grade Eight at school; she played regularly for services in Skipton.

And Andrew was among the guests, taking the place beside Olivia. She sat outwardly calm beside him through the ceremony, talking her part as Anne's matron of honour in a beautiful slinky maxi-dress Pippa made specially. Andrew drove the Defender on their drive back to Skellside for the reception, where he moved among guests, cutting his usual handsome figure. People who didn't know her well took him for her longstanding partner, probably from how he knew his way around and acted the host, and the fact the dog treated him as master. As the afternoon wore on to evening and the guests started the barn dance, he led her outside, away from the racket, to where the last apple blossom was carried off by the wind in the old orchard behind the barn. Raggedy grey clouds moved in the Wharfedale sky.

'Another paper's been accepted,' he said. 'The referees just wanted one extra set of data. We'll need to do one or two more sampling runs.'

'Here?'

'Skellside? This wasn't one of our sites. No, the moorland ones.' She stared at him. 'You're coming back?'

'Why not? Olivia, you're not—you aren't giving up on our project?'

'But you dumped me! You bloody dumped me!'

He stepped back a pace. His face made her wish she hadn't spoken. He replied solemnly, 'I did not dump you. I'm here. You're here.'

'We were as good as married.' Why couldn't she leave it alone?

'I never said we were married. I never wanted to be married. I explained. I can't be that sort of person for you, Olivia. If you really want, I'll go away and never darken your door again. Is that what you want? Personally, I want to be with you, I want us to work together, I love you, we're good together. But not in the same place for ever and ever. Not to be like a poor old pair of Yarkers, grumbling away their lives in the mud. There's a world out there I want to be part of, with you.'

He was serious. And at last, Olivia saw he was right. She admitted it, and his face relaxed.

They embraced at length.

Eventually, he said, 'Anne and Giles have done the romance thing. The hefted life suits them. You and I can subvert the genre, Olivia. We have more important things to do. You here as long as you want, me in various places. I'll come back, and I hope we'll travel together. It'll be more fun like that, believe me.'

'I do,' Olivia said.